My Knight

by

Lee Ann Dansby

LionHearted Publishing, Inc.
Zephyr Cove, NV, USA

With special appreciation to
Robert and Elizabeth Cook

LionHearted Publishing, Inc.
PO Box 618
Zephyr Cove, NV 89448-0618

Cover art by Joyce DeFord
Cover model George Haber

ISBN: 1-57343-007-2

Printed in the U.S.A.

To my mom, Pat Dansby,
who always believed in me,
and without whose encouragement
this book may never have been written.

And to my critique partners, Gerry Bartlett,
Audrey Compton, and Kimberly Rangel for
their unflagging patience and persistence
in helping me improve my craft.

Chapter One

✢ ✢ ✢

Ralston Manor, England, January 7, 1067

She prayed he would kill her.

Kaela stood in the center of the room, her hands lashed together, tied to a rope that hung from a center beam in the ceiling. She struggled to show no expression, trying to display a calm in deep contrast to the terror that filled her. She bit down on her lip to keep from begging for mercy and tasted her own blood. Her cries would only turn his rage to lust. Then the unthinkable would happen.

Dear Lord, deliver me from this torment. If only God would take her now, let the pain from the lash of his whip take her life. She welcomed death over the rape she knew would follow this beating. Kaela heard Broderick's cruel laughter as the lash ripped through the soft fabric of her bliaut. He had remarkable skill with the whip, and he stripped her to the waist without once cutting into her tender flesh.

He stood in front of her, lifted her tear streaked face, and said, "Ah, Kaela, tears I see, but no cries for mercy from thy lips?" He smiled, a cold vicious smile. "No matter, your screams will begin soon enough when I take your maidenhead. Did you really think you could hide behind Chaldron's walls forever? 'Tis the truth you escaped me three summers past with only a beating, but you are my captive now, milady. I offered you marriage then and you shunned me. Now you will pay."

Kaela fought to control the panic swirling inside her. *No fear... no emotion...* She matched Broderick stare for stare, and bit back the angry retort she knew would only provoke him. She had learned at a young age that to show this man anything save cold indifference was dangerous. Deadly.

Broderick's whip whistled through the air and came down against the wall with a loud crack. She flinched. He threw back his head and roared with laughter; a harsh, vulgar sound that scraped across her raw nerves.

"For three long years I've waited for this day. I practiced patience while you hid behind Chaldron's walls and Jacob's protection. There's no one here to protect you this time, Kaela," he said. He ran his callused hands possessively over her breasts. Pure enjoyment, though fleeting, flashed through his eyes. Now, she knew he wanted more. He wanted her.

Kaela trembled with revulsion; her worst nightmare had come true. She would never forget Broderick's first beating. She carried the scars from his whip not only on her back, but in her soul. He would have raped her if Jacob had not come. They had been hunting when Broderick separated her from the others and led her deep into the woods. He had proposed marriage and, when she'd scorned him, had gone into a rage. Now, once again, she found herself at the devil's mercy.

His whip hissed and cracked, the sound slicing through the air, and her soul; the stinging lash close to her flesh. Close… too close.

Dear God, deliver me from this madness!

As if in answer to her prayer, she heard heavy footsteps coming down the hall. The door crashed open. Walter, Broderick's second in command, rushed into the room.

"My lord," Walter said, "a legion of Norman warriors has been spied up on the ridge. They are preparing to attack."

"So, they are finally here." Broderick tossed his whip aside. "Aye, let the Norman bastards come. Call the men to arms, Walter. We will give them a fight they will not soon forget."

Broderick turned to Kaela, grabbed her chin and squeezed until she cried out.

"Alas, much as it grieves me, cousin, this little tryst will have to wait. Once I've taken care of these Norman bastards, I will at long last take care of you."

Pulling his sword from its sheath, he reached up and cut the rope from the cross beam. Kaela fell to the floor and curled herself into a protective ball to ward off the kick she knew would come.

He didn't disappoint her. His boot landed brutally in the small of her back. Pain splintered through her. A burst of white hot light clouded her vision. She sent a silent litany to the heavens in thanks for her deliverance, then her fervent prayers ceased as she sank into blessed blackness.

❖ ❖ ❖

East Ridge, Overlooking Ralston Manor

Cameron D'Abernon stood beside the campfire and assessed the warriors gathered round him. In full armor, they were a fearsome sight, one that would strike terror in the heart of a stranger. But Cameron knew them for their loyalty and strength of purpose. For the coming battle, there could be no better company. They seemed oblivious to the bitter cold as they discussed their plans. The full moon rode high in the sky, illuminating the perimeter walls of Ralston Manor in the distance.

Johnathan, a strapping man of six feet with hazel eyes and brown hair, looked to his leader, towering over him by several inches. "What say you of Broderick of Ralston, my lord? Will this Saxon give us much sport?"

"Aye," Cameron replied, fixing a steely gaze on his second in command. "'Tis said he is a fearsome warrior, but he lost over half his men in the battle at Hastings."

"Much favored by King Harold, he was, and fought at his side in that bloody battle," Patrick, another of Cameron's loyal vassals, added. "'Tis also thought this bloody cur is one of the leaders of the Saxon resistance and was behind the surprise attack that nearly took Baron Lloyd to an early grave last month."

The warriors looked up at the sound of a rider approaching. "Hail, Andrew!" Johnathan shouted. "How be the defenses at Ralston Manor?"

Andrew dismounted from his destrier, handed the reins to an eager page, and walked into the circle of men surrounding the fire. He looked directly at his brother, Cameron, and cast the cloak from his armor.

Johnathan laughed. "The dirty beggar turns once

more into the fearsome knight." Laughter echoed around the camp.

"My lord," Andrew said, "their defenses are greatly weakened. The reports of Broderick's losses at Hastings are true, and he lost several more in his attack on Baron Lloyd. I could count only sixty men left to defend the town. The northern wall appears the weakest. I saw several places where the wood was charred from a previous attack, and has yet to be replaced. The tower guard is half what it should be."

"What of their defenses?" Cameron asked.

"Four hoardings have been erected at the wall. They are well positioned, but their supply of boulders is low. They are working to remedy that, but to fully stock the galleries will take at least a fortnight."

"How long will their present supply last?" Patrick asked.

"No more than a few hours," Andrew said.

"What of catapults?" Cameron asked.

"I saw only one, and the supply of stones is less than half what it should be."

"What of the gate?" Johnathan asked.

Andrew smiled. "Double doors-studded with iron. No barbican, or portcullis. Our battering ram will easily see its way through. They have plenty of water, but their food supply is low."

Cameron acknowledged this information with a nod to his younger brother. The report confirmed his suspicions. He gazed around the campfire, looking each loyal vassal in the eye. Each met his gaze in return. Pride and affection welled inside of him for these men who had pledged their loyalty and their lives, and had fought so valiantly at his side.

"We attack. I am anxious to get this matter taken

care of. Our men have been in battle since we landed at Hastings in October, and the weather continues to grow bitter. This is the last holding William has ordered us to secure. I am eager to return to London and see our King. He has promised a large fief to me for our efforts and I am impatient to see our new home."

Patrick laughed, poking Cameron in his ribs. "Possibly you are eager to see the wench who comes with the holding. Our William is eager to marry off the wives and daughters of the dead Saxon warriors to help secure the holdings and unite England and Normandy."

Cameron scowled. "Nay, Patrick, you know I will not take a wife. William will not ask it of me."

Lesser men would have been cowed by the cold anger in Cameron's eyes, but his vassals knew him well, and understood his pain. Andrew stepped forward to take Cameron by the shoulders.

"Come, brother, put Elizabeth's treachery behind you. 'Tis years past. You must think of your future and an heir to all that will be yours in this new land."

"Nay, Andrew, I will leave the begetting of an heir to you, little brother. 'Tis happy I will be to bequeath all that is mine to a nephew."

Cameron knelt close to the fire and sketched his plan on the bare earth.

"Thorsen, you will lead the attack on the bastions. We will concentrate on the north wall. Patrick, you will move in first with the mantlets. Have the archers fire the wall. Once it's aflame, we will no longer have to worry about the missiles being dropped from the hoardings. When you've fired the wall, switch to arrows and aim for the men-at-arms. 'Twill give

Thorsen the cover he needs to reach the bastions with the scaling ladders. Johnathan, Andrew, and I will lead the charge on the gate."

With that, Cameron stood and took his helmet from his page. Mounting his destrier, he raised his fist in the air to signal his men. His voice, like thunder, pierced the night. "We ride!"

Chapter Two

❖ ❖ ❖

Ralston Manor, January 27, 1067

The nightmare woke her. Drenched with sweat, heart pounding, Kaela clutched the bed covers and tried to calm herself with several deep breaths. Eight long weeks had passed since Broderick abducted her and brought her to Ralston Manor. The nightmare had returned immediately upon her arrival, as if it had been waiting for her.

Shivering in the darkness, the nightmare still fresh in her mind, Kaela decided the demon in her dreams was worse than her real life nemesis. Thank God, the Normans had begun their siege over a fortnight ago. Broderick had been too busy with his defenses to bother with her. But her dreams she could not evade… not without the opiate. She had suffered the nightmare for months after the first attack, until she had finally concocted a sleeping draught strong enough to quiet the night demons. But she had felt ashamed to need it, had told no one about her weakness. She had no draught here, and the Broderick of her dreams was even more tormenting than the Broderick who lived and breathed and held her captive.

At times she wished Broderick would come and be done with her. At least the agony of waiting, of facing the nightmare night after night, would end.

The door to her chamber creaked open. Kaela tried to keep her breathing slow and steady, feigning sleep. Her heart raced at the thought that Broderick might have come at last.

"Milady," a soft voice whispered.

Kaela opened her eyes and smiled with relief at the old woman looking down at her.

"Oh, Maude, 'Tis you. I feared Broderick had returned."

"There, there, milady," Maude crooned, patting Kaela's shoulder. "'Tis only Arik and I."

Kaela looked past Maude to see Arik standing silently behind the nursemaid, his soft, childlike eyes peering into her own, a worried look on his face. Maude had been Kaela's nursemaid since she was a wee babe. Arik, Maude's simple-minded son, was ten years older than Kaela and never far from his mother's side. They had played together as children. She had been shocked and relieved when Maude and Arik had appeared at Ralston Manor not long after she was taken. They had pretended to be strangers lest Broderick send the old woman away. Fortunately, Broderick had been much too busy with the Normans to wonder about the old woman and her half-wit son. Kaela had Maude to thank for what comforts she had.

"What brings you here at this hour?"

Maude looked nervously over her shoulder and told Arik to close the door. She sat down on the bed next to her mistress and whispered, "'Tis time to make our escape, milady. The Norman troops have finally broken through the outer wall and will shortly breach the inner gates as well."

Kaela bolted upright. "We must hurry then. Is everything ready?"

"Aye, mistress, just as ye requested. The mules are hidden in the forest aback of the west wall. I have brought clothing for ye to disguise yourself as a boy. All is ready. Ye have only to change and we can be on our way."

"What of the guards at the west wall?" Shivering against the cold, Kaela quickly pulled the bed drapes and donned the boy's disguise.

"There was only one. Arik knocked him out. The rest have gone to help with the attack at the north wall."

"Then we must make haste." Kaela pulled back the bed drapes and stepped forward. "What say you?"

Maude gasped. "Why, I wouldn't know ye. Ye look like a lad, but you're the cleanest lad this keep has ever seen."

"'Tis naught to worry over. By the time we get through the secret passageway, I will be filthy," Kaela replied.

Smiling to herself, Kaela watched Arik push the bed aside to reveal the secret opening in the wall. She would be forever grateful to her father for telling her stories of his childhood escapades within Ralston's secret passageways.'Twas apparent Broderick had no knowledge of the hidden tunnel, else he would not have given her access to this chamber. Kaela picked up the torch from the wall sconce and led the way into the dark and dirty passageway. The air was stale and musty and she knew what kind of creatures called such a dark damp place their home. She would not contemplate going into such a place if she had a choice, but this passage held their only means of escape.

They stopped just inside the entrance and Arik pulled the bed back in place as Maude and Kaela picked up the bundles of food and supplies placed there earlier. Holding the torch high above her head to help light their way, Kaela slowly moved through the damp passage. Maude and Arik followed close behind her.

"What of Broderick?" Kaela asked.

"He was in the North Tower securing his defenses the last I saw him. I overheard him tell William to prepare for their escape. The dastard will ride into the hills before the dawn. He will continue to hide out and fight the Normans."

"'Tis foolish," Kaela replied. "He might as well resign himself to the fact the Saxon reign ended with Harold's death. William of Normandy has a legal claim to the throne. The deed is done."

"Aye, milady, but I am surprised ye take this news so calmly. After all, ye are heiress to Chaldron Castle. 'Tis a large and profitable shire and I know how much ye love the keep."

"'Tis true, Maude, the only happy times I remember were spent there with my mother and father. But they are long in their grave. Now that King Harold is dead, and England has been conquered by the Normans, it will make no difference that my father left Chaldron to me and to the husband of my choosing. Nay, all that has changed. I will be given in marriage to a man of the King's choosing. We can only hope we will be allowed to stay at Chaldron. As far as Broderick is concerned, I have known only abuse by his hand. He plans to ravish me. If he does not kill me, he will marry me off to one of his despicable friends, and my life will be a living hell. I will take my chances with the Normans. 'Tis said King William is marrying his barons to the Saxon widows and daughters. Mayhap, I will be lucky enough to be given in marriage to a very old baron, who will no longer want a maid to warm his bed. I can only pray 'Tis so, for I cannot abide any man's touch."

"Now lass," Maude replied, "ye have never known any other's touch except Broderick's. Not all men are as cruel and brutal. That man has a black heart, always has. Even when he was a young lad, I saw his cruelty with animals and his father's serfs. I also saw the way he lusted after ye. And hated ye, too, he did. He resents the inheritance your father left ye. He always felt Chaldron should go to him, even though he had no blood claim. I fear ye are wrong that Broderick would give ye to another. Nay, the cur plans to keep ye for himself."

Kaela felt sickened at Maude's words, and whirled around in the tunnel to face her. "What say you, Maude?"

"Aye, mistress, the filthy bastard planned to marry ye himself to gain your inheritance and after he had tired of ye, he planned to kill ye. Doubt me not, for I heard these black words from his very own lips not a sennight ago."

Kaela felt the color drain from her face. She swayed against the tunnel wall, dropping the torch. Arik reached out his big hands to steady her and snatched up the torch.

"Worry not, Kaela, I'll not let anyone harm ye." Arik kept his warm brown gaze on hers.

"Thank you, Arik." Kaela smiled up at him, knowing

in his child's mind he did not understand all Maude
had said. She resisted the urge to sob out all her hurt
and frustration. Now was not the time or place. With a
swipe at her tears, she straightened her backbone, and
took the torch from Arik. She didn't know why
Maude's words shocked her so. Since her parents had
died, she had come to expect the worst and had yet to
be disappointed.

"We must hurry now. We cannot be away too soon,
lest Broderick catches up with us. From what you say,
Maude, I am sure he plans to take me with him and
will soon discover I have escaped. If we are lucky, he
will be anxious to go into hiding and will not take time
to search for me."

"Aye, but he knows ye will return to Chaldron, and
he will come for ye there. His mind is twisted with
hatred and he will not stop until he has ye."

A cold chill passed through Kaela's heart at
Maude's words. "Mayhap by then I will be married to
another, a man strong enough to defend my home, or
Broderick will have already fallen to the Norman
sword."

"We can only pray 'Tis so." Maude sighed. "'Twas
by God's grace that ye have escaped Broderick's evil
hands once more. 'Tis sorry I am that Arik and I could
not have protected ye from him three summers ago,
milady. Ye will carry the scars from his whip to your
grave."

"I pray no man will want to bed me when he sees
my scars. Then the nightmare I suffered at Broderick's
hand would have been worth it," Kaela replied bitterly.
"You did protect me, Maude. 'Tis only because you
have helped me these last two months that I have been
able to preserve my virginity."

"'Twas your idea to rub the poison vines that cause the rash on your body, milady. I only brought them to ye."

"Aye," Kaela said and smiled at her. "It worked quite well, too. For more than a fortnight Broderick would not touch me, knowing how contagious I was. But 'twas your idea to put the herbs in the mutton that caused the severe stomach cramps. The fool never did figure out he had been poisoned."

"It took him days to get his strength back once the cramps finally stopped." Maude smiled.

They reached the end of the tunnel and Arik cleared away the cobwebs that covered the small hatch. Neglect made the hatch difficult to open and Kaela stepped back. Arik put all his strength behind forcing the small door open. Kaela doused the torch and waited while Arik cautiously stuck his head through the opening. At his signal that all was clear, they quickly climbed out into the dark, bitterly cold night. Arik shut the hatch, careful to make as little noise as possible, and covered it with dirt and branches, while Kaela looked to the outer wall for any sign that they'd been discovered. Once assured that no one was about, they hurried to the protection of the nearby trees.

Silently, they walked into the deep woods, to the place where Arik had hidden the mules. The journey to Chaldron was only a night's ride and Kaela was eager to return to her home. The last eight weeks had been hell and she would never forget them. She had lost her innocence while keeping her virginity.

A bitter wind blew from the north, so strong the trees whipped in a frenzy. They made their way homeward, giving the Norman camp a wide berth as they

circled around and headed south. Kaela wondered
about the Norman warriors who stormed Ralston and
wished them God's speed. Gossip said the Black Wolf,
the fiercest of the Norman knights, led the attack. She
had heard stories about him all her life, and although
probably only rumor that it was indeed him, she hoped
with all her heart it was so. Such an accomplished
warrior would be able to stop Broderick's escape and
slay him. Then and only then would she feel safe.

As they rode, she brushed against a tree branch and
winced when it slapped against her back, a cruel
reminder of Broderick's whip. A fortnight had passed
since Broderick had so brutally tormented her, but she
still felt the pain, still remembered his threats. She was
lucky that the Normans had attacked when they had,
keeping Broderick too occupied in battle to finish her
off. Whoever the Norman knight storming Ralston
Manor was, he had saved her life. Her own life she
would gladly give him in return for saving her from
Broderick's hands, but her maidenhead she would give
no man. At least not willingly. She would rather die at
her own hand.

Cameron and his vassals rode into Ralston Manor.
The battle had been over for hours now, and they had
just finished searching the countryside for Broderick
and his men. The coward had left the hall sometime
during the night with his most loyal men. From what
Cameron could gather from Broderick's steward,
James, the men had escaped through a hidden passageway.

Cameron knew the Saxons would soon be wiped

out. The resistance was not all that large. Many knights had been slain, and those who had lived had already pledged fealty to William. Only a few stubborn barons continued to fight. For now he must secure this holding and establish order. Then he could return to his king. He would deal with Broderick of Ralston later.

✛   ✛   ✛

Dark, angry clouds hung heavily in the sky, threatening rain. Kaela, Maude, and Arik made their way up the hill to Chaldron Castle. They had been seen by the guards who lowered the drawbridge with a loud rattle of chains. As soon as the bridge crashed into place, Windrey, the old gatekeeper, flung open the gates. The man wept openly, exclaiming over her return. Kaela nodded and smiled. He had been with her father since they were children and had stayed on to help her care for Chaldron after her parents' death, as had most of her father's people. Though old and few in number, her father's vassals served her well. All came out to meet them as they entered the outer bailey and a loud cheer rose from the crowd gathered there when they saw their beloved mistress return home safely.

Jacob came forward to help Kaela dismount, a look of relief on his face that quickly changed to a worried frown when he put his large hands around her small waist to help her dismount. Seeing the anxiety in his wizened old face, Kaela gave him a bright smile.

"'Tis not as bad as it looks, Jacob. All I need is some rest and a hot meal. Broderick was too busy with the Normans to pay me much heed. Besides, you know I am far too obstinate to stay down for long."

"Aye, Mistress," Jacob boasted, "I believe I know that only too well. Thank God ye are safe." He reached out and gave her a mighty squeeze, almost crushing the breath from her.

The man didn't know his own strength. She patted his arm affectionately as they walked together through the inner bailey towards the keep. Kaela felt so good to be home; she had feared she would never see her beloved Chaldron again. She felt warmed by the greetings from her loyal people.

A delighted squeal greeted her when she entered the keep and looked up to see Brenna flying down the stairs towards her. Her impetuous cousin threw herself into Kaela's arms and hugged her fiercely, tears of joy streaming down her face.

"Oh, cousin, 'Tis glad I am that you are home. I have done naught but pray for your safe return. Are you all right? Did that devil harm you? Were you very frightened? How ever did you escape? Did you kill the devil?"

Kaela shook her head, laughter bubbling up inside her. "Nay, Brenna, I did not kill the devil and I am much too tired now to give you the story of my trials over the last two months. Right now I want a warm bath, a hot meal, and a long nap. I will tell the tale this eve whilst we sup."

"Aye, Kaela, of course you need your rest. God's teeth, you do look a fright dressed in those filthy boy's clothes, and 'Tis obvious by the dark circles under your eyes that you have not slept in days. A bath and a nap are just the thing," Brenna said.

"I'll prepare one for ye right away, milady," Maude said.

"Nay, Maude, you and Arik are as travel worn as I.

You will both take to your beds immediately. Have Helen or one of the other girls take care of me." With that Kaela made her way up the stairs and down the hall to her chamber.

After her bath, Kaela put on a clean shift and climbed wearily into her bed. She had barely closed her eyes when she heard the door to her chamber open and looked up to see a tiny figure running toward her. Kaela sat up and held her arms out to pull the little girl up onto the bed and into her lap.

"Ah, there you are, Mattie. I was wondering when you would show up. God's truth, I missed you, sweet pea," Kaela said.

Mattie wrapped her arms around Kaela's neck and hugged her tightly.

"When I woke up from my nap, Nanny told me you were home," Mattie told her in a high sweet voice. Mattie's blue eyes were large and luminous as she gazed up at Kaela, a look of adoration on her chubby face. "I am so glad you are home, Kaela. Why did you sneak away like that?"

Kaela laughed and pulled Mattie close again, running her fingers through fat black ringlets. "I didn't sneak away my little sweet pea, but I did have to leave suddenly. I'm sorry that I didn't have time to tell you. I'm back now and I won't leave you again," Kaela said gently.

"Promise?"

"I promise, sweeting."

Kaela loved her youngest cousin with all her heart. Mattie was only four summers, but she had been with Kaela since she was a babe. Mattie and Brenna had come to Chaldron to live when their parents had died of the plague. Kaela, Mattie, and Brenna had all lost their parents to that terrible sickness three summers ago. Kaela had come to feel more like a mother to Mattie than a cousin or a sister.

Thanking God she had been able to return, Kaela held Mattie close, breathing in her sweet baby scent. Tears pricked her eyelids, quickly forgotten when Mattie began to squirm.

"Did you help Brenna while I was away?" Kaela asked, tickling the little girl until she squealed with delight.

"She's too bossy. I like you better, Kaela." Mattie stuck a thumb in her mouth and snuggled against Kaela's side.

Kaela laughed. "I think bossy is a good word for Brenna, but 'Tis not that she means to be so."

Mattie snorted. "Hmph! She likes to be boss!"

"Why don't you go and see if you can help her now, sweet pea. 'Twas a long journey home and I sorely need to rest."

"All right, Kaela, but hurry. I want to show you the doll Jacob made for me." Mattie hugged her one more time. She backed up slowly, scooted off the bed, and slipped quietly from the chamber.

Several hours later Kaela returned to the hall feeling much like her old self again. Thank God she had slept dreamlessly. Jacob and Brenna greeted her warmly and they sat down to a hearty dinner, obviously put together to please the long-absent mistress, as well as "fatten her up" as the cook said. Kaela briefly explained her ordeal with Broderick, skipping over the worst of it.

"We've heard naught of the siege, but there is no doubt the Normans will take Ralston," Jacob said. He shook his head. "If I know Broderick, he will run like the coward he is before the Normans breach the Manor's fortifications."

Kaela nodded her agreement. An unease inside told her that Broderick was still alive and well. "Aye, Jacob. He will flee to fight another day. He leads the Saxon rebels."

Jacob's face was grim. "I will warn the men to keep an eye out for him. While that cur lives you are in danger."

"You are right, something must be done about Broderick. I fear his mind has snapped. He will never give up." Kaela clasped her hands to stop their trembling. The concern on Jacob's face brought tears perilously close to the surface. She smiled tremulously. "Tell me, Jacob, how went your visit with William of Normandy? Did all go well?"

"Aye, my lady," Jacob replied. "I was received cordially, and King William accepted my pledge of fealty and loyalty to the new crown. He was not surprised that you wanted to pledge your loyalty and that of all Chaldron. He is familiar with the situation here. He knew your father. They met years ago in Normandy when Charles accompanied Edward the Confessor there. Your father preferred Norman ways, as did our King Edward, and recognized William's claim to the throne. Charles cared not that William was a bastard, and William appreciated his friendship. I am sure he will take this into consideration when he decides what to do with Chaldron."

"Did you explain to him my unusual circumstances?"

"I told him Charles had left Chaldron to you, and had given you the freedom to choose your own husband. God's truth, the King was greatly amused by this, as was Matilda, his wife. I believe they are most curious to meet you. As for honoring your father's request, I believe you know there's little chance of that, Kaela."

"I do not expect it, Jacob. That would be too much to hope for." Kaela sighed. If only she had been born a male. There would be no thought then of taking her home from her.

"Holy Saint Ambrose's bones, I don't see why not," Brenna exclaimed. "Your father was a wise and loving man. 'Tis natural he would want his only child to inherit his holdings. And why shouldn't you be able to choose your own husband? God's truth, no man will be choosing me if I don't want to be chosen!"

"'Tis not for you to worry over, Brenna. No man in his right mind would tie himself to that mouth of yours," Jacob said with a grin.

Brenna beamed back at him. "Aye, don't I know it, Jacob. The tongue can be a mighty sword, and most effective. Since I have no holdings and only a small dowry left to me by my dear parents, I do not think I have to worry overmuch. Nay, I will be choosing my own husband, and of course the fortunate man will only hear honeyed words from these lips."

"'Tis something I cannot wait to see," Kaela laughed.

"Aye, it will be something to behold, our Brenna wooing a man to her bed."

At that Brenna blushed deeply. "Jacob, such talk in front of ladies."

Jacob grinned with a devilish glint in his eye as he looked at Kaela. "My apologies, Kaela."

"Oh, you rogue," Brenna teased, "you will not rile my temper tonight. 'Tis too happy I am to have our Kaela home."

"William will let us know soon enough what his wishes are. Until then we will concentrate on running

Chaldron the way my father saw fit. The future will care for itself."

A dark shadow crossed Jacob's face. Kaela met his gaze and saw the guilt mirrored there. She reached over and took his hand in hers.

"You could have done naught, Jacob. 'Tis over now. Let it be." Her voice was barely above a whisper.

"Let me speak, Kaela. This needs to be said." Jacob sighed. When he spoke, his voice had gone soft and very gentle. Kaela felt her throat tighten, and knew without looking that tears streamed down Brenna's face. He continued to speak very slowly, holding her hand tightly in his. "I was out of my mind with worry when I returned to Chaldron and Brenna told me what had happened. My guilt weighs heavy for leaving you unprotected. Had I been here, I do not believe Broderick would have been so bold. I am not a young man any longer, but I still have my strength, and I know Broderick fears me."

Kaela started to silence him, but he raised his hand to stop her.

"God's truth, necessity bade me to go to William, and I know it was your decision to send me, but I will feel guilty for the rest of my life that I was not here to protect you, nor was I able to go after you. We do not have enough men to protect Chaldron in these unstable times, much less mount an attack on Ralston. Nay, the decision Brenna made to send Maude and Arik after you was a wise one," he said, smiling across the table at Brenna. "She knew Broderick would see the old servant and her simple-minded son as no threat and would allow them entrance into the hall. Brenna is most clever, just as you are. Broderick has always underestimated you, but Brenna didn't. She knew that if it was possible for you to escape, you would find a way. Thank God she was right."

"Thank you, Brenna. I owe my life to your cleverness."

"Nay, Kaela, do not thank me. I wish I could have ridden after you myself…" Brenna shook her head and dashed away a tear. "You have not told all that you suffered at Broderick's hand. I questioned Maude extensively this afternoon, and she left nothing out of the telling. As God is my witness, Kaela, that bastard will never again touch you. Aye, the whoreson will pay dearly for what he has done."

Kaela felt her control slipping as waves of shame washed over her. She looked away, unable to bear their scrutiny. Fighting the sobs that threatened to escape her, she remembered Broderick's hands on her body, and heard again his cruel laughter. "I should never have been so foolish as to leave the keep unescorted. I'll not do so again." She struggled to keep the tremor from her voice and turned to Brenna, giving her a hug. "Come, cousin, enough of such laments. 'Tis past and I am safely home. Why don't you see if you can beat this stubborn old man at chess?"

"'Tis out of pity that I let him win," Brenna said, with a wicked twinkle in her eye.

"God's bones, the girl is daft," Jacob replied, snorting.

"I wager my coin on Brenna this round, Jacob. You said yourself, she is a very clever girl."

"Why I am sure I never said any such thing about this brat."

"I will leave you to it then," Kaela said, as she walked toward the stairway leading to the third floor and her bedchamber. "This has been a very long day and I bid you good eve."

Once in her chamber, she dismissed Sarah, her maid, and stripped down to her shift. She wrapped herself in a blanket and pulled her chair very close to the fire. So many thoughts whirled through her mind she almost felt dizzy. Her whole future was so uncertain. What would King William do? She was sure he would give her in marriage. Chaldron was a large and profitable holding. William would award her lands to one of his best knights. Her practical mind realized that Chaldron needed a strong man to hold it and strong warriors to protect its walls.

She and Jacob had done a good job managing the shire since her father's death, but their freedom could not last. Her father had never intended for it to be so. She knew he had expected her to marry quickly. She had intended to herself… before Broderick's attack three years ago. Then the nightmares had come…

When suitors came to call, she inevitably found an excuse to send them on their way. Always she told herself she would soon take the time to choose a husband. Now time had run out and the choice would no longer be hers.

She wondered if she could use her father's relationship with William to help her cause, then sighed in frustration. King William did not know her at all, and she was a mere woman who wouldn't even be allowed to ask for an audience with her new king. She could only pray he would be kind to her.

Chaldron Castle, one of the largest holdings in England, and much advanced in its design and construction, had been built by her father, a man much before his time. He had started many new and innovative ways of farming.

King William would not give Chaldron to just any

man, but to one of his most loyal barons, one fierce enough to hold it at all cost. Would he choose the Black Wolf?

He was certainly the fiercest of all William's warriors. The thought alone gave her cold chills. Perhaps he already had a wife. She had no way of knowing. And even if he did, she had no guarantee William would not give her to another knight and Chaldron to someone else. She would pray that did not happen. As much as she feared being given to a man in marriage, she knew she could not bear leaving Chaldron and the people she loved so dearly.

She hated this war. So many noble Saxon warriors had been killed, their holdings lost. King Edward had surrounded himself with his Norman friends, as had her father. They both had a great dislike for Harold, who had no real claim to the throne. William of Normandy did, even if he was a bastard. Harold had been crowned King by the Witan because he was the most powerful Earl in England at the time of Edward's death.

Her father would have wanted William on the throne. If Harold had held the throne, he would have taken Chaldron away from her. Neither man would have allowed her to choose her own husband. No matter who reigned, she would lose. Kaela agreed with Brenna—how terribly unfair that women had no rights. She wished her future to be her own choice. Instead, the best she could hope for was an amiable husband, or one who ignored her.

Kaela pushed thoughts of the future away as she rose from her chair and crossed to the bed. She crawled beneath the covers and closed her eyes in exhaustion. Surely tonight she would sleep.

❖   ❖   ❖

He was closer. The footsteps more pronounced. She ran faster, stumbling in the dark passageway. She had to get away—up ahead a light beckoned her. She must reach the light. She must! Then she would be safe.

Her heart pounded with fear as she listened to the eerie sound of her name echoing down the passageway. She increased her speed once again, running toward the light. She stumbled and landed hard against the cold dirt floor. Something skittered across her hand and she screamed.

His laughter echoed back to her as she forced herself to her feet. She ran blindly now, searching for the light. Suddenly Broderick stood before her—his eyes, dear God, his eyes...

Kaela awoke with a start. Her eyes immediately searched the room. Alone. *The dream again. Sweet Jesu, would she ever be free of it.* She took a deep breath and tried to calm her racing heart. Her sweat-drenched body trembled violently and she swore an oath as she threw back the covers and crawled from the bed. She grabbed her cloak and made her way silently out of the keep. The moon lit her way to the drying shed where she kept her herbs and medicines. Once inside she crossed immediately to the table against the far wall and began to mix the sleeping draught, promising herself it would only be for tonight. She had controlled herself before, she could do so again. She would find the strength to overcome her nightmares. For now, however, she had to sleep.

She sent a silent plea to the heavens that God would be merciful with her.

God's mercy ran out one week later...

Chapter Three

✤   ✤   ✤

Kaela stood in the great hall giving instructions to Maude and Sarah regarding their duties for the day, when Jacob rushed in to tell her that riders approached. Together, Kaela and Jacob climbed to the walkway atop the outer wall and watched the riders coming in from the west.

"They're Normans," Jacob said.

"Aye," Kaela replied. "From the looks of the column, there is a whole army. What do you think this means, Jacob?"

"Mayhap they carry a missive from the King. Whatever it is, there is nothing to worry about, Kaela. William assured me all would be well. Take heart, girl, for we will know soon enough."

Jacob turned from her and issued orders to open the drawbridge and prepare to open the gates. Climbing back down the ladder, Kaela turned to Jacob.

"I will await word from you in my chamber. 'Tis best that you greet these visitors first and apprise me of the situation."

Jacob smiled and nodded in understanding. Kaela would watch the Normans and assess the situation before showing herself.

Once in her chamber, Kaela stepped out onto the parapet where she could view the inner bailey. She wore her heavy cloak to protect her from the harsh cold, the hood pulled over her head. Her whole body tingled with anticipation and dread as she watched the warriors approach. Well over ten-score, they all wore battle armor.

They made an intimidating picture. Had they been the enemy, she would have no hope for Chaldron. She did not have half as many warriors as she saw before her now, their armor glinting so brightly it blinded her when the sun peeked out from a cloud. Kaela looked at the banner the army carried—a snarling wolf emblazoned in silver, on a black background. The Black Wolf, she thought, and searched the warriors for a glimpse of the legend.

Five men broke away from the rest and rode their massive war horses across the drawbridge, entering the outer bailey where Jacob and his men stood ready to greet them. The men looked fierce and huge sitting astride their destriers. But the warrior in the center stood out above the other four who drew their horses in and lined up behind their leader.

The Black Wolf—Kaela had no doubt. Garbed entirely in black, he rode a black horse draped in black. The warrior's chainmail gleamed in contrast and his shield depicted the snarling head of a wolf.

Kaela watched Jacob step forward to greet the warrior. The man dismounted and stood next to Jacob, towering over him. She noticed how he observed all the activity around him.

Suddenly, the warrior glanced up and his gaze met hers. Stunned by his piercing blue eyes, she took a step back and leaned against the doorway. Why did she feel as if he could see into her very soul? Ridiculous, yet her body trembled.

The door to Kaela's chamber flew open and Brenna hurried in with Mattie in tow. "Kaela, did you see? There is a whole army out there," Brenna announced, stepping out on the parapet and leaning precariously over the balustrade, her red hair flying in the wind.

Kaela reached out and clutched Brenna's bliaut, pulling her back inside. "You fool, they can see you! Is that the kind of first impression you want to make?"

"Don't be silly, cousin. They're Normans. What difference does it make?" Brenna retorted.

"More than you realize, I think," Kaela replied.

Mattie tugged on Brenna's gown. "Hold me up, Brenna! I want to see. Is it the devil? Has he come back?" Her eyes were wide with fear.

Kaela swept Mattie up into her arms. "Nay, Mattie, see for yourself—these men are our new friends. They come from Normandy and were sent by our new King. They will not hurt us, sweet pea."

Mattie let out a squeal when she saw all the horses and warriors down below. "Look, look at the big man in black, Kaela."

"Where?" Brenna stuck her head out again.

"Down there, see him," Mattie said, pointing down and waving to the man. "He is looking right at us."

Mortified, Kaela looked down and met the warrior's gaze again. He looked astonished, then suddenly threw back his head and laughed.

Kaela whirled around, dragging Mattie and Brenna back inside her chamber. Her face burned with embarrassment.

"Take Mattie and change her gown, Brenna, and change your own as well," Kaela ordered. "We want to look our best when we greet these Normans. Dress Mattie in her blue bliaut, and why don't you wear your green one? It goes nicely with your hair."

"'Tis naught to worry over, Kaela. I fail to see what all the fuss is about," Brenna said, laughing over Kaela's embarrassment.

"I have sworn fealty to their Norman King. He is now our King, Brenna. 'Tis no secret that the Normans feel we Saxons are a backward people. I am determined to show them they are wrong in their assumptions," Kaela said, giving her cousin a blistering look. "Just do as I say, and do not go downstairs until you are summoned."

"Aye, your majesty," Brenna retorted, then took Mattie by the hand and led her out of the room.

✣   ✣   ✣

Cameron's sharp gaze missed nothing while he admired the size and magnificence of Chaldron Castle. He had never seen anything quite like the design and wondered about the man who had built it. The creator had obviously been influenced by Norman building methods, but the design was even more impressive. He had first glimpsed the Castle over two hours ago, when he had crested the western ridge and seen the crenelated towers looming in the distance. He sat upon his stallion for several minutes, gazing down on the view before him, amazed. The village, larger than he expected, looked well-kept and organized. The fields, as far as the eye could see, were being tilled and pre-pared for the coming spring planting.

A wooded area lay to the east and to the west with a beautiful meadow and a large herd of sheep grazing nearby. A small stream ran through the property, with a pond in the meadow's center. A large mill stood next to the pond. Out from the village, the land formed rolling hills. Atop the hills loomed Chaldron Castle, large enough to discourage all but the most determined enemy. The wall appeared to be over twenty feet high, with eight square bastions rising high above the outer wall. Two massive machicolated towers guarded the entrance passage, which was further defended by a drawbridge, a pair of iron studded doors, and two portcullises. A large moat surrounded the perimeter wall.

Now, standing inside the massive walls, he was appalled that so few knights had been retained here. Not even half the number needed to defend such a holding. He knew this must not have always been the case, for the castle could easily house at least three hundred men. The well-maintained garrison, located on the keep's first floor, had no more than sixty men-at-arms in residence.

Entering the great hall with Jacob and his men, he immediately noticed the cleanliness, quite a contrast to most keeps. Fresh rushes lay on the floor, emanating a most pleasant odor of fresh rosemary. The room was large, at least twice the size of the great hall at his home in Normandy. The castle rose four stories high. The barracks filled the keep's first floor with a long hall running down the center to divide the rooms. At the barracks' rear, a stone stairway led to the second floor and opened onto the great hall.

White-washed walls, covered with tapestries to help ward off the dampness, added a warmth to the large room. A massive hearth filled a large part of the back wall. The fire blazing there gave the room a warm and welcoming atmosphere. A long trestle table with several stools stood in the center on a raised platform, and there were several smaller trestle tables and benches positioned along the walls. Several large, high backed chairs stood in front of the hearth. A chess set topped a small table near the chairs. Cameron turned to Jacob and complimented him on the hall's coziness.

"'Tis Lady Kaela who is responsible for all that you see. She takes great pride in her home," Jacob answered.

"Where is this lady you speak of, Jacob? Why is she not here to welcome us?" Cameron grinned. He had seen the lady only minutes before when they entered the bailey. At least he presumed the woman standing on the parapet looking down at him to be Lady Kaela. He had no idea who the other lady might be, but the little girl laughing down at him had tugged at his heart, and he wondered about the child's identity. He had been told that Lady Kaela had yet to marry.

"Lady Kaela thought it best if I greeted you first, Baron, and inquired as to the reason for your visit," Jacob stated boldly.

"I have a message from the King, which I prefer to deliver to Lady Kaela myself, if you would be so kind as to fetch her, Jacob."

"Aye, Baron, if you will excuse me," Jacob said. He bowed to Cameron and turned toward the staircase that led to the third floor and what Cameron thought to be the sleeping chambers.

Cameron approached the trestle table and joined his men. A comely serving wench brought the men ale to quench their thirst, along with several loaves of warm, crusty bread, wedges of yellow cheese, and dried apples and figs. Andrew, Johnathan, Patrick, and

Thorsen were devouring the food, and eyeing the wench.

"Save some for your Baron," Cameron teased. He shouldered Patrick aside and helped himself to a piece of bread and ale.

"What think you of Chaldron Keep, Baron? I don't think I've ever seen anything like it."

"'Tis most impressive, Johnathan, of that there is no doubt."

"Aye, eight guard towers, and barracks large enough to house three hundred soldiers," Patrick said. "I would have loved to know the man who designed and built this fortress."

"So would I." Cameron nodded. "His defenses are impressive. Aye, the man had the mind of a warrior, but what amazes me is that he left it all to a mere woman. What could he have been thinking?"

"She is his daughter, Cameron, his only child," Andrew said.

"I'll not argue that, Andrew, but 'twas madness to leave his holding to a woman. 'Tis a miracle this keep has been managed so well. I am sure that is mostly due to Jacob. Did you notice how few soldiers are on retainer here? There are not enough men to defend even a small fortress. The wench must be mad to think she can defend herself with so few men. God's truth, a woman could not possibly know of defense and battle strategies. Nay, I think her father let softness blind him, to do such foolishness."

"What, you dare besmirch my father, you great Norman oaf?"

Kaela startled the men with her outraged cry. They turned, to see a woman storm towards them.

"How dare you judge my father? Doubtless you Normans are the devil's very own bastards. God's truth, you are not worthy to worship at my father's grave. He was a wonderful man, kind, caring, and considerate. He certainly wasn't so little minded as to think women useless as you Normans do. My father gave me the freedom he would have given a son. He encouraged me to use my mind."

"A grave mistake, that." Cameron replied with a tight smile.

"But, my lady, such a great mind as yours might also glean that we are hardly the devil's spawn, or even bastard born, though I'll grant you our Christian names do reflect our father's fondness for a foreign wench who he stole and made his lawful wife." His smile vanished. "Taking a foreign bride is not an uncommon practice among many a conquering lord, though doubtless such a fortunate woman should be chosen not only for her fair face but a sweet tongue."

"How dare you ridicule me or my lack of soldiers?" Kaela raged.

What a temper! Blasted female. She had literally spit her words at him, and in perfect French, too. Where did she learn to speak his language? Her incredible green eyes flashed with indignation. Although she was tall for a woman, he could see the hint of full breast and slim hips beneath her purple bliaut. Her hair, long, thick, rich with coppery highlights, hung loosely to her hips. A tightness gripped his body and he forced his vision from her hips to her outraged face, her look still spitting daggers at him.

Try as he might to fight it, his body responded and clear thinking became more difficult. He noticed he was not the only one affected by her beauty. His men each wore a stunned look, and something close to adoration shone in their eyes. Except for Thorsen—the

Viking always looked bored, a mask for his feelings.

"I sent five score knights I had on retainer to fight with King Harold at Stamford Bridge. They were brave Saxon warriors who fell in battle, you bloody Norman." Kaela couldn't remember the last time she had felt such fury.

Cameron arched one black eyebrow. "Are you finished, mademoiselle?"

"A… aye," Kaela stammered. Dear Lord, she had shouted at this Norman knight who towered over her. Now she looked up and really saw him for the first time. She gasped, and took a step backwards.

Her head barely reached the baron's shoulders. All the anger drained from her, replaced by fear. She trembled and had difficulty remembering how to breathe. She clasped her hands to stop their trembling and forced herself to meet his gaze. His eyes were mesmerizing, the blue so intense, with darker rings of indigo around the pupils. Kaela shook her head in an effort to clear it. The Norman was asking her a question.

"How is it you have learned to speak our language so well?" His voice sounded hoarse.

"My father traveled to Normandy several times with King Edward. He spoke your language and he saw that I learned the language as well. I was also tutored in Latin and write both languages as well as my own. Quite a feat for a mere woman, wouldn't you say, Baron?" Kaela asked, raising her chin.

Cameron realized this woman truly feared him, no real surprise since most women cowered in his presence. That she tried valiantly to mask her fear pleased him.

Cameron watched Patrick step forward, take Kaela's hand, and raise it to his lips. She flinched ever so slightly at his touch. Why? Patrick had always had a way with the ladies.

"Your French is perfect, my lady. You must forgive our earlier conversation. 'Twas not meant to slight you or your father. God's truth, we are amazed at all you have accomplished here. Isn't that so, Baron?" Patrick asked, giving Cameron a sly wink.

Cameron grunted and glared at Patrick, noting he still held Kaela's hand.

Patrick released her immediately and stepped back.

"Allow me to introduce my vassals, Lady Kaela. The bold one here is Patrick," Cameron told her. Patrick made a sweeping bow, a cocky grin on his handsome face.

"'Tis pleased I am to meet you, Patrick," Kaela said. She took a step closer to Jacob.

Cameron noticed how her hands trembled and he suddenly wanted to take her hand in his and comfort her. Scowling, he attributed his reaction to utter weariness.

He watched as a smiling Johnathan took over the introductions. Cameron felt an emotion very close to jealousy. Finding his own voice, he introduced her to Thorsen. The Viking had been his friend since childhood. In those days Thorsen's father had been vassal to Cameron's.

Looking up at the Viking, Kaela tensed and gripped Jacob's hand. Cameron wondered at her reaction, then decided the scowl on Thorsen's face intimidated her.

"Don't mind Thorsen," Andrew told her. "He always scowls, though he doesn't mean anything by it. 'Tis just his way."

Still, Kaela appeared very pale to Cameron, her trembling more pronounced. *What was wrong with her?*

Kaela felt dizzy with fear. Something about the

Norseman reminded her of Broderick—perhaps his pale blond hair and light eyes. Instinctively, she stepped backward.

Jacob recognized her fear and gently squeezed her hand. "You said you have a missive from the King, Baron?"

"Aye, King William requests your presence in London, Lady Kaela."

Kaela's eyes widened in surprise. "William of Normandy has requested to see me?" she asked, incredulously. All thought of Broderick and the Viking scattered.

"Aye, William sent a missive to Ralston Manor in which he requested that I inspect Chaldron's holdings and bring you to London with me. He and Lady Matilda are most anxious to meet you," Cameron explained. He watched her face closely and saw myriad emotions. Amazement, fear, and a certain wariness that made him long to chase the uncertainty from her life. A foolish thought, he knew. Sweet Jesu, but this woman did strange things to his senses.

"So, it was you at Ralston Manor?" Kaela asked, catching her mistake too late. She had no desire for Cameron to know anything about Broderick, and had demanded Jacob's silence on the subject.

Her words set Cameron aback. "You knew I was at Ralston?"

"Oh, I did not know you were there. You misunderstand me, my lord. I merely asked if you were there."

She dared to lie to him! He could see it in her face. How could she know of Broderick and Ralston Manor? Were they in league? If he found out the wench had aided the bastard... by God, he would strangle her! How like a woman to be devious and underhanded, the very reason he wanted nothing to do with the creatures.

Kaela's next question interrupted his thoughts.
"What know you of Broderick of Ralston? Was he
taken in the battle?" Cameron could see she was visibly
shaken now, her face pale, tears swimming in her eyes.

Cameron saw red. No wonder she was so afraid.
She knew of the battle at Ralston Manor and feared for
that bastard, Broderick. Disgust surged through
Cameron. This beautiful, intelligent woman could not
care for such a snake. But then, he would never
understand a woman's mind and did not wish to.

"The sorry bastard escaped before Ralston's defenses
were breached. He ran away, like the coward he is!"
Cameron roared at her.

Kaela trembled. The look on Cameron's face was
one of pure hatred. Did he hate Broderick as much as
she did? She didn't understand. Was he angry at her?
Why? Had she not sworn fealty to William, and
welcomed the Black Wolf into her home? Fire surged
in her veins, momentarily blocking out her fear. How
dare he treat her this way? She had done nothing to
provoke him.

"Don't you shout at me," Kaela blazed. "'Twas not
but a question. God's teeth, Norman, what is the matter
with you?"

"Never mind, I have heard all I want to hear from
you tonight, mademoiselle," Cameron said, sarcasm
dripping from each word. "We will finish this discussion in the morning. I expect a complete tour of your
properties, so I can give a full report to William. Jacob
tells me you have been acting as steward since your
father's death. You will ride along with us. My men
are weary and in need of rest. They will be occupying
the barracks for the time being. Prepare a chamber,

and have a meal sent up to me, along with a bath," he demanded.

Heat rushed to Kaela's cheeks, outrage firing through her. How dare he command her? England may be conquered, but she would be damned if he would conquer her.

"I have work to do, Norman," she said tightly, then shot a glance at Jacob. "See to his needs, Jacob." She turned and stormed out of the room... the same way she had stormed in.

❖   ❖   ❖

Fuming, Kaela spent the day in her chamber. She couldn't understand the change in the Norman. One moment he acted almost human, and the next he raved like a mad man. No wonder they called him the Black Wolf. She sent Brenna down to see to the evening meal and the men's comfort. A loudly protesting Mattie, she sent to the nursery. That heathen would never get anywhere near the little girl.

Moody and silent, despite Maude's attempts at conversation, Kaela took her meal in her room. Maude prepared her bath for her, bringing the wooden tub in and placing it next to the fire. Sarah and Eleanor brought up several buckets of hot water to fill the tub, leaving two buckets for Kaela to rinse her hair.

Finally alone, Kaela stripped off her clothing and eased into the tub. The warm water soothed her ragged nerves. God's truth, the Norman not only frightened her, he infuriated her. He also made her feel things she didn't understand. She had never seen eyes like his— so blue, and somehow so knowing. Kaela wondered if he could look into her mind and see her every thought.

He stood taller than the other men he had introduced her to, with the same massive proportions—broad shouldered, his chest incredibly wide, arms and thighs bulging with muscle. Kaela had no doubt he could snap her in half with his large hands. She knew all about being overpowered and helpless to fight against a man's strength. She had unwittingly angered him. Would he harm her? Somehow she thought not. Nay, it was the admiration in his eyes that frightened her.

Going to London to meet the King worried her. She feared she might never see Chaldron again. She had barely escaped Broderick and returned home. Now she must leave Brenna and Mattie again. Tears filled her eyes.

Kaela snatched up the rose scented soap Maude had left for her and scrubbed her skin vigorously, working out her frustration. She washed and rinsed her hair, but the tension never left her body. She stepped from the wooden tub and stood close to the fire to towel herself dry. She was completely surrounded by men. The black wolf, Normandy's fiercest warrior, slept down the hall. She had seen lust in his eyes. What if…

Kaela wrapped herself in a fur and crossed to her trunk. Though her hands shook, she reached for a vile of the opiate and drank the contents in one swallow. *Just for tonight,* she promised herself. *Just once more.*

She crossed back to the fire to try and erase the chill that reached to the depths of her soul. After a few minutes the potion began to take effect and she fell into a heavy sleep.

❖   ❖   ❖

Cameron stood before the hearth in his bed chamber, dressed only in his chausses, his chest bare. With his belly full and after a warm bath, he felt wonderful, but still tightly wound. That woman. Why did she affect him so? He had probably overreacted to her questions earlier. But Elizabeth had taught him not to trust women. A lesson he would never forget. Kaela had lied to him, damn it, and he intended to find out why. Obeying the King's command to see her safely to London would be a blasted inconvenience. Eager to return to London, he knew the girl would slow him down miserably. She probably couldn't even ride. Worse, he would have the very devil keeping his men from her. Frustrated, Cameron raked his hands through his hair.

God, he needed sleep for he had much to do on the morrow. Turning from the hearth, he started across the room to the bed when he heard a strange sound. He stood still and listened intently. Again, he heard a strange moaning sound.

Retrieving his dagger from the mantle, Cameron crossed to the heavy door and opened it, trying to get a sense of where the sounds originated. There, louder this time, the moans came from the chamber at the hallway's end.

Cameron crept down the hall and paused outside the door. The cries held an urgency, as if someone were in agony.

He tried the door. Unlocked. Quietly, he stepped into the room. His gaze flew to the big bed against the far wall. Empty. The cry came again and Cameron whirled. His breath caught in his throat when he saw her.

Damn. Lady Kaela lay on a bed of furs before the hearth. His heart pounded wildly, his loins tightened.

Naked, she had kicked aside the furs and curled on her side. The firelight bathed her body in soft golden light. Lord, she was beautiful. His body hardened painfully as he gazed at her breasts, full and softly rounded, with nipples a rosy pink that begged for a man's mouth. Slim waisted, her stomach flat, her hips smoothly curved… his mouth went dry. God, he wanted her, wanted to touch her soft woman's mound. Her copper hair fanned about her, highlights dancing in the firelight.

Cameron let his gaze roam freely, boldly. An image of her long legs wrapped around him as he plunged into her came unbidden into his mind, and he grew even harder. He couldn't remember the last time he had wanted a woman this much, so much he trembled. His shaft stood eager, aching, his breathing shallow and labored. He ran his hands through his hair. Frustrated, he forced himself to move away from her. He could not have this woman. William trusted him to bring her to London, the virgin he had found her, long protected by her giant fortress.

Kaela cried out again in her sleep, obviously lost in a nightmare's throes. If he woke her, she would be mortified to have him find her like this. Perhaps he should cover her with the fur and leave her alone. Surely, the dream would pass and she need never know he had seen her. He swept his eyes over her once again. Her beauty would haunt him for a long, long time. When he tugged on the furs, Kaela screamed again. Instinctively, he knelt to take her in his arms, to comfort her. The moment he touched her, she cried out and began to thrash wildly. An empty vial fell from her hand and rolled toward the fire. Cameron picked it up and took a cautious sniff. God's teeth, she had drugged herself.

Kaela moaned again and he turned back to her. Tears streamed down her face as she begged, the sound piteous. "No, no, no, noooo... don't touch me, stay away, stay away."

Dear God, what had happened to her? What terror would cause her to drug herself into a sleep so deep he doubted she knew yet that he knelt beside her? Cameron stroked her hair, trying to soothe her, yet afraid to try to hold her lest she cry out again. He murmured soft words and ran his hands through her silken tresses. He took a deep breath... she smelled like roses. How odd to smell roses in winter. Cameron watched her, a worried frown creasing his brow.

Kaela rolled over to her other side and curled her body into a tight ball. "No! No!" she cried.

"Holy Mother of God," Cameron gasped, horrified. Her back, her beautiful back! He couldn't believe his eyes. Ugly lash marks ran across her back from her right shoulder to her waist. The scars appeared deep, the edges smooth and shiny as if they'd been healed for a long time.

Sweet Jesu, a beating like this could have killed the girl.

Someone had whipped this beautiful, brave woman when she had been little more than a young maid. Rage at the unknown villain ran cold in his blood. Kaela... what courage she must have had to sustain her through such a beating. A deep respect began to grow within him, respect and something akin to tenderness. He reached out and gathered her into his arms, lifted her, and carried her to the bed. Ignoring her weak struggles against him, he placed her gently on the soft mattress.

She trembled with cold and Cameron lay beside her, pulling the heavy furs over them. Kaela didn't resist his touch this time, but sighed and snuggled closer to his warmth. Cameron wrapped his arms around her and held her gently to him, running his large hands over her smooth, shapely thighs and buttocks to warm her. He told himself he meant only to give her comfort, but his loins hardened again, and he knew he must leave her soon or he would not be able to stop himself from ravishing her.

She didn't deserve that; she had known enough brutality in her short lifetime. Gingerly, he ran his fingertips along the lines of her scars. Kaela flinched slightly in her sleep and let out a soft moan. Cameron pressed a tender kiss against her brow and promised himself he would avenge her. Carefully, he lifted himself from the bed and left the room before he gave into the lust that would make him no better than the whoreson who had whipped her.

Back in his own chamber, the turmoil in Cameron's mind denied him sleep. The girl had touched him, touched him deeply. But he didn't really care for her. No, he felt sorry for her, nothing more. Still, he made a silent vow to protect her from further harm. He owed that much to William.

He had his own wounds to heal, though they were not on the outside like Kaela's. The lashes against his heart had scarred him, closed his mind to women and the pain they caused. But something about her called to him. At the very least, he would find the bastard who had beaten her. When he did, the man would pay with his own blood.

Chapter Four

✛   ✛   ✛

Cameron awoke and knew someone had entered his room. When he rolled on his side to reach for his sword, he came face to face with eyes as blue and brilliant as the morning sky. Ah, the little nymph he had seen laughing down at him yesterday. She was perched on his bed, staring at him with eyes round with curiosity. She showed no fear, but scooted closer and placed her hand on his arm.

She tilted her head to one side. "My name is Mattie. Who are you?"

Cameron stared at her, astonished. He could not believe this little pixie had boldly marched into his bedroom, clambered atop his bed, and proceeded to question him. She poked him with one chubby finger.

"Are you awake yet?" she asked.

"Aye, Madam, I believe I am." He couldn't control a wide grin. She rewarded him with one of her own. What a beautiful child. Her smile brightened the room like sunshine.

"Well?"

"Well, what?"

"Who are you?"

"My name is Cameron. What is your name?"

"I already told you," she said, giggling.

"What did you already tell me?"

She frowned at him, but her eyes danced. "Mattie, my name is Mattie."

"'Tis pleased I am to meet you, Mattie. Now, would you mind telling me what you are doing in my bed?" Cameron pulled himself up against the head board and tucked the furs firmly around his waist.

Her face solemn, Mattie climbed onto his lap. "I came to see the devil. Kaela said you were not and so did Brenna, but I didn't believe them 'cause Kaela's scared of you. She stayed in her chamber all day yesterday, and I heard her crying last night."

Cameron stared at her in utter disbelief. What was the child talking about? He could see she was very serious.

"I am not a devil, Mattie. I am only a soldier, a Norman soldier. Your new King William is my friend and I have come on his behalf to see Chaldron, and to bring a message to the Lady Kaela. Does that answer your question?"

"Aye," she said with a sigh. Then she smiled again, that sweet trusting smile, and his heart turned over. "I knew you couldn't be the devil. I just wanted to make sure, that's all."

"What say you of the devil, Mattie?"

"He's the bad man who took Kaela away."

Cameron tensed, his senses alert. "Someone took Kaela away? When was this, Mattie? And who is Kaela to you? Is she your mother?"

"My mama died when I was a baby. Kaela's my cousin. I love her like a mama, though. Brenna's my sister. I love her, too, but she is very bossy."

Cameron laughed at that. "This Brenna, she's the

sassy red head I saw at dinner last eve, is she not?"
The girl had acted outrageously, much to his vassals
delight. She had quite a mouth on her, that one.

Mattie nodded.

"When did someone take Kaela away, Mattie, and
where did she go?" Frowning, Cameron repeated the
questions. Mattie's answers might explain the lash marks
he had seen on Kaela's back. Rage surged through him
each time he thought about what she had endured.

A curious look on her cherubic face, Mattie stared
at the mass of black hair on his chest. She extended
her hands and placed them there, curling her fingers
into fists and tugging.

"Ouch," Cameron yelped. "What are you doing,
you little minx?"

Mattie laughed up at him, tossing her shiny black
curls. "They're all springy, just like I thought. How
come you have hair on your chest?"

Cameron groaned. "God's truth, little one, many
men have hair on their chests."

"Oh, I've never seen a man's chest before. You
have many muscles, too. Why is Kaela afraid of you?"

"She isn't. I made her angry yesterday, that's all."

"Did you make her cry?" she asked him, frowning
again.

"Nay, she must have had a bad dream. I am sure
she will be all right. Now tell me about this devil,
Mattie." He tried not to sound exasperated, but extract-
ing information from this tiny girl required more
patience than training a war horse.

Mattie shrugged. "I'm not s'posed to know 'bout
him, but I heard Brenna tell Uncle Jacob a bad man
took Kaela away. She called him 'a bloody devil.'
Uncle Jacob got real mad. Everybody cried when

Kaela was gone. At first I thought she sneaked away, 'cause she didn't tell me good-bye. Brenna said she went on a journey, but I knew that wasn't true. Kaela always says goodbye." Her sky blue eyes stared anxiously into his.

"How long was she gone?"

"A long time." Mattie couldn't tell him more, he realized. Her child's mind would not know how to gauge time.

"When did she return to Chaldron?" he asked. "And was she alone when she came back?"

"'Twas over a sennight ago and Maude and Arik came home with her."

"Who are Maude and Arik? Did they leave with Kaela, too?"

"Nay, Brenna sent Maude and Arik to help Kaela. I know 'cause Arik told me. He's my friend. Maude is Arik's mama and Kaela's old Nanny."

"Is Arik little like you?"

Mattie giggled. "Arik's almost as big as you."

Cameron was sorting through all this information when Mattie reached over and grabbed his hand.

"I knew you were not the devil. 'Twas you who laughed at me yesterday and I remember Brenna called the bad man a giant, blond devil. Your hair is black like mine, so it couldn't be you. I'm glad."

"Why are you glad, Mattie?"

"'Cause I like you." Mattie reached up, put her small chubby arms around his neck, and gave him a squeeze.

"I like you too, little one." Cameron returned her hug, then lifted her off his lap and set her on the floor. "Mayhap you should go and wake Kaela. 'Tis sure she would love to see you this morn."

"Oh, Kaela's been up for hours. She went out to ride Sky. Her horse is beautiful and fast as the wind. Your horse is beautiful, too. What's his name?"

"Goliath."

"Can I ride him?"

"Nay, little one, no one rides Goliath but me. I will take you down to the stables with me later and let you see him."

Mattie's eyes widened with pleasure. "Thank you! But you must make friends with Kaela first. She won't let me near you," she told him. With a mischievous grin on her face, she backed slowly from the room. "You will, won't you, Cameron?"

"Aye, you can count on it, little one."

Cameron smiled to himself. Making amends with Kaela might prove an interesting task. With that thought in mind, he jumped from the bed and dressed quickly, anxious to find the lady in question.

✦   ✦   ✦

Cameron found his vassals with Jacob in the outer bailey, surveying the practice field. It was quite impressive. The large field had wooden stands built to one side. He overheard Andrew and Patrick organizing a tournament for the men to be held that afternoon. A good idea. His men were tired, battle-weary. They hadn't seen their families since they had left Normandy back in September. The match, both entertainment and exercise, would be good for them. Giving Andrew and Patrick his approval, he pulled Jacob aside to ask about Kaela's whereabouts.

"She went riding, my lord," Jacob said, a furious scowl on his face. "God's teeth, the lass is stubborn. I tried to get her to stay within the castle walls, or to let me send an escort with her, but she wouldn't allow it. The girl is headstrong, she is."

"I'm afraid I might have something to do with that," Cameron said. "Mayhap she thinks to avoid confronting me, Jacob. I greatly angered your mistress when we met."

"Aye, Baron, I'm afraid so. Kaela is sensitive about her father. She still grieves for him deeply, and you were harsh with her yesterday when she questioned you about Broderick," Jacob said, his brown gaze unflinching.

Cameron felt a surge of anger at the mention of Broderick's name. "What is her relationship to Broderick? Does she try to protect the cur?"

"Nay, Baron, Kaela and Broderick are cousins, but 'Tis no love lost between the two. She merely wanted to know what had happened to the man."

Intuitively, Cameron knew Jacob told the truth. Very well, he would take the knight at his word for now; after all, he had no reason to doubt him, but he hoped for all their sakes that his intuition was correct.

"Jacob, take Johnathan and Thorsen, and show them the stables, garrison, and storehouses. I am going to retrieve your wayward mistress. When I return, we will all ride out and tour the village and surrounding fields. Where will I find her?"

"Kaela usually rides along the west ridge toward the lake when she is troubled. Have patience with her, Baron. The girl has been through more than you know," Jacob told him.

Cameron gazed at the knight intently. "Is there something you wish to tell me, Jacob?"

"Aye, but I promised my mistress I wouldn't."

"I see." Cameron sighed. So Kaela didn't want him to know about her ordeal. He could understand that, but he intended to deny her desire. He was determined to know the truth.

Cameron stalked to the stables and saddled Goliath. His temperamental stallion didn't like anyone other than Cameron to be near him. The great black destrier snorted loudly as Cameron approached. Cameron mounted and rode out through the outer bailey. Once across the drawbridge, he turned west to search for Kaela.

It didn't take him long to find her after he crested the ridge. Her horse galloped with great speed across the meadow below, racing toward him. The day was cold and Kaela wore her heavy cloak, but the hood had fallen back and her coppery hair had escaped its binding to stream behind her. Cameron's heart quickened as he watched her. God's teeth, what a beautiful woman, filled with fire and defiance, and yes, vulnerability. Cameron understood why she wanted to keep her pain and fear hidden, but he couldn't allow her to hide the facts from him. He wondered if the cur who had hurt her was the "devil" Mattie had chirped about. He would know soon enough. He urged Goliath into a gallop down the ridge to join her.

Kaela heard the horse's hooves and turned to see the Black Wolf galloping toward her. Her breath caught in her throat. Lord, the man looked magnificent. He rode his stallion as if he and the beast were one.

Cameron called out for Kaela to halt and reined Goliath in beside her mount. He looked down at her, his eyes dancing with amusement.

"I see that I need not have worried," he said, giving her a smile that stopped her heart.

God's teeth, this man was too handsome for his own good. No doubt ladies swooned when he favored them with one of his magnificent smiles. He had perfectly straight white teeth, and a beguiling dimple in his right cheek. The conceited lout knew it, too, for he seemed quite full of himself. She would die before she let him know she found him handsome. Deliberately scowling, she answered him.

"What say you? Worried about what?"

"Your riding ability. I thought sure you would impede our journey to London, but I see I was wrong. You ride like a man, my lady."

Like a man, indeed. She would prove to this condescending oaf that she could do anything a man could do. Even so, she could not help smiling, proud to have won his approval.

When she smiled at him, pure joy swelled within Cameron's breast. Shocked, he realized this woman could invade his heart, but at the moment he wanted to taste her sweet, luscious mouth. Staring at her mouth, he realized she spoke to him. Her words were low and soft, carried away by the rising wind that whipped her hair around her face and shoulders.

"I beg pardon, mistress. What did you say?"

"Why are you here? Was there something you wanted?"

"I want to tour the village and surrounding fields. I told you yesterday I wanted you to escort me. Nor do I want you to ride alone again. In fact, I forbid it."

"You forbid me? By what right do you forbid me to ride on my own lands? I ride where I please, Baron. You will forbid me nothing, not while I am mistress of Chaldron." Her voice cold and controlled, Kaela stared defiantly at Cameron.

"Someone needs to tell you what to do, you little fool." Her words and the defiant look on her face angered him. He would teach this woman her place, though the teaching sorely tried them both. "Any idiot would realize that to ride unescorted outside the castle walls is dangerous. Curse the saints, woman, you try a man's patience. Saxon resisters still roam these lands, not to mention thieves and marauders. What do you think they would do to a woman alone if they came upon you?"

Dismayed, Cameron watched Kaela's face turn a deathly white. He feared she might swoon and reached out a callused hand to steady her.

"Are you all right?" he asked, gently.

"Aye, but I have realized you are right. I should not have come alone. You have my word, I will accede to your wishes, at least on this issue. Let's ride back now. We'll collect Jacob and your vassals and I'll show you the village and Chaldron lands."

She turned Sky and nudged the mare into a gallop. Cameron rode by her side back to the castle, unable to believe the effect his words had on her. He had expected her to fly back at him, furious that he dared forbid her anything. Instead, he had made her fearful. Perhaps she had remembered who had put those scars on her back, the "devil", as Mattie had called him. At least she listened to reason. She had shown such fear; Cameron cursed, realizing he did not like to see her weak and uncertain. He preferred the fiery wench who defied him.

Once again, he vowed to discover the devil's identity, for he had no doubt a mere mortal had done this terrible harm to her. What man would want to mar that beautiful skin, crush that spirit? A dark mood settled

over him. He could not force Kaela to confide in him.
Mayhap this Arik or Maude could be persuaded to tell
the tale. Surely, anyone who loved the mistress of
Chaldron Castle would be hot for revenge.

He watched Kaela urge her horse toward the safety
of the keep, and he felt an unaccustomed tightness in
his chest. By God, he would see the lady free from the
fear that gripped her, and soon. He pondered how best
to broach the subject as they rode back to the castle.

The Chaldron holding fascinated Cameron in the
same manner as did its mistress. Beyond question,
Kaela's father had been a man before his time.
Everywhere Cameron looked he saw things that
amazed him. They had started their tour with the
unbelievably well organized village. The cottages
were neat and clean. Many were made of wood, not
the usual sod. The villagers, curious about their visitors,
all stood out in the road. Cameron saw by the warm
expressions on their faces when they greeted Kaela
that they were fond of their mistress, who called each
one by name, asking after their health and their
families.

Johnathan, Jacob, and Thorsen rode with them.
Thorsen, a quiet man, maintained his usual silence.
Cameron noticed that Kaela kept her distance from the
Viking, urging her mount to the forefront next to
Cameron's. Johnathan rode beside Jacob, questioning
the knight in great detail about the farming procedures
in the well-tended fields. Although men were plowing
a large field to their right in preparation for planting,
two equally large fields lay fallow.

"Why leave these fields fallow?" Cameron asked.

"We use a three field system here. 'Twas my father's idea and has been most productive. With three fields instead of two in rotation, grain production has been thrice increased. This field is being plowed now for the spring planting of barley and rye." Kaela spoke with great pride in her voice.

"You will also notice horses in the field along with the oxen. The horses are collared and have a system of leather ropes we call harnesses, allowing them to work at full strength without strangling themselves. Although faster than the oxen, they require costly grain for feed and are more susceptible to disease. Using a balance of the two has proved most effective."

When Cameron looked at her, she blushed, her fair skin a becoming pink, and his heart beat faster.

"You truly astound me, Lady Kaela. First I learn you speak and write English, French, and Latin, a quite extraordinary feat in itself. God's truth, few of my knights can read or write with any true skill. 'Tis on priests we rely for such a service, but never have I known a woman who could do these things." He paused, gestured toward the men working. "Now I see before me well tended and productive fields, and agricultural methods unlike anything I have ever heard of. 'Tis quite remarkable."

Kaela's blush deepened. His intense gaze and charming smile set her body tingling. Confused by her reaction and determined he would not know his effect on her, she said, "'Tis not I who am remarkable, my lord, but my father. Everything I know I learned from him. The innovations were his."

"Aye, a remarkable man," Jacob added. "You should have been here when Charles first came. 'Twas nothing compared to what you see now. The castle is the finest in all of England. Several Norman barons have patterned their castles after Chaldron's design, but none compare. 'Tis your doing, my lady, that Chaldron remains as well-cared-for as in your father's day." Pride filled Jacob's voice.

"I am impressed, my lady," Cameron said, turning his mount. "We should return now. The hour grows late and my men have planned a mock battle for this afternoon. 'Twill be a welcome diversion. We will tour the mill and the outlying properties on the morrow."

"By your leave, my lord," Kaela replied, turning her horse beside his.

❖   ❖   ❖

The Black Wolf's soldiers and the keep's serfs filled the outer bailey. Brenna, Kaela, and Mattie sat on a raised pavilion where Maude and Arik joined them. Jacob was participating in the melee.

The soldiers had separated into two mock armies. A knight who felled his opponent won his match. A prize went to the knight who performed best in battle.

The first match to draw the ladies' eyes was between Jacob and Johnathan. While Brenna cheered loudly, Jacob and Johnathan hurtled towards each other, leaning forward on their mounts, spears leveled. The first point went to Jacob as he thrust forward, knocking Johnathan's lance to the ground. He made his pass by the stands where Brenna jumped up and down, and Mattie blew him kisses. He gave Kaela a jaunty salute, laughter and pride in his warm brown eyes.

However, Jacob was soon felled by Johnathan, which did not surprise Kaela. God's truth, the Norman knight was two decades younger than Jacob, and his prowess with his sword made the outcome inevitable. The crowd cheered as the two warriors saluted each other and rode off the field.

Andrew and Patrick drew the ladies' attention as they challenged each other. Kaela noticed the warm gleam in Brenna's eye when she looked at Andrew.

"Do you see something you like, Brenna?" Kaela teased.

"Aye, cousin. His name is Andrew. I met him at dinner last eve. He is beautiful, is he not?" Brenna said dreamily and waved boldly to Andrew. The handsome knight tipped both helm and lance to her.

"Beautiful? I do not think I would call the younger brother of the Black Wolf beautiful." Kaela couldn't help laughing.

"Brother? Oh nay! Don't tell me that handsome warrior is brother to his Excellency! 'Tis not so," Brenna wailed.

"His Excellency? 'Tis Cameron of whom you speak?"

"Aye, 'Tis what I call him. The name fits, don't you think? The way he lords himself around. I heard how he ordered you about," Brenna said in a huff.

"God's teeth, Brenna, don't be so judgmental. The man is accustomed to command and he was upset at the time." Kaela couldn't believe she had spoken in Cameron's defense.

"Well, I don't like him, although I have yet to meet him. However, his brother is most handsome." She returned her gaze to Andrew and sighed.

Unfortunately, Patrick unseated Andrew on the first pass. Too busy trying to impress Brenna, the younger knight failed to concentrate on his skillful adversary.

Patrick laughed as he helped his friend up. "You had best get your mind off bedding and on fighting, my friend."

"Aye," Andrew laughed. "But she is beautiful, is she not Patrick?"

"True, but that tongue, Andrew. Why, 'Tis a veritable sword."

"She speaks like an angel," Andrew replied, then drew his sword. Again, Brenna cheered and waved to him.

Johnathan, outweighing Andrew by almost three stone and a far more seasoned warrior, took the final match after a grueling battle. To the crowd's applause and cheers, they rode off the field.

When the winning army had been established, the soldiers began to drift into small groups. Chanting "Wolf" and "Viking" until the sound became a roar, they called for Cameron and Thorsen to join in battle. At Thorsen's nod, he and Cameron joined the melee and walked to the center of the field while stripping off their tunics.

The crowd cheered again when the two men began to circle each other.

Kaela couldn't tear her eyes away from Cameron's beautifully muscled, sun-bronzed body, or the wide triangle of black hair that narrowed at the waist band of his chausses. His dark tan contrasted Thorsen's paler skin. The blond Viking's chest had no hair. Equally muscled, Kaela thought the two men quite evenly matched.

Awed, she watched Cameron lunge and catch Thorsen's waist in a death-like grip. The blond Viking hooked Cameron's head in a fierce hold between his right arm and his upper torso. Cameron twisted, lifted

Thorsen's body from the ground, and threw him several feet. Brenna tugged on Kaela's arm and Mattie jumped up and down, more excited than Kaela had ever seen the child.

"Oh, Kaela," Brenna exclaimed, "never have I seen anything like them."

"I should hope not," Kaela replied. When she realized she wanted to reach out and touch the dark hair covering his chest, she gasped. Praise God, the sound went unnoticed as the crowd cheered louder.

Thorsen now had Cameron pinned to the ground. Kaela wondered if he would squeeze the very life from him. Cameron quickly brought his knee up and forced Thorsen off him. In one smooth motion, the Norman rolled to his feet, leaped on the Viking's back, and locked his arms around Thorsen's neck.

Kaela cheered for Cameron, and realized she too had risen to her feet. She watched Cameron throw Thorsen to the ground, whereupon Johnathan signaled the end of the match and declared Cameron the winner.

To Kaela's mortification, Cameron strode over to stand before her and made a low, sweeping bow. Mattie stood on tiptoe, holding out her arms and wiggling her fingers. She gave Cameron her brightest smile and laughed joyously as the warrior reached out and scooped her up. Kaela looked on in disbelief. To her knowledge, the two hadn't even met.

"You won, you won! I knew you would!" Mattie cried, hugging his neck.

"Aye, little mistress, I did, and just for you, too," Cameron said to the little girl, but his gaze locked with Kaela's.

"Mattie, you little imp," Brenna cried, breaking the spell. "What must the Baron think of you? Come here to me this instant."

"'Tis quite all right." Cameron laughed, but handed Mattie over to Brenna. "The little mademoiselle and I are fast friends. Isn't that so, Mattie?"

"Aye, my lord," Mattie said, her voice quite serious before she giggled.

"Oh? And just when did this friendship come about?" Kaela frowned first at Cameron, then at her small cousin.

"Why early this morning when I woke to find unexpected company in my bed."

"Oh, Mattie!" Kaela gasped.

"Oh, Mattie, indeed," Brenna exclaimed, throwing her head back and laughing. "You are shameless, little sister."

"You need not worry, madam, all was quite innocent I assure you." Cameron grinned broadly. "Come, Mattie," Cameron drawled. "I believe I promised you a look at Goliath, and now is a perfect time." He retrieved Mattie from Brenna's arms and strode toward the stables, the little girl on his shoulders.

"God's truth, I believe he has made a friend for life," Brenna said.

"Aye, the little traitor." Kaela felt a smile tug at her mouth.

That night Cameron and Kaela's loyal vassals filled the great hall. A jovial mood enveloped the entire company. Cook had outdone herself, preparing a huge feast of mutton, veal, and roasted goose. With Mattie snuggled next to her, Kaela sat next to Cameron at the main table. Jacob sat across from her on Cameron's left. Brenna, along with Andrew, Johnathan, Patrick, and Thorsen completed the table.

Cameron noticed how his vassals stared at Kaela.

He made no comment, for he could not take his gaze from her either. Brenna and Mattie entertained everyone with their accounts of the afternoon's melee, and Kaela smiled all through the meal.

"We will tour the mill tomorrow, Jacob, and the outlying area. There's no need for you to ride with us, Kaela. I want to leave for London day after tomorrow. 'Twould be wise to use the time to prepare for the journey."

"You are going to London, Kaela?" Mattie asked, wide eyed and clinging tightly to Kaela's arm.

Now he had done it. Kaela had wanted to tell Mattie about the journey to London. Her little cousin would be upset to be left behind again. Kaela shot Cameron a murderous glance before she pulled Mattie onto her lap.

"Aye, sweet pea," she said in her gentlest voice. "I have been invited to London to meet our new King. Is that not exciting?" Kaela did her best to sound cheerful, even though the idea terrified her.

"I don't want you to go, Kaela," Mattie cried, burying her head against Kaela s breast.

"What is this nonsense? Why does William want to see my cousin?" Brenna asked, staring coldly at Cameron. "Surely you do not plan to take Kaela to London unchaperoned."

"'Tis exactly what I plan to do." Cameron returned her icy stare with his own.

"I'm coming with you," Brenna said as she turned to Kaela.

Kaela shook her head. "You must stay and care for Mattie."

Cameron interrupted her. "Jacob, along with most of my soldiers, will remain to see that the Keep runs smoothly. Chaldron will be quite safe in Kaela's absence," he said, his voice showing his irritation. Ridiculous, the way they all clung to Kaela. The girl shouldered too much responsibility. God's teeth, anyone could see the stress she endured.

"But is Kaela safe with you, m'lord?" Brenna shot back.

Cameron raised an eyebrow. Andrew reached for Brenna's hand.

"'Tis not for you to worry, Brenna. Kaela will be well cared for."

"'Tis what I fear," she murmured.

Andrew frowned. "My brother is a man of honor, mistress. You speak without cause."

"Enough, Brenna. You need not frighten Mattie more than she already is. I will be fine, sweet pea." Kaela patted Mattie's back to soothe her. "I look forward to meeting our new King. I will take Sarah with me to act as maid and chaperon."

The worry on Mattie's face tugged at Cameron. "'Tis true, Mattie," Cameron said gently. "The King and Queen are friends of mine. William was friends with Kaela's papa. There will be much celebration while Kaela is there. I am sure she will have a good time and she won't be gone long at all." He smiled reassuringly.

Kaela's heart melted a little more. She couldn't believe this Norman warrior was trying to soothe a child. He had been so good with her today. Mattie had chattered all afternoon about her visit with Goliath and her wonderful Wolf. Mattie had never taken to another man the way she did to Cameron.

Mattie turned her large blue eyes on Cameron. "Are you coming back too, Wolf?"

using Kaela's endearment for her.

Mattie slipped away from Kaela and crawled up in Cameron's lap. "I want you to come back, Wolf," she said, her thumb in her mouth and her black curly head against his breast.

Cameron's chest tightened painfully. "Why, little one?" His voice sounded gruff to his ears.

"'Cause, I like you."

"I like you too, sweet pea."

Glaring at Cameron, Brenna pushed back her stool. "Come, Mattie, 'Tis time for bed. 'Tis obvious you're too tired to know what you are saying."

"I want Kaela to put me to bed." Mattie's mouth turned down in a pout.

"Come along then. I will take you." Kaela held out her hand.

Mattie wrapped her arms around Cameron's neck and gave him a very wet, very loud kiss on his cheek. "Night, Wolf."

"Good night, Mattie." Cameron watched them cross the room to the stairs that led to their bed chambers. Indeed, he needed to armor his heart against those two—he had neither time nor inclination to dally with the lovely mistress of Chaldron and her tiny, adorable cousin. He turned back to his men to find them watching him, amusement on all their faces. To his horror, he felt his face flush.

"The hour grows late. You may retire to your quarters, gentlemen." He dismissed them, daring them to make the teasing comments that so obviously hovered on their tongues.

Chapter Five

✣   ✣   ✣

A thousand stars twinkled in the sky. Cameron paused to gaze at them while he walked along the wall-walk. He had sought the cold night air to clear his head.

He pondered his reaction to Kaela and Mattie. His feeling for Mattie he understood. She reminded him of Peter in so many ways. But his reaction to Kaela mystified him. He wanted to protect them. He had seen many women pretend to be vulnerable, but there was no playacting here. God's truth, Kaela tried to hide her vulnerability. Her love for the child was genuine, and it softened him toward her in spite of himself.

What would happen to Mattie if Kaela were taken from Chaldron? Even Brenna's bravado and tart, wayward tongue were a defensive ploy. The girls had only Jacob, a fine man, and loyal to all three, but not a blood relation. He held no power, would have no say in what happened to them.

Nay, Cameron thought with a sigh, 'twas up to him. He would speak to William on their behalf. Once he explained their situation, the King would see that the three stayed together here at Chaldron.

He would give Kaela to some worthy knight who

would be happy to take her to wife, especially with Chaldron holding part of the bargain. Cameron felt sick at the thought another would touch Kaela. He cast the feeling aside—he had no reason to care. He did not want a wife.

Elizabeth had almost destroyed him, taken everything he loved. He could not endure such pain again. Nay, his life satisfied him. He would settle on whatever holding William saw fit to award him and continue to train his men and secure this land for Normandy. Soon, he would bring his mother and two younger sisters to live with him.

Cameron continued to walk the castle's perimeter, speaking to the men on guard duty. Still impressed by what he had seen today, he admitted he would love to own Chaldron, but not at the sacrifice of his freedom. Not even Kaela was worth that. He would put the girl from his mind, distance himself from her. In a sennight they would be in London. Once he turned her over to William, he would never see her again.

Aye, that is what he would do. He wanted his life back to normal, disciplined and organized. These unwanted feelings would cease. Feeling better, he smiled up at the star studded sky. He would walk the perimeter wall one more time and then seek his bed.

❖   ❖   ❖

Unable to sleep, Kaela paced her chamber like a caged animal. Her body craved the opiate, but she refused to give in. Not again. She would not let her fear of Broderick destroy her life. She had managed to overcome the dependence on the draught before. She would do so again.

An hour dragged past before she reached for her cloak and made her way to the north tower. She loved the view there, especially beneath a full moon, but tonight only stars would keep her company. She would have preferred a night ride on Sky and a walk around the lake, but she had given the Norman her word.

The last time she had ridden to the lake alone, Broderick had kidnapped her. A chill riffled up her spine when she remembered, but she could force him from her mind. If only she could deny him in her dreams. The opiate gave her rest, but did not keep the dreams away. She prayed with time they would fade.

She climbed the tower stairs and gazed out at the sky. A lump tightened her throat. Many times she and her father stood in this very spot, trying to identify the constellations. Her mother had teased them, calling them her "star gazers." Oh, God, she felt so alone.

She felt a presence behind her and turned to see the Viking staring down at her. With a strangled cry, she backed away from him, only to run into the wall. He reached out to steady her and she cringed from his touch.

"Why do I frighten you, mistress?" he asked gruffly.

"You do not frighten me, sir. God's truth, you only startled me," she replied, her voice barely a whisper.

"Methinks you lie."

"'Tis… 'Tis naught but truth I speak." Kaela hated that she stuttered. God, she had to get away from this man. He had Broderick's look about him, a resemblance that brought back ugly memories. If he sought to harm her, she had no way to defend herself. Slowly, she edged away from him.

"You need have no fear, madam. I have never

harmed a woman. 'Tis sorry I am to have frightened you, but I had no idea you were here. I came out only to have a walk before I seek my bed." He waited, but turned to go when she didn't respond.

Seeing the sincerity in his eyes, Kaela felt foolish. On impulse, she reached out and touched his arm. "Forgive me, Thorsen. Do not go on my account. If I seem afraid, 'Tis that you remind me of someone who once hurt me." Mortified she had admitted so much, Kaela felt tears on her face and turned away from him.

"Who hurt you?" Thorsen asked bluntly.

"You do not know him and 'Tis of no importance. Forget my foolish words. Please, Thorsen, I pray thee, say nothing about this to anyone."

"Why do I remind you of him?"

"I do not know—perhaps your fair hair and pale eyes, but you are nothing like him."

"Is this man still alive? Is he here at Chaldron?"

"He is alive, to my regret, but, nay, he is not here."

"You must tell me his name and I will avenge you."

"Oh, nay," Kaela gasped. "He is far away and cannot hurt me. I want only to forget."

"You must tell me if you see him again. I will protect you, my lady. You have no reason to fear. Nor will Cameron let any harm come to you. He cares for you."

Kaela stared at the Viking. "I doubt that your lord cares for me. I fear he sees me as a burden to him. He wants nothing more than to deliver me to London and be rid of me."

"Nay, he only tries to deny his feelings. He does not wish to care for you or any woman. Nevertheless, he will protect you, as will I. You must identify this man who has hurt you."

"Nay, say no more. You and Cameron will be out

"Nay, say no more. You and Cameron will be out of my life soon, Thorsen. There's naught you can do for me, but thank you for caring. I am thankful for Cameron's protection and his escort to London. I will bid you a good night. 'Tis sorry I am for my reaction to you. 'Twill not happen again. I hope we can be friends."

"Aye, my lady, friends we shall be." The Viking gave her one of his rare smiles and Kaela left him.

Late in the night Kaela crawled from her bed and made her way to her trunk. Her hands trembled as she reached for the vile. Her confrontation with Thorsen brought memories of Broderick too close, and she was unable to rid herself of her fear. Promising herself it would be the last time, she drank the potion. Sleep— she must have sleep.

Cameron awoke to the sound of Kaela's cries. *Damn!* He reached for his chausses. *So much for keeping my distance.* He went to her chamber and quietly entered. The fire had gone out in the cold, pitch black room. He could not see her, but he heard her cries from the bed. He quickly crossed the room and pulled back the furs to climb in beside her. She quieted against him, letting out a low moan.

By the Virgin's nightrail, you would think a maiden would awake when a man entered her bed, but not this one. She must have drugged herself again. At least this time she was wearing clothing. Cameron gathered her into his arms to share his heat. His presence seemed to comfort her. He would stay for a few moments longer, then build up the fire for her before he returned to his own bed.

❖   ❖   ❖

She heard Broderick's cruel laugh as he chased her down Ralston's dark secret passageway. His footsteps kept coming ever closer, paralyzing her with fear. She ran on, stumbling toward the light she could see ahead. A light she must reach. She was closer now. Someone stood in the light, his arms outstretched, beckoning her to him.

Cameron! He would protect her from Broderick, if she reached the light and the safety of his arms in time.

"Cameron, I'm coming… help me…"

Cameron awoke with a start, surprised to find himself still in Kaela's bed, his arms around her. Breathing heavily, her body drenched with sweat, Kaela clung to him, calling his name. He tightened his arms around her, and spoke soothingly.

"I am here, Kaela. No one can hurt you. You're safe, love. Hush, hush, 'Tis all right."

Cameron held her in his arms. Broderick could not hurt her now. Warm and protected, she saw Cameron smile at her, those beautiful blue eyes gazing into hers. He cared about her. He would keep her safe.

Kaela reached up, drawing his head down to hers, and kissed him. His lips were so hard and warm, her whole body seemed to catch fire. She could not get enough of him. She pressed her body closer to his and sighed deeply.

As soon as her lips parted, Cameron deepened the

kiss, rubbing his tongue against hers. She was so soft and so hot. He could not believe she was clinging to him, kissing him this way. He had never felt such raw desire. God, she tasted so sweet his head was spinning. He ran his hands down her back, cupping her firm round buttocks and pulling her up against his hard and throbbing manhood.

"Safe, so safe," Kaela murmured against his lips.

"Aye, Kaela, I will keep you safe," Cameron murmured. He pulled away slightly, gazing down at her. Dawn's half light filled the room and he saw she still slept. Cameron groaned. It was the drug that allowed her to react so freely. Keep her safe from his lust, indeed. God's truth, he was ready to ravish the girl. His loins felt on fire with his great need. With a last effort at control, he pulled away from her.

She followed him, pressing her body against his.

Cameron smiled. At least in her sleep she wanted him. The opiate freed her of any inhibitions. She would be mortified if she were awake, and frightened. Perhaps in sleep she would reveal that which, awake, she would never tell him. He whispered, "Who follows you, Kaela? Who wants to hurt you?"

"Broderick," she mumbled, her body trembling again.

Damn! She had asked about that whoreson, not from concern, but fear. Cameron had hated the Saxon before, thought him a coward for running away, but now his fury turned cold. The bastard would pay for what he had done to Kaela.

He drew her to him again and rubbed her back, whispering to her, "You are safe, Kaela, safe with me. Broderick will never touch you again."

She relaxed against him and her breathing slowed

until she slept deeply again. He rose from the bed and covered her, then quickly returned to his bedchamber and dressed for the day. He intended to seek out Jacob at once. To protect Kaela he had to know everything he could about Broderick. The old man would answer truly this time.

When he entered the great hall, he met Thorsen.

"You are up early, friend," Cameron said in greeting.

"I need to talk to you, Baron. 'Tis about Lady Kaela."

"What about her?" Cameron asked, alarmed.

"Not here. Let us go outside away from any prying ears."

The two men left the Keep and walked through the inner bailey to the courtyard.

"What is this about Kaela?"

"I came upon her last night in the north tower. She was afraid of me, Cameron, very afraid."

"I see."

"She tried to deny it when I questioned her, but I would not let her."

"What did she tell you?" Cameron clasped Thorsen's shoulders.

"She said a man had hurt her, one who had blond hair and light eyes like mine. For that reason, I remind her of him. I assured her, I would never hurt her, Cameron. I asked her who this man is, but she refused to say. She did tell me that he still lives, but he is not here at Chaldron. I could get nothing else out of her. I told her we would protect her, that she must tell you who this man is."

"She already did, though she does not know it," Cameron replied.

"What do you mean?"

Cameron sighed. "Kaela has nightmares, terrible

nightmares. I went to her room last night when I heard her crying. I found an empty vial beside her. I could not believe she drugs herself. We could storm the castle and she would not hear. Apparently, she relives the attack in her sleep. When I asked her who hurt her, 'twas Broderick's name she spoke."

"Broderick of Ralston?" Thorsen sounded incredulous.

"Aye."

"Slimy bastard. I thought him a coward when he deserted his castle after our attack, but now... God's blood, Cameron, only a coward would harm a woman. How badly did he hurt her, do you know?"

"If you mean did he rape her, I don't know, but I assume that he did. I know he whipped her," Cameron said, his body trembling with suppressed rage.

"Whipped her?" Thorsen bellowed. "By Thor, I will kill the bastard with my own hands."

"Nay, friend, that pleasure will be mine." Cameron spit out the words, clenching his fists at his side.

"She told you this?"

"Nay, I saw for myself. She has terrible scars on her back from the lash."

Thorsen's face grew pale. "I cannot believe that beautiful girl has been flogged. What kind of whoreson would do such a thing?"

Cameron shook his head, afraid he might lose control if he spoke.

"How did you see her scars, Cameron?"

"I told you, she can sleep through a battle. The first night I heard her cry out, I found her asleep before the fire in her chamber. She wore no clothing. 'Twas then I saw her scars."

"And did you behave honorably? I know you are

attracted to the lass."

"Of course I was honorable. What do you take me for? I would never ravish an unwilling maiden and you know it," Cameron retorted angrily.

"I apologize. Something about the lass melts my heart. I do not want to see her hurt, Cameron."

"Aye, friend, neither do I. Let us go and find Jacob. We will tour the outlying lands at once. Before this day ends, we will know Mistress Kaela's story. She may have sworn Jacob to secrecy, but he will tell me all, even if I have to strangle the words from him."

✧   ✧   ✧

Kaela awoke to sunlight streaming through the window. Lord, she had slept late. Always an early riser, 'twas not like her at all, but she had slept so deeply. Yawning, she stretched lazily, then pulled back the furs and climbed out of bed. She felt wonderful, almost like a new person.

Then it dawned on her. She had not had the nightmare, at least she did not remember having dreamed. If she had slept the night through, she must be getting better. Thank God that He had heard her prayers. The opiate had never stopped the dreams before. Perhaps her talk with Thorsen had helped to clear her mind. Surely he would keep her secret. Some future time would be soon enough to tell Cameron about Broderick. With the pain still fresh, she could not share something so personal and degrading, not with the Norman. She would not have told Brenna and Jacob had it not been for Maude.

Thinking of Cameron brought a smile to her lips. Yesterday, he had been kind to her, and good with

Mattie. She treasured his compliment on the way she had overseen Chaldron. Despite his tendency to order her about, the day in his company had been pleasant. Under other circumstances, she might have come to care for the handsome baron.

Throwing open the door to her chamber, Maude interrupted Kaela's daydreaming. "'Tis time to be about, Mistress. The day is wasting and there is much to be done to prepare ye for your trip to meet our new King."

"Aye, Maude, I cannot believe I slept so late." Kaela smiled warmly at her old nurse.

"Lady Brenna and Mattie have both been asking for you. Come, break your fast, and we will be about your packing."

❖   ❖   ❖

A brisk wind blew at their backs when the three knights reached the lake, and tied their horses beneath a tree. Standing at the water's edge, Cameron gazed out across the water where sunlight danced and shimmered upon the rippling surface. In the distance a fish broke from the water and reentered with a soft slap. Wind rustled trough the mighty oaks whose massive branches hung low over the water's edge. He understood why Kaela loved this peaceful place.

"This is where he kidnapped her?" Cameron asked, his voice edged with steel. Grim-faced, he had listened during their ride while Jacob recounted Kaela's ordeal with Broderick.

"Aye, Baron," Jacob answered. "Kaela often comes to this lake. 'Tis one of her favorite places. Broderick must have watched the Castle for some time. He obviously knew I had taken a number of my men and left for London to see King William. The cur never would have taken her had I been here."

"You say she was being held captive at Ralston when I laid siege to the Castle? God's teeth, she could have been killed." Cameron ran his hand through his hair in frustration.

"Aye, 'twas your siege that saved her. Kaela told me her ploys had finally run out. Broderick was tormenting her, readying the whip for her back, when his second in command interrupted to announce your arrival. The bastard meant to rape her."

"My God!" Cameron said, sickened by the thought.

"Kaela would never have lived through the ordeal," Jacob said.

"But why, Jacob? Why did Broderick want to hurt her?" Once again, blinding rage filled Cameron.

"Broderick has been a problem since childhood." Jacob shook his head. "I caught him once, and the lad no more than ten summers, torturing a mother cat and her kittens. He wished to terrorize Kaela, but she always had her parents' protection. Charles recognized Broderick's sickness and kept his daughter away from the boy whenever possible. She never traveled to Ralston without Charles or her mother. Broderick's father, a weak-willed half-brother to Marissa, Kaela's mother, did not discipline the boy. His mother, a sickly little mouse, wanted nothing to do with him."

Cameron picked up a stick and tossed it into the water. "What else?"

"Broderick resented Kaela's wealth. As the closest male heir, he felt that Chaldron should have been his. Kaela was only sixteen summers when her parents died. Broderick lost no time in proposing marriage. He

brutally, thinking to cow her into doing his bidding."
Jacob frowned fiercely. "He underestimated her. She
would die first." His eyes bleak, Jacob looked at
Cameron. "'Tis all my fault, Baron. I found them in
the woods and pulled the whoreson off her. I should
have killed him."

"'Tis too late to repine. Go on." Cameron put his
hand on the man's shoulder.

"Broderick would not give up. He petitioned King
Edward for the rights to Chaldron, but King Edward
was a great friend to Charles and upheld his wishes. If
I had realized Broderick would try something so
desperate as to actually kidnap the girl, I never would
have left her," Jacob said sadly.

"She held him off for almost two months!" Thorsen
exclaimed. "'Tis quite amazing, that."

"Aye, I still don't know how she managed. The lass
has spirit, but Broderick has taken much from her.
Kaela knows fear now."

Cameron gazed out across the lake, no longer
aware the sun danced upon the water. He wondered
what Kaela had been like before she had learned to
fear men. Determined to free her from her fear, he
would do everything in his power to help her.

"She will be well, Jacob. My men and I will protect
her with our lives, and I will speak to William on her
behalf. She will have no need to fear unwanted attentions from any man while she waits to be given in
marriage. I doubt that William will take Chaldron
from her. He valued her father's loyal friendship, and
William rewards such loyalty."

"My thanks, Baron. 'Tis a relief to know that she
will be under your protection. She is an exceptionally
beautiful woman, though she knows it not, and will be

beautiful woman, though she knows it not, and will be most sought after at court. I fear you and your men will have no easy task in keeping the hounds at bay. Mayhap, the King will see fit to give Chaldron and Kaela to you. I can think of no better man for my Kaela, than the one I see before me."

Cameron grimaced and looked away. "I do not seek a wife, Jacob."

"But, Baron..."

"Let us return to the keep. The hour grows late and we have much to prepare for tomorrow's journey," Cameron said stiffly, then mounted Goliath.

Chapter Six

❖   ❖   ❖

Before morning dawned on Chaldron castle, the outer bailey teemed with activity. Many villagers had turned out to see their mistress depart and to get a last look at the notorious Black Wolf. Maude, efficiently giving orders, saw to packing the food stuffs for the week-long trip. One hundred men would accompany the Baron to London, while the other two hundred remained under Jacob's command to protect Chaldron.

Kaela entered the outer bailey with Mattie and Brenna in tow just as the soldiers were mounting their destriers. Arik led Kaela's mount to her. When Cameron strode forward, Mattie held her arms out and he took the child from Kaela. Arik handed Kaela the reins and put his big arms around her.

"I want to go with you, Kaela," he said. "Who will take care of you?"

"Why look at all these soldiers, Arik," she said, her smile warm. "I will be perfectly safe. I need you here to help Jacob, and to look after the horses." She gave him a quick hug. "I will not be gone long this time, Arik. I will be back before you can miss me."

Maude dabbed the corners of her eyes with her apron. "I still say I should go with ye, milady. I can take better care of ye than Sarah—the girl's too skittish for my likes."

Kaela placed her hand on Maude's shoulder. "Sarah will do just fine. 'Tis settled, Maude. I'll not have you traveling in this harsh weather. You have yet to fully recover from our hardships at Ralston."

Maude glared at Cameron. "See that she gets back to us, Baron."

"Aye, she had best get back safe and sound, 'Your Excellency,' or you will answer to me," Brenna told him boldly.

"Your wish is my command, 'Princess'," Cameron teased. To Mattie's delight, he gave Brenna a mocking bow.

Mattie hugged him and whispered softly in his ear, "You come back too, Wolf, and take care of Kaela."

"Kaela will be safe." Cameron handed her to Brenna. He couldn't bring himself to tell the child he would not be returning.

Jacob strode over and placed his hand on Cameron's shoulder. "God's speed," he said, giving Cameron a knowing look. Turning, he embraced Kaela and lifted her onto Sky.

Perilously close to tears, afraid her voice would betray her, Kaela smiled, but said nothing. She took a long look around the bailey as Johnathan, Thorsen, Patrick, and Andrew rode forward.

"Are you ready?" Cameron asked. He wanted these difficult moments behind them.

"Aye, Baron."

"Let us ride," Cameron called, raising his hand and giving the signal. Jacob ordered the drawbridge lowered. The soldiers fell in line behind them, while Cameron and Kaela rode side by side through the gate.

The long, tiring day passed slowly, but Baron Cameron's vassals had helped to ease the boredom. Every hour or so a man appeared by her side to regale her with stories about Normandy, or some battle fought. She thought them most considerate, but could not help noticing Cameron's scowl. Patrick rode beside her now, entertaining her with a story about his last trip to court and his valiant efforts to win a lady fair, only to be passed over for Johnathan.

"Can you believe, my lady, that the demoiselle in question would turn away this handsome face for one so ugly as Johnathan's?" Patrick teased.

Kaela laughed. "Nay, sir, I cannot see the maiden's reason, except mayhap her sight was poor," she teased, giving Johnathan, who rode on her other side, a broad wink.

"Mayhap the lady in question knew a true knight when she saw one," Johnathan boasted.

Kaela sighed and tilted her head to one side. "Had I the decision to make, 'twould be difficult indeed."

Cameron rode up to the trio, a deep scowl on his face. "Johnathan, ride point for the column. Patrick, fall to the rear and relieve Andrew. He has eaten our dust for the last two hours. Perhaps a little dust will help you close that mouth of yours."

Johnathan and Patrick exchanged a knowing glance and hurried to do his bidding.

"What has you so cross, Baron?" Kaela said, tossing her coppery tresses over her shoulder. "Your men were only being kind in helping break the monotony of this long day."

"I am not cross, Madam. My men need to see to their duties. I will ride with you awhile, if you do not find my company too boring."

"I shall try and suffer through," she said, watching his eyes turn darker, and so mesmerizing that she immediately regretted her remark. "What would you like to talk about?" she added softly, still unsure as to why this man could fire her temper one minute, and have her trembling the next. She forced the disturbing question aside and tried to concentrate on his words.

"Tell me more about your childhood growing up at Chaldron."

Desperate to ignore the flutter in her stomach, Kaela stared off into the distance and pulled her thoughts away from him. Gazing at the sundrenched land, she recounted the happier times she had known at Chaldron.

The sun had set fire to the western horizon before Cameron finally called a halt to the day's trek. They had followed the main road, a sorry path at best, on the grueling ride. Kaela, unused to being in the saddle for such long hours, felt stiff and sore. Cameron reached up to help her dismount. When her feet touched the ground, Kaela realized she would not be able to stand. She leaned into him for support, placing her hands on his massive shoulders, and instantly regretting her actions when she felt the hard ripples of strength burn into her palms.

"Forgive me, Baron," she started, then swayed as the day's excursion sapped her strength.

Cameron pulled her closer. His voice gruff, he said, "The feeling will return in a moment, Kaela. Lean on me. 'Tis sorry I am you have had such an exhausting day. The men will have the tents up shortly. You can sit by the fire to have your evening meal."

"Thank you, Baron, I think I can walk now. If you will excuse me, I will find some privacy."

Regretfully, he released her. She walked away, her hips gently swaying. He could still smell her scent... roses...

Cameron found Johnathan and Thorsen overseeing the erection of the tents and ordered them to place his at the edge of the clearing away from the others. When he orderd Patrick to place Kaela's things in that tent, Johnathan lifted one eyebrow in inquiry. Thorsen stopped his question, placing a hand on Johnathan's arm.

"I will explain later. Let it be, Johnathan."

"I do not think 'Tis wise after what Mistress Kaela has been through," Johnathan said, glaring at his lord.

"She has nightmares, Johnathan. Cameron only desires to comfort her. She is safe with him. Besides, mayhap 'twill help our cause."

"Aye, did you see him scowl when Patrick and I teased her?" A sly smile on his face, Johnathan's warm brown eyes danced.

"I saw the same scowl when I rode with her," Thorsen answered. "I believe the strategy is working."

When Kaela returned to the clearing, the tents were pitched, and several fires burned. Soldiers stood in groups around them, warming themselves. Cameron motioned to her and she joined him at the fire with Thorsen, Johnathan, Andrew, and Patrick. They ate their meal in relative silence, discussing briefly their plans for the morrow. Kaela's eyes grew heavy once she filled her stomach.

Cameron placed an arm around her waist to steady her.

"Come, my lady, I will show you to your tent. We must rise at dawn to continue our journey."

Bidding the others good night, Kaela followed him

to the tent at the clearing's edge. Made from animal skins, the hides blocked the cold waning winter wind. Furs placed on the ground inside the tent made an inviting pallet. Kaela turned to thank Cameron for going to such trouble and to bid him a good night. Surprised, she saw he had followed her inside.

Instinctively, she stepped away. Walking across the tent, she found her belongings neatly stacked. She noticed some clothing that did not belong to her and next to the clothing, a shield engraved with the snarling wolf. Slowly, she turned to face him. "Where is Sarah?"

"I sent her to bed with the other servants. She will be here in the morn to tend to your needs."

Kaela fought to keep her voice steady. "Why is your shield in my tent?" she asked, her voice low, wary.

"Where else would it be?"

"In your own tent, Baron."

"This is my tent." Cameron moved toward her.

"Then why are my things here?"

"I wish you to stay with me and share my tent."

"Oh, nay, I will not!" Kaela tried to back away from him, from the overwhelming fear that froze her blood when he reached for her. His eyes flashed indigo fire in the dim light, singeing her with nothing more than a glance. He meant to rape her. She dodged around him and ran toward the tent opening.

Cameron caught her in his arms. She struggled against his crushing strength, her hands pushing against his chest.

"Let me go... please, you cannot do this." Terrified, she spoke in little more than a whisper.

"Kaela, calm down, you are overreacting. I am not going to harm you."

"I will not sleep in this tent with you, Norman! I must have my own tent. Please!"

"If I give you a tent, what will you do when my men come running at the sound of your screams?" Cameron still had his arms around her and he pulled her to him. Putting a finger under her chin, he lifted her face to his.

"You cry out in your sleep, Kaela," he said, his fingers gentle on her cheek.

Kaela's head spun. She could not think clearly when he stood this close.

"You lie, Norman. I do not cry out."

"Aye, you do."

"How do you know I scream in my sleep?" Afraid to believe him, she had to ask.

"I have heard you, Madam. God's truth, I am surprised all of Chaldron has not heard you screaming."

Kaela began to tremble. Cameron's smile disappeared. He reached for her, closing his arms around her again. This time, when he stared down at her, she saw the fire in his eyes had cooled. In the deep depths of blue, she saw herself, wild, frightened, and it startled her, even more than his nearness. What had she let Broderick do to her? Nay, he had not stolen her virginity. He had taken something more precious. Her courage.

"I know you have nightmares, Kaela," he said, his voice rich, understanding. "If you tell me about them, mayhap I can help you."

Kaela held his gaze. She wanted to trust him, to let him comfort her, to have him hold her this way. Tentatively, she rested her head against his shoulder.

"Nightmares," she whispered.

"Aye, Kaela, will you tell me about them?"

"Not now, Cameron, I do not want to talk about

them now," she told him softly, rubbing her cheek against his chest. "How can staying in your tent with you help my dreams?"

"You become quiet when I hold you."

"What?" Kaela's green eyes widened as she pulled back to look up at him. "What do you mean?"

"The first night I heard you scream, I went to your bedchamber." He pushed her head gently against his chest again, afraid to see the look on her face. She tried to pull away, but he tightened his hold. "Let me explain before you pass judgment. I tried to wake you from your sleep, but you wouldn't awaken. 'Tis true, woman, you could sleep through a bloody siege."

"'Tis absolutely absurd... you jest with me. I would know if a man held me or crawled into my bed."

"Mayhap you would, if you did not have the need to drug yourself. I have slept with you every night since I came to Chaldron, and you have not once known that I held you. I found an empty vial in your hand the first night I came to your room. There is no need to deny it."

Kaela pulled away from him, her face red, her hands covering her burning cheeks. "You don't understand. I need the draught to help me sleep, but I have not slept with you. I have not! Nay, I would know if I had."

"Kaela, please," he pleaded, "I swear on my honor as a knight that nothing improper happened." His eyes never left hers. "I am an honorable man. I would never ravish a maiden. I wanted only to calm you. I understand why you need the draught. 'Tis a terrible nightmare. When I lay beside you and put my arms around you, you quieted immediately. I left each morning before you awoke. You seem to have this nightmare every night and I knew no other way to calm you."

"Dear God," she said, closing her eyes. "I have been sleeping with a man."

She looked so horrified, he had to smile. "Aye, sleeping, naught else." She began to tremble again. He took her in his arms, but to his dismay, she began to cry.

"Hush now, sweetheart. 'Tis all right," he whispered moving to the fur pallet and kneeling on the soft furs. Cradling her on his lap, he spoke very softly.

"On my honor, Kaela, I will never harm you and I will never let anyone else bring harm to you. Please tell me your dreams. I am sure talking about them will help you."

She shuddered… the tears fell faster.

Oh God, Cameron groaned. What was he to do now? Slowly, he rubbed her back. Her tears soaked through his tunic but, oblivious to the damp, he tried to calm her. "You can tell me, Kaela. 'Twill help you to tell me."

"I can't… what he did was too horrible," she said, trying to control her tears.

"Whatever happened, I am sure you were not at fault." He wanted her to trust him enough to tell him of her own accord. He sat quietly, rubbing her back, waiting for her to speak.

When she began to speak, she barely whispered. "Once, long ago, a man hurt me. 'Tis of him I dream."

"What happened, Kaela? Did he rape you?"

"Nay, but that was his intent. Jacob rescued me before he could take my maidenhead. But he hurt me, Cameron, horribly." She shuddered. "The man is truly evil. I suffered much before I escaped from him. In my dreams I relive what he did to me." Kaela could not bear to tell him Broderick had whipped her. He would be repulsed by the scars on her back. She so wanted to be beautiful in his eyes. Drying her eyes with the back of her hand, she pulled away from him. She looked up into eyes filled with tenderness and compassion.

"Sometimes in my dreams he chases me. I know when he catches me, he will finish what he started and I will die. I will die!"

"Tell me who this man is, Kaela, and I will see that he never hurts you again."

"There's naught you can do, Cameron. He hides with the other Saxon rebels. Once we reach London, you will no longer be responsible for me. I will be given to some strange man as his wife." Kaela sobbed. "I don't want a husband, Cameron. He will be allowed to hurt me."

"Nay, William would not give you to someone who would hurt you."

"If marriage is so wonderful, why do you not desire a wife?" she asked, her eyes still filled with tears.

He grimaced. "My preference to live without a wife has nothing to do with you."

"You want only to be rid of me."

Lifting his hands gently to her face, Cameron drew her closer. Get rid of her? Aye, he should, and soon, for his own sake. Very softly he pressed his lips to hers. Kaela tried to pull away, but he held her and whispered against her lips.

"Let me show you what can be between a man and a woman." He pressed his lips to hers.

Kaela forgot to resist. She felt like she was drowning, swirling down into warm, welcoming water. He rubbed his thumb against her lips and, the moment they parted, slipped his tongue into her mouth.

He caught her gasp and groaned softly. Without realizing what she did, Kaela stroked his tongue with hers. When he groaned again, she slipped her hands inside his tunic to caress his chest.

God, he loved the way she responded to his touch. He had only meant to show her a man could be gentle and a kiss could be pleasant. But his desire for her consumed him. He wanted to learn all her secrets, to satisfy himself then and there. The kiss turned hot, intimate. His mouth slanted over hers repeatedly, starting a rhythm that echoed his heartbeat. Cameron knew he was going to lose control if he did not stop now. With his usual iron self-control, he forced himself to pull away from her.

Kaela followed him, wanting more. God's truth, she had never dreamed kissing could be like this. Her body on fire, she seemed to be chasing some elusive thing. She opened her eyes, ready to protest because he pulled away from her, and immediately came to her senses, blushing deeply.

He smiled at her. "You see, 'Tis not always bad between a man and a woman."

Unable to speak, Kaela said nothing. She could only stare at him, her eyes wide with wonder. She hadn't known a kiss could be so incredible. Wanting more, she watched him shake his head as if to clear it before he pulled her to him again. She knew she should resist, but she felt boneless, incapable of pushing him away.

"Tell me the name of the man who hurt you, Kaela. Let me help you. I give you my vow you shall be avenged."

"Now you sound like Thorsen," she said shyly. She could not believe how wonderful she felt, warm and safe. She loved the comfort of his massive arms. No one could hurt her as long as he was near.

"You told Thorsen of this man?"

"I did not tell his name, but I told Thorsen I had been hurt. He forced me, for he sensed I feared him. He reminded me of my attacker. I no longer fear your friend. He also vowed to avenge me."

"Who haunts you, Kaela?"

She laid her head on his shoulder, her eyes tightly closed. "Broderick of Ralston," she whispered, "my cousin, a horrible man. When I refused to marry him, he abducted me and held me captive in his castle. Your attack on Ralston enabled me to escape. I owe you my life, Cameron."

"That is why you questioned me the night we met?"

"Aye, though I could not tell you then. 'Tis a very hard thing to talk about, and I did not know if I could trust you."

"Do you trust me now, Kaela?"

"Aye, I trust you. I know now you will not hurt me. If you wish, I will sleep in your tent until we reach London."

He hadn't known how much he wanted her trust until she said the words, words that filled him with an unspeakable joy.

"I will never betray your trust," he said, his voice husky, raw. "Come now, 'Tis growing late. We must get some sleep. 'Twill be another long, hard day's ride on the morrow."

Cameron stood and removed his tunic, still wet from Kaela's tears. Her eyes widened at the sight of his naked chest. When she looked away shyly, Cameron grinned. The girl was innocent, but so filled with passion. Remembering her kiss, he wondered if he were mad to want to lie down with her. She would sleep, unaware of the pain her nearness caused him. He pulled the furs aside and crawled in, motioning for her to join him. Her eyes huge, Kaela slowly moved toward him.

"You will be uncomfortable unless you remove your gown, Kaela. I have seen you in your chemise before. You are safe. In the dark, I can hardly see you anyway."

She hesitated. "But I—"

"Trust me."

Turning her back, she stripped down to her chemise, and lay down beside him.

With the furs over them, Cameron gathered her in his arms, her head on his shoulder. Kissing the top of her head, he sighed deeply.

"Good night, Kaela."

"Good night, Cameron."

Within minutes, she slept. It was the first time he had known her to do so without the sleeping draught.

A long time passed before he could forget how her lips felt against his. Her breasts, covered only by the thin chemise, burned his flesh. He turned her so that she would not feel the part of him that was rock hard with his longing. Curse the saints, no man had ever endured a worse torture than lying with this warm, soft woman curled against his side. She trusted him. If she could read his thoughts at this moment, she would run screaming from the tent.

Cameron awoke just before dawn. He lay on his side, his arms around Kaela. He knew she still slept.

Her buttocks pressed tightly against his groin. God, how he wanted to reach out, stroke her full breasts, her smooth thighs. Even, the thought made him hard with desire. He had to leave her, now, before he lost control and relieved the ache in his groin.

Quietly, he eased from the pallet and dressed. Slipping through the tent opening, he went to a nearby stream and splashed cold water on his face. Breathing deeply, he finally mastered his lust and returned to camp to build up the fire. As the flames started to catch, he sensed a movement behind him. Turning, he saw Thorsen and Johnathan making their way toward him. He nodded a greeting before giving orders for striking the camp.

"I want to leave within the hour, Johnathan. See that the men are ready," Cameron told his second in command, who strode off to see to their departure. Cameron turned to Thorsen, and placing his arm on his friend's shoulder, he smiled.

"She has begun to trust me, Thorsen." Cameron's voice swelled with pride. He felt glorious, as if he had won a great battle.

"She has confided in you?"

"Aye, 'twas hard for her, but she told me about Broderick. She did not mention that he whipped her, but she admitted in the nightmares he still pursues her. She fears he will take her again, that no one can stop him, but she is wrong. That bastard will never touch her again." Grim faced, Cameron looked into Thorsen's pale eyes.

"Aye, Baron. He will never harm her again. Does she have any idea where the villain might be?"

"She said he joined the Saxon rebels, which I am sure is true. We will add his name to William's list of rebels when we reach London. Broderick wants Chaldron. He will try to take her again. We will keep a close watch, Thorsen. I want you to inform Johnathan, Andrew, and Patrick of the situation. One of us must be with her at all times."

"No harm will come to the lass, Cameron. You have my word. Trust us to care for her."

When Cameron entered his tent a few moments later, he found Kaela awake and dressed for the day.

"Good morning, my lady, I trust you slept well," Cameron said, smiling.

Kaela blushed at the mention of the night past. She still could not believe she had spent the night in his arms, but she had, and had slept safely.

"Aye, my lord, I slept well, and am ready for our journey. I trust I did not wake you with my nightmares," she said softly.

"Nay, lady, you slept like the dead. Mayhap talking about your fears has already begun to allay them."

⁜   ⁜   ⁜

Their days fell into a routine, always beginning at dawn and ending with the setting sun. Cameron rode beside Kaela much of the time, and when he was not with her, one of his vassals rode by her side. Kaela enjoyed their company and soon trusted each one.

Cameron's men differed greatly from one another. Thorsen, the most serious of the lot, became her favorite. She thought Johnathan kind-hearted and most intelligent. He could read and write, had traveled extensively, and entertained her with stories of the places he had visited.

Andrew and Patrick, both full of life and mischief,

teased each other endlessly. Andrew told her about his home and family. He answered her questions about his and Cameron's youth. No one elaborated on the unfortunate marriage in Cameron's past, and though she wanted to ask questions, she did not.

As much as she enjoyed the company of his men, she longed most for Cameron's presence. She cherished the hours they spent riding together, talking about everything from their childhood to the running of Chaldron. When he was not with her, she constantly searched him out. Many times, she felt his gaze on her.

Kaela looked forward to her nights alone with Cameron. He had not kissed her again, but each night they lay wrapped in each other's arms, sharing their warmth. And with each passing day they grew more comfortable with each other.

On their sixth night out, they set up camp in a beautiful meadow surrounded by trees. A small stream flowed nearby and Kaela excused herself to see to her toilet. Dusty and grimy, she longed for a bath, an impossibility in the frigid water. She knelt at the stream to wash her face and hands. She sat upon a boulder, freed her hair from its braids, and began to brush it vigorously.

Cameron went in search of Kaela when she did not come back to camp as quickly as he thought she should. Damn—the woman knew the danger in being alone. One would think she would be more cautious after all she had been through, he grumbled to himself. He stopped abruptly at the sight of her, his breath catching in his throat. Lord, she was lovely. She sat on a boulder, brushing her hair. The setting sun played on her coppery curls. Rooted to the spot, Cameron watched her.

Kaela sensed his movement and turning, saw Cameron staring at her. She smiled at him shyly. "Have you come to look for me, my lord?"

"Aye, my lady, it soon grows dark, and you should not be in the woods alone. 'Tis not safe." His voice sounded hoarse. He came forward and knelt beside her to drink from the stream. Then he plunged both hands into the icy water and splashed his face.

Kaela watched him run his strong callused hands through his hair. No longer afraid of his strength, she felt safe and protected instead. Safe… and something more that she could not define.

"I could not resist the water, Baron. God's truth, I long for a bath. The water is frigid, but refreshing. 'Tis sorry I am if I worried you," she said shyly, her eyes never leaving his face.

"Aye, it is refreshing." He smiled at her, and rising to his feet, he held out his hand. "Let us return to camp."

Kaela put her hand trustingly in his and they walked back to camp together.

That they entered the clearing hand in hand did not go unnoticed by Cameron's vassals. Andrew and Patrick nudged each other, satisfied smirks on their faces.

"I would say our plan is working, Thorsen," Johnathan boasted, smiling at his friend.

"Aye, and none too soon for we reach London in another two days," the Viking answered.

"I have decided to speed things up a bit," Patrick stated.

"What do you have in mind?" Andrew asked.

"You will see in a moment. Just go along with me," Patrick whispered as Kaela and Cameron approached.

Their Baron still held Kaela's hand, although they both seemed oblivious to their action.

Cameron and Kaela joined the knights at the fire to eat their evening meal of bread and cheese washed down with ale.

Patrick stepped across Andrew and strode over to kneel before Kaela. "My lady, when I groomed your horse this eve, I noticed a stone bruise on her right fore foot. I fear she will be lame after another day of hard riding."

"God's teeth, poor Sky! I will see to her at once." Kaela started to rise.

"There's no need, my lady. I checked your mount myself and even though what Patrick tells you is true, the mare will be fine. I do suggest, however, that you ride with one of us tomorrow and allow your mount a rest. We will tie her lead to one of the other horses and slow our pace a bit," Johnathan stated, looking to Cameron who nodded approval.

Patrick stood up and grasped Kaela's hand. "You can ride with me, my lady. I do not mind."

Andrew stepped forward, a grin on his handsome face, and bowed low before Kaela. "I would be greatly honored if you would ride with me, Lady Kaela. I have several amusing stories yet to share with you."

Frowning ferociously, Cameron glared at his vassals. "This can be decided on the morrow. The hour grows late and the lady needs her rest. Come, Kaela," he commanded. Jerking her hand from Patrick's, he pulled her toward their tent.

Kaela looked up at him, her eyes twinkling. "God's truth, my lord, you gave me no chance to say good night."

Cameron shrugged, pulled her into their tent, and

closed the flap against the amused glances of his vassals. His men behaved like fools over this woman. So they wanted her, did they? Hell, he wanted her himself. Any man would. In a few days the King would solve all their problems and Kaela would wed another man. Fine—that's what he wanted. Angrily, he stripped down to his chausses and lay on the fur pallet. His gaze roamed over Kaela's silhouette while she removed her chainse and bliaut in the darkness. A few more days and he could get on with his life. No more would he be concerned about her. No longer would he have her warm soft body snuggled next to his at night.

"Come, Kaela," Cameron said, his voice hard with anger. "The night grows colder. Let us sleep." He held back the furs for her to slip in beside him.

She lay on her back, her eyes closed. In a small frightened voice, she said, "Have I done something to displease you, Cameron? Why are you angry with me?"

Cameron did not know if her voice trembled from the cold or from fear. "'Tis not anger. I am tired, that is all. Good night, Kaela."

Kaela sighed her content. "Good night, Cameron."

Cameron did not know if exhaustion from their long days, or if the security of sleeping by his side had prevented Kaela's nightmare during their journey, but he was thankful she'd had a respite.

This night, Cameron once more awoke to her terrified scream. She lay on her side, her back to him, and he took her in his arms to soothe her. Her body drenched with sweat, she shivered violently. He stroked her back and spoke to her, his voice soft, soothing. Gently, he kissed her forehead and nuzzled her ear as he whispered, "You are all right, Kaela. I have you. You are safe. Broderick can't hurt you, sweetheart."

Clinging to him, she moaned again and again.

"Kaela," he whispered, "Kaela, wake up… you are dreaming again."

Dazed, Kaela slowly opened her eyes. "Cameron?"

"I have you, Kaela, you only dreamed. You are safe now."

She shuddered, already clinging, sobbing, "'Twas the dream again. He is after me, Cameron. He will always be after me."

"Hush, sweetheart, 'twas only a dream. No one is after you. You're safe, I am here," he told her, placing soft kisses on her face.

"I am so frightened, Cameron. I do not want to be afraid anymore."

"I will protect you, Kaela, please don't be afraid."

"Hold me, Cameron, make the fear go away."

With her breath warm against his neck, his whole body filled with a consuming white heat. When he slanted his mouth over hers, she welcomed his kiss with a soft sigh and parted her lips the instant his tongue sought entry. Cameron groaned his delight and slipped his tongue into her warm, sweet mouth. God, she tasted so good, he could not get enough of her. His tongue mated with hers again and again.

A warmth began to grow deep inside Kaela, and spread through her body down to her toes. Lord, she loved Cameron's kisses. She wanted to be close to him, to feel his heat. She pressed closer to him, let her fingers caress his stern face.

Cameron groaned and tangled his hands in her hair. Kaela returned his kisses with innocent passion, slipping her tongue inside his mouth, tasting it. Trailing kisses down her neck, he lifted his hand to her breast, and teased her nipple until it was taut with desire. Kaela instinctively arched into him when his mouth covered her breast, nipping through the thin fabric. Cameron loosed the ribbon that fastened her chemise, pulling the fragile garment down to her waist. Kaela moaned with unbridled desire as his tongue came in contact with her swollen nipple.

Flame seared through her. She buried her hands in his hair, holding him tightly to her. God, she had never felt such heat. She wanted more, wanted her body to melt into his.

Cameron eased his knee between her legs and she clasped him between her thighs. He settled himself against her very center and Kaela felt his hard, hot manhood. He groaned his desire, lifted his head from her breast, and took her mouth once more.

Kaela accepted his kisses with a yearning she didn't understand. When his mouth slanted over hers again and again, she wanted to belong to him body and soul. Instinctively, she thrust her hips against his and heard his startled groan.

Cameron, fully aroused and filled with desire, took a moment to recognize the familiar sound of someone stamping his feet outside the tent. Abruptly, he pulled away from Kaela. When she started to protest, he placed his hand gently over her mouth.

"What is it?" he called.

"Baron, 'Tis almost dawn. The men are preparing to ride. Lady Kaela should break her fast before we leave," Thorsen said.

"Aye," Cameron said, smiling tightly down into her startled face. "We will be out in a moment." He listened for Thorsen's departing footsteps, then rolled away from Kaela.

"Oh God," Kaela sighed, covering her face with her hands. What had she done? She would never be able to face Cameron again, not after what had passed between them.

Cameron sat up and gazed down at Kaela. The lady was most embarrassed, he noted, smiling. He watched her sit up, pull up her chemise, and carefully tie the ribbon. Cameron placed one finger under her chin and lifted her face to his.

"Good morning," he said softly, placing a warm gentle kiss on her lips. Then he saw the tears on her cheeks. "Curse the saints, woman, do not cry."

"I have shamed myself, and you, Baron." Kaela choked out the words.

"Nay, sweeting, do not berate yourself. 'Tis natural for a man and a woman to desire each other. Though I should never have allowed what we shared to go so far, nothing happened to cause you shame. Forgive me for taking such liberties. My only excuse is that I lost my head." Cameron knew he would have taken her maidenhead, if not for Thorsen's interruption. He had lost his head, indeed. Seeing Kaela's distress, he realized she must be horrified at what had almost happened.

"You had another nightmare, and when I sought to comfort you, I forgot myself for a few moments. 'Twill not happen again."

An aching emptiness overwhelmed Kaela at his words. He regretted what he'd done. God help her, but she wished Thorsen had not come so soon. She treasured each hour she had spent in Cameron's arms, yet he seemed determined to turn her away. He desired her too. He did not even deny his lust, as if his feelings and she were both inconsequential. If he did not want her, then so be it. Hell would freeze before she would show him her desire again. Without another word to Cameron, Kaela stood and dressed in the gray morning light.

Holy Saint Ambrose's bones, what did the woman expect from him? 'Twas not his place to teach her about carnal desire.

Now she would not even look at him much less speak to him. Cameron snatched up his sword, stormed from the tent, and stomped past his men. Ignoring their greetings and knowing grins, he headed for the stream to cool his anger.

Cameron chastised himself all the way back to camp. Hell, he had spent every night sleeping by Kaela's side since he'd arrived at Chaldron. No wonder he had lost control. Very well, he would let his men amuse the lady from here. He could trust them to do what he could not.

Entering the clearing, he swiftly changed his mind. His trusted vassals... hah! The idiots! Thorsen, Johnathan, Andrew, and Patrick had mounted and with silly looks of adoration on their faces, each man beckoned to Kaela to ride with him.

Kaela stood in the center of the meadow, hands on her hips, laughing at them. Making up her mind, she strode towards Thorsen. Mayhap during the long hours ahead, her Viking friend would enlighten her about the Black Wolf's distaste for women.

Before she could reach Thorsen, Cameron charged up on Goliath and, leaning over, grabbed her around the waist, and lifted her up onto his lap. She settled against his thighs with a thud. God's teeth, the man was a barbarian, she thought angrily.

"She rides with me!" he shouted, daring his men to challenge him. They wisely remained silent as

Cameron rode to the head of the procession, but behind his back they exchanged knowing winks and nods. Turning their mounts, they fell into formation. "An excellent idea, Patrick," Johnathan said.

"Aye," Andrew agreed, laughing. "'Twould seem the lady is beginning to get to my thick-headed brother."

"Aye, and a day in the saddle with the beautiful lady in his lap will not help him ignore her."

"I would say things are proceeding nicely, wouldn't you, Thorsen?" Johnathan slapped his friend on the shoulder.

"'Twill be a most interesting day, Johnathan, most interesting" Thorsen agreed with a nod.

Chapter Seven

❖   ❖   ❖

Riding with Cameron was torture. Granted, a sweet torture, but torture, just the same.

Kaela sat rigidly for the first hour, determined not to lean against him. Although, angry at his high-handedness, she soon realized Cameron's actions were those of a jealous man. She smiled at the thought. Perhaps she might yet melt his heart. With a sigh, Kaela relaxed and leaned against his broad chest. Through his hard muscles against her back and her thighs molded to his, she sensed he was still angry, and decided to leave him to his thoughts. The horse's motion and the warmth of Cameron's body made her drowsy. She rested her head against his chest and closed her eyes, content. Within moments she slept.

At the sound of her even breathing, Cameron relaxed and slipped his arm around her waist to hold her more securely. He tried not to think of the sensuous feel of her round soft buttocks pressing so intimately against him. The morning had been overcast and a light rain began to fall. When he pulled his cloak around them, she snuggled closer to his warmth, resting her head in the hollow of his neck. With her breath whisper-soft and soothing against his skin, Cameron felt an inner peace quite foreign to him. How right he felt, holding this girl in his arms. He frowned at his foolishness, knowing he had no right to such thoughts.

"Is something bothering you, Baron?" Thorsen asked, riding up to Cameron's side.

"Shh! You will wake her. The lady had a restless night. Have the men keep a close watch, Thorsen. We near the city where we are more likely to run into trouble."

"Aye, Cameron, but our party is large. I think we have little to worry about."

"Perhaps." Cameron wished he could say the same. He had much to worry about, he thought, looking down at the girl asleep in his arms. She trusted him so completely. That trust had become a burden. He wanted her... he should take what he wanted and damn the consequences.

They camped just outside the city that night and Cameron posted extra guards around the perimeter. The rain did not let up, so they were unable to have a fire. Kaela ate a cold supper in the tent, then curled up under the furs of their pallet. Cameron came in briefly to change from his wet tunic to a dry one of heavy wool.

"I am taking part of the guard duty, Kaela," he told her, not meeting her eyes. "We are close to London now and there is more traffic on the roads. If we are to have trouble it will be more likely to happen here." Taking some cold mutton and a loaf of bread, he left her alone.

She knew what he said was true, but he had no reason to take the guard duty, not when he had so many men with him. No, he welcomed an excuse to stay away from her, she thought sadly. Overwhelmed with loneliness and uncertainty, she knew this would be her last night with Cameron, and he chose to stay in the rain while she lay on the pallet they had shared, cold and very alone. God only knew what would happen to her once they reached London. Trying not to think, to keep her fears at bay, she resisted the urge to take the sleeping draught, crying herself to sleep.

Cameron leaned against an ancient oak, gaining some shelter from the rain, and scanned the camp's perimeter. Cold and tired, he could think only about Kaela. He knew she felt his withdrawal from her, but damn, he did not know what else to do. How else could he protect himself? They would reach the palace tomorrow, and he would put her into the King's care. He felt a deep sadness at the thought and shook his head in anger.

"What troubles you, Baron?" Thorsen asked. He had come up so stealthily that Cameron jumped at the sound of his deep voice.

"God's teeth, I must be losing my concentration. I did not hear you approach."

"Aye, I think your mind is elsewhere. Perhaps on a young lady with copper-colored hair who probably at this moment is very cold and very lonely."

Cameron groaned. "I cannot go to her, Thorsen. Already, she has come to depend too much on me and tomorrow will be difficult enough for her. We must stay close by her side until all is settled."

"Aye, Jacob was correct in his assumption. Kaela is a beautiful woman and comes with a fine holding. Many men will want her," Thorsen said, closely watching his friend.

Cameron grunted. "No one will touch her until she is wed."

"Not even you, Cameron?"

"What do you think I am doing out in the rain." Cameron glowered at Thorsen.

"I think you are being a very stubborn, foolish man."

"What else can I do, Thorsen? I have vowed never to marry again and Kaela is not a woman to be bedded outside wedlock. She deserves someone who is gentle and kind, someone who can love her. I am not capable of love, nor do I want it. I learned that lesson well a long time ago." Cameron clenched his fists at his sides, frustrated to his very depths. God, what a mess he had made.

"Why can't you admit you care for the girl?"

"Aye, I care for her, but I do not love her, nor do I want a wife. I refuse to endure that hell again, not even for Kaela," Cameron said gruffly, a pained look on his face.

Thorsen stared at his friend for a long time, trying to assess how far to push him. "'Twas long years past, Cameron. You are a different man now, older and wiser. Kaela is not like Elizabeth. Elizabeth was a cold-hearted, conniving bitch, her beauty only an illusion. Kaela's beauty comes from deep within her soul. She is a woman of honor."

"You sing her praises so highly, Thorsen, mayhap you will take her for your bride," Cameron said, sneering. He wanted to knock his well-meaning friend to the ground.

"I would be honored to have Kaela for my wife, and I would challenge for her in a minute, since you are too stupid to do so. But I know King William will honor her father's request and award Kaela along with Chaldron. Such a prize will only be given to one of his most powerful barons. I have no chance. Who would you give her to, Cameron? What knight do you find worthy to play the role of loving husband?"

"How the hell should I know?" Cameron shouted. "God's blood, there must be someone worthy. William will decide who is best."

Thorsen placed his large hands on Cameron's shoulders and looked him in the eye. "I will say this one more time, Cameron, then I will not speak of it again. Let go of your hatred for Elizabeth. 'Twas of an age past. You deserve a happy life with a wife and children of your own. Kaela is the right woman for you. She has suffered as much as you have. She deserves someone loving. You cannot tell me you do not care deeply for her, for I know you do. God's truth, it shows in your face every time you look at her, and I believe she cares for you."

Cameron's eyes widened. "How do you know she cares for me? Has she told you this?"

Thorsen shook his head. "Are you blind, man? Can you not see the way the lass looks at you. Whenever she is given the choice, she turns to you. God's truth, she trusts you. You are the one she poured her heart out to. Can you not imagine the fear she must feel? Her whole future hangs in the balance. She has lost her parents, been whipped by a monster, had her country taken from her, and tomorrow she meets a new King who will give her to some stranger who fully expects to bed her. How can you desert her like this?" Enraged, Thorsen glared at his friend.

Cameron threw up his hands and shouted back. "I won't desert her, Thorsen. God's teeth, man, there has to be a logical solution to this mess and I shall find it. Let me be!" With that he stormed off into the night with no real direction in mind, but a few minutes later he found himself in front of his tent. Hell, why should he spend their last night stomping about in the rain?

He entered the tent and stripped out of his wet clothing. He heard Kaela's deep breathing, interspersed with hiccups. She had cried herself to sleep. Guilty and desperate for the feel of her, he took her in his arms and cradled her head against his shoulder. She was everything Thorsen said she was. Kaela rubbed her cheek against his chest and snuggled closer. She was so warm and soft and so very vulnerable.

"Do not worry, Kaela," he whispered softly against her ear, "I will let no harm come to you. Somehow, I will work this out. Please God, let me find a way to work this out."

In her sleep, Kaela softly spoke his name and pressed her thigh against his groin. He hardened with desire. God, the night would be unending.

"Lady Kaela, 'Tis time to arise and be on our way. We will reach London by early afternoon."

Waking to Thorsen's voice and his hand gently shaking her, Kaela opened her eyes. She sat up, pulled the furs securely around her and rubbed the sleep from her eyes. She looked about for Cameron, then realized he had not even come to bed last night.

"Where is he?" she asked, raising pain-filled eyes to Thorsen's.

"The Baron took several men and rode ahead to see that the roads are clear enough for passage. The rain has finally stopped, but the roads will be very muddy."

Kaela's eyes never left his. "So that is the way of it

then," she said, more to herself than to him.

Thorsen looked as if he wanted to strangle his friend.

"Come, my lady, we will leave shortly, and catch up with Baron Cameron on the road."

"Give me a moment, Thorsen, and I will be ready." She gave the Viking a timid smile, marveling at the gentleness in the giant man.

Thorsen left the tent and gave the men their orders. Kaela rose slowly from the pallet, her body as heavy as if she were drugged, and made her way to the stream. After washing her face in the chill water, she squared her shoulders. With grim determination, she walked back to camp and gave Thorsen her bravest smile.

"Now, let us be off—my destiny awaits me." Her smile wavered, then disappeared.

Thorsen lifted her onto his destrier and mounted behind her. "'Twill be nice to share your company this day, my lady."

"I fear I will not be very good company, Thorsen, for I am filled with worry over what the King plans for me."

He patted her arm. "You have nothing to fear. William is a fair man and a good King. He will treat you justly and Cameron will speak to him in your behalf. You are still under our protection and will remain so until things are settled."

"Your Baron plainly wants nothing to do with me. God's truth, I do not understand him, Thorsen." She sighed, leaned her head against his chest.

"Cameron is a complex man, Kaela. Having known betrayal in his life, he does not trust easily. 'Tis naught to do with you. Cameron fights his own private battle with himself, one I believe he is destined to lose."

His words made no sense and she turned to look at him. "I don't understand."

"He cares for you, lady, and will not desert you. Remember, too, that I also look to your care."

"'Tis a good friend you are, Thorsen," she told him softly, once again resting her head against his broad chest. "What say you of this woman whose memory torments him so?"

"'Tis Cameron's place to tell you about what is past, not mine. Given time, perhaps he will confide in you, even as you confided in him."

Kaela doubted that, but said nothing more. Although Cameron's withdrawal greatly saddened her, she could do nothing to change him.

When they saw him an hour later, he smiled and bid her good day, but he made no move to take her from Thorsen's arms. He rode at the front of his troops and she did not see him again until they entered the outer bailey of William's Castle in London.

After directing his men to see to their mounts, with Thorsen and Johnathan at his side, Cameron escorted Kaela. Inside, he ordered a message be taken to inform William of their arrival. Taking Kaela's hand, he led her down the north corridor to the chamber assigned to her. He instructed the serving maid he found there to prepare a bath for Kaela and find her illusive servant, Sarah. The girl hurried from the room to do his bidding. He looked to Thorsen and Johnathan who stood flanking the entrance, worried looks on their faces, and dismissed them with a nod.

Kaela stepped away from him and looked about the room. A window looked out into a courtyard. A beautiful tapestry covered the large bed. A small chest stood in one corner and several pegs on the walls served to hang clothing. Kaela turned back to Cameron when he spoke.

"A warm bath will do much to revive your spirits," he said as he turned to leave.

Cameron heard the tremor in Kaela's voice when she said, "Thank you for seeing me safely here, Baron. W-will I see you again?"

Cameron's resolve almost melted at the fear he saw in her eyes. Running his hand through his hair, he said, "Of course you will see me again, Kaela. Johnathan will collect you this evening for dinner. You will dine with me and my vassals. One of my men will be with you whenever you leave this room. There will be a guard at your door until William decides your future. You will not be left alone. You will be presented to the King this evening. I wish you to dress accordingly." He tilted her face to his and ordered, "Rest this afternoon, for I do not like to see those dark circles beneath your eyes. I will not have William think I did not take proper care of you."

"Aye, my lord."

Cameron bowed. "Until this eve, my lady."

✤　　✤　　✤

As Cameron had promised, Johnathan came for her. Kaela smiled, satisfied, when she saw the stunned look on the knight's face.

"You look very beautiful, my lady," he said, extending his arm to her.

"Thank you, Johnathan. Think your King William will approve?"

Her shining copper hair fell unadorned to her hips.

Her low-cut gown, a rich deep violet, made her eyes shine like emeralds. Johnathan gulped as he gazed at the soft swell of her breasts. A heavy gold belt hung low on her hips and her jeweled dagger rested there.

"Aye, Kaela, King William will be most impressed, as will every other male in the great hall. Baron Cameron awaits us. He has been in conference with the King most of the afternoon and will present you to him. The King has invited us to dine at his table this eve. 'Tis quite an honor, my lady."

Kaela clutched his arm. "I am nervous, Johnathan. I know naught to say to this Norman King."

"Be yourself, Lady Kaela, and your grace and charm will win him over anon, as you won all of us." He winked at her.

"Why, Johnathan, you are flirting with me," she said, and wanly smiled at him.

"Aye, but do not tell my Lord, for he would surely have my head."

"I think not, Johnathan. Cameron cares naught for me. I'm only a responsibility that will soon be lifted when he turns me over to the King."

"We shall see, my lady."

✢   ✢   ✢

Cameron sucked in his breath at the sight of her, as did every other man in the room. He watched her glide toward him, her back straight, a stiff smile on her pale face.

The great hall, noisy with conversation and revelry a moment before, fell silent. Staring at the lovely young woman who stood before them, people began to whisper, asking who she might be. Several knights started to make their way towards her until she stopped before the Black Wolf. Then 'twas whispered this must be the Lady Kaela, the Saxon noblewoman William intended to give in marriage. The hall buzzed once again with gossip.

Kaela, oblivious to the stir she had caused, saw only Cameron as he reached out and took her hand in his. His piercing blue eyes roamed over her, slowly taking in every detail of her appearance.

"Well done, Kaela. William will be most impressed. Come, my lady, your King awaits you." Cameron put his hand to her waist and guided her through the throng. Kaela failed to notice the men ogling, but Cameron did not. He scowled at the men who had open lust on their faces.

The King's guard pushed the heavy oak doors aside and announced their presence. They entered the throne room, just off the great hall, where William sat in a large, high-backed chair in the center of the raised dais. He rose slowly to his full height and waited while Cameron and Kaela crossed the room. He never took his gaze from the girl who glided toward him. Kaela walked to the edge of the dais and curtsied deeply before her King.

"William, may I present Lady Kaela of Chaldron," Cameron said. He saw the admiration in his King's eyes and frowned. Although totally devoted to his Matilda, William never ignored a pretty face.

"Your Majesty, I am honored to meet you," Kaela said, her head still bowed. "I pledge you my loyalty, Sire, and that of Chaldron as well."

William held out a big beefy hand and commanded her to rise. "'Tis a pleasure to meet you at last, Lady Kaela. I see the rumors of your beauty were not exaggerated." He smiled charmingly, his brown eyes soft with sympathy. He was a large man, as tall as Cameron but much heavier, with gray-streaked hair. Wrinkles creased the skin at the corners of his eyes, but when he smiled at her he looked almost youthful.

"Ah, my lady," he said, looking up as a very short woman entered the room, "come and meet our Lady Kaela. Kaela, may I present my lovely Queen, Matilda."

Lord, she was a tiny woman, Kaela thought, curtsying to her Queen. "Your Majesty."

Matilda came forward, her dark brown eyes never leaving the girl before her. She reached out one tiny hand and gripped Kaela firmly by the shoulder. "Arise, my child, and let me get a good look at you."

Kaela rose. Matilda, so short the top of her head barely reached Kaela's shoulder, was very plump and wore her brown hair bobbed short and curly. Kaela looked into her eyes and saw much warmth and amusement there. This is a kind woman, she thought.

"'Tis true, William, she is a very beautiful woman. Our barons will be fighting with each other for her hand," Matilda said, laughing up at her husband.

Kaela's face paled and she swayed slightly. Cameron stepped forward, his hand on her waist to steady her. Matilda took her hand, patting gently.

"There, there, child. You have no need to worry. Our Norman knights are noble men, quite as chivalrous as your Saxon gentlemen. William will choose wisely for you."

Cameron grimaced at her words and tightened his hold on Kaela, hoping his expression escaped William's notice. The King chuckled. Cameron had already given William his report on Chaldron. He had gone into much detail concerning Lady Kaela, telling him about her ordeal with Broderick of Ralston. His tale succeeded as William's heart had gone out to the girl, evoking a fierce protectiveness in the King. Her father had been a good friend to William. As King, he assured Cameron he would see the Saxon's daughter well cared for. When he shared these thoughts with Kaela, Cameron saw her relax somewhat, but she stayed very close to his side while she listened. Cameron did not move away either.

"You must still be weary from your long journey, Lady Kaela. Cameron, take Lady Kaela for a walk in the garden before we sup. I believe the night air will refresh her and bring some color back into her cheeks." He dismissed them with a wave of his hand and Cameron bowed to his King and led Kaela from the room.

"What think you, William?" Matilda asked, taking her husband's large hand in her small one. "Did you see the way Baron Cameron looked at her?"

"Aye," William chuckled. "He reminds me of myself when I first saw you."

Matilda beamed at her husband. He was so tall she had to lean back to look up into his face. The top of her head just reached the middle of his massive chest.

"I remember well the looks you gave me," she said, laughing. "So full of adoration."

"And have they changed over the years, wife?"

"Nay, and they had better not, husband. Tell me what you know of Baron Cameron and his feelings for this girl. I can see there is a story here. 'Tis true, William, I never thought to see a look like that on Cameron's face."

"Neither did I. He has been extremely bitter over Elizabeth, and still is, but this girl has touched him."

"Will he marry her, do you think?" Matilda asked, her voice hopeful. She dearly loved Cameron and thought him her husband's most loyal knight. Her heart had gone out to him over Elizabeth's treachery. She had given up hope of seeing him happy with a woman. Lord knew, many a woman had tried to breach the wall he had built around himself, but none had succeeded, not even Lady Constance who still chased in hot pursuit.

"He says not. The fool is determined never to marry again, although he is much concerned over my choice for Kaela. He has asked to be allowed to assist me in my decision," William said, chuckling. "Per chance there is hope yet for our Baron."

"Aye, husband, we will see what we can do to help him along. She is a beautiful girl, but filled with sadness, I think, and there is fear in her, William."

"You are most perceptive, Madam. The child has reason to feel fear. Come, let me tell you what Cameron relayed to me. I will need your wisdom and insight to help me with this one, love," he said, and sighed as he hugged her to him.

"I doubt it not, my love," Matilda replied.

Cameron pulled Kaela's cloak tightly around her and, taking her hand, walked with her into the garden. Out in the cold, biting night air, he pulled her to his side, placing his arm around her shoulders to keep her warm. The full moon spilled its soft light upon her upturned face. Cameron felt a now familiar tightening in his chest. To give this woman to another man would be very difficult.

"You did well with William, Kaela. I am very proud of you."

"I am afraid, Cameron. I can't bear the thought that William will give me to some man I do not know." Strain filled her soft voice.

Cameron lightly squeezed her shoulder. "'Twill be all right, little one. I could see the concern in William's eyes for you. He will treat you fairly. You will have ample time before your wedding night to get to know the man who is chosen."

Kaela stiffened in his arms, terrified by the thought of a man touching her. Except for Cameron. She loved it when he held her and kissed her. The memory of their nights together came flooding back to her and she blushed.

"'Twas very lonely without you last night, Cameron. I missed you," she said, looking away to hide her embarrassment. "Why did you not sleep with me?"

Her bold question surprised him. He turned her face to his, rubbing his hand against her cheek. Her skin felt like the rarest silk. "You were already asleep when I came to bed, Kaela. I did not wake you, but I held you in my arms until I had to leave to check on the roads."

Her eyes widened. "You were there? You did not leave me alone all night?"

His heart turned over at the look she gave him. "Aye, but I will no longer be able to come to you. There are many eyes here in the Castle and it would not do to have your reputation tarnished."

"What about the nightmares, Cameron? What will I do?" The fear in her voice ate at him. He wanted desperately for her to be at peace.

"Your nightmares have been less frequent of late. Perhaps they are fading. You will be guarded so you need not worry for your safety." He cupped her face in both his hands. "Kaela, you must promise me you will not go about unattended. Not all men are honorable, as you well know, and I do not want you harmed."

She buried her head against his shoulder. "I will do as you say, Cameron. I don't want to leave you." She raised her eyes to meet his gaze, whispered, "I don't want to ever leave you."

His throat constricted. God's teeth, she tempted him. He placed his hands on her shoulders to step away from her, but he made the mistake of looking at her lips, so soft and beguiling in the moonlight. His body disobeyed his mind and his lips took hers.

Kaela sighed. Her mouth opened, and his tongue swept in to mate with hers. She melted in his arms, passionately returning his kiss. Cameron groaned. No woman had ever made him feel this way, as if he drove her wild. Gently, he pulled away and gazed down into her passion-glazed eyes. He should never have kissed her. Guilt sickened him. When he spoke, his voice sounded hoarse, his words gruff.

"Come, Kaela, the King awaits us. We must not be late to his table." His movements rougher than he intended, he hurried her inside.

Chapter Eight

❖   ❖   ❖

A large crowd filled the great hall to capacity. Trestle tables lined the walls and servants were bringing out large platters filled with tempting fare. The ale flowed freely and everyone seemed to be in high spirits.

Kaela clung to Cameron's arm as he helped her through the crowd toward the massive hearth at the other end of the room. She could see Thorsen's white-blond head above the crowd. He leaned against the mantle, a mug of ale in his hand. Johnathan, Andrew, and Patrick stood close by his side. Smiling broadly, they looked toward her when she and Cameron approached.

"We wondered where you had gone," Patrick said, his gaze roving over Kaela. "My lady, you are a vision to behold. The hall has been buzzing with nothing but talk of your beauty." He bowed before her and taking her hand in his, placed a kiss upon her palm.

Kaela tried to return his smile, knowing he said the words to make her forget her circumstances.

Cameron said nothing, but his eyes scanned the hall and he saw the hungry way many men appraised Kaela. God's teeth, he would gladly pluck their eyes from their leering faces.

Andrew ordered a serving wench to fetch mulled wine for Kaela. He smiled warmly down at her. "What think you of the new Castle, Lady Kaela, and how was your visit with our King?"

"God's truth, it is most impressive, Andrew. I remember visiting London once before as a small girl. My father was great friends with King Edward, you know. My meeting with King William and his Queen went quite well. My, the lady is short, is she not?"

Cameron heard his name being called and turned to see several battle-scarred knights motioning for him to come and drink a cup of ale with them. He bowed to Kaela. "If you will excuse me, Madam, I will leave you in my vassals' capable hands for a moment and say hello to some of my friends."

Kaela acknowledged him with a nod and turned back to his men. He heard her laughing tentatively at one of Patrick's outrageous comments.

Baron Joseph clasped Cameron warmly by the shoulder and pulled him forward into the circle of men. "Ah! 'Tis good to see you, my friend. We hear that William has kept you well-occupied with one siege after another since Hastings."

"Aye, that he has, Joseph, but I am sure all of you have been as busy securing England for Normandy."

Baron Frederick, another of Cameron's favorite knights, laughed heartily and slapped Cameron on the shoulder. "But you are the lucky one, Wolf. William has given you a duty that has made us all most envious."

"Aye, Cameron, we have all heard about Lady Kaela and Chaldron Keep. I must say I was quite taken by the lady's beauty when I saw her enter the hall this evening on Johnathan's arm," Joseph said.

"Every man in the room was taken, Joseph. 'Tis a

pity you and I are already married, old friend. I'd love to challenge you for the fair maiden's hand," Frederick teased.

"There will be no challenges for the lady," Cameron said, his voice hard, a dark scowl on his face. "William plans to award Kaela and all her family's holdings to one of his most trusted barons. Her father befriended our King and he will see her well-cared for."

Frederick and Joseph exchanged surprised glances. Lifting one eyebrow in question, Joseph asked, "And are you among those being considered for the lofty title of husband, my friend?"

"Nay, Joseph, you know I will never marry again."

"'Tis glad I am to hear that, Cameron, for your abstention greatly narrows the competition."

Cameron turned toward the snarling voice behind him. His gaze came to rest on Baron Thomas, a man he neither trusted nor liked. He schooled his features into a bored facade. "As I said, King William will give the lady to a loyal baron who will take good care of her." His voice, dangerously soft, plainly showed he detested this man. He could not understand how the man had found favor with their King. 'Twas true he was a fierce warrior and had won many battles, but to Cameron's knowledge, the man had no honor.

"There is no baron more loyal to William than I, D'Abernon, and I assure you, I will take great care of the lady in question. Aye, I plan to keep her quite busy writhing beneath me in my bed," Thomas said, sneering.

Cameron's hands clenched at his side, and a muscle twitched in his cheek as he stared at Thomas. With iron control, he refrained from striking the man. *You'll touch her over my dead body.* The thought cheered him, for he had often bested Thomas in the lists. He turned his back, choosing to ignore the man, and smiled at his friends.

"William has invited the lady and me to dine at his table this eve. 'Tis best I go now and collect her," he said, before he left them.

"Most interesting, wouldn't you say, Joseph?" Frederick said, watching Cameron walk away.

"Indeed, Frederick. I am anxious to see what worthy knight is allowed the fair lady's hand."

Cameron's eyes filled with anger when he saw the crush of knights surrounding Kaela. The fools were fighting amongst themselves trying to speak to her. He pushed his way through the crowd, but his anger died immediately when he saw the bewilderment on her face. Her eyes wide and startled, she pressed firmly against Thorsen's side. His Viking friend gazed down at Kaela, a wide grin on his face, but he kept a wary eye on her suitors.

Kaela had never been besieged by so many men, all clamoring to speak with her. She wished Thorsen would send them away. When she glanced up and saw Cameron, she smiled with relief.

One glare from the Black Wolf and the crowd dispersed. No man in his right mind would challenge the warrior.

Still glaring, Cameron offered Kaela his arm. "The King awaits us, madam. Shall we dine?"

"Aye, my lord."

"Well done," Cameron said, glancing back at Thorsen. The Viking merely nodded and followed his baron.

At the table with William and Matilda, Cameron and Kaela were seated next to each other. Cameron shared his trencher with her, feeding her the choicest bits of meat. Kaela ate heartily, for more than a sennight had passed since she had eaten a good meal.

The King had many questions for her. When he asked about the farming techniques used at Chaldron, she explained them in detail.

At last, William turned his attention to his wife. Kaela drank deeply from the wonderful wine in her cup and allowed the serving wench to refill the goblet. She smiled warmly at Cameron when he teased her about all she had eaten.

"Aye, my lord, you almost starved me to death on our journey," she said. Cameron, smiling warmly, turned his attention to Johnathan as his vassal spoke to him. Kaela sat contentedly at Cameron's side and drank her wine. Warm and secure, she wished she could always be beside him this way. He had been kind to her in the garden, she thought drowsily, and he had looked at her with admiration when she had entered the hall on Johnathan's arm.

Cameron felt Kaela lean into him and turned to see that she had fallen asleep, her head resting on his shoulder. He chuckled and glanced up to see Matilda's laughing eyes upon him.

"I believe the lady is quite exhausted, Baron. Why don't you see her to her chamber?"

"Aye, the journey was hard on her. If you will excuse us." Cameron gently took Kaela by the hand, shook her awake, then guided her from the room up the stairs to her chamber.

"I am sorry I fell asleep, Cameron. I hope I did not embarrass you," she murmured.

"Nay, Kaela, William and Matilda understood."

Cameron entered her chamber, crossed to the bed, and pulled back the tapestry. Dismissing Sarah, telling her he would see to the lady, he unfastened Kaela's gown and pulled it over her head. Trying not to look at her body in the thin chemise, he helped her under the covers.

Kaela, warm and fuzzy from the wine, looked up at Cameron, trying to focus on his face. "Will you stay with me until I fall asleep?"

"Aye, I will stay, by the look of you that will not be long." Even as he spoke, he could see her drifting off. He sat very still for several moments and watched her, listening to her even breathing; her hair spread out across the pillow, the sweet smile on her face. Cameron leaned over and placed a kiss on her forehead. Closing the door behind him, he quietly left her chamber.

Cameron gave orders to the King's guard stationed outside her door to let no one enter, and then made his way to his own bedchamber. He lay in bed for a long time, thinking about Kaela and the time they had spent together. He remembered the feel of her soft body next to his and the sound of her laughter. He had been touched by her expression when, surrounded by William's knights, she looked up to see him approaching. She had seemed so uncomfortable with their attentions. He had never known a woman to react that way. She seemed to be interested only in him. While he tried to tell himself that that boded ill, he felt elated. When he finally fell asleep, he dreamed of her.

Kaela awoke several hours later to the sound of her own cries. Her heart raced so hard in her chest, she feared it would explode. Covered with sweat, she shivered under the covers. She sat up when a man's voice called to her from outside her door. With a sigh of relief, she realized the King's guard had heard her screams. She went to the heavy door and called to the guard that everything was all right, but, afraid the dream would come again, she did not return to her bed.

Instead she retrieved a vial of the sleeping draught from her trunk and crossed to the window. She breathed deep of the cold night air to try and stop her trembling, and silently cursed Broderick of Ralston. Gazing out at the courtyard, she wondered if her life would ever be normal again.

Broderick had stolen her courage—she wanted it back. With Cameron's help she had begun to face her fears, but now he would be leaving her. She must find the strength to put her past behind her, the courage to face her future. She glared at the vial of opiate clutched in her hand, and with resolve stiffening her spine, threw it out the window. Before her nerve dissolved, Kaela crossed to her trunk and retrieved the remaining vials, sending them the way of the first. "I'll not let you beat me in this way, Broderick," she vowed.

"Please, God," she prayed fervently, "let me overcome this fear of Broderick. Take these nightmares from me. Help me find my strength." Kaela leaned against the window and stared out at the night for a long time, thinking of all she had been through and what might yet be ahead of her.

❖   ❖   ❖

Cameron awoke with a start. He had been dreaming of Kaela. The fire had died in the hearth and cold pervaded the room. Thinking how much he missed her soft warm body snuggled next to his, he cursed aloud. He dressed quickly and crossed to the window. Not quite dawn, but soon the sun would rise.

He left his chamber and made his way quickly to

the north wing where he approached Kaela's chamber door. The guard at attention, nodded in recognition.

"Has all been well?" Cameron asked.

"The lady screamed something terrible during the night, Baron. I called out to her and she answered me after several moments that all was well. After that, I heard nothing else from her," the guard said.

Cameron dismissed the man with instructions to find Johnathan and send the knight to him. He entered the bedchamber, only to find the bed empty. His heart leapt to his throat. Turning, he gazed around the room. He found her then, lying on the floor by the window, her body curled into a tight ball. Cameron rushed to her side, knelt, and lifted her in his arms. God's teeth, she was so cold her body was shaking. He quickly laid her on the bed and pulled the covers over her.

Kaela came slowly to awareness. Opening her eyes, she saw Cameron's worried face. "Cameron?" she whispered. "What are you doing here?"

The dark circles under her eyes worried Cameron. He could see she was still quivering from the cold. Holding her hand, he asked, "What were you doing on the floor, Kaela?"

"The floor?"

"Aye, I found you lying on the floor by the window." His voice sounded hoarse to his own ears.

"The nightmare came again. When I screamed and woke myself, the poor guard must have been scared to death. I dared not sleep again for fear the nightmare might return."

"You took the sleeping draught?"

"Nay, I threw it out the window. I want my life back, Cameron. I'll not allow Broderick to control me any longer. The last thing I remember was looking out the window, waiting for the dawn," she said, her smile weak. "You must think me extremely foolish for falling asleep there."

"I think no such thing. I should never have left you alone. Now we must get you warm and you must rest. You look ill, Kaela."

She frowned, but he ignored her and went to build up the fire. When he returned to her side, she still trembled. Cursing, he pulled back the furs and crawled in beside her, pulling her into his arms.

"Cameron?"

"Hush, Kaela, and go to sleep," he told her angrily. He rubbed her back very gently and she fell asleep. When the tremors ceased, he went back into the corridor to wait for Johnathan. He soon heard heavy footsteps and looked up to see his second in command striding toward him, Thorsen fast on his heels.

"You summoned me, Baron? Is anything wrong?" Johnathan asked.

"Aye, it's Kaela," Cameron told them, concern evident in his voice. "She had the nightmare again last night. Too frightened to go back to sleep, she spent half the night gazing out the window. I found her this morning, crumpled on the floor, freezing to death. 'Twill be a miracle if the foolish woman doesn't get sick," he grumbled.

"What do you want us to do?" Thorsen asked.

"I am not leaving her alone again. I want you to speak to the Captain of the guard, Johnathan. Tell him our men will guard Kaela. Then I want you, Thorsen, Andrew, and Patrick to take turns guarding her room at night."

"And where are you going to be, Wolf?" Thorsen asked.

Cameron flushed. "I am going to sleep with her. She only had the nightmare once while we were traveling and I am sure they lessened because she felt my presence."

"What about her reputation, Baron?" Johnathan asked, frowning at Cameron.

"That is why only you four will stand watch here. After I retire, and those in the castle sleep, I will come to her room. You must wake me before dawn to return to my own chamber."

Cameron's two vassals smiled broadly.

"Damn you, 'Tis the only way I can be assured she will be all right. Go and make arrangements with the guard, Johnathan. Thorsen, you stay here and guard the door. She sleeps now and I want to make sure she gets a few hours' rest. When her maid comes, send her away, but with strict orders to return in four hours with a hot bath and food."

Thorsen nodded and Cameron slipped back into Kaela's chamber. He lay beside her and held her in his arms. She looked so pale and the shadows under her eyes were dark. Truly worried, he prayed she would not become ill.

❖   ❖   ❖

"Too short?" William roared.

"Aye, the man is too short," Cameron stated.

"Baron, you have sorely tried my patience. We have been through this list twice. God's toenail, we have discussed almost every eligible bachelor in Normandy and you have come up with a reason to reject each one. Now you are telling me that Baron Lexton is not suitable for marriage to Lady Kaela because the man is short."

William's eyes bulged. At first he looked outraged, then appeared as if he was about to laugh.

"We have not discussed all the bachelors in Normandy, Sire," Cameron grumbled. "Only your most loyal barons are to be considered. Lady Kaela deserves the best Normandy has to offer, at the least, a husband who is taller than she."

God's teeth, he had to control himself. He had made himself look the fool before his King. Every time William mentioned a name and he pictured the man with Kaela, he felt uncontrollable rage. Hence, he was reduced to stupid excuses.

"Baron Cameron, you have made my head pound. 'Tis enough of this nonsense for today. But I tell you this, and hear me well, on the morrow we will name a husband for this lady. If you cannot agree, then the decision will be mine. Do you understand me?" William roared.

"Aye, Sire, we will decide on the morrow. I am sure someone must be suitable."

"In the meantime I am going to the great hall and announce that tomorrow I will name a husband for the fair lady. God's teeth, I have knights out there tripping over themselves petitioning me for her hand."

Cameron's felt his face pale. William smiled as he exited the room.

Cameron stormed to the stables and had a groom saddle Goliath. *Damn women anyway.* Their lot in life was to make a man miserable. Now he had acted the idiot because he could not find Kaela a suitable husband.

Cameron rode Goliath hard until, at last, the tension drained from his body. Thank God Kaela's appearance had improved by the time he had left her to her bath. He wondered what she did now and whether or not Andrew cared for her properly. Andrew—hah—what did he know of women. Frowning, Cameron reined the horse around and retraced his path. He would see for himself how Kaela fared in his brother's care.

❖　❖　❖

Kaela laughed delightedly at Andrew, her eyes sparkling with mischief. "Andrew, you are teasing me. No one loves Brenna more than I, and I quite agree with you that she is a beautiful woman. But you go too far to call her a 'most docile creature', 'sweet and timid.' 'Tis not the Brenna all Chaldron knows and loves."

Andrew grinned. "Perhaps she is not so timid, but, madam, she is quite sweet. Tell me, does the lady have any suitors?"

"None that I know of at the moment, Andrew. We Saxons have been fighting a war, you know."

"'Tis true, but now that you have lost, I fully intend to introduce Lady Brenna to the fine art of courtship." He winked at her and laughed.

"You must promise to be honorable, Andrew, or I will have your head."

"My intentions are most honorable, I assure you."

The two stood near the back of the hall. Andrew had been most attentive and made several introductions. Kaela noticed Johnathan and Thorsen had not been far away all afternoon, and had kept the overly amorous knights at bay. Patrick, in true form, flirted outrageously with every female in the room. Kaela had not seen Cameron since late that morning. She wondered if he was still in conference with the King and if she was the topic of their conversation.

She felt Andrew stiffen and looked up to see an unfamiliar man approaching. He was tall, but not nearly as tall as Cameron. Kaela would not call him handsome, but his features were not displeasing. He had light brown hair and hazel eyes, and his build was on the slim side.

He stopped directly in front of her and lifted her hand to his lips, placing a rather wet kiss there. Kaela disliked him immediately and pulled her hand away.

"Allow me to introduce myself, my lady, since this young imbecile is not going to do so. My name is Baron Thomas. I believe we will soon know one another quite well."

He smiled then, but Kaela noted the smile never reached his eyes. Something cold and slimy about this man revolted her and she shivered. The way he had insulted Andrew angered her.

"I have no desire to know you better, Baron. If you will excuse me." Kaela began to move away, but Thomas reached out to stop her. Andrew immediately stepped to her side and Kaela could see Johnathan and Thorsen approaching.

"I don't believe the lady desires your company, Thomas," Andrew said, his voice filled with sarcasm.

"'Tis Baron Thomas to you, Andrew. Don't forget that. As for the lady, she had best get used to my company," he said, sneering.

His eyes roved over Kaela, and she moved closer to Andrew.

"What say you, Baron?" she demanded. Thorsen and Johnathan joined Andrew by her side and she took comfort in their nearness. Something about Baron Thomas made her skin crawl.

"King William has announced he will award you to one of his barons. I mean to have you." When Kaela gasped in outrage, Baron Thomas laughed.

Cameron had entered the hall only moments before, instantly alert. As soon as he saw Baron Thomas talking to Kaela, he sensed trouble. Making his way across the room, he saw Thorsen and Andrew standing on either side of her and Johnathan directly behind her. In effect, she was completely surrounded.

"'Tis true, my lady. I have won many battles for William and am one of his most powerful Barons. The King will not deny me."

Feeling faint, Kaela trembled. Dear God, William could not give her to this man. Surely Cameron would protest.

"Baron Cameron does not want you," Baron Thomas said, as if he read her thoughts. "He told me so himself. No one stands in my way. Aye, you and Chaldron Castle will be mine."

At that moment Cameron stepped between Kaela and Thomas, effectively blocking her view. She had never been so glad to see him in her life. She immediately gripped the hem of his tunic and began to twist it nervously. Andrew and Thorsen stepped forward, standing shoulder to shoulder with their baron. Johnathan stepped around her and took a position next to Thorsen. They had built a human wall to separate her from Baron Thomas. She realized they were protecting her, but she couldn't see a thing. Kaela stood on her tiptoes and tried to see over Cameron's shoulder. Cameron reached behind him and gave her waist a hard squeeze, telling her to be still. Kaela stepped back and began to pace back and forth behind her protectors, grumbling to herself. She tried to step around Andrew, but he grabbed her arm and pressed her back behind him. She turned in disgust and began to pace back to Johnathan's end of the wall hoping for better luck. When she brushed against Cameron he reached back and pulled her firmly up against his back. His steely warmth felt so good, she sighed her defeat and decided to stay put.

Cameron folded his arms across his chest and glared at Thomas. "What is this, Thomas?"

"I merely informed the lady of my intention to wed her," Thomas drawled, glaring back at Cameron.

"Over my dead body, Baron," Cameron growled.

Kaela had never heard sweeter words. Busy sending silent thanks to God, she almost missed Baron Thomas's next words.

"'Twould give me great pleasure, Cameron, but you have said you will not marry the Saxon Wench. I fail to see your concern."

"Lady Kaela remains under my protection until she is given in marriage."

"As I told you yesterday, ere long the lady's beautiful body will belong to me. I assure you she will be screaming with delight in no time."

Kaela's knees buckled. She would have fallen if Johnathan had not caught her.

Cameron wanted to strangle the bastard, but Thorsen denied him that pleasure.

The Viking brought one powerful fist down on Baron Thomas's head. The man crumpled to the floor like a falling leaf. Cameron turned to Thorsen and roared, "I was going to do that!"

"Aye, but you were taking too long," Thorsen replied calmly.

Several of Baron Thomas's vassals ran over when

they saw their baron fall. "What is the meaning of this?" one of them bellowed.

"Get this sorry bastard out of my sight or he will feel more than a headache when he wakes up," Cameron said, his voice cold.

"You will pay for this, Baron Cameron. Baron Thomas will not go unavenged."

"I will gladly meet your master on the jousting field anytime."

The Baron's men picked him up and carried him from the hall.

"How long do you think he will be out?" Andrew asked, chuckling.

"The last man Thorsen punched remained unconscious for over an hour," Johnathan stated, his voice filled with pride.

"Serves the bastard right," Andrew said.

Cameron turned to face Kaela. "Are you feeling well? You look quite pale. You can release her now, Johnathan." He glowered at his young friend.

Kaela placed her hands on her hips, her eyes spitting fire.

"Did you tell that horrible man you would not have me?" She wanted to shout at him, but whispered instead because everyone in the hall was listening to their conversation.

"Nay, I merely said I would never remarry. 'Tis no secret, Kaela. Hell, woman, I have told you that myself." Cameron's face flushed darkly.

"I see," Kaela replied, her head swimming. "I believe I need some air. Thorsen, would you escort me to the garden?"

"'Twould be my pleasure, my lady." The Viking offered Kaela his arm.

She left without even a passing glance at Cameron. He cursed her under his breath.

Andrew crossed his arms over his chest and glared at Cameron. "Brother, I never thought to say this, but you are a damned fool."

Kaela could not stop shaking. Sweet Jesu, she had been such a fool. Baron Thomas's mocking words played over and over in her mind. Cameron would not have her. Holy Mother of God, would King William give her to that vile man? If not to him, would her future husband be someone who wanted only her body and her lands? She felt weak with fear and with a building anger. Curse men, anyway. Why couldn't a woman choose her own way in life? Brenna was right... life was not fair. Kaela knew she could run Chaldron as well as any man.

"Kaela, are you well?" Thorsen shook her gently.

Looking up into his worried face, she bit down hard on her bottom lip to keep from crying, then smiled tremulously. "'Twas quite a blow you gave that weasel. I do not believe he knew what hit him. My thanks, Thorsen."

He only shrugged, embarrassed by her praise. "Kaela, about Cameron..." he murmured.

"I don't want to talk about him, Thorsen," she said in a small voice. "'Tis all for naught. The man has made his feelings perfectly clear—he does not want me."

"'Tis not true, Kaela, 'Tis just that..."

Kaela reached up and put her hand over his mouth, taking him by surprise.

"Enough, Thorsen, I can bear no more. I need to be alone for a while. I need to think."

"I can't leave you alone, Kaela, 'Tis not safe," he

told her.

"Is there a chapel here, Thorsen? Surely I would be safe there. You could wait outside the door for me. I think mayhap prayer is what I most need right now."

"Aye, my lady, there is a small chapel. I will take you there."

"I don't know what I would do without you," Kaela sighed.

They had been standing in the garden off the great hall. Thorsen took her hand and led her toward the west wing.

Neither noticed a man standing in the shadows near the garden wall. Almost completely hidden by overhanging branches, he watched them turn from the garden and enter the building.

Chapter Nine

❖   ❖   ❖

The chapel was small, intimate, and quite deserted. Kaela knelt before the altar, buried her face in her hands, and wept. She had never been so frightened, except when Broderick had held her captive.

Thorsen stood outside the chapel door, his arms crossed over his chest, a deep scowl on his face. Time was quickly running out and Cameron remained mulishly stubborn. Even if the Viking could get an audience with the King, he had no idea what to say that might help the situation. He heard footsteps approaching. Surprised, he saw Queen Matilda walking toward him, unescorted, which was most unusual.

"Ah! There you are my Viking friend. I have been looking everywhere for you. I understand you guard Lady Kaela," she told him, her brown eyes flashing.

"Aye, Your Majesty, she prays in the chapel."

"Hmph! I would imagine the lady feels much in need of divine intervention about now."

"She is most upset."

"I am sure she is. Tell me something, Thorsen, how do you think your liege lord feels about Kaela? William tells me he refuses to marry the girl."

"He loves her, but he is too stubborn to admit he

wants her," Thorsen grumbled.

Matilda graced him with a warm smile. "Well, I see we are in agreement then. Don't worry, Thorsen, William and I will not let Cameron be so foolish as to throw away this chance at happiness. Now I believe I had better see if I can't bring this 'divine intervention' about." Matilda winked at him and placed her finger to her lips. She slowly opened the chapel door and slipped through.

Kaela's silhouette was barely visible in the dim light. The sound of soft weeping came from near the altar. Matilda walked to the front of the chapel and placed her hand on Kaela's shoulder, startling the girl.

"Come my dear, dry your eyes. 'Tis time we talked about your problem."

Unable to believe her eyes, Kaela blinked and shook her head.

Matilda laughed softly. "Come now, sit over here by me," she said, moving to the chairs provided for herself and the King. Kaela followed. "We have much to discuss before this evening."

Kaela stared at her. "I don't understand, Your Majesty."

"Please, call me Matilda. I believe we are going to be great friends. Now, my dear, I have come to talk to you about Baron Cameron."

"There's nothing to discuss. He does not want me," Kaela said forlornly.

Matilda smiled. "I fear you are wrong, my dear. The man wants you so badly he is making himself daft."

Kaela shook her head.

"There is much you do not know about Baron D'Abernon. It is Cameron's place to tell you about his past, and therefore, I shall not. I will tell you another woman in his life once hurt him very deeply. The man is bitter and, for that reason, he has decided never to marry again. William and I feel he must move beyond his pain, begin to live again. Tell me, dear, what think you of Cameron?"

Kaela blushed. She hardly knew this woman, but she sensed Matilda's kindness. The Queen reminded Kaela of her own mother.

"I know not what it means to love a man. I have never felt that, but Baron Cameron has been very kind to me." Kaela kept her gaze on the floor. She did not know how to tell the Queen all that had happened to her, but she forced herself to apeak. "I don't feel very comfortable around men. I was very close to my father and mother. They died three years ago, and I have been, for the most part, on my own. I—I was hurt by a man." Kaela choked on the words.

"I know what happened to you, child, for William told me."

Kaela's cheeks flamed. Matilda patted her hand. "Do not be embarrassed, I understand exactly how you feel, my dear. I know what it is to be helpless and overpowered by a man."

Kaela's eyes widened. "You do?"

Matilda nodded. "When I was seventeen, my father promised me to a horrible man whom I despised. Oh, I am sure my father did not realize what a scoundrel he was. My father saw only that he came from a good family, and had riches. The brute constantly tried to get me alone. When he looked at me, I always felt as if I were naked."

"I know the feeling well," Kaela said softly.

"One night he caught me unaware in the stables

and tried to rape me. I fought him well... I am very small but you would be surprised at my strength," Matilda said, her brown eyes twinkling. "Anyway, I could not fend him off. He ripped my clothes off my body and dealt me several blows. He would have taken me then but, by the grace of God, a most wondrous knight came to my rescue. A large, handsome brute of a man. He had been visiting an uncle who lived with my family at the time. We had never met before that night. He pulled the man off me and beat him to a bloody pulp. Then he covered me with his cloak and carried me back to the keep. Needless to say, my father no longer held me to the betrothal, and my 'most wondrous knight' asked my father for my hand. I gave the man a merry chase before I said yes, but he has had my heart ever since that fateful night." Matilda fell silent, smiling at her memories.

"Your wondrous knight was William?"

"Aye, he was my William," Matilda said.

"You love him very much, don't you?"

"Aye, my dear, with all my heart and soul." Matilda stood and began to pace back and forth in front of Kaela. "Let us return to the matter at hand. You were telling me your feelings for Cameron."

"As I said, he has been kind to me. I have been so afraid around men since Broderick, but Baron Cameron is different. He makes me feel safe, and I trust him. I was able to tell him about my ordeal with Broderick. God's truth, he dragged the tale from me. The man is very persistent."

Matilda laughed. "I am sure he is. Would you wish to have him as your husband?" The queen watched Kaela very closely.

Kaela blushed to her toes. "I am not afraid when

Cameron kisses me—'Tis a fact, I rather like his kisses."
She glanced up at the Queen, but Matilda only smiled
and waited for her to continue.

"He is very good with my four-year-old niece,
Mattie, and she adores him. I am sure he would be a
good father, and he was very interested in Chaldron.
'Tis a certainty he would make a good husband. If I
must marry someone, I would prefer Baron Cameron.
But this is pointless, Your Majesty. The man has
already told the King he doesn't want me."

"We shall see about that, my dear." Matilda smiled.
"Aye, we shall see."

✥　　✥　　✥

Cameron cursed aloud as he dressed for dinner.
Not even his hot bath had relieved the tension he felt.
He had to choose a husband for Kaela by tomorrow,
and now she was not even speaking to him. Not to
mention the fact that his vassals were giving him icy
stares. Curse the saints, he did not deserve this
treatment.

He heard a knock at his chamber door and threw it
open.

"What is it?" he asked the guard standing before
him.

"The King wishes to see you, Baron, immediately,
in his chambers."

"Thank you, I will come right away," Cameron told
the guard, dismissing him.

"Now what?" Cameron grumbled, making his way
to the King's chambers.

"You wished to see me, Sire?"

"Aye, Cameron. Tell me, what think you of Baron

Robert Malet?" William asked, a smug look on his face.

Cameron thought for a moment, trying to place the man. Then he smiled. "I have only met Malet once or twice, but he seemed a good man. Why?"

"Matilda thinks very highly of him. He has been friends with her family for years. He is tall and quite good looking, wouldn't you say?"

"True." Cameron scowled, anticipating where William's questioning would lead.

"Malet has a large holding in Normandy, but he has a younger brother who could manage the estate. The Baron fought with me at Hastings, you know. Matilda thinks he will make a good husband for Lady Kaela. I agree with her, and now that I have your approval, I see nothing standing in the way."

"What?" Cameron roared. "The man is married!"

"He's widowed," William said, smiling broadly.

"Widowed?" Cameron gulped. God's teeth, he was going to be sick.

"Aye, he lost his dear wife just a few months ago. I have approached him about Lady Kaela. He seemed most enthusiastic. I have invited him to dine at my table this eve so the two can get to know each other. I believe our problems are solved, Cameron." William smiled when his vassal's brow creased.

"William, I do not feel the man…"

"Hold!" William bellowed. "I have had quite enough of your objections, Cameron. You said yourself he is a good man and quite handsome. He is a baron and a land holder. Besides, Matilda likes him, and she is a very good judge of character. After all, she chose me for a husband," William said, his eyes twinkling.

"I have sent an escort for Lady Kaela. She will dine at my table tonight with Baron Malet. You will not," he told Cameron sternly. "I want none of your interference."

"William… I—I—"

"I do not want to hear it, Cameron. The only way Kaela will not marry Robert Malet tomorrow is if you marry the girl yourself. That is all I have to say on the matter. You are dismissed," William said, waving him away.

Cameron knew better than to argue with his King. Numb, he walked back to the great hall very slowly.

Kaela will marry Robert Malet. 'Tis all over. He should feel relieved. Kaela would marry Malet, a good man, who would take care of her. Now Cameron was free, but he felt so empty.

"I believe the meal is ready to be served, Cameron. Should I go and get Kaela?" Johnathan spoke first when he and Thorsen joined their baron.

"Nay, the King has sent his guard. She dines at his table this eve."

"Without you?" Thorsen studied his friend's face and saw the misery there. He did not know exactly what Matilda was up to, but thought watching would be most interesting.

"I don't understand," Johnathan said.

"The King has chosen a husband for her. She sups with him tonight."

"Who is this man?" Thorsen asked.

"Robert Malet."

"A good man… I met him at Hastings. 'Tis good news, Cameron. Now you can put this bothersome interruption behind you," Johnathan said, giving Thorsen a knowing look. "I am starving. Let us join Andrew and Patrick."

The men looked up and saw Kaela enter the hall

with the King's guard. She walked gracefully across the room to the King's table. Cameron could not take his eyes off her. *She looks more beautiful every time I see her.*

"She looks lovely," Johnathan said.

"Aye, Malet is a lucky man," Thorsen added.

Kaela wore a vibrant blue bliaut and her copper-colored tresses glowed under the rushlights. She smiled warmly at William and Matilda. Cameron felt as if he had been punched in the gut when a tall, handsome man took Kaela's hand in his and raised it to his lips.

"Let us join the others," Cameron ground out, wondering how the hell he would get through the meal. He sat in stony silence as the men around him ate and talked with one another. His vassals tried several times to draw him into the conversation, but he seemed oblivious to them.

"He has not taken his eyes off her," Patrick whispered to Andrew.

"'Tis most telling, is it not?" Andrew said, smiling.

Thorsen looked happier than his friends had ever seen him, and he ate everything in sight.

What is he saying to her? Why does she smile and laugh so? Holy Saint Ambrose's bones, he had never felt this miserable. Pushing back his stool, he rose and left the hall.

Smiling, Matilda watched Cameron leave the hall and reached over to pat Kaela's hand. "I do believe he has taken the bait, my dear. The poor man appears most upset to me."

William threw back his head and laughed. "I have never seen a man so disturbed. I do believe he will come around before we see the dawn."

"Do you really think so?" Kaela asked. She was

afraid to hope.

"I do indeed, my lady." William smiled at her.

"Whatever happens, you will not be wedding Baron Malet on the morrow."

"Aye," Robert said. "My wife is an understanding woman, but I do not think she would stand for that, Lady Kaela."

"I wish I could have seen his face when you told him Robert was a widower." Matilda grinned at her husband.

"'Twas something to see, my dear."

Cameron paced the wall walk, ignoring the cold night air. After tomorrow Kaela would belong to another man. He would never see her again, hold her in his arms. Unable to stand the thought, he cursed soundly. He could not let her go, but he had vowed he would never marry again, never love another woman. If he loved Kaela, he would become vulnerable. Something inside Cameron told him he could trust Kaela, that she would not hurt him, but he refused to listen.

He turned at the sound of footsteps and saw Thorsen coming toward him. God's blood, the last thing he needed was another lecture. "What do you want?"

"I thought you might want someone to talk to, my friend."

"There's naught to say. She marries Malet on the morrow, and that's the end of it."

"Why can't you admit you care for the girl?"

"You know I do," Cameron said, running his hand

through his hair, "but I don't want that kind of pain again."

"Why does it have to be painful, Cameron?" Thorsen asked. "You care for her, and she trusts you. You don't have to love her to marry her. Does Robert Malet love her? Of course he doesn't. God's teeth, he only met her this eve. No matter who Kaela marries, the man will not be in love with her. Why not wed her yourself?" Thorsen could see he had Cameron's attention. He hoped his lopsided logic would get through to the man.

"True, Malet might grow to love her, but you are a good man, Cameron. Would you treat the lady any less kindly than if you were in love with her? I think not. And think about the good you could do at Chaldron. The place needs an army as strong as yours—it was built to house such strength. You would love the challenge—to be master of such a holding.

"And there is little Mattie. I saw the look on the child's face when you left her. She needs a strong man in her life, one who will care for her. How do you know that Malet will even allow the child to stay? You were wonderful with Peter," Thorsen said softly, and watched Cameron blanch at the memory of his small son. "You could bring great joy and security to the child."

Listening to Thorsen's words, Cameron felt hope kindle, then build to a consuming flame in his heart. "I can marry her. I won't have to love her," he said, more to himself than to Thorsen.

"She already trusts you, Cameron, feels safe with you. Think of how she will feel going to this man that she does not know. What will Malet think when he sees the scars on her back? Mayhap, he will not want her any longer. How can you desert her?"

"I can't. You are right, Thorsen, she needs me," Cameron said, a broad smile forming on his lips. Sweet Jesu, he felt as if the world had been lifted from his shoulders. He did not have to give Kaela up. Elated, he wanted to shout. Instead, he said calmly, "I can marry her and be a good husband. I don't have to love her to do it." He slapped Thorsen on the shoulder. "By the Saints, I will wed her."

Thorsen grinned from ear to ear. Thank God for fools, he thought, following Cameron back inside.

Eager to reach Kaela's chamber, Cameron moved silently through the corridors, Thorsen at his heels. The hour was very late and even though she was angry with him, he knew she was afraid to be alone.

Things would be different now. He smiled in the darkness. He would tell her he intended to marry her. God, he felt wonderful.

Kaela's eyes flew open when a hand clamped over her mouth. She gazed in pure terror at the man leaning over her. Recognizing his cold hazel eyes, she tried to scream.

Baron Thomas placed his other hand on her throat and squeezed. "Keep your mouth shut, bitch, or you will die this night," he snarled. "I watched you tonight as you dined and laughed with Robert Malet. The man is not half so powerful as I, yet William thinks to give you to him. Nay, I will not be denied." Baron Thomas straddled her hips, pressed his weight against her body, and brought his face within inches of hers.

"I will have you, wench. Your fine Baron Cameron will not stop me. He will die for the humiliation he caused me this day, and that Viking bastard with him," Thomas vowed.

Kaela gasped for breath and forced herself to go limp. God help her, where was Cameron? What had happened to Andrew? She had left him standing guard outside her door. *Dear Lord, please don't let him be hurt. Please help me get away from this man.*

"Afraid?" Thomas said. "Little slut, I'll make quick work of you." He reached for the fastening of his chausses.

The moment his grip loosened, Kaela lunged forward taking Thomas by surprise and knocking him off balance. She scrambled from the bed, and ran toward the fire.

My dagger, I have to reach my dagger! Kaela had left the jeweled blade on the mantle. She heard a strange keening, and realized the sound came from herself. As if she were moving in slow motion, she reached forward.

A few feet from the hearth, Thomas grabbed a handful of her hair and yanked her back against him. She fought like a woman possessed, biting and scratching at his exposed flesh.

"Bitch!" he growled. "So the King does not think me good enough. I'll show him! I'll show them all." He whirled her around, and slammed his fist into her stomach.

Gasping at the searing pain in her stomach, Kaela screamed Cameron's name. Then Thomas's body crashed down on hers. She continued to fight, digging her fingernails into his face. Thomas howled, struck her again, and ripped her chemise from her body.

"I will have you now, you bloody bitch. Your precious Cameron cannot help you. Go ahead, fight me. I like to feel a woman's flesh beneath my fists."

He leaned down and sank his teeth into the soft flesh above her right breast. Kaela screamed again.

She felt as if she stood outside herself, watching this animal ravish her. She heard him grunt, knew his hands ran down her body to force her thighs apart. His heavy body smelled sour with sweat.

Then she could fight no longer, could feel nothing but a strange numbness.

✣   ✣   ✣

Cameron cursed when he saw Andrew crumpled in a heap on the floor outside Kaela's chamber door. His heart in his throat, he knelt at his brother's side and placed his hand on his neck. Feeling a strong pulse, he sighed with relief. Someone had knocked Andrew unconscious.

"Holy mother of God—Kaela!" Cameron heard her scream and lunged for the door, only to find it barred.

"Help me, Thorsen!"

The two men threw their shoulders against the heavy oak door and Cameron heard it splinter. One more thrust and they charged into the room.

Cameron's eyes took in the scene before him and he roared his rage. Thomas had Kaela on the floor in front of the hearth. The bastard was on top of her. Lunging forward, Cameron grabbed the man by the neck and threw him across the room.

"You bloody bastard, I will kill you for this,"

Cameron grabbed Thomas by his tunic, lifted him to his feet, then slammed his fist into his face and heard the satisfying sound of the man's jaw breaking. He hit him again and knew he had broken his nose as well when blood splattered across his tunic.

He turned in surprise when he felt Thorsen's large arms encircle him, pulling him away from Thomas. Long since unconscious, the man slithered to the floor.

"Leave him! Kaela needs you now, Cameron," Thorsen said, his voice filled with concern.

"Oh God!" Cameron turned and saw her lying so still upon the rushes. He crossed to her, softly calling her name. She opened her eyes and stared at him blankly when he lifted her in his arms. "God's blood," Cameron moaned. "What has he done to you?"

She didn't make a sound as he carried her to the bed and sat down, cradling her in his arms. He pulled a fur from the bed and gently wrapped her in it.

"Call the guard, Thorsen," Cameron said, taking control of the situation. "Get that sorry bastard out of my sight. Put him in the dungeon. William will deal with him tomorrow, or by God, I will. And see to Andrew immediately. Thomas must have hit him very hard for him to be unconscious so long. Send word to Matilda, and ask her to send her physician."

Thorsen looked down at his friend, watching as he held Kaela to him. Cameron had not looked so distraught since the night Peter died. Nodding, the Viking left the room and called for the guard.

Cameron carried Kaela to the hearth and sat down in the high backed chair, pulling it closer to the fire. He held her in his lap and pulled back the fur, checking her quickly for broken bones. He found none, but grimaced when he saw the bite marks on her breast.

Gently, he wiped away the blood, all the while soothing her with soft words. She sat unmoving in his arms, staring into space. God, he thought desperately, 'Tis as if she is not here.

"Kaela, you are all right. I am here, sweetheart. 'Tis Cameron. You are safe now. Please, Kaela, talk to me." He rocked her back and forth, caressing her arms and back, telling her over and over she was safe. Relief flooded through him when she began to tremble. She made a high wailing sound that chilled his blood. He hugged her to him, and rocked.

"'Tis all right, sweetheart. I am here," Cameron whispered. Please God, he prayed, bring her back to me.

She began to cry, huge racking sobs, and Cameron breathed a sigh of relief.

"Cameron?" she whispered, and moaned.

"Aye, sweetheart, I have you. You are safe, Kaela. 'Tis going to be all right, sweeting. I will to take care of you." He placed his hands on either side of her face and gazed into her frightened green eyes. "I will not leave you ever again. Do you understand me?"

She only stared back at him, not saying anything. He took a deep breath and tried again. "I am going to marry you, Kaela. You will be my wife. No man will ever harm you again. You are mine, Kaela. Do you hear me? You are mine now."

She leaned into him and sobbed against his chest. "I was so afraid, Cameron. He woke me up. I tried to fight him. I could not reach my dagger. He was so s-strong," she sobbed.

"Hush, little one. You are safe now. I know you tried to fight him. He will never hurt you again. No man will ever hurt you again." Easing her head back, he placed soft kisses on her face, and tasted the salt of her tears. "You belong to me and no one will ever hurt you," he said, elated when he felt her arms slip around his neck. Cameron heard a great commotion in the corridor, then watched Thorsen hurry into the room, with William and Matilda at his heels.

"She's all right," Cameron said, in answer to Thorsen's inquiring look.

"Thank God for that. Bring her to the bed, Cameron. Here is Metford to see to her." Matilda briskly took charge.

"Good God, Cameron, I can't believe this," William bellowed. "Are you sure the poor thing is all right? I will have that bastard's head for this."

Matilda turned and pointed to the doorway. The heavy oak door had splintered clear through and barely hung in place. "Out," she said. "I will not have Kaela upset further, William. Go bellow in the hall while I see to her injuries."

William gave her a sheepish look and left the room. Thorsen followed right behind him.

"You, too, Cameron."

"Nay," Kaela said, clinging to his hand. "Don't leave me, please."

"'Tis only for a moment, child, until Metford can see to your injuries. He will be right outside the door," Matilda reassured Kaela as she motioned Cameron out the door. He leaned down and kissed her forehead. "I will stand at your door, sweetheart." He left the room to join William and Thorsen.

"How is Andrew?"

"He has a hell of a headache, but other than that, he is fine."

"I cannot believe Baron Thomas would do such a

thing," William said. "I heard about the trouble you two had in the hall and the bastard threw a fit this afternoon when I refused to give him her hand, but I never thought him capable of this."

"What will you do?"

"God's truth, Cameron, you have already beaten the man to a pulp," William answered.

"Aye," Thorsen said. "He has a broken jaw and a broken nose."

"He disobeyed me openly when he attacked the girl. I told him he could not have her. This is a flagrant violation of his oath of fealty. Kaela has sworn her oath of allegiance and is under my protection. Baron Thomas will lose his head."

Cameron nodded his approval. "I will wed Kaela on the morrow."

"Ah! So it took a near rape for you to come to your senses," William said, one eyebrow arching in question.

"Nay, 'twas the threat of Robert Malet. I will let no other man have her. I had decided to wed her before Thorsen and I found her with Thomas."

"I am glad," William said, smiling warmly. "You will not regret your decision, Cameron. She is a fine lady."

"I know." Cameron smiled back at his King.

William frowned. "Are you sure she is all right?"

Matilda came into the corridor and stood next to her husband. "She will be fine. Metford gave her a sleeping potion and dressed her wound. The bastard bit her, William," she said, her brown eyes flashing indignation. "I want his head on a pike."

"You will get your wish, my love."

Matilda nodded her approval and turned her attention to Cameron. "And you will stop this nonsense and marry the girl."

"I will wed her on the morrow," Cameron said, bowing to his Queen.

"He had already decided, Matilda," William said, placing his arm around his wife and drawing her to his side. "The threat of Malet brought him to his senses. Come, wife, let's be off to bed. We have a wedding to see to on the morrow."

Cameron could hear her laughter as she left with her husband. He turned to his friend. "Get her trunk, Thorsen. I am moving her to my chamber for the night. The lady no longer has a door to guard."

He lifted Kaela in his arms and cradled her head against his shoulder. When he reached his chamber, he placed her in his large bed, disrobed, and joined her.

"Never again, sweetheart," he whispered, taking her in his arms. "I will take care of you, always."

Chapter Ten

✤   ✤   ✤

Slowly, Kaela opened her eyes. Groggy and disoriented, she turned her head and met Cameron's gaze. She smiled, her mind still fuzzy.

"Hello," she said.

"Good morning. How do you feel?"

"My head hurts." She looked around the room. "Where am I?"

"You are in my bed at the moment, madam." Cameron grinned, but then his expression became serious. "Do you remember last night?"

Memory came flooding back and Kaela gasped. Her eyes filled with pain as she looked at him. "Oh God!"

Cameron gathered her in his arms. He had been awake for hours watching her, this beautiful woman who would soon be his wife. His wife! Knowing she would be frightened and confused when she woke up, he had stayed with her. "'Tis all right, Kaela, you are safe now."

Kaela tensed and shuddered, thinking how close she had come to being raped. "If you had not come when you did, Cameron…"

"I know sweetheart, but I did come in time. 'Tis all

over now. No one will ever hurt you again. Do you remember what I told you last night, Kaela?"

"You told me you were going to marry me."

"That's right."

Kaela felt warm and tingly all over. Then Thomas's face loomed before her and she shuddered.

"Make the feel of him go away, Cameron. I still feel his dirty touch," she cried, clutching him.

Cameron moaned. Sweet Jesu, how he hated to see her tormented. "You are free of him, Kaela. He will never touch you again. No other man will ever touch you again. Only I have the right to do that."

"Make the thought of him go away. I want to feel only you," she whispered, clinging to him.

Cameron understood then. She wanted to be cleansed of Thomas's memory. He cradled her beautiful face between his hands for a moment and stared deeply into her eyes. "You have the most bewitching eyes I have ever seen." He leaned down and pressed his warm lips against her trembling ones.

Kaela opened her mouth and slid her tongue inside his, desperate in her need to have him kiss her. And kiss her he did, slanting his mouth over hers again and again. Kaela felt a deep ache of desire spread its warmth all the way to her toes. She moaned softly and ran her hand down his muscled back.

When she pressed closer to him, Cameron groaned, so hard with desire that he couldn't think. Reluctantly, he pulled away from her and smiled down into her flushed face.

"Soon, sweetheart, soon we will enjoy each other, but now is not the time. Today is your wedding day, and you have much to do to prepare yourself. Tonight will be soon enough to lose your maidenhead. You will come to my bed a virgin bride," Cameron said, teasing her.

Kaela blushed to her toes and Cameron let out a lusty laugh, pulling away from her and leaving the bed. He pulled on his chausses and tunic, then turned to find her watching him. "Believe me, my lady, I will think of nothing else this day."

"Cameron, why are you marrying me? Is it because of what happened last night?"

"I am marrying you because it is the right thing for both of us, Kaela. Is it not what you want? Would you prefer Baron Malet?" He held his breath. What if she refused him?

Looking away, she twisted the sheets into knots. "'Tis you I prefer for my husband, my lord," she whispered.

"Good, 'Tis settled then. Get dressed now, for 'Tis time to be about. Thorsen waits to escort you to the Queen's chambers. Matilda has taken favor with you, Kaela. You are to prepare yourself for the wedding in her chamber. Come now, our Queen is not known for her patience."

He is marrying me out of pity. Resentfully, Kaela pulled her bliaut over her head. *He does not love me, but he is kind and will make a good husband. Mayhap in time he will love me.* She prayed it would be so.

✣   ✣   ✣

Kaela had never felt so pampered. A hot bath had been prepared for her when she reached the Queen's chambers, and three servants waited to attend her. She soaked in the rose-scented bath for over an hour, letting the warmth ease the tension from her body. Sarah scrubbed her with scented soap and helped Kaela wash her hair. After Kaela's bath, Sarah wrapped her in a soft robe and led her into another room where she found Matilda waiting for her.

"Ah, my dear, you look much refreshed. Come and join me in some lunch and I will tell you about the wedding." Matilda smiled broadly at Kaela.

"Thank you, Your Majesty," Kaela said. Her stomach rumbled when she smelled the cooked meats and fresh bread.

"We are alone now, Kaela. Please call me Matilda. Are you feeling better, child?"

"Aye, the bath helped. 'I am thankful for your help last night, Matilda," Kaela said shyly.

"Think nothing of it, my dear." Matilda waved her hand in a deprecating gesture. "I am glad you are all right and that the filthy bastard had no opportunity to harm you further."

Kaela shuddered, remembering Thomas's hands on her body.

"The memory will fade with time, Kaela. Cameron will help you forget. There is much joy to be found in the arms of a loving man, my dear."

Kaela's head came up and she stared gravely at Matilda. "The Black Wolf does not love me. He vows never to love again."

Matilda could see fresh pain in the girl's eyes. She smiled, remembering how miserable being young and naive had been.

"Perhaps, but you will be surprised what the love of a strong woman can do to a man."

"I don't love him," Kaela said defiantly, surprised the words did not ring true, even to her ears.

"Be patient with him, Kaela. Cameron is a good

man and will be a good husband. He prizes loyalty
above all else—you must remember that."

"I will try."

"Now, my dear, I think you will be quite pleased
with the beautiful gown I have chosen for you. I know
Baron Cameron will." Matilda clapped her hands. In a
moment, Sarah entered the room, the wedding dress
draped over her arm.

Kaela had never seen anything like the shimmering,
light as air fabric. She stood very still while Sarah
settled the pale cream-colored gown around her. Cut
low, the gown hugged her breast and waist, then flared
into a full skirt at her hips. Matilda placed a beautiful,
hammered gold belt inset with diamonds around her
and a matching diamond necklace sparkled around her
throat. A wreath of white roses around her head held a
long veil made from the same shimmering material.
Her long copper tresses shone with highlights and
swirled loosely to her hips.

Matilda and Sarah clapped their hands and gazed
with pleased awe at their handiwork.

Among the throng that filled the chapel, Cameron's
warriors waited to witness the marriage of their Baron.
Cameron stood on the raised dais with the Bishop and
William. Andrew stood at his brother's right.
Johnathan and Patrick walked up to join them.
Everyone turned to stare when Matilda entered and
made her way to her husband's side.

"We are ready to begin, William."

William nodded to the musicians at the back. They
began to play a soft religious melody on their lutes.

Thorsen entered with Kaela on his arm. Cameron could not believe the vision coming toward him. Never had she looked more beautiful than at this moment in her splendid, shimmering wedding dress. Later, he would swear she had floated to his side. He also heard every man in the room suck in his breath at the vision she made.

The look on Cameron's face made Matilda pinch William, giving him a wide smile. The King returned his wife's smile, then focused his attention on the ceremony.

Thorsen put Kaela's hand in Cameron's, giving his baron a teasing wink before stepping to one side to join Johnathan and Patrick. The Bishop pronounced the sacred words of the marriage ceremony. Kaela heard Cameron's deep responses and responded in kind. The exchange of vows was over very quickly and Cameron leaned over her, slanting his lips over hers.

William stepped forward to proclaim in a booming voice, "Lords and ladies, may I present Baron and Baroness Cameron D'Abernon." Kaela heard a resounding cheer and then William hugged her. She turned from the King only to be swept up in Thorsen's arms. The big Viking squeezed her and whispered his congratulations in her ear, then passed her on to Andrew, Patrick, and Johnathan. She could see Matilda standing next to William, smiling broadly, and Kaela returned her smile.

The next few hours flew by. The musicians played and the ale flowed. Toasts were made to the happy couple, and Cameron's vassals came one by one to kneel before her, pledging their loyalty to her and to Chaldron. Kaela, overwhelmed with emotion, struggled to fight back her tears. Cameron never left her side, and she slipped her hand in his, smiling up at him.

"Are you happy, Kaela?" he asked her tenderly.

"Aye, my lord, very happy," she replied.

The wedding supper was a feast to behold. Servants carried out large platters of every kind of meat and fowl. There was a large array of vegetables and breads, and the wine flowed freely.

Cameron and Kaela sat with the King and Queen. William regaled them with stories about his courtship of Matilda. Kaela sat close to Cameron, content that he fed her from his trencher. She placed her hand on his thigh, and he smiled down at her, cocking one dark brow. "Are you anxious to retire to my bed, wife?"

Kaela blushed, and drew her hand away, only to have him put it back.

Matilda interrupted them. "Come, Kaela, 'Tis time for the women to leave the hall. The men will keep your husband busy with toasts for the next hour."

Kaela followed Matilda from the hall and down the corridors to Cameron's bedchamber. A fire burned in the hearth and the furs had been pulled back on the bed. Crossing the room, Matilda lifted a beautiful chemise from the bed. "'Tis for you, my dear."

Kaela gasped at the beautiful sheer material, then blushed and thanked the Queen.

"Put it on, Kaela, and await your husband. I doubt you will wait long. The man has been making love to you all night with his eyes," Matilda said, softly. She hesitated, then asked, "Kaela, do you know what to expect in the marriage bed?"

"I have a good idea."

Matilda patted her hand. "You have nothing to fear, my dear. Cameron will be gentle with you. There will be some pain the first time, and blood when he breaks your maidenhead."

Kaela blanched.

"Do not be afraid. 'Twill only hurt the first time and then only for a moment. I promise you will enjoy what is between a husband and wife." She patted Kaela's cheek, turned, and left her.

Sarah helped Kaela out of her gown and into the chemise Matilda had given her. Kaela dismissed her, and crossed to stand in front of the fire. What if she hated mating with Cameron? Would he think her ugly when he saw the scars on her back? Her hair would keep her scars covered, if she were very careful. She could do nothing to hide the ugly bite mark above her breast, but that would heal in a few days and leave no permanent mark. Shuddering, Kaela turned when she heard the door opening. Twisting her hands in front of her, she gazed at Cameron, her eyes wide with fear.

God, she was lovely. Cameron gazed at her, standing in front of the fire, where the light shone through the soft, sheer material of her chemise. Sucking in his breath, he crossed the room and took her trembling hands in his.

"Have I told you how very beautiful you are, wife?" he asked softly, watching the firelight play on her hair.

"Nay," Kaela said. She looked into his eyes. She loved the dark blue ring that surrounded the irises. "I hope our children have your eyes," she whispered, not realizing she had spoken aloud.

He drew her into his arms. "Ah, Kaela, I believe we will do well together."

He felt her tremble and thought he must go slowly with her. Determined to make this a pleasurable experience for her, he guided her to the chair on the other side of the hearth and sat down, pulling her into his lap.

"Don't be afraid, sweeting. We have all night to love each other. I won't hurt you, Kaela." Gently, he kissed the tips of her fingers.

"Matilda said you would, at least the first time," she blurted, blushing furiously.

Cameron smiled. "Aye, there will be a little pain, but I will be gentle with you and the pain will not last long."

Cameron reached up and ran his hands through her hair. "You have the most beautiful hair, wife. 'Tis full of a copper flame when the firelight hits it, and 'Tis soft as silk."

"Yours is as black as a raven's wing," she said, running her fingers through his dark locks.

Cameron moved his lips softly over hers. "Open your mouth, wife. I want to kiss you."

Kaela obeyed, and he felt her shiver with desire when his tongue entwined with hers. Cameron kissed her gently at first, until he felt her respond. He deepened the kiss, all the while stroking her neck with his fingers. Kaela moaned, and Cameron felt his manhood grow hard with desire. God, she tasted sweet. He wanted to know her passion, and slanted his mouth over hers again. Slowly, he untied the ribbons holding her chemise. The soft material fell to her waist, baring her breasts. Cameron's eyes glazed with desire as he looked at the creamy flesh. Lifting his hand, he caressed one rosy nipple until the sweet bud hardened.

Kaela snuggled closer to him, marveling at the way he made her feel.

Cameron placed his hands on her waist and lifted her. "Straddle my hips with your legs, Kaela."

She obeyed him, and felt the hard shaft of his

manhood press against her when he lowered her to his lap. Kaela placed her hands around his neck and lowered her lips to his, kissing him deeply. Cameron groaned in response and reached up with both hands to cup her breasts. He drew lazy circles around her nipples with his fingertips, and Kaela felt a shiver of delight. A white heat began to build inside her and, wanting more, she pressed closer.

Cameron almost lost control when she wiggled against him. He lifted her onto her knees and took her right nipple into his mouth, sucking until Kaela threw her head back and moaned. God, she was responsive. He ran his hands down her back to softly knead her buttocks, all the while suckling first one rosy breast, and then the other.

Kaela, beside herself with need, strained for something. She did not know what, but her desire soon reached an uncontrollable pitch. "Cameron, please…"

Cameron carried her to the bed. "Ah, sweetheart… you are so very beautiful." His gaze roamed over her body while he quickly stripped off his clothes.

Awestruck, Kaela watched his skin turn to bronze and gold in the glow of the firelight. She gazed at the magnificent rippling muscles in his arms, shoulders, and thighs. Her eyes widened in fear when she saw his bulging manhood, thrusting out from his body. "Nay, I cannot…"

Cameron laughed softly and lay beside her, pulling her into his arms. "Don't be afraid, little one, just feel," he said, kissing her passionately.

Kaela lifted one trembling hand, tracing the hard line of his jaw, following it to his smooth lips. She gazed into his scorching eyes, desire making them a deeper blue, and felt strange emotion sweetly unfolding inside her, warming her until it burst into a wild vibrant need. She trembled with the fierceness of it.

"You are so beautiful," Kaela whispered huskily.

Cameron's raging desire increased a hundred times at her touch and her voice. "Open your legs for me, sweetheart," he said hotly. His fingers delicately probed amidst the curly triangle between her thighs, seeking entrance.

She opened her thighs, responding to the deep need she heard in his voice. Shivers of delight raced through her. His fingers parted her, slipping deep inside her wet warmth, tenderly and skillfully pleasuring her.

He settled himself between her long lovely legs, and sighed his contentment. "I have dreamed of this night since the first time I met you," he whispered.

In wonder, Kaela gazed up at him. The warrior whose name made men tremble, touched her with such tenderness. She ran her hands down his back, marveling at the feel of his hard muscles beneath her fingers. She listened to his raspy breathing and felt his heart pound in rhythm with her own.

"Tell me what to do, Cameron," she whispered, her hips pressing against him.

Lord, how she pleased him. His hands shook and the ache in his groin became a painful pleasure.

He chuckled, "Quit moving against me like that or it will all be over too soon, Kaela."

Her soft body turning against him almost shattered his control, but she gave the most wonderful feeling he had ever experienced. God, he wanted to touch her everywhere. He kissed her deeply as he ran his hand up her thigh. Then he lowered his head and again suckled her breast. Kaela arched against him and buried her hands in his hair, pressing him tightly to her.

She felt so hot, the need inside her building by the moment.

Cameron moved lower, placing soft kisses on her stomach. She gasped as his fingers again found her soft woman's mound.

She started to protest, but he shook his head and gently parted the soft wet folds of her womanhood. Kaela whimpered and pressed against his hand.

"That's the way, sweetheart, let yourself go. I want to feel your pleasure."

Kaela could not stop herself. Wild with desire, she tossed her head from side to side against the pillow. A tightness grew in her stomach, radiating a white heat all the way to her toes. A startled gasp of pleasure escaped her.

Cameron slipped a finger inside her, and almost spilled his seed when he felt her hot, moist flesh. She was wet with desire, ready for him. God, she was so tight and small.

He would have to enter her soon. Parting her legs wider, he buried his face against her soft woman's mound. Kaela gasped, and tried to push him away. "No, Cameron, no… you cannot."

Cameron looked up, seeing the desire in her eyes. "Hush, wife, and let me love you." He removed his finger and replaced it with his mouth.

Kaela arched against him, forgetting all about her embarrassment when hot flames engulfed her. His tongue found her most sensitive spot and stroked her rhythmically. Waves of desire washed over her. Kaela felt the pulsing deep inside her suddenly explode in wild, piercing pleasure that racked her body with wave after wave of sensation. She called his name, arching against his mouth.

Cameron, almost beyond thought, his need was so great, told himself over and over to be gentle. He came to his knees and inched his throbbing shaft into her incredible warmth. He felt her tight sheath expanding to encase him.

Kaela felt the pressure of his manhood filling her, and her eyes flew open. He was so hard, so hot, so huge. The warm knot inside her began to expand.

Cameron found her mouth and kissed her deeply. Slowly, he entered her until his manhood pressed against her maidenhead.

"Relax, sweetheart," he said, breathing heavily. His body was covered in a fine sheen of sweat. She was so hot, and so tight, he was beside himself with wanting her. "I am going to break your maidenhead now, Kaela. Relax and the pain will be over in a minute." He kissed her and made one powerful thrust. He felt her maidenhead tear before he buried himself deep within her.

Kaela clung to him, biting back a cry of pain.

"Be still, Kaela," he said when she tried to move against him. "Give yourself time to adjust to me. The pain will be gone in a moment." With iron control, he kept from thrusting deeply into her. He placed soft kisses over her face and whispered sweet words of love to her, telling her what he would soon do to her.

Kaela felt the pain recede and the need begin to build in her again. Her hips moved against him and she moaned her pleasure.

Cameron lost his control then. He began to move deeply within her, pulling out slightly and then burying himself in her. They fell into the age old rhythm of lovemaking as Kaela moved her hips with his. He tried to go slowly, but she wouldn't let him.

Lost in her desire, she ran her hands down his long muscled back, cupping his buttocks in her hands, pressing him to her as she lifted her hips to meet him.

With a groan deep in his throat, Cameron plunged into her again and again. Kaela met each thrust with wild abandon, mindlessly seeking the pleasure he sought to give her. Cameron pulled away slightly, and placing his hand between their joined bodies, began to stroke her with his fingers. She cried out his name. Cameron felt her spasms caress his shaft, clenching and pulling against his engorged manhood. With his arms wrapped around her, he held perfectly still to increase her pleasure. When her spasms began to subside, he drove into her again, no longer able to control the force of his thrust. Shouting her name, he found his release, spilling his seed inside her. He collapsed on top of her, for a moment stunned by the depth of his feeling. He had never felt this with any other woman. He had always been able to control his reactions. With Kaela, control had been totally abandoned. Beyond coherent thought, he did not want to move.

"Cameron, you are too heavy," Kaela said, pushing against his chest.

He slowly withdrew and propped himself on his elbows to relieve her of his weight. Sighing, he kissed her forehead. His scent mingled with hers; he liked that. He gazed down at her, startled to see tears in her eyes.

"Did I hurt you?" Gently, he wiped a tear from her cheek.

"Only a little."

"Why are you crying, Kaela?" Gazing into her eyes, he saw the wonder mirrored there, and a tenderness that deeply touched him.

"I can't believe something I have feared for so long could turn out to be so wonderful."

Cameron grinned at her then, a boyish grin, and Kaela reached out to smooth a lock of hair that had fallen over his brow. He rolled onto his back bringing her with him, and she snuggled against his side, using his shoulder for her pillow.

"Cameron?"

"Hmmm?"

"Did I please you?" She spoke so softly, he could barely hear her.

He smiled, hugging her to him. "If you pleased me any more woman, I would be dead."

She laughed, rubbing her hand across his chest. "You pleased me, too."

"I know."

"How do you know?"

"You were quite vocal, madam."

Kaela blushed. "I was wild," she said, mortified.

"You are a passionate woman, wife. You have nothing to be embarrassed about. I consider myself a lucky man."

Kaela beamed her pleasure. He might not love her, but he was pleased with her. They had made a start.

"Good night, sweetheart." Cameron fell sound asleep in seconds, completely sated.

Kaela lay awake for a long while, enjoying his warm body pressed tightly against her. His even breathing comforted her. She was no longer alone. *Please God, let us be happy. Help me find a way to make him love me.*

✤   ✤   ✤

The King's guard did not notice the lone figure moving stealthily along the eastern wall. There was no moon and the night was dark. He wore a cloak, his face completely hidden by its hood. He ran his hand along the wall until he felt the opening to the hidden passageway. Very slowly, he eased the stone aside and slipped through the small opening, then made his way quickly to the cover of the trees. He walked due east until he reached an isolated hut, and whistled sharply to announce his presence to the man by the campfire.

"What took you so long?" The man never took his gaze off the fire.

"The Norman bastards were awake later than usual, celebrating a marriage. That slut married the Black Wolf," the cloaked man growled, his voice filled with hatred.

"Broderick will go crazy when he hears this."

"'Tis not all. 'Tis rumored William leaves for Normandy within a fortnight. The bastard is going home to celebrate the slaughter of our Saxon brothers. Now is the time to make our move. You must leave at dawn and ride for Wales. Broderick will be anxious for this news. Tell him Kaela and her new husband are expected to leave for Chaldron immediately."

"Does no one suspect your loyalties, then? You are going back?"

"Aye, there is still much I may be able to learn. The Norman fools do not suspect my loyalties lie elsewhere. I will learn all I can before I join our men in Wales."

While waiting for the sun to rise, the two men sat together in front of the fire and discussed their plans for war.

Chapter Eleven

❖   ❖   ❖

Deep in thought, Cameron rode Goliath up to the ridge top. He had left his wife to ride beside Thorsen and gone ahead to scout out a place for his men to make camp.

God, he was married. He still could not believe he had wed again, although three days had passed since he said his vows.

He still felt numb with disbelief. He never thought to find himself with another wife. And what a wife. His loins hardened at the thought of her passion. He smiled. She pleased him. Timid and shy the morning after he had taken her for the first time, when he touched her, she lost her inhibitions and became a wild woman again. Amazed at the lust he felt for her, he still could not control himself, a thought that displeased him—a warrior must always be in control. And he would be, he comforted himself, as soon as his feelings began to fade, as soon as he got used to her.

Extremely fond of Kaela, William and Matilda had made it very clear they expected him to take good care of her. Cameron vowed he would do that, and frowned. Broderick. His gut told him they had not seen the last of the bastard. Kaela had not had her nightmare since their wedding, and he hoped with all his heart she never would.

His mind filled with plans for Chaldron, he rode back to join Kaela and his men. Proud to be the new master of such a holding, he wanted to continue to improve and update the properties. His first priority would be to see to the roads. More than meager paths strewn with rocks and impossible to traverse in rainy weather, he and his men would build real roads, accessible in all seasons.

William had encouraged his Barons to build castles to help fortify England. Cameron knew there would be much travel and activity while the Normans made England their own. Men would pass through Chaldron's properties because fine roads made their travel much easier. He would charge a toll for the use of the roads to help increase Chaldron's coffers.

He was also eager to buy horses and breed them, something his father had always talked about. If he could breed animals from different stock, he would improve the animals' stamina and speed. Cameron shared his father's enthusiasm. He could put the theory to the test, now that his time would not be taken with war.

His mind returned to his parting discussion with William. Leaving shortly for Normandy, William had told Cameron he could not return before the following winter. He had charged Cameron, along with four other of his most trusted knights, to keep the peace. The King's brother, Odo, would be overseeing matters of the realm until William's return. He had admonished Cameron and the other trusted few to assist Odo in any way they could. William, aware of the growing rebel movements, charged Cameron to keep a sharp eye out for trouble. The King expected Cameron to send his army to patrol the outlying regions, and if there was trouble, which he knew there would be eventually, he would be expected to squash any infant rebellion. He only hoped the trouble would not be too severe. He did not relish leaving Chaldron and his wife so soon. With that thought, Cameron urged Goliath into a gallop and rode back to his wife's side.

Wales

Broderick roared his outrage at the news of Kaela's marriage. He paced back and forth in the entrance to the cave that was their hideaway. The rebels were in Wales, a half day's ride from the English border. The cave was large, its entrance well-hidden in the cliffs.

"So the little slut married that bastard. She will pay dearly for it." His pale eyes filled with uncontrollable rage. He took several steps away from the entrance and gazed broodingly at the sky. The clouds, dark and heavy, promised more rain before midnight.

God's blood, how he hated this land of endless rain. He scanned the unforgivingly hostile peaks of the Black Mountains that loomed in the distance. "That whoreson will pay dearly for taking what is mine, as will all the bloody Normans for stealing England from us. 'Tis because of them we are forced into exile in this godforsaken place."

He kicked angrily at the boulder at his feet, then turned his icy stare on his vassal, Walter. "We will ride to the ridge that borders Chaldron and Ralston holdings. The forest is dense there, a good place for ambush. We should see them clearly when they enter the valley below. Aye, 'twill be a good place." Broderick sneered, rubbing his hands together for warmth. "Kaela will not return to Chaldron as D'Abernon's wife. She is mine, and I will have her, Walter. I may have to wait until we reclaim our country before I can possess Chaldron, but I will not wait to plow that little bitch's belly. Nay, I have waited long enough."

"My lord, our spies report the Black Wolf travels with over one-hundred warriors. To attack Baron D'Abernon at this time is unwise. The attack on Herefordshire is close upon us. New men arrive daily and we have much to do to prepare for our attack. We should not deploy so many men to England at this time."

Broderick stepped forward and slapped Walter across the face. Rage contorted Broderick's features and his pale blue eyes looked wild.

"You dare to question my orders?"

"Nay, Baron, I but wonder if we should try to take Lady Kaela so soon. Mayhap, we should wait until we have overtaken Herefordshire and established a stronghold there." Rubbing his jaw, Walter backed away.

"You will do as you are commanded, Walter. We ride for England at first light with one-hundred-and-fifty men. The rest remain here to continue our preparations."

"Aye, my lord, I will see to it." Walter, looked uneasy at his baron.

"Walter," Broderick said, his voice deadly soft, "'twould be most unwise of you to question my orders again."

Walter nodded and scuttled off to do his lord's bidding.

Broderick turned back to the cave entrance and made his way through the dark tunnel to the large cavern that had become the headquarters for the Saxon rebels.

Smiling, he anticipated Kaela's reaction to her soon-to-be new home. He would have her. Nothing would stop him. He thought of her beautiful body and the fear in her eyes when she looked at him. Though she tried desperately to hide her fear from him, when he saw her tremble, he had a sense of overwhelming power. She had let that whoreson touch her and she would pay dearly. He would have to be careful not to kill her, to prolong her torture for as long as possible. Aye, he would keep the bitch with him for a long time before he finally killed her. And when she died, her death would come slowly and painfully.

The thought made his loins ache. His manhood pressed tightly against his chausses. He strode to the back of the cavern to find that little serving wench, Mary. He had kidnapped the girl, a virgin, on their last raid, and when he had raped her, he had thought of Kaela. He would have her now and think of Kaela as he took her. He laughed cruelly, thinking about what he would do to her. The wench might not live through the beating this time, but no matter. In a few days he would have Kaela in his power, and would no longer have need of Mary.

Cameron's brow creased with worry as he watched Kaela. He noticed the dark circles under her eyes and the paleness of her skin. The pace of the return had been hard on her. Thank God they would reach

Chaldron by nightfall. His fist clenched around his destrier's reins as he remembered her screams of the night before, the first night since their marriage she'd had the nightmare. Calming her had taken a long time. He knew she had not slept again, and she seemed distant and withdrawn this morning. Quickly he drew his mount up to hers when he saw her slender body begin to slump forward. Reaching out, he lifted her from her horse and placed her in front of him. Sighing, she leaned back against him.

"I am sorry, my lord, I cannot seem to stay awake," she murmured.

He held her against his chest. "Rest, sweeting, I do not mind holding my wife for a time." Gently, he rubbed his chin against her hair. "You slept little enough last eve."

"The dream was so vivid, Cameron. I fear Broderick plots against us."

"You are exhausted, Kaela. We will reach Chaldron by nightfall. There you can have a proper rest. Hush now and try to sleep."

They rode in silence until the sun arced high in the sky. Kaela slept fitfully in his arms. Finding an open area, Cameron called a halt to the procession. "We will rest here for a few minutes," he said, and dismounted with Kaela still in his arms.

"You can put me down now."

"Nay, wife." He strode across the meadow towards a small stream. Gently placing her upon a boulder at the stream's edge, he knelt on one knee and splashed the cold water on his face and arms. Then he turned her and began to splash the chilling water over her face. She squealed when the water touched her skin, then laughed.

"Thank you, husband."

"Are you feeling better now?" He gazed at her intently. Her coloring seemed better and he felt relieved, until he noticed her worried frown.

"What is it, Kaela?"

"I know not, Cameron. Mayhap I am having trouble forgetting last night's dream. I feel such dread. I hope all goes well at Chaldron."

Reaching up, Cameron smoothed her hair back from her lovely face. "I left two hundred warriors with Jacob. I am sure all is well at Chaldron. What will your people think of their new master?" he asked, hoping to distract her.

She laughed and, giving him a mischievous look, squeezed his hand. "The villeins will be happy to have the fearsome Black Wolf for their protector. However, Brenna will probably scream the walls down upon our heads and try to murder you in your sleep."

"Ah, but I shall have you sleeping by my side to protect me," he said, his grin devilish. Delighted, he watched a red flush stain her cheeks.

"Come, wife, we must be on our way if we are to reach Chaldron by nightfall."

Kaela mounted Sky, assuring her husband that she was rested enough to ride her own mount, and they set off for home once more.

✤   ✤   ✤

The day turned bitterly cold. Kaela grew increasingly anxious as they neared Chaldron land. Cameron ordered her to the back of the procession and sent Patrick to ride beside her. She thought Cameron had grown tense, also. He constantly scanned the horizon.

She gazed out over the stark winter landscape and shivered with apprehension. On Chaldron land now, a large meadow loomed before them. Kaela's gaze went to the eastern ridge and scanned the forest edge. The trees, bare of leaves, looked stark against the gray sky.

Startled, she heard Cameron's deep voice barking orders and saw the warriors begin to move into formation. Her eyes widened in terror when she saw Saxon warriors pouring over the ridge ahead and bearing down on the column. Dear God, they were being attacked. Kaela, too stunned to move, saw Patrick grab Sky's reins and pull her with him to a cluster of trees.

"Stay here, Kaela, until I can see what Cameron wants to do," Patrick yelled, then turned his destrier and rode toward his leader.

Pale and terrified, Kaela watched the Saxon warriors charge out of the forest. Cameron and his men had almost reached the center of the meadow before the attack began and had no chance to turn back. Her breath caught in her throat as she heard her husband's battle cry. Watching in despair, she saw the Norman warriors draw their broad swords and battle axes to meet their enemy. Metal clashed against metal to create a deafening noise. Kaela searched frantically for Cameron and was relieved to see him riding towards her with two other soldiers. She fought for control to keep from flinging herself into his arms, so great was her fright.

"Stay here within these trees, Kaela, where you will be safe," Cameron said. Turning to the two soldiers, he commanded them to guard her with their lives. Before she could reply, he turned Goliath and sped back into the battle. Kaela had never known such fear as she watched him draw his sword and engage in the fighting. Dear God, what if he were killed? Her guardians raised their shields and moved in front of her, blocking her view.

"Nay," Kaela cried, "I will watch my husband." She forced Sky forward between their mounts and pushed with all her strength at their shields. They did not move. "We are far from the battle, out of harm's way. Please," she begged, her eyes pleading, "I would see what is happening."

The warriors moved their shields to allow her a view of the battle. Warriors raced to and fro over the valley floor, weapons flashing. Amid the great din she heard the wounded scream, their cries mingling with shouts of victory when an enemy went down. Searching frantically for Cameron, Kaela's heart turned cold when she saw Broderick on the field.

"God's blood!"

"What see you, my lady?"

"Broderick," Kaela gasped, horrified. She saw him advancing toward Cameron. She clutched the man on her left by the arm, pointing with her other hand toward her cousin. "You must warn Baron Cameron that Broderick of Ralston is behind this attack. 'Tis him with the shield of the raven."

"I cannot leave your side, my lady."

"My husband must be told that he is here, I tell you. Cameron does not know Broderick on sight. My cousin will not fight with honor. Cameron must be warned. I demand you obey me. This far from the fighting, I need but one warrior here with me. You must hurry!"

Unsure and wary of disobeying his lord, the warrior looked at her. Making his decision, he galloped down into the valley to warn his baron.

Kaela kept her eyes on Cameron and watched him wield his sword with deadly accuracy. She sighed with relief when her guard reached his side and pointed to where Broderick stood, engaged with two Norman soldiers. She screamed when Broderick brought down his sword against one Norman. The man crumpled at her cousin's feet. In mere seconds, the other soldier fell. Broderick searched the field, then made his way toward Cameron. Oh God, she had to do something. Before the soldier guarding her could move to stop her, she spurred Sky into a gallop and charged toward the battle. He spurred his horse after her, but could not catch her in time and was immediately engaged by a Saxon warrior.

Kaela, in the thick of the battle, knew that men all around her fought for their lives, but her gaze never left Broderick. She was determined to reach her cousin before he could get to Cameron. When Broderick's eyes met hers, she watched them first widen with surprise, then narrow in recognition. He started toward her, his bloody sword in one hand, his shield in the other.

Kaela slid from Sky's back to search for a weapon. She ran to a fallen soldier and reached for his broadsword. When she could not lift the heavy weapon, she cried out in frustration. Straightening to continue her search, she felt a heavy blow to her head and slumped to the ground. Waves of nausea and dizziness washed over her. Struggling to her feet again, she stumbled over a dead Saxon warrior and pulled a dagger from his body. When she looked up, Broderick had almost reached her. The demented look in his eyes made her blood run cold.

"God's blood, you little fool, you have joined the

Norman fight?" She heard his roar above the battle.

"I will not let you harm my husband." Kaela thrust the dagger forward.

Broderick laughed when he saw the puny dirk, then dropped his sword, and raised his fist. A twisted smile soured his face.

Lowering his shield, Cameron cried out when he saw Kaela ride into the melee and make her way toward Broderick. With his heart lodged in his throat, he turned Goliath. Praying he would reach her in time, he cut a zig-zag pathway through the death scene around them. Choking back an uncontrollable fear, he watched Kaela thrust a dagger toward Broderick. Goliath leaped forward, reaching her as she lunged forward to attack. Thanking his Maker that the Saxon dropped his sword in favor of his fist, Cameron met Broderick's gaze for one brief moment before the Saxon lunged for his sword, his eyes promising death.

Cameron reached down and plucked Kaela from her feet. He heard her startled gasp when he slammed her across his saddle and spurred Goliath away from the fighting.

Kaela fought him like a wild cat until his shouts reached her and she realized her husband held her. She collapsed against him as they rode toward the trees' protection. Once they reached safety, he slid from Goliath's back and violently shook her.

"By the Virgin's nightrail, Kaela, have you gone mad? What did you think you were doing?" In the next instant, he hugged her so fiercely she could hardly breathe.

"I couldn't let him hurt you," she rasped.

Blood dripped from a gash in her forehead. Gently, Cameron wiped at the wound.

"'Twas naught you could do, Kaela. God's teeth, woman, the man is a warrior and twice your size. Did you really think you could harm him with that dagger?"

"I didn't think, Cameron, I just reacted."

Cameron groaned, frustrated, when he saw the tears streaming down her face. He hugged her to him once more and then set her firmly away. "You are to stay here, wife. Do not move from this spot until I come for you. I will send two of my men to protect you."

"Cameron, please…"

"Hush, Kaela, 'Tis almost over. You can see we are winning." He turned and started back to his destrier.

Kaela scanned the battle field. They were indeed winning, but her mind rebelled at the carnage before her. Then, from the fighting behind Cameron, she saw a Saxon warrior riding toward them, his bow aimed at her husband's back. She screamed and instinctively threw herself between Cameron and the charging Saxon. The arrow pierced her side and she fell at her husband's feet.

Cameron bellowed his rage and reached for his sword. Stepping over Kaela's body, he ran to meet the Saxon bastard who had harmed his wife. He raised his sword and severed the man's arm with one mighty blow. A second thrust finished him.

Cameron's anguished cry echoed down the valley. Lifting his unconscious wife in his arms, he realized the battle was winding down. Thorsen and Andrew hurried toward him. "How bad is it?" Thorsen asked, reaching Cameron's side.

"She has taken an arrow in her side." Anguish filled Cameron's voice.

"At least she has fainted. 'Tis a blessing she won't

feel the pain when you remove the arrow," Andrew said, removing his cloak and placing it on the ground.

"Let me tend her wound, Cameron. I have had more experience with this," Thorsen said.

"Nay, do not touch her," Cameron said, and laid her on the cloak. "She is mine. I will care for her. 'Tis because of me that she is hurt." His voice filled with pain, he whispered, "She was trying to protect me. The little fool rode into battle to try to protect me from Broderick. I still can't believe her courage."

Using his dagger, Cameron cut away her bliaut to expose the wound. He bit his lip, then quickly broke off the protruding arrow head and pulled the shaft from her body. Kaela's scream tore at his heart. Thorsen handed him cloths to press against her side.

"She has lost much blood," Andrew said.

"Aye, we must remove to Chaldron immediately. Thorsen, find Johnathan and have him see to the wounded and the necessary burials. We will take twenty of our best men and leave now for Chaldron. Andrew, you come with us. Bring Goliath and once I have mounted, hand Kaela up to me."

Quickly, they followed his orders. When Andrew lifted Kaela into Cameron's arms, she moaned, but did not regain consciousness. He held her to him and whispered, "We will be home soon, sweetheart, just hold on."

With his heart lodged in his throat, Cameron held his unconscious wife against his chest. He concentrated on taking slow steady breaths to gain control of his rampant emotions. Over and over he insisted his reaction was logical. This fierce protectiveness was perfectly normal. She was his wife, her safety his responsibility. He ignored the gnawing fear she might not survive, and gently rubbed her arms. Immense relief washed over him when he saw the lights of Chaldron Keep in the distance. He signaled to Thorsen, and the knight rode ahead, bellowing their identity to the gate keeper, requesting entry. The drawbridge was lowered and Cameron rode swiftly into the outer bailey. Jacob met them there, but his welcoming grin vanished when he saw Kaela.

"What happened?"

"She was injured in battle," Cameron answered. "Quickly, Jacob, we must see to her wound. Call for Maude and order the medical supplies she will need. I will take Kaela to her chamber."

Cameron took the steps two at a time, moving quickly down the hallway to Kaela's chamber. When he reached the bed, he laid her on top of the furs. She stirred and a moan escaped her lips. Rubbing his knuckles against her cheek, Cameron spoke soothing words to quiet her.

He turned when he heard someone approaching and glanced at the entrance to see Jacob come through the door, Maude and Brenna close at his heels.

Maude crossed herself. Rushing to her mistress's side, she examined her wound. "Oh, my poor babe, my poor sweet babe." The old woman removed the bloodied dressing and shook her head when she saw Kaela's torn side.

"What have you done to her, you monster?" Pale with shock, Brenna screamed at Cameron.

Cameron leveled a gaze cold as ice on Brenna. "You shall cease your screaming this instant, cousin." He spoke in a deadly soft voice.

"Cousin?" Brenna gasped.

"Aye, Kaela and I are married. You and I are related

now," Cameron said, unable to suppress a smile at the dismayed expression on her face. "I am lord of Chaldron, Brenna, and you will do well to remember that." The command in his voice left no room for question.

"A fine husband you are, my lord. I can see what you have allowed to happen to your wife," Brenna said, fuming.

Ignoring her harsh accusation, Cameron crossed the room to stoke the fire. He spoke directly to Maude.

"The arrow pierced her side. I removed it, but the wound has not been cleaned and she has lost much blood. Do you know what to do for her?"

"Aye, milord, I will see to my mistress. First we must clean the wound. I will need ye to help me hold her down."

Cameron returned to the bed and placed his hands on Kaela's shoulders, while Maude searched through her basket and pulled out a bottle of liquid. "Jacob, you hold her feet. The pain will be great and she must be as still as possible if we are to stanch the bleeding."

"Oh, God."

"Keep quiet, Brenna, or I will order you to leave."

Brenna scowled warily at Cameron and backed away from the bed, her hand over her mouth, but she did not leave.

When Maude poured the liquid over Kaela's wound, she cried out, lunging forward to elude the fiery pain. Cameron forced her down against the furs and she fainted again.

"What is that vile smelling potion?" Cameron never took his gaze off Kaela.

"'Tis root of peony mixed with vinegar, sulfur, and oil of roses. 'Twill draw the poison from her blood,"

Maude said, taking cloths from the basket and dipping them in a bucket filled with hot water that Sarah had brought into the room. Maude pressed the hot cloth against Kaela's side to clean the wound, then used a cold one to stop the bleeding. After a few tense moments, she lifted the cloth and smiled. Once more, she applied the vile smelling potion.

"I believe the bleeding has stopped. Ye can release her now, for the lass has fainted again."

"Will she be all right?" Jacob's voice broke slightly.

"'Tis too soon to tell, but Kaela is strong and will fight. I must stitch the wound and bathe her. Brenna will stay to help me," Maude said, dismissing the men.

"Nay, she is my wife. I will stay."

Her brown eyes soft, Maude said, "'Tis only for a little while, milord. Kaela faces several days of fever. We will all be needed to help nurse her. I promise to call you once she is settled."

Cameron stared at her for a long moment. "Very well, I will see to my men. Send for me in the great hall." Reaching out, he placed a hand on her shoulder. "Take good care of her, old woman."

Brenna watched him leave with Jacob, then turned back to Maude. "What make you of that?"

"I think the mighty warrior has fallen," Maude said, smiling.

"Aye, it truly looks as if he cares for her." Brenna's face softened with an answering smile.

✤   ✤   ✤

Cameron crossed the great hall to the hearth where a serving wench passed ale to Thorsen and Andrew. He threw himself into a chair beside them.

"How is she?" Thorsen asked.

"The wound has been cleaned. Maude stitches it now. We can only wait and see." Cameron raked his hands through his hair, wincing when the front doors slammed open.

Johnathan and Patrick strode into the hall and stood before Cameron while Johnathan made his report. Saddened, Cameron learned they had lost ten men in the battle, low numbers compared to the Saxons. Johnathan had counted over thirty of their enemy slain.

"What of Broderick?"

"The whoreson escaped. We found no trace of him."

"Send out scouts at first light, Johnathan. We must discover where these Saxons are hiding."

"Broderick dropped his sword when Kaela attacked him. I saw with my own eyes and still I cannot believe it." Johnathan stated. "What make you of that, Baron?"

"He chose not to kill her. I believe he is obsessed with Kaela and ambushed our train to kidnap her. He could have killed her, but dropped his sword in favor of his fist." Cameron's eyes filled with hatred.

"He knew we were on our way from London. There's only one way could he have known that."

"Aye, Thorsen, a spy has infiltrated Williams new castle. See that William is notified immediately."

"What was she doing on the battlefield?" Andrew asked. "God's teeth, 'Tis a miracle she wasn't killed."

"She wanted to protect me, the little fool," Cameron said bleakly. "Then she threw herself in front of an arrow meant for me. I do not understand her."

"Perchance she loves her husband," Thorsen said.

Cameron glared at the Viking, but said nothing, then fixed his stony gaze on the hearth. When Sarah came into the hall to say Maude had summoned him, Cameron left without another word.

"What make you of that?" Johnathan asked.

"I think my stubborn brother is in love with his wife," Andrew said. "Let us pray she lives."

"Aye, and pray also that our baron faces his feelings and puts the past behind him."

They all nodded.

Cameron entered the well-lighted bedchamber where wall torches cast the shadows even from the corners. He crossed swiftly to the bed and gazed with worried eyes over Kaela's still form. She looked so pale and fragile lying there. He lifted the blanket to examine her wound. "You have done well," he said to Maude, who stood at his side.

He placed his hand upon Kaela's brow and his gaze flew to Maude. "She is afire."

"Aye, milord, the fever has begun."

"Tell me what to do."

"She should be bathed often with cool cloths, but ye must keep her well covered. Cook is stewing up a fine broth, for we must keep feeding the lass liquids. Naught else will help, but to pray, milord," Maude said, her wizened old face creased with worry. "I will stay with her through the night."

"Nay, Maude, I will nurse my wife this night. Get some sleep. You have done well." Cameron escorted her from the room and closed the door behind her. He moved to the hearth, added a large log to the fire, and then, going back to the bed, shed his clothes and slipped in beside his wife. He cradled her fevered body in his arms and tried to push his relentless fear from his mind. *She will get well.* "I will not lose you now, Kaela," he whispered, burying his face in her soft hair.

Cameron awakened to find Kaela's violently shaking body draped over his. Cursing himself for falling asleep, he rolled her onto her back. She burned with fever and thrashed back and forth, mumbling unintelligibly. Cameron raced to build up the fire. Taking a bowl of water and a clean cloth from a nearby table, he returned to the bed and tried to cool his wife's body. As he ran the damp cloth over her arms and legs, he raised his gaze to her face. Startled, he saw fevered green eyes staring back at him.

"Nay, I will not let you hurt him," Kaela shouted. She began to fight with unbelievable strength, grabbing his hand and pushing it from her body. "Stay away from me, stay away." Crying out, she lurched forward until the pain in her side immobilized her. She fell back on the bed in agony, moaning softly. Quickly, Cameron covered her and, taking her face in his hands, spoke sternly. "Kaela, 'Tis Cameron, you are safe. Kaela, can you hear me?"

Kaela's eyes cleared for a brief moment and she whispered his name, her voice raspy.

"Aye, sweetheart, I am with you," he answered.

"You are safe?"

"We are both safe… we are home now," he said, cradling her head in his arms. He watched, dismayed when her eyes glazed and she again moaned and thrashed in his arms.

Cameron lost count of how many times he bathed her fevered body and spoke soothing words to ease her fevered dreams. Sometime in the night, he dressed to help ward off the cold and pulled a chair up to her

bedside. Near dawn the fever seemed to break somewhat and Kaela fell into a more relaxed sleep. Cameron
sat in the chair and stared at her for a long time.
Something deep within him opened, overwhelming
him with pain, sadness, and fury at the thought he
might lose his beautiful new bride. Quickly, he pushed
the feelings aside, cursing aloud. She would live, she
had to.

Sometime later, Cameron felt a light pressure on
his knee. Forcing his eyes open, he found a pair of
brilliant blue ones staring up at him.

"Hello, Mattie. I wondered where you were."

The little girl eyed him for a moment and then her
gaze fell to the bed. She whispered, "What's wrong
with Kaela?"

Cameron patted her shiny black curls. "She is hurt.
An arrow pierced her side, but I took it out and Maude
cared for her."

When Mattie burst into tears, Cameron scooped her
up and cradled her in his lap.

"She's dying," Mattie said, gulping back her tears,
"just like my mama and papa."

"Nay, sweet pea. Kaela is very sick, but she will
not die."

Mattie wrapped her pudgy little arms around his
neck. "How do you know?"

"Because I am her husband and I will not let her."

His words made perfect sense to Mattie. If her
"Wolf" said Kaela would be all right, then she had no
doubt he spoke the truth. "When will she wake up?"

"I know not, sweet pea, mayhap not for several
days."

Mattie gazed at Kaela's sleeping face for a few
minutes, then turned her cherub's face back to Cameron.

"You will stay with us now that you belong to Kaela," she said emphatically. Cameron felt his heart warm when she broke into a dimpled smile. "You are mine now, too."

"Aye, little one, and you are mine." He squeezed her until she squirmed, delighting in her childish giggles. "Would you like to hear about the King and Queen, and the wedding in London?"

"Aye," Mattie said, settling her small body against his chest. She listened intently while he told her of their adventure.

Kaela opened her eyes slowly. Intense heat burned through her whole body, and she felt weak with thirst. "Water," she said, in a voice barely above a whisper. In seconds, a cup pressed her lips and a trickle of cool water slid down her throat. She focused briefly on Maude's wrinkled face. The old nurse eased Kaela's head back on the pillows and she smiled her gratitude. Turning her head to the side, she noticed Cameron sitting in a chair pulled up to her bed-side. Mattie was curled in his lap and they were sound asleep. Kaela smiled weakly. Her husband's gentleness never ceased to amaze her. She wanted to ask Maude what was wrong with her but she felt too weak to say the words. Thinking what a wonderful father Cameron would be, she drifted back into oblivion.

For three days and nights the fever raged, rising so high she became delirious and thrashed wildly upon the bed, then dropping down for a while, allowing her to sleep like the dead. Cameron never left her side. Maude, fussing and fuming, did everything she could to get the stubborn man to take to a bed for some much-needed sleep, but to no avail. He allowed Maude and Brenna to nurse her during the day, but barred the chamber door at night and cared for her alone. Chaldron's affairs, he turned over to Jacob and Thorsen.

In the midnight hours of the second night, Cameron woke to Kaela's clinging arms and urgent pleas. Her fever burned high again. He tried to disengage himself to bathe her, but she held to him fiercely, pressing her body so tightly against his, it seemed she would mold them into one.

When she screamed Broderick's name, Cameron realized the nightmare had claimed her again. In a commanding voice, he reassured her he was with her and she was safe. Kaela opened her fevered eyes and called his name. Wrapping her arms about his neck and pulling him to her, she kissed him with a raging passion. Shocked into complete stillness for a moment, Cameron then tried to pull away, for he understood she had no idea what she was doing. Kaela moaned in protest and deepened the kiss, thrusting her tongue between his lips.

Cameron groaned when desire for her blazed into life. His whole body absorbed her heat. He returned her kiss with all his pent-up passion. Kaela moaned his name again. He slid his hand down her thigh and came in contact with her bare skin where her nightgown had ridden up to expose her soft pliant flesh. Kaela ran her hand down his bare chest, over his taut abdomen, and boldly caressed his straining manhood. Cameron groaned. His whole body rigid with pleasure. Exerting all his control and willpower, he pulled away from her.

When he left the bed, Kaela began to cry. Returning quickly with a cool cloth, he laved her fevered body. She soon fell into a deep sleep. Cameron eased back into bed and held her in his arms. Sighing deeply, cursing himself for his weakness, he knew he should find another bed but could not bear to leave her side. His body ached for her touch and he looked forward to the day he could make love to her. "You will get well, Kaela," he whispered to her. "I command it."

Chapter Twelve

✣   ✣   ✣

Warm and happy, Kaela slowly surfaced from her dream. She had been riding Sky, racing across the western ridge toward the lake. Her father had been with her. Even when she opened her eyes, she could still hear his laughter, and she smiled. Surprised, she stared into Cameron's brilliant blue eyes.

"Good morning." She lifted her arms to stretch lazily, but grimaced at the sharp pain in her side.

"What happened?"

"Welcome back to the land of the living." Cameron carried her hand to his lips, kissed her palm, and returned her smile. "You took an arrow in your side. Don't you remember? The wound heals nicely, thank God, but for a time, I—we feared we might lose you."

Puzzled, she shook her head and shuddered. An arrow? Someone had shot—Fear curled around her spine. Slowly, an image swam upward through her mind. The ambush... the noise... She remembered. She had faced her enemy with only a dagger. Cameron must think—blushing, Kaela looked up into his worried face.

"Broderick," she whispered.

"Aye, Broderick."

"May I have some water, please?" Trying to distract her scowling husband, Kaela quickly changed the subject.

Cameron turned to the small table beside the bed and poured some water for her. "Sip very slowly," he said, holding the cup to her lips.

Cool and soothing, the liquid trickled down her throat.

"Are you hungry?"

"I am starving." She smiled shyly.

Cameron crossed the room in three long strides, threw open the door and bellowed for Maude. In mere seconds she appeared, her face alight with joy when she saw Kaela awake and sitting up. "Bring some broth for your mistress, Maude. She is ravenous."

"Aye, milord," Maude said, hurrying to do his bidding.

Returning to the bed, Cameron sat beside Kaela and held her hand. "'Twas three days your fever raged."

"Three days? I remember naught." Kaela's heart turned over at the concern she saw on his face. Heat raced through her body as though the fever had returned. She flinched when he brought her hand to his lips and kissed each finger. More tingling warmth raced down her spine. "Were you with me the whole time?"

"You are my wife. Of course, I stayed with you."

She smiled.

"I wanted to throttle you when I saw you charge onto the battlefield." Brusquely, Cameron interrupted, returned her hand to her lap, and pulled away from her. "I cannot believe you were so foolish as to face Broderick with nothing but a dagger. Of all the stupid—"

"Stupid? Don't you dare call me stupid." Resenting his withdrawal as well as his tone, she glared at him.

"Don't interrupt me, wife. I demand your promise; you will never again do anything so stupid."

"I promise no such thing." Infuriated, she crossed her arms over her breasts.

"Then I shall order a guard to be with you at all times."

"You wouldn't."

"Try me."

They matched each other glare for glare, until Kaela conceded.

"Oh, very well, you have my promise." Hoping her expression matched his fierce scowl, Kaela sank back on her pillow.

"Good. Your respect for my wishes pleases me, wife. Now where was I? Aye… like an idiot, you blatantly disobeyed my orders and charged into the fray."

Kaela started to protest, but he placed his palm over her mouth. Too surprised to move, she stared at him.

"At last, I have your attention. You have put me—all of us—through hell this three days past. I shall speak my mind, wife." A wicked twinkle gleamed in his eyes.

Kaela sighed, resigned.

With a triumphant grin on his face, he removed his hand. For the next five minutes, she remained silent while he informed her she would henceforward obey his every command. Under no circumstances would she ever leave the keep without an escort.

Kaela decided not to argue with him, not until her strength returned. Besides, his tired, drawn face and obvious worry touched her.

Bustling into the chamber, Maude interrupted Cameron's tirade. Kaela's mouth watered when she smelled the broth's tantalizing aroma. She glanced pleadingly at Cameron.

"Very well, I have made myself clear and will leave you now. Chaldron has been neglected long enough. I will return this eve, wife. You are not to move from that bed until I say you are fully recovered." He leaned above her, brushed his lips across her forehead, and took his leave.

Her mouth agape, Kaela watched him go.

"'Tis some man ye married, that 'un."

Smiling and shaking her head, Kaela opened her arms. Caught in Maude's embrace, Kaela whispered, "'Tis so good to be home."

"'Tis good to have ye back, mistress. All Chaldron has been praying ye would recover.

"Where is everyone?"

"Ye needn't worry, milady. Ye'll have company all the day long, with all o' them so anxious to see ye. Brenna and Mattie will be along any moment. Now eat up yer broth, for 'Tis strength ye need."

"Order a bath for me, Maude, and stay to help me dress," Kaela said, sipping from the cup.

"Nay, Kaela, the Baron wants ye to stay in bed and in bed ye ought to stay. I have not e'en taken out yer stitches, child."

"I shall have a bath, and you shall help me dress, Maude." When Maude frowned at her, she added, "You've no need to worry. I promise to stay abed for the rest of the day, but I will go down to sup. Please send Cook up to me. We must discuss tonight's meal. 'Twill be my first at Chaldron with my new husband, and I want it to be special."

"Ye are happy with him then, mistress?"

"Aye, Maude, very happy."

"He never left yer side while ye were sick with the fever, Kaela. Tended ye himself, at night, he did."

"I know." Kaela smiled. "I know."

Although a little weak when she entered the great hall that evening, she moved with a light step and a smile on her lips.

When she had awakened this morning and found Cameron by her side—his eyes so full of concern, she'd realized she had given him her heart. The knowledge that she truly loved him filled her with joy. More than anything she wanted to have the kind of marriage her parents had. Now she dared to hope.

✣   ✣   ✣

A resounding cheer from those present greeted Chaldron's mistress. Wide, welcoming grins on their faces, Thorsen and Andrew rushed to her side.

"We did not expect to see you this evening, Kaela. Cameron said you would stay in your chamber for a few more days."

"As you can see, Thorsen, Baron Cameron was mistaken. I truly feel quite well and I wish to dine with my friends."

"You look wonderful." Andrew's glance approved her vivid blue bliaut. "Are you sure this isn't too much for you?"

"I am fine. A little sore 'Tis all."

"Does our Baron know what you have planned?" Thorsen asked, his eyes twinkling.

"Nay, 'Tis a surprise." Kaela winked at the Viking. Entering the hall, Patrick whooped when he saw her. He swept a courtier's bow, gallantly placing a kiss on her fingertips.

"My lady, 'Tis good to see you have recovered. Despite the fright you gave us, I believe you have grown more beautiful."

Laughing at his exaggerated compliment, Kaela made a low curtsy. "'Tis good to see you all again. Come, let us drink a toast to friendship and to Chaldron, our home."

When Cameron entered the hall, Johnathan at his side, he bit back an outraged cry. His beautiful, defiant wife stood with his vassals before the hearth, a mug of ale in her slender hand. 'Twas all he needed, a frustrating end to a terrible day. During her illness, he had consoled himself that once she recovered, he would put her from his mind and get on with running Chaldron. But no, she had intruded on his thoughts the whole day. He did not wonder his mood had been foul.

He had planned to go straight to their chamber, order a hot bath, then share a meal and the quiet evening hours with her. He had missed their talks, sharing his thoughts… he had missed her. Now, she stood amid his men while the dimwits ogled her. Anger in every stride, he crossed the room and glared down into her questioning eyes.

"I ordered you to stay in bed. Mayhap I have gone blind, lady, but I see no bed here."

"Don't be angry with me, husband. Your sight serves you quite well, but I feel so much better and am happy to be home. I wanted us to celebrate with our friends." She took a step closer and, to his surprise, slipped her arm around his waist. "I have ordered a wonderful meal prepared, our first at Chaldron as man and wife. Please, Cameron…"

He grunted, not trusting himself to say anything. Her nearness, the fragrance of roses, and her smile drove him to madness. He couldn't think. Clutching her hand, he led her to the table. The look he shot his men dared them to laugh at the way his wife affected him.

Cameron took his place at their table with Kaela on his right, sharing the food from his trencher. He watched her, pleased that she ate with good appetite. Jacob sat across from them, relating what had happened in their absence. A few minor disputes among the villeins would require Cameron's attention, but nothing else had been amiss. When Cameron explained his ideas to improve the roads, Jacob responded with admiring approval.

Brenna and Andrew, seated beyond Jacob and Thorsen, whispered to each other throughout the meal. Seeing Brenna blush at some remark Andrew made, Cameron grinned. They would make a good match, his brother and his wife's impetuous young cousin.

Kaela sighed. He choked on his venison when she placed her hand on his thigh, absently stroking from hip to knee. Fire raged through his body at her touch. From the sweet smile she gave him, she had no idea what her caress did to him. He placed his hand over hers to still her movements before he made a fool of himself.

"Are you tired, Kaela?"

"Aye, husband, tired and happy. Thank you for not banishing me to our chamber." Her eyes, soft and gentle, gazed into his.

Cameron clasped her hand and rose from the table. Leaning over, he whispered, "'Tis time for bed, wife."

Kaela blushed. Without a word, he lifted her in his

arms and started up the stairs to their chamber. His men cheered and she buried her face in his neck.

With the door closed behind them, he set her on the fur-covered bed. Happy to see a bath awaiting him, he stripped off his clothing. Sighing, he sank down into the soothing water.

Never taking her gaze from his beautiful body, Kaela undressed and slipped between the covers. Warm to her toes, she watched his muscles ripple and glisten in the glow from the fire.

"Tell me about your day," he said, smiling at her.

She tried to keep her voice even while she told him about the gossip from the village and her visit with Brenna and Mattie. Watching her husband towel his body dry and cross to their bed, she swallowed a lump in her throat.

He stood there a moment, naked, and gazed down at his wife. He read the hunger in her eyes, lifted the fur aside, and stretched on his side next to her warmth.

"'Tis too soon after your injury, Kaela. I do not want to hurt you," he said, his voice strained, his eyes dark with desire.

A moan escaped Kaela's lips. Pulling him to her, she wrapped her arms around him and caressed his back and shoulders. She smiled when he sighed. The steely evidence of his need pressed against her thigh.

"Please, Cameron, I need you."

When she stroked her hands over his buttocks, he pressed her onto her back. Covering her body with his, he raised up on his elbows, brought his mouth down to hers, and kissed her deeply, tenderly. "I will try to be careful."

Kaela, caught up in the raging emotion of the moment, knew only that she loved him, loved him deeply. The overwhelming joy of her love expressed itself in her passion. Trembling with her desire for him, she pulled him closer, ran her hands over his hard, muscled body, devouring him with her fingertips.

Cameron released her mouth, dipped down to capture the nipple of one creamy breast. Kaela moaned her pleasure as he suckled and her nipples grew taut. Cameron rolled to his side, taking her with him. Conscious of his weight, not wanting to hurt her, he trailed soft kisses against her scar.

"You should never have been wounded, sweeting, should never have been hurt, not for me," he whispered.

His tender words brought tears to Kaela's eyes. She lifted his face to hers and feathered kisses across his brow.

"Why do you weep, sweetheart?"

She shook her head, slanted her mouth over his, and kissed him deeply.

Cameron groaned. Smoothing his hands down her thighs, he parted her legs and caressed her. She cried out when he slipped his finger inside her. When she arched against him, he knew she craved more. He could hold back no longer.

With a powerful thrust, he entered her, then rolled to his back. Astride his hips, she arched her back to take him deeper inside, deeper, until she gasped with pleasure.

With his hands on her hips, Cameron lifted her up and down on his shaft, teaching her the rhythm. Kaela ran her hands through the dark hair on his chest and tweaked his nipples. He groaned again, his thrusts deeper and faster, taking them to the edge of fulfillment. He began to stroke her womanhood with his fingers.

Deep spasms racked Kaela's body and she cried out her release. Cameron stiffened beneath her, then spilled his warm seed into her.

She collapsed against him, holding him to her, listening to his pounding heart... never had she felt so close to anyone.

After several minutes, Cameron lifted her from him and rolled away. He sat up and examined her side to make sure they had not disturbed the wound. His lips curved in satisfaction, he lay down again, drawing her to him. Kaela laid her head on his shoulder, tracing his jaw with her fingers. Neither said a word, content to hold each other. Kaela drifted to sleep. Cameron lay there for a long time, listening to her steady breathing.

When he'd thought she would die, fear had overwhelmed him. His grief over Peter's death had come rushing back, fresh, painful, and as deep as when his son had died. Sucking in his breath, filled with an aching tenderness he had prayed he would never feel again, he watched her. Poignant beyond words, the emotion made him far too vulnerable. Panic washed over him.

No, he would not love her. He would not. He would deny his feelings, distance himself from her. She left him no other choice.

Cameron drew away from Kaela and turned his back to her. She curled against him as if seeking his warmth. For the third time, Cameron groaned aloud. Denying her would be the hardest thing he had ever done, but he would close his heart to her... he would not love again.

❖   ❖   ❖

Aware morning had come, Kaela reached for her husband, only to find his side of the bed cold and empty. Frowning, she opened her eyes and glanced around the room. No Cameron. He must have gone to the great hall to break his fast. Surprised, because the dawn had barely grayed the sky, she left their bed and dressed. Smiling, Kaela remembered the passion of their lovemaking. Her heart light and filled with hope for their marriage, she wanted to give her handsome husband a warm greeting.

Entering the great hall, she found the vast room as barren as their chamber. She called to Maude, who was on her way to the kitchen, and asked Cameron's whereabouts.

"He left several moments ago, milady, on his way to the stables. Seemed to be in quite a hurry, he did, though why he'd be about without so much as a crust of bread to eat, I do not know." Shaking her head, Maude scurried on toward the kitchen.

Kaela hurried up to their chamber to don her cloak, then ran back down the stairs and out the heavy front door. She crossed the inner bailey, nodding briefly to the servants who greeted her, and reaching the stables in time to see Cameron mount Goliath. Johnathan and Thorsen stood well away from the stallion's dancing feet.

"Good morning, my lord." Trying to catch her breath, Kaela joined the two men.

Cameron scowled. Curse the saints, why did the woman have to look at him with those innocent, intoxicating green eyes. He had rushed this morning, hoping to leave the keep before she awoke. He didn't want to deal with her now, not when he felt so torn by his emotions.

"Why have you risen this early? I have much to see about and no time for your woman's foolishness." Cameron saw the hurt and dismay in her eyes at his gruff, impatient words. Guilt gnawed at him, but he pushed the feeling away.

"I but wished to break my fast with you before you began your day, husband." Kaela wondered at his grim countenance; had she somehow displeased him.

"Nay, we leave now, as you can see." Cameron glanced at Thorsen and Johnathan, but chose to ignore their frigid glares.

"When will you be home?"

"I know not."

"I will see you this eve then, my lord. God's speed." Reaching up, she placed her hand on his thigh while her troubled gaze clashed with his stony one.

Unable to endure her touch or the pain in her eyes, Cameron spurred Goliath into a gallop. He never looked back.

Thorsen and Johnathan mounted, nodded to Kaela. Their faces somber, they followed their baron.

Puzzled and half-angry, Kaela returned to the keep. She had done nothing to deserve Cameron's strange, rude behavior. Their night together had been wonderful, filled with tenderness and passion. Truly, she did not know him well enough to gauge his moods. Ah, well, she had much to do and little time to waste in worry. If she had displeased him, he would tell her soon enough. Inside the hall, she called to Maude to join her at the table.

Maude brought a loaf of warm bread, some fruit, and cheese to place before her mistress.

"I will fetch ye a cup of ale, milady."

"Bring one for yourself, too. I wish to discuss what

must be done today. Chaldron needs much attention. Have Sarah go and wake Brenna, please, for she will be needed as well."

Half an hour later, Maude, Brenna, and Kaela still sat at the table.

"Your husband begins his day early," Brenna said. "What is he about that takes him from the keep at so ungodly an hour?"

"I overheard Johnathan and Thorsen say last eve they planned to inspect the mill this morning. I can only surmise that was their destination. The baron did not inform me of his plans." Kaela regretted the pique in her tone. She knew Brenna would take offense if she perceived an intentional slight in Cameron's actions.

"What? Well, he certainly should have *informed* you. You have run Chaldron almost single-handedly these two years past. He'd best not be planning any drastic changes around the estate. Chaldron is fine the way it is."

"I know not what he plans and, until he tells me differently, Chaldron's affairs proceed as usual. We will not discuss my husband, Brenna, not with so much to do." Kaela rose and began to pace before the hearth, absently twisting her clasped hands. When she realized Brenna and Maude were watching her nervous actions, she gave them a look that dared them to comment.

"The rushes must be changed today, Maude. Send one of the girls to fetch the dried rosemary from the shed to mix with them. Also, the interior walls are smoke-stained and need be cleaned before the white-washing is begun. I want the tasks finished ere the week is out.

"I think it is time we have new tapestries for

Chaldron, Brenna. Much has changed in our country now, and in our lives. We have a new heritage to record for our children. No one is more skilled with a needle than you, cousin. We will meet this afternoon and work out several new designs. Please tell the spinners to provide the proper yarns and have the weavers prepare the background fabrics. The other cloth we need has already been made and stored away. I see no reason why we cannot begin work on the tapestries."

"You know I love the needlework, Kaela. Tell me more about what you have in mind."

"I want something very special that will please my husband, make him feel Chaldron is truly his home. I've been thinking… perhaps a banner with Cameron's crest, and large enough to cover the wall above the hearth."

"Aye, that should please him, indeed, and Mattie, too. My little sister has taken quite a liking to her 'Wolf.'"

"And he to her. He is very good with her, Brenna." Kaela smiled. Something softened inside her each time she saw Cameron and Mattie together. "'Tis all for now, and time we get started. I will be in the storage rooms should you need me this morning. The baron's men have put quite a dent in our larder. We must restock with enough supplies."

"Aye," Brenna said, "the Viking alone eats enough for ten men."

The day passed quickly. Kaela tried not to think about Cameron or his attitude toward her, but she could not keep him from her thoughts. Late in the afternoon, she ordered a bath and set about making herself presentable for her husband. She opened her chest and took out a turquoise chainse with a matching bliaut a shade deeper. The color complimented her skin.

Smoothing the material over her hips, Kaela felt her confidence return. The gown became her. She let Sarah brush her hair, but knowing Cameron's preference, decided to wear it down. She went downstairs to the hall where Cameron's vassals cast their approving glances toward her. Seeing her husband standing near the hearth, Kaela made her way to him.

His eyes narrowed, Cameron watched her cross the hall. Sweet Jesu, the woman had no right to sway her hips in that provocative manner. The looks his men bestowed on her made his blood boil. How dare she behave as other women, constantly vying for a man's attention?

"Good eve, my lord." Expectantly, Kaela looked at him, her eyes soft and shining.

"My lady." Cameron bowed his head slightly. She stood very close, too close... the familiar rose scent quickened his pulse. Silently, he cursed. He had driven himself and his men the whole day hoping to rid his mind of her, to no avail. Now here she stood, all softness and curves, drawing him under her spell.

"How was your day, husband?"

"Busy."

Thorsen glowered at his friend, but gave Kaela a rare smile. "I can see you have been busy, Lady Kaela. The hall is fresh with new rushes, and my poor stomach growls aloud in response to the delicious smells coming from the kitchen."

"Thank you, Thorsen. We have worked hard this day to make the baron's new home a welcoming one."

Cameron made no comment and continued his conversation with Johnathan. Frowning at his back,

Kaela turned her questioning gaze to Thorsen. He shrugged, then made an obvious effort to distract her.

"I have noticed, my lady, there are no hounds in the hall. 'Tis most strange and rather pleasant."

"My mother would not tolerate animals fouling the keep. There are kennels behind the stables where the hunting dogs are sheltered and fed." Touching his hand, she lowered her voice. "I know what you seek to do, Thorsen. Thank you, but I must learn to deal with my husband's moods." Though her hand trembled, she reached for Cameron's arm. "Come, my lord, let us dine." Determined to lighten his mood, she sat beside him and poured his ale. At her signal, the servants brought in platters heaped with pheasant pasties and roasted wild boar, tureens of mutton stew, and loaves of fresh hot bread.

The food at Chaldron was the best Cameron had ever eaten, but he did not compliment his wife. He had no need. His men were tripping over their own tongues to do so.

Kaela's spirits deflated with each passing moment. Cameron grunted or answered with a single word her attempts at polite conversation. His behavior not only puzzled her, but hurt her deeply.

When the meal finally ended, Cameron's soldiers filed from the hall on their way to the barracks. Kaela chose that moment to lay her hand on Cameron's arm.

"I have ordered a bath for you, my lord, if you are ready to retire to our chamber."

"I have no desire to retire, madam. I will order my own bath when I am ready for it." His voice hard and scathing, he pulled away from her.

Kaela's face flamed at his rude manner. Mortified, she knew Johnathan and Andrew had overheard. She glanced down at her hands for a moment, then forced a smile to her face and tried again.

"If you are not ready to retire, my lord, perhaps you would care to play a game of chess with me. I can promise you my skill is great enough to make the play a challenge."

"Nay, I have business to discuss with Johnathan. You have my permission to retire, now. I will come up when I am finished."

He had dismissed her. Bewildered, Kaela said nothing. Her back painfully straight, she rose from her chair and walked toward the stairway. She feared her voice would break if she tried to speak. He had embarrassed her enough for one evening… she would not let him see her cry. Slowly, she made her way to their chamber. She had no idea what had caused this distance between her and her husband, but she intended to find out. Undressing, she slipped a nightrail over her head and slid beneath the covers to wait for Cameron. This nonsense would soon end.

But not this evening.

Late in the night, Cameron finally entered their chamber. The fire had almost died and he added a log to the embers. He watched his sleeping wife, appreciating the curve of her hip and thigh. Not wanting a confrontation, he had stayed away until he felt certain she slept. He had nothing to say to her. Damn her anyway, she had no right to look so innocent, lying there with her coppery hair fanned across the pillow. Cameron turned from her and stripped off his soiled tunic.

The bath she had prepared for him still waited by the fire. He dipped his fingers in the water. Cold as ice. Fine.

Aye, a cold bath was just the thing. Cameron lowered his body into the frigid water, his mind in turmoil. Quickly, he bathed and dried himself, then crawled into bed. Surely with time his riotous feelings would subside. He and his wife could learn to live together with some degree of harmony. Until then, he would keep his distance, ignore her.

Kaela sighed in her sleep, burrowing against him. He echoed her sigh. His damned traitorous body heated at her touch. Ignore her? Nearly impossible, he admitted.

Cameron took his wife in his arms and tried in vain to sleep.

Chapter Thirteen

✣   ✣   ✣

The sun's first ray's of light spread across the awakening dawn. Kaela opened her eyes to memories of last night's frustration. He had escaped her again. Grumpily, she stared at the empty bed next to her. She smoothed her hand over the still warm sheets, comforting herself with the knowledge he had slept by her side. Then a sense of loneliness washed over her. Cameron had placed a terrible distance between them.

Gathering her determination, she slipped from the massive bed and padded on bare feet across the chamber to throw open the door. She called to Maude, ordered a bath, and then crossed to the hearth to build up the fire.

Within the hour, Kaela sat at the trestle table in the great hall. A worried frown on her face, she broke her fast. A tentative smile greeted Jacob when he joined her a few minutes later.

"Have you seen my husband this morn, Jacob?"

"Aye, Kaela, he rode out just moments ago with Johnathan and Thorsen"

"My husband does not deem it necessary to tell me his plans. 'Tis most annoying. He has not once asked me to go over the accounting with him, nor has he been to check the barley fields. I know not if he intends to take over all the duties of running Chaldron. The man is infuriating. He knows I have acted as steward for the last two years, yet he does not discuss his plans with me. What think you of his actions, Jacob?"

"I think your husband is a most intelligent man, Kaela. He has seen how well Chaldron is managed and knows to whom the credit belongs. However, I am sure he wishes to make his mark here as well. 'Tis his right. He is master of Chaldron now."

"I know he is master. God's truth, I do not wish to fight my husband for control of Chaldron. I know my place, Jacob," Kaela said, pushing her trencher away in disgust. "Still, Chaldron is my home. I have managed the estate for the last two years. Until my husband tells me differently, I will continue to do so. I want to ride out and inspect the fields today, Jacob. 'Twill soon be time for spring planting."

Jacob eyed her warily. "'Twould be best to wait until the Baron returns, Kaela. You should consult your husband as to his wishes."

"Nay, my husband deliberately avoids me. So be it. Two can play at his game. I shall ride to the fields. Will you come with me?"

"Aye, I give you my support and my loyalty. I have a feeling you will need both before this day is over."

Kaela turned and smiled at Jacob as they crossed the hall together. "Even anger from my husband is preferable to being ignored, Jacob."

He took her hand in his and gave it an affectionate squeeze. "You may retract those words before the day ends, Kaela."

✣   ✣   ✣

Cameron slowed his pace as he and his vassals rode through the village. He looked again with admiration at the well-built cottages, the overall neatness of the village. Chaldron was a well-run shire and he swelled with pride that it was now his. His wife's management of her father's properties would ease his assuming control. He had ridden over the property since dawn with Johnathan and Thorsen, seeking their advice on placing the new roads. Excited over his plans, Cameron wanted to begin construction right away. He had made the right decision in marrying Kaela. She would give him strong sons to carry on the D'Abernon name and they would have a fine heritage. He had not wanted to leave his wife this morning. The image of her soft body burned in his brain. Perhaps he should rethink his position. The more he tried to ignore her, the more the little vixen invaded his thoughts. Denying himself accomplished nothing. Besides, once he was used to having her, his desire would fade.

But what if it doesn't? What if your feelings for her continue to grow and you find yourself vulnerable to her every action? What then?

Cameron gripped Goliath's reins and increased the animal's pace, heading toward the fields. He knew only too well the answers to those questions. Nay, he would deny his desire for Kaela, no matter what his abstinence cost him.

"Are you ready to check the fields now, Baron?" Johnathan's question interrupted Cameron's thoughts.

"Aye."

"What does Kaela say about the spring planting? I

would think the time grows near. Have the serfs completed preparation of the soil?" Thorsen asked.

"I have not asked my wife. 'Tis no longer her concern. She has run Chaldron well, but she is a woman and will attend to those things that are proper for a woman of her station. I am Master of Chaldron—I will see to its running."

Thorsen looked out over the fields. His solemn face broke into a smile. "Have you informed your wife of her new duties, Baron, or shall I say, instructed her in the lack of them?"

"Nay, she is my wife. She knows her place."

Grinning, Thorsen directed Cameron's attention to the figures on horseback riding through the fields to the south. Cameron cursed when he followed Thorsen's gaze and recognized one rider as his stubborn wife.

"What the hell does the woman think she is doing?"

"'Twould seem she makes preparation for planting. Perhaps she does not realize she is a mere woman and therefore not up to the task."

Cameron glowered suspiciously at his straight-faced friend, then turned his horse and raced toward his wife.

"We had best see that he does not kill her." Thorsen chuckled and gave Johnathan a knowing smile.

"Nay, Thorsen," Johnathan said, laughing as they turned their mounts and followed Cameron. "We had best see that she does not kill him. I vow the lady has reason."

When Kaela saw her husband riding toward her, prickles of apprehension raced up her spine. Pleased by his dark scowl, she said, "God's truth, 'twould seem he has noticed me, Jacob."

"Aye, mistress, I fear so." Jacob nudged his mount closer to hers.

"What do you think you are doing, wife?" Cameron reined in his mount beside her. His cold, steely glance matched his tone.

"Good day, my lord husband." Biting back her urease, Kaela spoke calmly. "Jacob and I have been inspecting the fields. 'Tis time to begin the spring planting."

"I am aware of that, woman. I don't need you to tell me."

Ignoring her angry husband, Kaela dismounted and knelt to pick up a handful of dirt.

"I didn't think you would, my lord, but since you have not informed me of your plans, I thought it best to proceed with my duties as usual."

Cameron jumped from Goliath's back and came to stand directly in front of his kneeling wife.

"You thought wrong, madam. You are no longer responsible for the running of Chaldron. I am master here, and I will see to Chaldron's needs." Slowly, calculatedly, Cameron let his voice rise to a near-roar.

Rising, Kaela stood before her husband, her hands on her hips, her chin raised in defiance. "You need not shout at me, my lord. I assure you there is nothing wrong with my hearing. If you desire to oversee the planting, then do so. Pray, tell me, my lord, what are my duties to be?" Her voice was quiet. Too quiet.

"You will see to my comfort, and you will give me strong sons. Those, my lady, are your only responsibilities."

Cameron watched Kaela draw herself up and cross her arms under her breasts. Though she grew more angry by the minute, he wanted nothing more than to scoop her up and carry her away to some secluded place where he could ease his desperate thirst for her.

"I see, and what am I to do with the rest of my time, husband?"

Cameron shrugged. "Whatever you women do."

"What we women do? I can't speak for other women, my lord, but I can assure you looking after my idiot husband will leave me with more time for leisure than running Chaldron ever did."

Blinking, Cameron took a step back. His wife was actually yelling at him. He couldn't believe Kaela would advance on him like a raging storm, shaking her fist in his face. Had she taken the time to look behind her, as he did, she would have seen Jacob, Thorsen, and Johnathan struggling to hide their laughter. Stunned, Cameron looked from his wife to his men, and back again.

"My responsibility for the welfare of our people is as great as yours. For two years I have run this shire quite well *without you.* I refuse to sit back now and watch you ruin it."

When Cameron opened his mouth to answer that insult, Kaela shocked him even more by reaching up and holding her hand over his mouth.

"Let me finish," she said, poking her finger at his chest. "You are a warrior, Cameron, mayhap the best in all Normandy." She stopped for a moment when he beamed at her comment. God's teeth, why did he have to be so handsome? She shook her head to clear her thoughts. "But you probably know nothing of farming, my lord. Tell me, is this soil ready to be planted with seed?" she asked, picking up some dirt and thrusting the loose grains into his hand.

Cameron looked down at the dirt for a moment and

then raised his eyes to his wife's. Her undisciplined outburst wearied him. She must be taught a wife's proper place.

"The soil looks fine to me," he said, his expression deliberately bored.

"Ha! You know nothing. This field has yet to be fertilized. There's a shed full of manure that the villeins must spread and till into the earth before we can plant seed for barley and rye. If you wish to run Chaldron, husband, you had best learn to do so properly." Kaela knew her gloating tone would antagonize him, but she didn't care.

Cameron seized her wrist and yanked her against his chest. She felt the heat radiating from his hard muscled body, and knew the effort to control his temper cost him dearly.

"'Tis enough, Kaela. I am your husband, by God, and you will treat me with respect," he said in a voice so deadly soft, she had to strain to hear him.

"'Tis a double-edged sword, my lord. If you want respect from me, you will treat me with respect." Her fiery green eyes looked into his smoldering blue ones.

"I could beat it into you, wife."

"You will not beat me."

"What makes you think I won't?"

"You are a man of honor, Cameron. You would never beat a woman," Kaela said.

Cameron drew a deep breath, caught his wife's hands, and helped her mount her horse. "Go home, Kaela. You have made your point. After dinner we will discuss the running of Chaldron, but mark my words well, wife. There can be only one master here." His hands caressed her waist and Kaela placed her hands over his, caressing them. Her touch sent sparks of desire racing down his spine.

She leaned down and whispered to him very softly. "I would have it no other way, my lord."

With those parting words she left him, Jacob trailing behind her. Turning to mount, Cameron saw the amused glances of his vassals.

"Not a word from either one of you."

Thorsen ignored his friend's warning, threw his head back, and laughed.

"Aye, my friend, I would say the lady does not understand she is a mere woman. Were I you, Cameron, I would count myself lucky she does not."

"Aye, Baron, life with your lady wife will never be dull," Johnathan added.

Cameron glowered at them. "I never thought it would. The question is, will I survive?" He shook his head, still amazed by her outburst, and began to laugh. "I never knew my wife could be such a hellion."

❧   ❧   ❧

Kaela felt tense all through dinner. Her husband remained pleasantly aloof and she had no idea what he was thinking. Her cheeks grew hot when she remembered her outburst earlier in the afternoon.

Cameron interrupted her thoughts, taking her hand and leading her away from her untouched meal.

"Come, wife, 'Tis time we talked."

Kaela followed her husband down the hall to the small room where she stored Chaldron's records. She had spent many hours here pouring over the parchments, assessing Chaldron's needs, and keeping track of her family's wealth. Watching her husband sit behind her small desk, she could not help thinking how his large frame overpowered the piece of oak. She made a mental note to commission Henry, one of the castle's woodcarvers, to build a new desk for her husband.

Cameron commanded Kaela to sit. She pulled up a chair before the desk, patiently waiting for him to seek her advice. Half-an-hour later, he looked up from a parchment and motioned her to his side. Pointing to a column of numbers, Cameron asked, "What do these numbers signify?"

Kaela placed one hand on his shoulder and leaned over him. Her hair fell against his arm and he reveled in its softness, loving the sweet scent of roses that washed over him. He longed to take her in his arms, and realized he was losing his battle. Kaela was too much woman to be ignored.

"'Tis the amount of winter wheat collected from each villein last harvest. The next column shows how much wheat is used each month." When Kaela breathed in her husband's scent, her hands itched to caress him.

"You have managed well, Kaela. Your work makes assuming control much easier for me. I wish to learn more about your methods for record-keeping. Although I will appoint a new steward soon, I intend to keep a close hand in the running of our shire."

"*Ours,* my lord?" she asked, unable to believe he had said the word.

"Aye, wife, 'Tis ours. I have considered the words you spoke this afternoon. I have come to realize I do not want a lazy wife who does nothing. I would have you at my side to advise me," Cameron said, looking into her questioning eyes.

Honored by his words, Kaela didn't know how to

respond. She stared at him for a moment, then looked away.

"Thank you, husband." She fought to keep her voice from trembling.

"Don't misunderstand me, Kaela. I am master here, and what I decide is law. Since you are an intelligent woman, I will seek your advice from time to time. When I hold court to hear the villeins' grievances, I expect you to sit at my side and give your opinion when requested, but only when requested. Do you understand?"

"Aye, husband, I understand."

Without warning, Kaela sat on his lap, her soft lips placing kisses on his cheek. He pulled away.

"Stop that, wife." Despite his vow, his arms went around her and he held her to him.

When Cameron continued to speak, he still held her.

"At the end of each day, we will discuss the day's events. You will have charge of the keep. I expect an accounting from you each evening."

"Aye, husband."

"There will be changes, Kaela. I will make Chaldron mine."

"Chaldron is already yours, my lord." Kaela laid her cheek against his shoulder, wanting never to move.

Cameron whisked her from his lap and set her on her feet, but he gave her the first smile she had seen from him since the morning of her recovery.

"Off with you now, wife. I have business to discuss with Johnathan."

"Will you be as late retiring as you were last evening, husband?"

"We shall see, wife. We shall see."

❖   ❖   ❖

Cameron moved down the hall toward the chamber he shared with his wife. He remembered her standing before him, her face red with rage, shaking her small fist in defiance, and he smiled.

Aye, he was married now, for better or worse, and Chaldron belonged to him. Stopping in the nursery to check on Mattie, he found her sound asleep, her arms around her doll. He could not resist reaching down and running his fingers through her soft curls. He marveled at how quickly she had bonded with him. Her "Wolf"… he liked the sound of that.

Entering their bedchamber, Cameron stopped short when he saw Kaela. Desire jolted through his body as he gazed at her. She wore the shimmering gown that she had worn on their wedding night. He could see her every curve through the sheer material. She stood close to the fire, the dancing flames reflecting in her hair.

Cameron smiled in appreciation, despite his conflicting emotions.

"I have prepared your bath, husband."

"I see that you have." Cameron crossed the room to take her in his arms. "Will you assist me, wife?"

Kaela pulled away from him and, hiding a smile, began to undress her husband. "Of course, my lord. 'Tis a wife's duty to see to the comfort of her husband." Her hands trembling, Kaela pulled Cameron's tunic over his head, and dropped the garment to the floor. Entranced by his sculpted perfection, she tentatively ran her hands over the coarse hair on his chest and up his smooth bronzed shoulders.

"You are beautiful, husband."

"Nay, wife, you are the one who is beautiful. I am much scarred from battle." Cameron ran his hands down her back, bringing her closer to him. Despite his need for her, he tried to concentrate on what she was saying.

"Your scars are marks of valor, husband. They are beautiful to me. My scars are scars of shame, and will always remind me of my weakness." Choking back a sob, Kaela tried to pull away from him.

"What are you talking about, Kaela? The scar from the arrow is insignificant. Every time I see it, I remember only your bravery in trying to protect me. How could that detract from your beauty, wife?" Cameron drew her to him, feathering kisses across her brow, but Kaela pulled away from his embrace.

"'Tis not just the scar from the arrow, husband," Kaela said, unable to look at him. During her illness, he must have seen her back, but she could not voice her fear that he had been repelled.

"Ah, you mean the scars on your back from the flogging you suffered at Broderick's hand." Cameron drew her back into his arms, cradled her head against his chest.

Kaela sobbed against him. "How did you know they were caused by Broderick's whip?"

She trembled in his arms and Cameron's chest tightened with his need to comfort her. He lifted her chin, until her troubled gaze met his.

"Sweeting, I have known about the scars on your back since the first night we met. I saw them when I came into this very room and found you lying here before the fire."

"And you married me knowing how scarred and

ugly I am?" she asked in disbelief. "I never told you
Broderick whipped me, Cameron—how did you know?"

"You talk in your sleep, wife." He turned her in his
arms, pulled her long hair to one side, and placed soft,
sensuous kisses along her neck and shoulders.

Kaela melted against him, overwhelmed by his
words and what his warm lips were doing to her body.
On fire with desire for him, she could not believe he
could ignore the ugly lash marks that crisscrossed her
back.

Cameron, sensing her feelings and determined to
comfort her, pushed the thin straps of her gown from
her shoulders, and let the soft material slide to the
floor.

Kaela gasped and tried to pull away. Knowing he
had a full view of her naked back in the firelight, she
desperately wanted to hide from him.

"Nay, wife, I would look at you." His voice kind,
Cameron continued to caress her shoulders. He bent
his head, placing velvety kisses down her spine,
touching each scar. "I have seen the marks many
times, Kaela. You are wrong to think they are ugly. As
the scar from the arrow reminds me of your bravery,
so do these marks from the lash. God, what you have
suffered at the hands of that monster, yet you are still a
gentle, loving woman. You found the strength within
yourself to survive his beatings, to escape him. You
found the courage to trust again. I will never betray
the trust you have given me. Nay, wife, these, too, are
marks of valor. They could never alter your beauty."
Cameron, having reached the base of her spine, continued to caress her. Kneeling, he ran his hands down her
silken thighs.

He could call her scarred body beautiful and make

her believe the words. Tears streamed down Kaela's face. Turning in his arms, she sank to her knees, took his face in her hands, and kissed him with all the love and passion she dared not speak of. She ran her hands down his muscled chest, quickly untied the laces of his chausses, then pushed them over his hips.

"The bath water grows cold, my lord." Kaela smiled and rising, pulled him to his feet.

Cameron stepped into the wooden tub and watched his beautiful wife step in after him. Kaela wrapped her arms around his neck, pressed her fevered body against his. Cameron brought his lips down to hers, kissing her with all the gentleness he possessed as they eased down into the warm water.

"I like the way you help me with my bath, wife. Will you scrub my back?" He gave her a coaxing smile.

Kaela straddled his hips, rubbing her breasts against his chest. She reached for the soap and lathered his chest, scrubbed his back and arms, slowly, methodically, all the while teasing kisses upon his lips. Cameron reached for her breasts and Kaela moaned her pleasure when his tongue flicked over one taut nipple.

On fire for his wife, Cameron could stand this sweet torment no longer. With one smooth motion, he lifted her in his arms and stepped out of the tub. He reached for the towel and, joining his wife in front of the fire, began to dry her body and his own. When they were both dry, Kaela took his hand in hers and glanced toward the bed.

"Nay, wife, I would love you here first." Cameron drew her to him and claimed her mouth in a drugging kiss. His tongue plunged violently into her mouth to love hers with fierce abandon. All his pent-up anxiety and fears culminated in his reckless passion for her. She moaned when he began to caress her neck, and threw her head back to give him better access. He trailed a line of kisses down her neck, stopping in the hollow of her throat where he could feel her pulse beating wildly.

"Ah, Kaela, you are beautiful," he murmured. "I can't get enough of you." Once hand captured a breast and, lowering his head, he captured the other with his mouth.

Kaela moaned again and ran her hands through his hair, bringing him closer to her.

Cameron eased her gently to the soft fur rug, then covered her body with his own, parting her legs and lying between them. He continued to caress her breasts, building the heat in Kaela to a fevered pitch. Arching against him, she tried to pull him closer.

Knowingly, Cameron smiled at her. He trailed kisses over her belly until he reached her womanhood, then tenderly used his mouth and tongue to love her. To his delight, a rapturous cry escaped her lips as she thrashed beneath him.

"Does that please you, Kaela?"

"Aye, Cameron, don't stop." Pushed toward the sun and helpless to stop her flight, she writhed while his tongue stroked her flesh until she moaned with desire. The feather-soft touches of his tongue, his lips, against that most secret part of her drove her wild. She could not bear his loving, yet she thought she might well die if he stopped. Then his mouth hurled her toward release and she cried his name.

"Aye, sweetheart, come with me," Cameron murmured when her body began to spasm beneath him.

He swept her up, carried her to the bed, so hot for her, his need so great, he could hold back no longer. He laid her on her stomach and, spreading her legs, quickly covered her. He stretched her arms above her head, clasping her hands in his. Breathing in heavy gasps, he rained fiery kisses over her shoulders and her back.

"I need you, Kaela. Come to me, sweetheart," Cameron murmured.

When Kaela lifted her hips, he entered her with one powerful thrust. Groaning his pleasure, again and again he plunged into her, unable to control his wild need for her. Firmly holding her against his hips, he concentrated on slowing his pace. He slipped one hand down to stroke the sensitive pearl of her womanhood. Determined to bring her to fulfillment once more before he found his release, he smiled when he heard her throaty cries and knew her need was as wild and desperate as his own.

They found release together, crying out for one another. For long minutes afterward, neither could speak.

Cameron lay back and crushed Kaela to him, listening to the heavy pounding of her heart against his. He had never felt such ecstasy, never known such joy. The passion in this woman he had married frightened him.

Kaela clung to her husband, fighting the tears that threatened. Her heart filled to overflowing, she longed to tell him she loved him. But she knew Cameron did not want to hear those words from her. If she spoke, he would surely turn from her. He had each time before when she thought their closeness finally secure.

Resting her head against his shoulder, she drew lazy circles across his chest. She inhaled Cameron's rich, sensual scent and gloried in her contentment. Her husband held her so tightly, she could hardly catch her breath. Playfully, she pinched his chest.

"Cameron, you don't know your own strength."

"I'm sorry sweetheart, you make me forget myself," Cameron said, his voice husky. He relaxed his hold, smoothing his hand over her arm, in an easy caress.

"I never knew a woman could feel this way," Kaela said, giving him a lazy smile. "Did you mean what you said, husband?"

Cameron gave her an inquiring look.

"You told me you need me. Did you mean the words, or were they only spoken in passion?"

Cameron clasped her to him. Hesitantly, he answered her. "I meant the words. I did not know until I said them, but 'Tis true."

"I need you, too, more than you will ever know. You can trust me, husband. I will never betray you."

Cameron remained silent, although Kaela waited several minutes for his response. When she realized he would not answer her, she said, "You believe me, don't you?"

Cameron smiled, his eyes full of tenderness, but Kaela could see the wariness in them. He rubbed his knuckles against her cheek and leaned to kiss her lips.

"I believe we need each other, wife. This need is not an emotion a warrior wishes in his life. Trust is not an easy thing to give, and I am honored that you trust me. Loyalty is something earned, Kaela, along with respect. Our relationship is very new. I will not hold you to your words until we know each other better."

Kaela wondered if hearts really do break. She could do nothing to keep him from pulling back, putting that forbidding distance between them. They had shared need, and though she had given him her love, she would have to be satisfied with what he offered. She sighed. Cameron had much to learn about her, but she would show him her loyalty and her love, and he would come to love her. Without that hope, she could not exist.

"In time, you will come to believe my words, husband. For now, 'Tis enough to know we need each other." Kaela offered him her lips.

"Aye, wife, 'Tis enough, for now."

Chapter Fourteen

✣   ✣   ✣

Over the next several weeks, turmoil and confusion filled Kaela's life. Quickly, she came to believe her handsome husband was a very fickle man. Each time she felt she had made progress with him, a glance or a word set him off, and he withdrew from her again. One day she would find him kind and loving, the next, withdrawn and distant. He drove her insane. Kaela knew with certainty she loved him, but the only thing that remained constant in their stormy relationship was their lovemaking. No matter what their days brought, whether growing closeness or Cameron's cold indifference, he filled their nights with passion. This one stabilizing force in their marriage kept Kaela's hopes alive. All the love she stored in her heart for her husband expressed itself in their passion-filled nights.

Cameron, constantly unbalanced by his feisty little wife, had never known such happiness. At the same time, he had never been so miserable. Kaela intruded on his every waking thought. His emotions ranged from tenderness to rage, but she was always the cause. Every time he thought he understood his wife, and had his feelings for her placed within comfortable guidelines, she did something unexpected and a new quandary

opened for him. Their lovemaking? Cameron often
smiled when he thought of his nights with Kaela. His
wife continued to surprise and delight him in bed. For a
shy, inexperienced woman, his wife turned into a little
wanton in the throes of passion. She had disproved his
theory time and again. No matter how often he satisfied
his lust with her, he never tired of her, and he doubted
he ever would.

Brenna, Jacob, and Cameron's vassals watched the
pair with growing amusement. Chaldron Keep had
never been livelier.

One bright morning in early April, Kaela awoke
alone, as she did most mornings. She had always
thought herself an early riser, but her husband rose
before the sun. On the occasional morning when she
awakened to find him still lying beside her, he would
draw her into his tender embrace. His early-morning
lovemaking was always poignant and so intensely
sweet, Kaela wished she would awake to find him
with her more often.

That was not the case this morning, however, and
Kaela hurried to dress and make her way to the stables
before her husband discovered her intentions.

He had been in a particularly foul mood the day
before. She had been in the south tower chamber,
which she and Brenna had converted to a sewing room
where they could work on the new tapestries.

Kaela decided she wanted to surprise her husband
with the new tapestries once they were completed and
so they had moved all their supplies and helpers to the
south tower, well out of Cameron's way. Kaela heard a
commotion coming from the outer bailey and poked
her head out the narrow window to see what was
going on. Her eyes grew wide with dismay as she

watched Cameron drag one of the stone masons out of the masonry hut by his hair.

She flew down the stairs as fast as her feet would carry her and entered the outer bailey in time to hear the Baron shouting at the man. He had the lad pressed against the outer wall of the hut and was shaking him by the shoulders.

"You dare to sleep while you are supposed to be in my service," Cameron said, ice in his voice. Kaela was sure he could be heard all the way down in the village. His face was mottled with rage and she was afraid he was going to hurt the lad.

She started to step forward to try and reason with her husband before he let his temper get the best of him, but she was stopped by a steel hand on her shoulder. Kaela turned to find Patrick frowning down at her.

"Do not interfere, Kaela. The Baron knows what he is doing," Patrick told her sternly.

"The lad is hardly more than a boy, Patrick. I do not want Cameron to hurt him."

"'Tis time the lad became a man, Kaela. Cameron found him asleep at the mason's wheel. The lad could have severed a hand or worse. He reeks of ale and you can see for yourself that he is hung over. 'Tis not to be tolerated. The boy is a danger to himself, and to those who work with him. Cameron knows what to do."

Kaela nodded her understanding and stood at Patrick's side to see what her husband would do next. She was amazed to see him throw the boy over his shoulder like a sack of grain, and carry him to a watering trough next to the stables where he unceremoniously dumped him in. The youth came up sputtering and Cameron jerked him to his feet.

"God's blood, you are not man enough to carry out

the duties that have been given you, lad. For the next two fortnights you will be assigned to the labor crews under Johnathan's supervision. The men work in three hour shifts, but you will work all three daily shifts to build our new roads. Mayhap the hard labor will help you to overcome this passion you seem to have for the drink. If you perform well and learn to obey orders, I will consider letting you train with my warriors. If you do not, you will be sent back to the village to find your own means of support. Is that clear?" Cameron growled.

"Aye, Baron," the lad replied weakly as Johnathan came forward to take him away.

Wide-eyed, Kaela had stared at her husband. He could be a hard man, but she had to admit he had handled the situation well.

Cameron had spent most of his days working with his men from dawn to dusk. He would train his warriors starting from midmorning, after he had returned from a hunt, or surveying the fields, until early afternoon. Then he always rode out to supervise the road construction and never returned before dusk, many times covered in grime from toiling alongside his men.

Only in the last few days had Kaela noticed that Cameron had been spending time inspecting the different workers' huts inside the bailey. He had inspected the armorer's hut, made several changes and ordered swords crafted to his specifications. He visited the wheelwright, carpenters, and farriers. Kaela had found him one afternoon in the brew house consulting with Joseph over the recipe for the ale. They'd had quite an argument over that. The recipe Kaela used had been her grandmother's favorite and she refused to change it. Everyone knew Saxon ale was superior to Norman, she had told him. She had won that battle, but it was one of the few she could attest to.

The servants informed her that her husband had been in the wagon shed, piggery, and even the storehouse. This all seemed very odd to Kaela since her father had never interfered with what he considered her mother's domain, but she assumed he only wanted to acquaint himself with the way Chaldron was run and let his presence be known. She drew the line at her herb garden though. Kaela took great pride in her garden and was depended upon by her people for her medicinal herbs. If he put just one of his big feet on her carefully tended soil, he was going to pay dearly.

What had sent her rushing to the stables this morning was Arik. Last evening, she had heard Cameron tell Johnathan he intended to inspect the stables, when he returned from his morning ride. Kaela had been very careful to keep Arik out of Cameron's way, afraid of how her husband might react when he discovered Arik was simple-minded. She did not want Arik ridiculed, or worse, turned out. Arik loved horses and Kaela had given him the responsibility of seeing to the animals' welfare long ago. He took great pride in her trust.

Confident she had time to locate Arik and send him on some errand before Cameron returned, Kaela hurried through the stable's massive double doors, Arik's name on her lips. She came to an abrupt halt when she saw Arik in the center of the stables, deep in conversation with her husband.

"God's teeth," she gasped.

Both men turned at the sound of her voice. Arik's face broke into a huge smile. Coming forward, he lifted her off her feet giving her a bear hug. She held him tightly, gazing over his shoulder at her husband's scowling face.

"Good morn, Kaela, you are here early. Do you want me to saddle Sky for you?" Grinning, Arik set her down.

"Nay, Arik, I came to talk to you." Kaela's gaze never left Cameron's.

"What seems to be the problem, wife?"

Kaela rushed to her husband, frantically wondering what she might say to soften his attitude toward Arik. Her giant friend followed along behind her.

"The Baron asked me about what I do here at the stables. I told him about each of the horses and how they like for me to care for them," Arik said, his voice filled with pride.

Kaela stood between the two men and looked at her husband with pleading eyes. "'Tis true, Cameron, Arik is very good with the horses."

"I am aware of that, wife. Now, if you will excuse us, I want to explain Arik's new duties to him." Cameron turned from her and walked to Goliath's stall. Arik followed him and Kaela tried to hold back her panic.

New duties! Cameron meant to take Arik from the stables. Arik would be devastated. She had to do something. Following Cameron, she took his hand in hers.

"I would like to stay and hear about these new duties. Do you mind, Cameron?" Mayhap if she stayed beside him, he would be more careful with his words. If his plans were too harsh, she intended to plead Arik's case.

"Suit yourself, wife." Cameron shrugged. "As I said, Arik, you have done a wonderful job with the horses. You seem to have a magical way with the animals. I have plans to enlarge the stable to twice the size it is now, with at least twenty new stalls. I want to bring in horses of different breeds and do some cross-breeding."

Seeing Arik's eyes alight with excitement, Kaela stared at her husband. Relief washed over her. If he praised Arik for his work, mayhap he would let him stay on.

Cameron ignored his wife and continued.

"I am promoting you, Arik, to head stable master. We have five other stable boys now and will increase their number. Jacob has the list of duties you are to perform each day. You must report any problems you have to Jacob, who will then report to me. Do you think you can handle these new duties?"

Arik's face beamed with pride. "Aye, Baron."

"You will have your very own room at the back of the new stables, Arik. You must consult with Kaela. She will help you furnish it so that you will be comfortable."

"Thank you, Baron," Arik shouted, slapping Cameron on the back with enough strength to knock a lesser man down. Then he swung Kaela in his arms as if she were a child.

"Did you hear that, Kaela, a room of my own, and I am going to be the stable master," Arik beamed.

"I am so proud of you, Arik. 'Tis wonderful." Laughing, Kaela grasped his shoulders. If he didn't stop swinging her in circles, she would be sick.

"Put my wife down now, Arik, and saddle another horse for me. You must groom Goliath and put him away."

"Aye, Baron," Arik said, settling Kaela in her husband's arms. "Goliath and I are great friends." He marched off to the tack room to get the Baron's saddle.

Kaela hugged her husband until she thought her arms would break. He dragged her arms from his neck and stepped away.

"What is that for?" he asked, smiling broadly.

Kaela flung herself at him again, hugging him fiercely.

"Oh, Cameron, I feared when you realized Arik was simple-minded, you would cast him out. You have not only accepted him, but have honored him as well."

More than anything Kaela wanted to tell her husband how much she loved him. She put her arms around his neck, then tugged lightly on his hair to bring his mouth to hers. She kissed him with all the love and passion inside her.

Another piece of the wall around Cameron's heart crumbled. Kissing her, he felt the now familiar knot of desire expand in his chest and reluctantly pulled away from her. He smiled when he saw the passion in his wife's emerald eyes. Reaching up, he placed his hands on either side of his wife's lovely face.

"You amaze me, Kaela. How could you think I would cast Arik out? Do you know me so little? He cannot help how he is. Not only is he wonderful with the horses, he is a loyal servant and a loyal friend to you. I have not forgotten that Arik followed you to Ralston Castle and helped you escape from Broderick. I know the man would lay down his life to protect you. I would never do anything to harm him. Besides, Arik deserves this position—he has earned it."

Kaela blushed. "You are right, husband. I am sorry I doubted you. 'Tis just that I have seen so many taunt Arik and I did not know how you would feel. Please forgive me," Kaela pleaded.

Cameron hugged her to him and chuckled. "There's naught to forgive, sweetheart." He turned her around and patted her delectable bottom. "Now be on your way, wife, before I forget my duties and carry you back to our chamber."

Kaela glanced over her shoulder and gave him a promising smile. "I will see you this eve, my lord." Happy, she hurried back to the hall, eager to tell Maude the good news.

Late that afternoon, Patrick rode out to the road construction to inform Cameron that the scouts he had sent to track Broderick had returned. Cameron returned to the keep, anxious to meet with the men.

"What did you find, James?" Cameron asked his vassal. The men were bone weary, and in much need of baths and food, but Cameron needed to know his enemy's whereabouts.

"We have no doubt the rebels are in Wales, Baron," James said. "From what we learned, they have a series of camps set up in caves about a half-day's ride from our border. They move easily from one location to another. 'Tis difficult to say when they plan to move against Chaldron. We saw several parties make forays into England, only to return within a sennight."

"I see. Know you not what area they were scouting?" Cameron clenched his fists at his side. He wanted to attack Broderick so badly he could taste it, before the bastard tried again to kidnap Kaela.

"Nay. They rode north and judging by how long they were gone, I would say Herefordshire, but 'Tis only a guess, my lord."

"You have done well, all of you," Cameron said, nodding to each man. "Get some rest and something to eat. Johnathan and I will meet with you later and go over your report. One last thing, James. What of their numbers?"

"'Tis hard to say, my lord. We counted almost two hundred men, but there may have been many more."

Cameron nodded, dismissing his man.

Kaela watched the exchange from the parapet of their chamber. She had no idea who her husband was talking to, but she could tell by his movements he was upset. She watched him mount his horse and again leave the keep. She expected him to return to the road construction, but he turned west toward the lake. Sighing, she left the parapet and crossed back to the bed to lie down. Her husband must find the lake as soothing to the nerves as she did. Had she the energy to join him, mayhap he would talk with her and share his troubles.

All this worry over her husband had made her ill. She had been so tired lately. More often than not, she sneaked in an afternoon nap when everyone else was too busy to notice. The dizzy spells concerned her, too. She was never sick. Worrying so much about him did no good. He would come around... in time.

Kaela's worries grew when she saw her husband's face that evening. His fierce scowl would intimidate anyone. Kaela noticed how the servants stayed out of his way. His men also left the great hall as soon as they had eaten. Cameron had not said three words over dinner. When she tried to interest him in some food, he gave her a glacial stare. Kaela's eyes glazed with tears. She rushed from the hall before she shamed herself by crying. She should be accustomed to Cameron's bad temper by now, not weeping over his lack of consideration.

Kaela paced back and forth in their chamber.

Cameron still had not made an appearance and she wondered if he was sulking somewhere. Too nervous to sleep, Kaela decided she would check on Mattie. When she reached the nursery door, she found it open. Stepping over the threshold, she entered the room and stopped. Her husband sat on a stool before the fire, Mattie in his lap, their heads bent closely together. Mattie sobbed softly and Cameron spoke gently, soothingly while he used his dagger's tip to work a splinter from her palm.

He had the little girl laughing by the time he finished. Kaela thought she would burst with joy at the sight of them. If she did not know better, she would think they were truly father and daughter.

"What is this?" Kaela asked. She smiled tremulously at the pair before her as they raised their gazes to her misty one.

"Cameron took a splinter out, Kaela. It didn't even hurt," Mattie boasted.

"You're a tough one, sweet pea." Cameron ran his hands through her bouncy black curls. "Now it's off to bed with you, little one."

"One more story, please, Cameron?" Mattie's blue eyes pleaded.

"Nay, Mattie, 'Tis already past your bed time. I came to tuck you in."

Mattie stood up and reached for Kaela's hand. Turning, she took Cameron's hand, too.

"I want both of you to tuck me in."

Kaela smiled at her husband. Her knees trembled at the soft look in his eyes and the tender smile he gave her. When Mattie slipped under the covers, they both kissed her and said good night. She fell asleep before they left the room.

Hand in hand, Cameron and Kaela made their way back to their bedchamber, each lost in thought. A few minutes later they lay in their own bed, sharing passionate kisses. For the moment, they needed only the comfort they found in each other's arms.

Kaela opened her eyes the next morning, so sick she could barely get out of bed. Waves of nausea washed over her. She lay very still waiting for the feeling to pass. The sickness abated after a few minutes, and she dressed for the day. When she entered the great hall, several of Cameron's men were still at the table eating some of last night's left-over mutton. The greasy meat's odor reached her nostrils, sending her flying back to her chamber. She reached the chamber pot just in time. After several minutes, Kaela dipped a cloth in cool water. Wiping her flushed face, she sat down on the bed.

Suddenly enlightenment came and Kaela's hand instinctively went to her stomach. *Could it be? Am I with child?* Caught up in the many changes in her life, she had not thought about missing her monthly flow. Now she realized she had not had her woman's time since her marriage. Kaela leaned back, stunned. She carried Cameron's baby. Her eyes filled with joyful tears.

"A baby," Kaela whispered softly. "Our baby."

How would Cameron feel about a child? Surely he would be pleased. He had said he wanted her to give him sons. He would be a wonderful father. *Now he will love me... how can he not?* She felt so happy she thought she would burst. How should she tell him? The words must be very special. They should be alone... yes, she would try to find a moment alone with him today, or perhaps she should wait until tonight when he came to their chamber. Until then, she would try to find the right words.

Kaela did not see Cameron that morning. He was gone from the keep. Then he trained on the quintain with his men all afternoon. Frustrated, she chided herself for her impatience. They would be alone tonight. That would have to be soon enough.

Deciding she would take extra care with her appearance, Kaela ordered a bath just before dinner. The days had grown warmer with spring's arrival. Stripping off her clothes, she sank gratefully into the warm soothing water. She felt very tired, for she had not been able to sneak in her afternoon nap. She ran the sponge over her body, marveling at the soreness of her breasts. Placing her hands on her stomach, she thought of the child growing inside her and smiled. Leaning her head back against the rim of the tub, she closed her eyes for a moment.

When Kaela didn't make an appearance at the dinner hour, Cameron went in search of his wife. He had not seen her all day, and he wondered if she were ill. Opening the door to their chamber, he found her sound asleep in the bath tub. He shook his head as he crossed the room and knelt down beside her to gently shake her awake.

"Kaela, are you all right?" he asked, breathing a sigh of relief when she gave him a lazy smile.

Cameron lifted her from the tub, soaking his tunic in the process. He grabbed a towel and began to dry her.

"What an unusual wife I have. Not only can you sleep through the loudest of battles, you even sleep in a tub of water." He laughed softly.

Kaela covered his mouth with hers and kissed him

tenderly, wrapping her nude body around him and holding him close. Cameron dropped the towel. In two strides, he reached the bed and deposited her there.

"Are you not hungry, wife?" he asked, a wicked gleam in his eyes.

"Aye, my lord, I am starving for my husband." Kaela gave him a look that sent his blood rushing through his veins.

Cameron removed his clothes and joined his wife on the bed, his eyes roaming greedily over her luscious curves. "Then of course, sweetheart, let me feed you." Cameron groaned as his mouth slanted over hers.

Kaela rubbed her tongue against his, then ran her hand down his bare chest, and lower, taking his already throbbing shaft into her hand and stroking him.

Cameron went a little wild, kissing her deeply and growling low in his throat to let her know he liked her bold action. He wanted… needed… to be inside her, to feel her hot, tight sheath encasing him. He knew he could not wait much longer.

Turning Kaela on her back, he parted her thighs and, dragging his lips from hers, he moved down to caress the very heat of her. Already wet with her desire for him, she moaned her pleasure when his tongue began to stroke the sensitive nub hidden within the slick folds of flesh. Then he pressed high inside her and Kaela arched up against him, calling out his name.

"Cameron, please, come to me now…"

Cameron answered her with one smooth motion and buried himself deep inside her. His pleasure was so intense, he didn't think he could bear it. He buried his face in her hair and plunged into her again and again. He felt as if he were coming apart.

Kaela clung to him, wrapping her legs around his hips and losing herself in the pleasure of him. They both reached fulfillment at the same moment. Beyond thought, Kaela cried out her love for him.

"I love you, I love you."

She could no more hold back the words than hold back the tide. Filled with love for him, she wanted to tell him she carried his child.

Cameron froze at her words, then collapsed on top of her. Her words echoed in his mind. She loved him? God, she loved him. Her declaration caught him by surprise. Overjoyed and desperately afraid at the same time, he searched for words to respond. He felt strongly about his wife, but he did not love her... could not love her.

Cameron said nothing, but rolled away from her and lay on his back, staring at the ceiling.

Suddenly very cold, Kaela wondered how she could have been so stupid. She had not meant to tell him, but the words had just tumbled out. What was he thinking? She reached out tentatively and placed her hand on Cameron's shoulder.

"Cameron, are you all right?" she asked, her voice barely a whisper.

"Of course, I am. Are you? I wasn't too rough with you, was I?" He did not look at her.

"I am fine," Kaela answered. Dear God, he would not even look at her.

Cameron jumped up and began to dress. "I am starving, Kaela, and I have to meet with Johnathan and Thorsen this evening. Do you want a meal sent up to you?"

"Nay, I will come down to the hall to have my dinner," Kaela said, her voice flat. So much for telling him about the child tonight. He was extremely uncomfortable with her, and she had only said she loved him. Dismally, Kaela watched him search for a dry tunic.

"I will see you at table then," Cameron said, and he was gone.

Kaela left the hall as soon as she could. Brenna and Jacob had joined her while she ate her meal, but she was not in the mood for pleasant conversation. Filled with turmoil and indecision, she needed time alone to think.

On this beautiful spring night, the crisp air refreshed her. Overhead a blanket of stars twinkled, giving her an odd reassurance. She had walked the perimeter of the castle along the wall-walk. The exercise had helped to clear her head. Not wanting company, Kaela climbed the stairs of the north tower and squeezed herself into the narrow window ledge to peer out at the night sky.

Kaela always thought about her parents when she came here. She smiled. How happy her mother and father would have been to know that she was with child. They had always wanted more children, but were unable to have them. A grandchild would have been most welcome. Kaela realized she desperately wanted this child.

Mayhap she had overreacted to Cameron's response when she had told him she loved him. Although she had not meant to voice her feelings, she did not regret her words. After all, they were true. Knowing how she felt, perhaps he would more easily come to love her.

The deep rumble of male voices interrupted Kaela's

reflection. Looking down, she saw Cameron and Thorsen walking along the wall-walk toward her. She started to call out, but realized by their gestures that their conversation was not a pleasant one. Not wanting to intrude, Kaela leaned into the darkness and waited for the two men to pass. To her dismay, they stopped directly below her. Before she could move away, their words drifted up to her.

"I do not understand your attitude, Cameron," Thorsen said, angrily.

"Well, you should. God's teeth, Thorsen, a shire the size of Chaldron is a huge responsibility."

"Cameron, we have known each other since we were children. You and I both know that the responsibility of Chaldron is not what is bothering you. You could run the whole damned kingdom without any qualms. 'Tis truth. You thrive on the challenge being lord of Chaldron offers. Drop this pretense—tell me what really bothers you. 'Tis your lady wife who has you in this mood, is it not?"

"Don't press me," Cameron growled.

Thorsen placed his hand on Cameron's shoulder. "I care too much about you and your lady to keep silent. Talk to me, Cameron. Let me help you."

Raking his hands through his hair, Cameron stepped away from his friend.

"There's naught you can do, Thorsen. No one can help me."

"The lass has given you her heart."

Cameron turned and leaned into the castle wall. He was quiet for several minutes. When he spoke, sadness filled his voice.

"It seems that is so and I am sorry for it. You know I cannot return her love, Thorsen."

"Cameron, if you would only—"

"Nay," Cameron shouted. "We have had this conversation too many times. You said yourself I could marry Kaela and not love her. I gave her back her home and kept her from marrying some stranger. She has my protection. That has to be enough."

"If it is enough, then why are you so angry?"

"I don't know. Damn her, she is so innocent. What do I say to her when she tells me she loves me?"

"Only you can answer that, my friend. But I think you are dishonest with yourself."

"Don't tell me what I feel, and do not tell me what I can give," Cameron said, his voice hard. "I know what I am capable of. You have not been where I have been, Thorsen. You have no right."

"'Tis truth that I know not your pain, but I can't believe you are incapable of loving again, if you would but allow yourself."

"All the love I had to give died with my son Peter." Cameron's voice cracked. "I refuse to discuss this with you. I married the girl because I saw my duty. The deed is done and I will try to be a good husband to her, but do not ask me to love her. I cannot, Thorsen, and I have no desire for her to love me. 'Tis something between Kaela and me. You will not interfere."

"Perhaps when she gives you another son…"

"Another son?" Cameron choked on the words. "No child will ever replace Peter in my heart. I will never betray my love for him. God curse you for even suggesting—"

"Calm down, Cameron. I didn't mean you would forget Peter. If you would only—"

"Enough!" Cameron glared at his friend. "You will not speak of this again, Thorsen. If you do, I will not be responsible for my actions."

"Aye, then let us walk, my lord. 'Twas not my wish to upset you so. I would give my life for you."

"I know you would, my friend. I would give my life for you as well. Let us speak of other things." Their voices faded as they continued their walk.

Kaela clasped her hands over her mouth to stifle the sobs that racked her body. Tears streamed down her face, blurring her vision. She watched her husband and Thorsen walk away. When they were out of sight, she slowly lowered herself to the floor and leaned back against the cold stone wall. Despair washed over her, a thick mist, completely shrouding her heart. She wrapped her arms around her knees and rocked back and forth.

Cameron's words echoed through her mind, over and over. He did not love her. He never would. He had given all his love to his son, a dead son Kaela had known nothing about. He had nothing left to give. No love to give their child, the babe she carried inside her. Dear God, what had caused this kind of grief? She had loved her parents with all her heart and had known the grief of losing them, and yet she was full of love for her husband. She had given love freely to Mattie and Brenna, and to Jacob. Kaela could not fathom a pain so great you could never love again.

Cameron had married her out of pity. He did not want her love, had cringed when he had heard her words. He took her body freely, but wanted no part of her heart.

"Oh, God," she sobbed, "help me. 'Tis more than I can bear."

Kaela had never felt more alone, more empty. She did not know how long she sat there. She knew she had to do something, but what? Finally, she stood and descended the tower steps, no real destination in mind. Surprised, she soon found herself in Mattie's room. The little girl lay sound asleep, snuggled under the covers.

Kaela undressed slowly, leaving on only her chemise, lifted the covers, and lay down beside Mattie. Taking the little girl in her arms, Kaela kissed her sweet-smelling hair. She needed human contact, and Mattie's sweet, sleeping warmth soothed her. After a time, she fell into a restless sleep.

Chapter Fifteen

✛   ✛   ✛

Cameron paced in their bed chamber. Where the hell was Kaela? 'Twas very late. 'Twas not like her to disappear this way. She could not be upset. Hell, he knew he had frozen when she had blurted out her love for him, but he didn't think he had been that obvious. He had not meant to hurt her... no, he was very fond of his wife. She had known enough pain—he would never deliberately cause her hurt.

But she was being ridiculous, Cameron grumbled. Whatever he had done, nothing warranted her disappearance. He would find her and bring her back where she belonged. On that thought, Cameron left their bedchamber and went in search of his wife. He found her in the nursery with Mattie, lying beside the child, both sound asleep. Kaela's clothing lay in a heap on the floor.

"What the hell?" Cameron crossed the chamber and came to stand at the bedside. He watched them sleeping for several minutes. Two little innocents, but what had brought his wife to Mattie's bed?

If she were upset with him because he did not say he loved her this afternoon, she was being too sensitive. Finding a way to appease her would be difficult, but he would not lie about his feelings.

When Cameron leaned over and shook his wife, she did not respond. How deeply she could sleep. The castle could burn down around her and she would sleep through the fire. He shook her again. "Kaela, wake up."

She slowly opened her eyes. Dismayed, Cameron saw they were red and tear-swollen.

"What is wrong, wife? Why are you here?" He kept his voice soft, trying to hide his impatience.

Kaela stared at him, silent, misery and grief in her gaze.

"Come back to our chamber, Kaela. We will talk."

"I don't want to talk to you, Cameron. Go away," Kaela said, her voice void of emotion.

"Come, Kaela, 'Tis nonsense, this. Surely you are not upset about what passed between us earlier."

His wife continued to stare at him and his frustration grew. He opened his mouth to argue further, but Kaela stopped him with a chilling look when Mattie began to stir.

"You will wake her, Cameron, and she will be frightened. Go away. I wish to stay here tonight."

"Kaela…"

Cameron could not believe his eyes. His wife had turned her back to him. She was dismissing him! He stormed from the room, cursing her under his breath all the way back to their chamber. Once there, he slammed the door so hard it almost came off its hinges. Stripping off his clothing, he threw himself on the bed. If that was the way the hellion wanted to act, so be it. He did not need her. He could sleep just fine without her soft body beside him. God's teeth, the woman was nothing but a nuisance. What had he done that was so horrible? Let her sulk and hide from him—he could play the same game. If she wanted to be ignored, he would show her how well he could ignore her.

Three hours later, tired of tossing and turning in the big empty bed, Cameron gave up. His wife belonged at his side, and damn it, he intended to have her there. Completely oblivious to his nudity, he left their bed and stormed back to the nursery.

Crossing to the bed, he found Kaela staring at him, her green eyes wide. Ha! She couldn't sleep either. Served the witch right.

Cameron didn't say a word. He simply scooped his wife up in his arms. Kaela didn't struggle, but lay passively against him. Neither said a word to the other on the trip back to their chamber.

Once inside their room, Cameron set his wife on her feet. He grabbed the hem of her chemise, pulled it over her head, and threw it to the floor. Then he lifted her and placed her in their bed, getting in beside her. He took her unresisting body in his arms and pulled her head to his chest.

"'Tis where you belong, Kaela. You will not leave me again."

Kaela did not answer. Cameron did not understand her behavior, but he was glad she did not fight him. He would talk to her in the morning, get this matter straightened out.

After a while, Kaela heard the deep even sound of his breathing and knew he had fallen asleep. Very carefully, she eased her body from his and rolled to the edge of the bed, as far away from him as she could get. Only then did she let herself sleep.

Cameron awoke shortly before dawn to find his

wife hugging the far edge of the bed. He rolled over pulled her sleeping body into his arms. He would have been content to hold her for awhile, but her backside pressed tightly against his groin. He felt intoxicated by her sweet fresh smell. He couldn't help placing soft, lazy kisses against her neck. When a sigh escaped her lips and she turned in his arms, the enticement became too great to ignore. He caressed her and before Kaela fully awakened, Cameron was making slow, sweet love to her.

Cameron lost himself in the intense passion he felt for his wife. Her body was so warm and inviting, she was so giving in her love for him, he could not get enough of her. Passionately, he kissed her, again and again. Once she awoke, Kaela returned his kisses with equal passion, thrusting her tongue into his mouth.

He had a desperate need to be inside her and, with one quick motion, he pulled her under him and parted her thighs. He called her name when he entered her hot, wet sheath. Pressing soft kisses over her face, he claimed her lips once more. He wanted to soothe her injured feelings with soft words, but couldn't find his tongue. Instead, he clung to her, their mouths melting together in fervent kisses. Repeatedly, he plunged into her, his need wild and hot.

Kaela clung to him, wrapping her legs around his hips and arching up against him. Her heart ached when his harsh words of the night before rang in her ears, but she was helpless in her need for him. She loved him—nothing could change that. The only way she had to express her need for him was through their lovemaking, and she held nothing back.

They reached their fulfillment at the same time. Kaela heard Cameron whisper her name as he poured his seed into her. She fell back against the sheets and Cameron collapsed on top of her. Kaela held him while hot tears dampened her cheeks. He had felt pity for her, had married her out of some misplaced sense of duty. She wished with every fiber of her being that love, not duty, drove her husband. She had his protection, believed he would always be loyal to her, but she wanted his love more than she had ever wanted anything. His love... the one thing he could not give her.

When Cameron's heart finally stopped racing and he regained his senses, he eased his weight off his wife and kissed her. Chagrin swept through him when he tasted the salt of her tears.

"Why do you weep, sweetheart?"

Kaela hastily wiped her tears away with the back of her hand. She shook her head, pulled the sheet to her chin, turned away from him, and closed her eyes.

Cameron placed his hand on her shoulder.

"Kaela, please tell me what is wrong between us." He had never felt so dismayed.

"'Tis naught," Kaela said. "Naught that you can repair. I am tired, Cameron. I would go back to sleep now."

He could not stand to see her this way, yet he knew not how to reach her. She had closed herself away from him. He was wide awake and the sun was coming up, but he couldn't bear to leave her. Before Kaela could protest, Cameron pulled her into his arms and held her. He rubbed her back and arms, offering the only comfort he knew how.

Kaela allowed his touch. Needing his comfort, she let herself relax against him. Within a few moments she was asleep.

✣   ✣   ✣

The midmorning sun streamed through the window before Kaela again opened her eyes. She couldn't believe she had slept so late. As the fog of sleep began to clear, memories of the previous night rushed in. Kaela sat up and immediately wished she hadn't. Nausea churned inside her. She lay back against the pillows and moaned her agony. At the moment, she did not know which was worse, the pain in her heart or her cramping stomach. Be thankful the nausea will pass soon, she chided, for the heartache will not.

She heard a knock at her door. Before she could answer, Maude bustled in carrying a trencher.

"I worried about ye, mistress. Ye never sleep late like this. Are ye ill? I brought ye some nourishment," the old nurse said briskly, a half-smile on her wrinkled face.

Fixing her attention on Kaela, Maude lost her smile.

Kaela waved the food away as soon as the smell reached her. "Get that away from me, Maude, and bring the chamber pot—quickly."

Maude did as she was bid and held Kaela gently by the shoulders until the gagging stopped. She found a cloth, dipped it in the water basin, and washed her mistress's pale face, all the while speaking soothing words to her.

"How long have ye known?" Maude asked.

"Known what?"

"About the babe ye carry."

"I only realized yesterday what was wrong with me. Did you know?" Kaela's eyes widened with surprise.

"I thought that might be the case. I have noticed

your afternoon naps, and your appetite changes. Have ye told the Baron yet?"

"Nay, and I am not going to, at least not for awhile."

"Why not, milady? 'Tis glorious news. Surely the Baron will be happy to know ye are carrying his son."

"'Tis a long story, Maude."

"Now, Kaela, 'Tis me ye are talking to. I have raised ye since ye were a wee babe. There's nothing ye can't tell me, love. What is the matter?" Maude, her hands on her hips, gave Kaela the same no nonsense look that her mother had always given her. Kaela burst into tears and the old nurse flew to her side and took her in her arms.

"There, there, child," Maude crooned, patting Kaela's back. "'Tis not as bad as that, love. 'Tis only natural for your feelings to be tender when ye carry a babe. Why, I remember when I carried my Arik. I drove my poor husband crazy with my constant blubbering."

Kaela smiled at that, pulled away from Maude, and wiped the tears from her face.

"Cameron does not want this baby," Kaela said, her voice forlorn.

"Nonsense, of course the man wants children," Maude said. Her tone left no room for argument.

"I overheard him last night talking to Thorsen. He had a son named Peter who died. He told Thorsen he would never love another child," Kaela sobbed.

"I didn't know the baron had been married before."

"He told me he had an unfortunate marriage, but until last night I had not known there had been a son. 'Twould seem I know naught of my husband. Everything is such a mess, Maude. I don't know what to do. I have tried to get Cameron to tell me about his past, but he won't. I don't know if he was married to this woman who hurt him very badly, or not. He is still devastated over the loss of his son."

"Have ye told him what's in your heart, lass?"

Kaela nodded. "How did you know?"

"'Tis obvious to anyone with eyes that the two of ye are in love."

Kaela shook her head. "My husband does not love me. He has made that very clear. Why do you think I am so miserable?"

"He may think he doesn't, but his actions prove otherwise. Don't look at me like that, Kaela. I know what I am talking about. The Baron has had many changes in his life recently and so have ye. Give yourself time to adjust. 'Tis truth, all will be well in time. I am sure he will be pleased about the babe once you tell him."

"I am not going to tell him, Maude. I don't want to tell anyone. You must keep my secret."

Maude shook her head at her young mistress and lifted her plump body off the bed.

"I will do as ye wish, milady. But ye will not be able to keep it a secret forever."

"I know, but 'tis what I wish for now."

"God's truth, I am thrilled at your news, Kaela. 'Twill be so nice to have a babe in the keep again. I know your mama and papa would be pleased, too."

"Aye," Kaela said, her eyes misty. "They would be. I am happy about the babe, Maude. I will be a good mother to this child, and give it all the love I have in my heart."

"I know ye will child, I know ye will. I will send up a nice bath for ye. 'Twill make ye feel better," Maude said as she left the room.

Kaela soaked in the hot bath until the water began

to grow cold. She did feel better, but her mind was still in turmoil. After she dressed, she made her way to the stables.

Searching Arik out, she asked him to saddle Sky. She planned to ride to the lake where she could enjoy the calming effect her special place always had on her. Her work would have to wait this day, because she needed time to herself. Mattie had begged to go with her, but Kaela had denied her, promising to play a game with her later in the afternoon. Brenna, busy with the tapestries, had hardly noticed when Kaela said she intended to ride.

The day was sunny with hardly a cloud in the sky. As Kaela rode by the orchards, she feasted on the beauty of the blossoming trees. She always felt better when she was outdoors close to nature. She urged Sky into a gallop and flew over the meadow toward the lake, relishing the feel of the wind in her hair.

She smiled over her success in leaving the castle unescorted. She had told Windrey, the gate keeper, she was meeting her husband at the mill. The old man had not questioned her and had lowered the gates immediately. Now she was free to enjoy these next few hours. She rode Sky at a break neck pace all the way around the lake before she stopped to let the mare rest.

Kaela slid to the ground and went to sit on a log by the water's edge. Questions filled her mind. She desperately needed to learn about Cameron's past. She would never understand him if he kept her in the dark. She considered asking Thorsen again, but knew he would not give in. She considered each of Cameron's vassals and finally chose Andrew. Cameron's brother would surely know all there was to know about his brother's past. Besides, she could argue, Andrew was her brother now, too. She would have to be careful though, find the right way to approach him. Kaela decided she would ask him on the morrow. Today she had to deal with her husband and her feelings toward him.

She did not want to see Cameron, but knew that was not an option. He had made it very clear last night that he would not be ignored. How could he make such passionate love to her and not care for her? He had told Thorsen he cared about her, he just didn't love her. He had pitied her and married her out of a sense of duty.

The pain rushed back again, and Kaela cried out her sorrow. She had so many unanswered questions. Had Cameron been married to this Elizabeth... had he loved her? What could a woman do to cause a man such bitterness? How had Peter died? How old had the child been?

Kaela vowed she would have the answers. Until she did, she would protect herself from her husband. If he did not want her love, she would bury it deep inside herself. She would nourish her love for their child and concentrate on its future.

Kaela could not deny her husband the physical love he needed. Aside from being her duty as his wife, her own body would not let her deny him. But she would not show him her vulnerability. Somehow, she would find a way to live with this sorrow. She had learned to live with fear after her ordeal with Broderick. She would learn how to live with Cameron's rejection of her love. She had no choice.

The sound of horses hooves intruded on her thoughts. She looked up, dismayed to see her husband galloping toward her. He looked furious. She had been found out. Kaela told herself that she would not let him get to her. Watching him dismount, she gulped, her courage faltering.

When Cameron stood in front of her, he reached out and pulled her to her feet.

"What do you think you are doing?"

"I came for a ride. 'Tis a beautiful day for being outside, is it not?" Kaela asked, her face expressionless.

"Windrey said you told him you were meeting me. God's teeth, Kaela, I thought for a moment you had been kidnapped again."

Cameron couldn't seem to keep the tremor out of his voice and the muscle in his cheek began to twitch. Kaela watched, fascinated.

"As you can see, my lord, I am fine. I wanted to come to the lake and so I did. I will not be a prisoner in my own home." Though Kaela spoke defiantly, her eyes held no emotion.

Cameron, used to seeing sparks flying from her green eyes, wondered where her fiery indignation had gone.

"Don't be ridiculous. You are not a prisoner."

"I am glad you agree."

"That does not mean you can leave the keep unescorted. You were foolish to do so and you know it."

Cameron's tone had warmed, but Kaela knew he was still very angry. Sweet Jesu, why could he not care for her? Kaela wanted only to be held in his arms, but remembering his words to Thorsen, she quenched the desire.

"I have been known to do foolish things," Kaela said. She had fallen in love with him—nothing could have been more foolish than that.

"You will not do it again, do you understand me?"

"I will not live in fear of Broderick any longer. I have always come to my lake when I have wanted to be alone. I want my life to be as it was, Cameron."

Puzzled, Cameron sensed something was very wrong. He had been worried about her feelings this morning, but she had been so passionate when they made love, he thought everything was all right between them. Now her behavior had thrown him off balance and he did not like the feeling.

"We will discuss this later, Kaela. Let us go home now."

He would have helped her mount, but Kaela pushed his hand away and climbed into the saddle.

She urged Sky over the meadow toward the keep. Cameron easily kept stride with her, but she ignored him. Once they entered the outer bailey, she slid from Sky's back and handed her reins to Arik. Without a word she left her husband and entered the keep to search out Mattie and play the game she had promised her.

More confused than ever, Cameron watched her walk away, but when one of his men called to him, he dismissed his wife from his mind. He would talk with her later, and demand an explanation for her strange behavior.

Kaela sat quietly through dinner, speaking to her husband only when he asked her a question. She challenged Thorsen to a game of chess after their meal and Cameron got the distinct feeling she intended to avoid him.

Later that night, when he got in bed beside his wife and she turned her back to him, he had no doubt that something troubled her. An exasperated sigh escaped his lips as he stared at her back.

"Why don't you tell me what is bothering you, wife?"

"There's naught. I am tired," Kaela said, still refusing to turn and acknowledge him.

Cameron placed his hand on her shoulder, turning her to him.

"Kaela, we have a marriage between us. We need to be open with each other. You should tell me when something concerns you."

Kaela ached just looking at him. She could not tell him she had overheard his conversation with Thorsen, nor could she tell him about the baby. She could not bear to hear him say he did not want their child.

"If you want our marriage to be open, Cameron, you can start by telling me about your past. Perhaps you would like to tell me about your life in Normandy. Why don't you tell me about the women you have known?" Kaela watched Cameron's face turn cold, the softness leave his eyes. He said nothing.

"'Tis as I thought. Good night, Cameron." Stonily, Kaela again turned her back to him.

Cameron said nothing, but he stared at her back for a long time. Even after the sound of her even breathing told him she was asleep, he continued to watch her. Finally, frustrated beyond endurance, he rolled over and forced himself to sleep.

❖   ❖   ❖

Over a fortnight passed and things were no better between Cameron and Kaela. In fact, Cameron thought dismally, they were worse. Kaela was more withdrawn than ever. At first he had considered her distancing herself from him a blessing. He needed the time to better understand his feelings for her. But he had long since given up that notion. She was constantly in his thoughts. He noticed she ate very little. Some mornings there were dark circles under her eyes, as if she hadn't slept.

He'd swallowed his pride after the first week, and tried to draw her out. Kaela resisted him at every turn. She went out of her way to avoid him, and everyone knew it. The only time she did not turn away from him was when he made love to her. Their unions were still filled with passion, but Kaela never initiated their intimacy and when it was over, she immediately pulled away from him.

Cameron was miserable. He missed his wife. He wanted to hear her laugh again, and see her green eyes blazing with mischief. He missed her companionship and the pleasure of talking with her. He noticed that, although she did not laugh anymore, she did not try to avoid anyone else. She still played with Mattie, and Brenna was often at her side. She even seemed to seek out the companionship of Thorsen, Johnathan, Andrew, and Patrick. No, the only one she wanted nothing to do with was her husband.

Cameron had no idea what had caused this distance between them. He treated Kaela the same as he always had, even better now, as he tried to get her to soften toward him, but nothing worked. Cameron found his moods turning blacker with each day. Amazed, he realized his wife's withdrawal hurt him. He had sworn he would not let another woman cause him pain, but somehow this wife of his had touched him.

This revelation made his mood even blacker, and his men began to go out of their way to avoid him. Only Mattie seemed to be oblivious to his bad humor, and they grew closer with each passing day. Mattie was the one bright spot in his life. He often sought out the little girl to tell her a story or play a game.

Cameron felt more empty with each passing day. He sat in front of the fire in the great hall late one night, unable to bring himself to climb the stairs and face his wife. He knew he was sulking, but could not stop himself. He had to do something to end this distance between himself and Kaela, but he was at a loss.

Engrossed in his thoughts, he did not hear Mattie approach. He jumped in surprise when she crawled into his lap and leaned back against his chest. He put his arms around her.

"What are you doing up, sweet pea? 'Tis long past your bed time."

"I woke up and couldn't go back to sleep. I went to your chamber, but you were not there. Kaela was asleep, so I came to look for you. Why are you here, Wolf?"

"I couldn't sleep either."

"Kaela is sad," Mattie said.

"Aye, sweet pea, she is, but I don't know why." Children were too damned perceptive.

Mattie turned in his arms and put her small arms around his neck, using his chest for a pillow. She yawned.

"Maybe you should play with her like you do me," Mattie suggested.

"Mayhap I should." Cameron laughed and gave Mattie an affectionate squeeze.

Kaela awoke in the middle of the night, alone. She panicked, thinking something must be wrong. Cameron had never left her alone at night before. She could tell his side of the bed had not been slept in. Putting on a robe, she hurried down the corridor to the nursery. Her panic grew when she found Mattie's bed empty. She ran down the stairs to the great hall on her way to the garrison to wake Johnathan and Thorsen.

Half-way across the hall, something caught her attention. Turning, she slowly walked toward the hearth. Her breath caught in her throat and her eyes grew misty at the sight before her. Her fierce warrior husband sat in the large chair before the fire, sound asleep. His cheek rested against Mattie's small dark head, one large hand buried in her hair.

Kaela stood for several minutes, watching them. Tears rolled down her cheeks. She felt something soften inside her at the sight of the two of them, these two people she loved so dearly. Innocent little Mattie had found a place in her husband's heart.

"If there is room for Mattie, husband, then perhaps your heart is not as dead as you believe. Mayhap there is room for me also," Kaela whispered. "I know there is love in you, Cameron. You give it in so many ways. I vow, husband, I will find a way to make you love me, or die trying."

Kaela stepped to Cameron's side and placed a hand on his shoulder. He came instantly awake, a startled look on his handsome face.

Kaela smiled down at him and Cameron thought his heart would shatter. It had been so long since he had seen her smile. God, he had missed her so.

"Come to bed, Cameron." She reached to take Mattie from his arms, but he stopped her.

"I will carry her."

"What are the two of you doing down here?"

"I couldn't sleep. Apparently Mattie couldn't either, so she joined me."

"You and she have grown quite close."

"Aye, she is a delightful child," Cameron said, cradling Mattie in his arms.

"I am glad. Mattie needs a father." Cameron made no reply, but her words affected him deeply. They put Mattie to bed and made their way to their own chamber. When they climbed in bed, Kaela rolled into his arms and lay her head on his chest.

"Good night, husband."

This was the first time she had called him *husband* in weeks. Cameron smiled in the darkness and drew her closer to him.

Chapter Sixteen

✦ ✦ ✦

The next morning Kaela went in search of her brother-in-law. She found Andrew in the outer bailey practicing at the quintain with Patrick.

"Andrew, could I speak with you, please."

"Aye, my lady, what can I do for you?"

"I would like to ride this morning. I thought you might be so kind as to escort me to the lake. 'Tis truly lovely this time of year."

"'Tis a wonderful idea, Kaela. Why don't I invite Brenna and Patrick to join us? We could make a picnic out of it."

"That would be nice, Andrew, and I would love to do that another time. But could we go alone today? I want very much to talk to you."

"Of course, Kaela," Andrew said and they made their way to the stables.

They rode slowly out to the lake. Andrew told her how he had grown to love Chaldron. Kaela teased him about his growing relationship with Brenna. When Andrew confided he intended to ask for Brenna's hand in marriage, Kaela smiled and gave him her blessing.

Once they reached the water's edge, they dismounted and stood while their mounts drank the cool water.

Then Andrew led the horses to a tree and tied their reins so they would not wander off. Kaela took his hand in hers and began to walk slowly around the lake's perimeter.

"I have always loved this place. My father taught me how to swim here the summer I was six years. My parents and I used to picnic here quite often. It has always been a place filled with happy memories. I find peace here when I am troubled."

"And you are troubled now, Kaela?" Andrew released her hand and put his arm around her shoulder. Hugging her to his side, they continued to walk.

Kaela sighed. "Aye, Andrew, I am greatly troubled. More than you know."

"It has not gone unnoticed, this sadness of yours. Brenna speaks of little else. We have all noticed, Kaela. Tell me how I can help you."

"I need to know about Cameron's past."

"What about it?" Andrew asked, his expression wary.

"I need to know about Elizabeth and Peter. Please, Andrew, tell me what happened."

Andrew sucked in his breath. "How do you know about Elizabeth and Peter? Has Cameron mentioned them to you?"

"Nay, that is the problem. Matilda told me about Elizabeth. Cameron will not tell me anything. I know that his past eats at him. He has a wall around his heart, Andrew. I don't know how to fight this hardness in him and find a way into his heart."

"He was hurt badly in the past, Kaela. I am sure with time he will confide in you."

"Nay, things have only grown more strained between us, Andrew. Surely you see that. Please, I am at my wit's end."

"'Tis Cameron's place to tell you of his past, Kaela. Surely things are not as bad as you think. I know my brother cares for you."

Kaela was desperate. She knew her only hope of saving her marriage was in understanding her husband's past. She decided to be honest with Andrew. She told him all that she had heard Cameron tell Thorsen. The tears flowed unchecked down her cheeks and she grasped his hand tightly in hers.

"Andrew, I am with child," she said, her voice soft.

"What?"

"I am carrying Cameron's babe within me."

"Kaela, 'Tis wonderful. Does Cameron know?"

"Nay, I found out the same day I overheard his conversation with Thorsen. He made it very plain that he had no love left to give another child, much less a wife. He had sworn his love to his dead son. How could I tell him I carried his babe? I could not bear to see the rejection on his face."

"He did not mean what he said, Kaela. He will love this child, I promise you. You do not understand what Cameron has been through."

"I know that. 'Tis why I am asking you to tell me what happened. How can I work this thing out with Cameron if I don't know what I am dealing with? Please, Andrew, I am begging you. Not only for my sake, and Cameron's, but for the sake of our child. Please, won't you help me?"

Andrew wiped away her tears, and, with a resigned sigh, said, "Aye, Kaela, I will help you. Cameron may never forgive me for betraying his confidence, but you need to know. Cameron must not lose you. He needs you desperately. Come, let us find a place to sit down.

'Tis a hard story to tell and mayhap even harder to hear."

"'Tis not my wish to cause problems between you and your brother, Andrew, but I don't know where else to turn," Kaela said, leading him to the shade beneath the trees. The May sun shone high in the sky and the day had grown quite warm.

They found a comfortable spot under an oak tree and sat down, leaning back against the giant trunk.

"To truly understand all that Cameron is feeling, you must still hear his story from him. However, I will tell you what I know."

Taking a deep breath, he began. "Our father died when Cameron was twenty years of age. He had been gone from home for many years, first training with William, then fighting at his side. Because of my father's illness, my parents called Cameron home when he was nineteen. Father had become too weak to oversee our vast properties. The responsibility fell to Cameron.

"The family grew closer during that long year. My father made it known on his death bed that he had chosen a wife for Cameron, a gentleman's agreement with the girl's father. They had trained together as squires, and had always hoped their children would marry. Her name was Elizabeth, a distant cousin to Queen Matilda. Naturally, William and Matilda favored the match. Cameron agreed, not only to please our father, but also the King. The two had never met and I remember Cameron was quite nervous about meeting his future bride. We teased him relentlessly, dreaming up visions of fat, ugly women.

"After my father's death, William called Cameron to court to meet his betrothed. Our whole family traveled with him. I will never forget the night William introduced Cameron to Elizabeth. He was entranced by her beauty. We all were. She was very fair, her hair so blonde it appeared almost white, and she had large blue eyes. Although Cameron was infatuated, Elizabeth behaved quite rudely to Cameron when she first met him. Enamored by her beauty, my brother hardly noticed.

"Elizabeth's father, Baron Lacy, had given her to Cameron. In the conceit and naivete of youth, Cameron was confident she would soon respond to him. Their marriage took place within a sennight, and we returned home.

"Before half-a-year passed Cameron realized he had made a terrible mistake. Elizabeth was mean, vindictive, and nothing he did pleased her. He became obsessed with making her love him, to no avail. Before the year was out, William sent for Cameron. Having had difficulty with his border properties in the north, the King took Cameron with him to settle the disputes. Matilda invited Elizabeth to court, and Cameron's wife went gladly.

"When Cameron returned after several months, he learned that his wife had been unfaithful to him with not one, but several members of the King's court. Elizabeth did not deny her infidelity. She threw her faithlessness up to him, ridiculing him as a lover. Devastated, Cameron felt he had lost face with his friends at court. He brought Elizabeth home and things between them quickly became intolerable."

Appalled at what she was hearing, Kaela stared at Andrew in bewilderment. He continued, so deeply lost in his memories, she knew he was no longer aware of her.

"Elizabeth said she had been in love with another man and had been denied that love because of her forced marriage to him. The man in question had married Elizabeth's cousin instead. When she had seen him at court, she begged him to bed her and the man refused.

"I think Elizabeth went a little crazy then. In her twisted thinking, Cameron had caused all her troubles. My brother was devastated. He believed himself to be truly in love with his wife. Within two months of their return from court, Elizabeth discovered she was with child. She taunted Cameron relentlessly during her confinement, telling him the child would not be his.

"I can't tell you how he agonized over her words. After Peter was born, 'twas soon apparent to everyone that the boy was truly Cameron's. The babe was the very image of his father.

"Outraged, Elizabeth closed her heart to the child. She even refused to nurse her son. Cameron was forced to bring in a wet nurse. Elizabeth became increasingly withdrawn and more hateful. She taunted Cameron at the evening meal in front of his family until Cameron finally started taking his meals in the nursery with Peter. He and the child became inseparable.

"Peter was a delightful child, full of life. He was greatly loved by all of my family. Once he learned to talk, he never stopped, questioning everything he saw. By the time the boy was two, Cameron had him learning to ride a horse. When he rode out in the afternoons, Cameron always took Peter with him.

"Just before Peter's third birthday, Cameron was called back to William's side. Peter cried the night through when his father left. To our amazement, Elizabeth seemed to take an interest in her son while

Cameron was away. She would coax him to come and sit with her in the evenings. Within a few weeks, she began taking him out in the afternoon and not returning to the keep until just before the sun set.

"One day, a few weeks before Cameron returned, I found her near the stream that runs through our property. She had pulled a switch from a nearby tree and was beating Peter. She had stripped the boy and raised welts on his skin. One of his eyes had been blackened and he was screaming hysterically. I wrested the child from her and brought him back to the keep. Mother tended his wounds. We did not allow Elizabeth to be alone with him again. When Cameron returned, we informed him of Elizabeth's behavior. God's truth, they had a terrible fight. We could hear Elizabeth screaming all the way down in the great hall. I don't know what she said to Cameron, but he struck her. He had never hit a woman before and has not done so since. He was filled with remorse that he had lost his control so completely.

"I was surprised he had not hit her sooner. She made his life a living hell, Kaela. Cameron told me later she had screamed her hatred for Peter. She could not forgive the child for being Cameron's. I am sure she resented the closeness the two shared. The child brought his father great happiness and Elizabeth hated Peter for that."

Kaela pressed her hands to her stomach, as if to reassure her babe. "I cannot imagine hating my own child. Please, Andrew, go on. What happened next?"

"Two nights later Elizabeth ran away. She took Peter with her. To this day we have no idea of her destination. Her father was no longer alive and she was estranged from her mother. I have always believed she had a lover and was on her way to him. She took the child out of spite, knowing his loss would hurt Cameron more than anything. She did not get far. 'Twas winter and a torrential rain set in not three hours after she left. I rode with Cameron as soon as we discovered what she had done, along with our brother Jean and several of Cameron's vassals. Thorsen is the best tracker I have ever seen, but even he could not find a trace of her in that downpour.

"Near dawn, we finally found them. Elizabeth was dead, her neck broken in the fall. Her horse must have been frightened by the storm and thrown her, or mayhap the beast missed its footing. Little Peter lay several yards away, unconscious. He had injured his head on a rock and there was blood. I will never forget the look on Cameron's face when he saw his son lying there, lifeless.

"I have never seen such a look since, Kaela, and I hope I never do again. Few people ever experience agony that deep.

"Cameron wrapped Peter in his cloak and we brought him home. He lived for a fortnight, never once regaining consciousness. He raged with fever and would call out for his father. 'Twas more than I could bear." A tremor shook Andrew at the memory and Kaela placed her hand over his.

"Cameron never left his side," he went on. "Not one bite of food passed his lips in all that time. I never once saw him sleep. He stood vigil over his son's small body until the very end.

"After Peter's burial, Cameron closed himself off in his chamber and drank himself into a stupor. Emaciated and ill from lack of food, he took a fever. He had lost his will to live. For days we thought we would lose him, but his fever broke and he recovered.

"Afterward he would not speak of Peter. 'Twas three years ago and he still won't talk about his son. Cameron threw himself into his work, running the family holding and training his men for battle. He pushed himself relentlessly. God's truth, he still does. When William announced his plans for Hastings, Cameron immediately joined him.

"There has never been another woman in his life, until you, Kaela. Many women wanted him, especially those at court, but none captured his heart. He might take one to bed, but never more than once, and he never gave any woman reason to think he would be interested in her. He swore he would never marry again; then he met you."

Kaela sobbed. Her heart bled for Cameron, but she had no idea how she could help him work through such grief.

"Cameron married me out of a sense of duty, Andrew. Nothing more," Kaela said, dully.

"Nay, Kaela. 'Tis what he tells himself, but 'tis not true. You must trust me in this. I know my brother. He cares very deeply for you. He has from the very beginning. There is this bond between you that is impossible to deny. I am not the only one who feels this way, Kaela. Thorsen, Johnathan, and Patrick have all noticed. Cameron needs you. I believe your love may be his salvation. If anyone can teach him to love again, you can.

"He loved Peter with all his heart, but he never truly loved Elizabeth. What he felt for her in the beginning was foolish infatuation. In the end, I am sure he hated her for what she had become, and for what she did to their child. Cameron is tormented by the past, but with you he has a future, a bright future. Please don't give up on him."

"I love him, Andrew. I could never give up on him. But I don't know how to reach him." Kaela had never felt so desperate.

"Be patient with him, and love him. I know you will find a way to reach him."

"I pray you are right, Andrew."

"This child you carry will help. Cameron will respond to his child. You see how he is with Mattie."

"Aye, mayhap you are right, but I don't want to tell him about the baby yet. Mayhap 'tis selfish of me, but I would like to know that he loves me, for myself. I will wait to tell him about our child."

They sat together in silence for awhile, needing to collect themselves. Kaela was overcome with grief for her husband and for the sweet little boy she would never know. Such a senseless death. She wondered how Cameron could bear his loss, and prayed for a way to help him.

The sun sat low in the sky when she and Andrew mounted their horses and rode slowly back to Chaldron.

❖   ❖   ❖

Kaela found a soothing comfort in the deserted chapel's quiet serenity. The warm afternoon sun streamed through the windows, casting patterns of light across the floor. The jewels inlaid in the heavy cross upon the altar sparkled with fiery brilliance. Kaela knelt before the altar, reflecting on the story Andrew had told her. The grief she felt was physical, reaching down to the quiet part of her soul to cause almost unbearable pain.

Tears streamed unheeded down her cheeks. Choked with despair and compassion for her husband, she poured out her heart to her maker.

"I cannot fight this battle without you, Lord. Please show me the way to reach Cameron. Help me find a way to heal his pain. I love him so, but I fear my love will not be enough to heal him. Help him, Father. Help me to reach him. I need him desperately. Our child needs him. Open his heart to us."

Time passed slowly while Kaela knelt in the stillness of the afternoon waiting for the inner peace she so desperately needed. When she began to feel the healing comfort she always found in prayer, she closed her eyes once more and offered thanks. Having found the strength she needed, she rose to her feet and soundlessly left the chapel, thankful that she was no longer alone.

When Cameron entered the great hall that evening, he took one look at his wife and knew that something had changed. She smiled warmly from across the room and looked genuinely glad to see him. His heart leapt in his chest, but he forced himself to keep his pace slow and steady as he crossed the hall to stand before her.

Kaela handed him a mug of ale and her smile broadened when she greeted him. A warm glow spread through Cameron's body. He ached to take her in his arms. He had missed her attention, and this change baffled him. If indeed she had changed. Mayhap her openness was a figment of his imagination. He scowled, and Kaela placed her small soft hand in his, gently squeezing his fingers.

"Why are you frowning, husband? Have you had a hard day?"

Her husky voice sounded like music to his ears, and his body grew taut with wanting her. She smelled like roses again and she wore her hair down, the long coppery tresses falling past her waist.

"Nay, wife." Cameron, oblivious to his vassals and the servants around them, replaced his frown with a grin. "'Tis good to see you smile." When she tried to release his hand, he clasped her fingers and placed them on his arm.

Maude had brought out several platters of delicious-smelling food and they crossed to the trestle table hand-in-hand. Kaela sat close to her husband, sharing his trencher. He and Thorsen were deep in conversation, but Kaela, consumed with his nearness, only listened half-heartedly. He kept his arm around her wile they ate, and once the trenchers were removed, Kaela rested her head against his shoulder, content to listen to the comforting sound of his voice. Relieved and happy to be close to him again, she drank in the sight and feel of him.

As a servant refilled their mugs with ale, Kaela leaned into her husband and placed her hand on his thigh. She whispered softly in his ear and Cameron felt his body harden in response.

"I am going to retire now, husband, and leave you to your men."

Cameron did not trust himself to speak. He could only nod when his eyes met hers. He saw some flicker of emotion mirrored in those green depths, but he could not define it. He followed her progress across the hall until she disappeared. A deep chuckle drew his attention.

He gazed across the table at his two best friends, answering their wide grins with his own.

"What has gotten into that lovely wife of yours, Wolf?"

"I know not, Johnathan, but whatever it is, I am thankful."

"'Twould seem you are back in her good graces, my lord," Thorsen said, giving Cameron a wink.

"Aye, it does at that." Anxious to retire, Cameron turned his attention to the necessary business of running the Chaldron's holdings. "Give me your report on the mill production, Johnathan. We will discuss our patrols on the morrow."

An hour later Cameron took the steps to his chamber two at a time. He did not dare hope Kaela would be waiting up for him, but perhaps this time she would not pull away from him after he made love to her. Oh, yes, he definitely planned to make love to her. His whole body ached to feel her touch.

❖   ❖   ❖

Kaela quickly dried the water from her body and wrapped herself in a soft blanket. Picking up her comb, she crossed to the hearth and knelt before the flickering firelight to dry her hair. She was as nervous as she had been on her wedding night. Somehow she felt as if she were giving herself to Cameron for the first time. She had come to terms with her love for her husband. Now that she understood the reasons for his behavior, she felt free to express her love for him.

She was afraid, but at the same time she felt hope for their future. Cameron might not feel he could love again, but she saw the love he tried to bury inside himself. She clung to the hope that she would be able to break down the wall he had built around his heart.

As for herself, she was through hiding her love for him. She would not pressure him with the words, but she would not hold back in expressing her feelings. She intended to love her husband openly, with the natural joy that welled up inside her. She would leave the rest to God.

Kaela had finished freeing the tangles from her hair when she heard Cameron enter the room. Her gaze met his for a long moment. She rose slowly to her feet, holding the blanket firmly around her shoulders.

"I thought you would already be asleep." Cameron's voice sounded hoarse.

"I was waiting for you."

"Did you want to talk?" he asked, moving toward her. When he stood before her, he took a strand of her hair and rubbed it between his fingers, bringing it to his lips for a moment. He devoured her with his eyes.

Kaela reached up on tiptoe and placed a soft kiss on the corner of his mouth, then, leaning back to gaze into his eyes, she released her hold on the blanket and let it slide to the floor.

"Nay, I am hungry for my husband."

Cameron's eyes feasted hungrily on her lush body. "God in heaven, but you are beautiful."

Kaela wrapped her arms around his neck and pulled his mouth down to hers for a searing kiss.

Molten desire coursed through Cameron's body. Both puzzled and delighted by her boldness, he felt intoxicated by the scent of her. He ran callused hands up and down the soft, smooth skin of her shoulders, then dipped down to caress the round curve of her buttocks.

Kaela moaned softly and with deft fingers began untying the laces of his tunic. Once they were freed, she pulled the soft fabric over his head and dropped it to the floor. She buried her hands in the coarse hair of his chest and ran the pads of her thumbs over his nipples. He groaned low in this throat.

Encouraged by his response, Kaela followed her hands with her tongue, placing light caresses that left a fever in his flesh wherever she touched him.

Cameron sucked in his breath when he felt his wife's hands move lower to remove his chausses. He brought his hands down to help her and Kaela pushed them away.

"Let me," she said, her eyes filled with passion.

He complied with her command, giving himself over to her caresses. She made him feel weak and powerful at the same time.

Kaela pressed her body into his and nuzzled his neck, then leaned down and took his nipple into her mouth, sucking hard.

Cameron thought his knees would buckle. Tangling his hands in her hair, he held her to him.

"I want to love you, Cameron, the same way you love me," she said, trailing feathery kisses down his taut stomach. Before he could catch his breath, she knelt before him, stroking his manhood.

"Kaela, don't…"

"Shh, Cameron." Holding his throbbing shaft firmly in one hand, she closed her soft sweet mouth around the tip of his arousal.

White hot desire raced through Cameron's body and he trembled from the mindless ecstasy. One moment his hands were fists at his side, the next they were buried in her hair, pressing her to him.

Kaela loved him wildly, running her tongue and hands down the hard hot length of his shaft, taking him over and over again into the deep recesses of her mouth.

Cameron went wild, pressing against her and groaning with the pure pleasure of what she did to him. When he could bear the sweet torture no longer, he lifted her to her feet.

"Kaela…" His voice sounded raspy and harsh with his need.

In one smooth motion he lifted her and brought her down on his hard pulsing shaft. Kaela wrapped her legs around his hips as he took her nipple into his mouth and began to suckle. She was so tight, so hot, that Cameron was desperate for fulfillment.

"I can't wait… Kaela." He found his release and spewed his seed into her.

Kaela clasped him tightly to her and placed soft wet kisses across his brow.

Cameron opened his passion-filled eyes to find her staring down at him.

"You will pay for that, wife." Smiling he carried her to the bed.

"Is that a promise?" Kaela's laughter quickly became a delighted moan when her husband knelt between her thighs. He lifted her legs over his shoulders and, taking her bottom in his hands, he gave her a wicked smile and brought his mouth down to suckle.

He loved her as fiercely as she had loved him. Kaela thought she would die from the pleasure his hot moist tongue brought her. He stroked her over and over, each caress bringing her closer to the sun. She called out to him, lost in the passion he created within her, and he answered with sweet love words of his own.

Once she had found her release, he entered her quickly and brought them both to fulfillment once more. They collapsed against each other.

When Kaela finally recovered her senses she was nestled in Cameron's arms, her head on his shoulder.

He ran his hands down her back. He couldn't stop touching her and his voice was hoarse when he spoke. "Kaela, why?"

Kaela placed a finger to his lips. "Don't question me, Cameron. I did what I did because I wanted to. Was—was it all right?" she asked, sounding very unsure of herself.

Cameron chuckled. How could she feel unsure after what they had just shared? "Had it been any more 'all right', wife, I would be a dead man. You have been so distant lately, Kaela, and now this sudden change. Why?" he asked, lifting her face to his.

"I have decided I am not going to fight my feelings for you any longer. I won't tell you things you do not want to hear, husband, but I won't hide my feelings either."

"Have I asked you to hide your feelings?" His heart ached as he watched a single tear trail down her cheek.

"You had naught to ask."

Cameron gently reached out with his thumb and wiped the tear away. "'Tis not my desire you hide your feelings, Kaela. I have missed you terribly." He kissed her then, a long lazy kiss that ignited the fire of her passion once again.

This time they loved each other slowly and tenderly. Kaela reached her fulfillment first, and she watched Cameron's face, inches above hers, when he poured his seed into her and called her name. They fell asleep still entwined in each other's arms.

❖   ❖   ❖

The next several days were pure bliss. Cameron did not understand the change in his wife, but he was grateful for it.

She surprised him one afternoon with a picnic at the lake. He made passionate love to her there under the shelter of the trees. He had never known such wild abandon. Kaela was completely uninhibited when she was in his arms.

In the afternoon Kaela often took Mattie and rode to the road construction. Cameron would take the laughing little girl up in front of him, and the three would ride to inspect the crops before returning to Chaldron. Cameron had never felt so at peace with himself and dwelled on the past less and less.

His wife delighted in teasing him and he relentlessly returned her teasing. Their nights were filled with passion, their days with love and laughter.

Kaela never once told him she loved him, but she showed him in a hundred ways. Unknowingly, Cameron returned her love, measure for measure.

Chapter Seventeen

✠   ✠   ✠

The hot June sun blazed down on the weary travelers. Skirting the top of a ridge, Baron Guy raised one hand to call a halt to the procession.

"'Tis about time you showed some mercy, brother." Lady Constance reined in beside him and mopped the sweat from her brow with her handkerchief.

"Behold Chaldron, dear sister." He swept his hand out before him. "We have arrived."

She shaded her eyes from the glaring sun and gazed down at the castle below with a glint of greed in her icy blue stare and smiled.

"God's teeth, Guy, you were right. 'Tis a veritable palace. I still cannot believe William let that little Saxon slut remain."

"Be careful, sister, your jealousy is showing."

"Don't you dare laugh at me." Constance turned her cold gaze on her brother. "Cameron D'Abernon should have been mine and you know it. I should be mistress of this keep, not some little Saxon slut whose father had ties to William. I still can't believe William would marry his finest warrior to a Saxon. I spent months wooing Cameron at court, then endured traveling to this godforsaken country to ensure he would be mine. I know Matilda was behind their marriage. You know she has never liked me."

"Perhaps that is because you have such a difficult time keeping a civil tongue in your head when you are in the presence of other beautiful women," Guy said, smirking.

"As you have a difficult time keeping your hands to yourself, brother," Constance retorted.

"Ah, but you ladies love being pursued, dear sister. Perhaps Cameron's new wife will be refreshing to look upon and already tiring of her husband."

"No woman in her right mind would choose another man over him."

"I had no trouble with Elizabeth. She seemed to love my roaming hands."

Constance smiled at her brother, but her eyes remained cold, hard.

"We have been seen, sister. I can hear the horns announcing our arrival. Be careful of your actions, Constance. 'Tis weary I am and in need of a pleasant night's rest before we continue our journey."

Cameron watched the riders from the wall walk and cursed fluently when he recognized Baron Guy's colors. Curse the saints, this was the last thing he needed. The man was an imbecile, a lecher. He was quite sure that Baron Guy had been among the many who had cuckolded him with Elizabeth. Things were finally going well with Kaela again and he did not want to see anything upset their new found peace. He grew even more distressed when he recognized Lady Constance among the riders. The woman was a thorn in his side.

He never should have coupled with her. The wench had been driving him crazy ever since with her ploys.

God's truth, he never would have slept with her in the first place if she had not plied him with wine and then accosted him in the dark passages of William's castle in Normandy. The woman had shoved his hand down her gown and rubbed up against him. Any man would have succumbed, he reasoned. He had done nothing to encourage her and had not taken her up on her offers since.

A feeling in his gut told him there would be trouble. Sighing, he ordered the gates opened. With any luck, their unwanted guests would stay only one night. He went to warn his wife they had company.

He found her several minutes later fast asleep in their bed chamber. God's teeth, 'twas the middle of the afternoon. Was she sick? He crossed the room and sat down beside her. His eyes roamed over her beautiful face as he caressed her hip. He laid his hand upon her forehead and was relieved to feel her cool to his touch. He shook her gently.

"Kaela, love, wake up. We have guests."

He smiled when she moaned and rolled onto her back. She didn't open her eyes and he knew she was still sound asleep. He chuckled deeply and began kissing her awake. After several minutes, he felt her smile against his mouth. He raised his eyes to see her lazy green ones looking back at him. She pulled him closer and kissed him deeply, running her hands through his hair.

Cameron, groaning low in his throat, reluctantly pulled away from her.

"Are you not feeling well, wife? I am surprised to find you sleeping in the middle of the day."

"I am fine, husband." Kaela stretched lazily.

Watching her, Cameron clamped down on his

growing desire.

"'Twas early this morn when you woke me with your lovemaking, husband. I was just catching up on my rest." She smiled and pulled him to her mouth once more.

Cameron kissed her again, running his hands down her warm body. All thoughts of the unwanted guests were forgotten for the moment. "'Tis truth you are getting fat and lazy, wife," he said, teasing her. "Aye, I believe you have gained a few pounds, sweeting. Perhaps married life agrees with you." He laughed aloud when Kaela blushed. He was surprised when she sat up abruptly and pulled his hands away from her waist.

"Why were you looking for me, husband? Was there something you wanted?"

"We have guests, wife. I am sure they are down in the great hall by now."

Kaela struggled to get off the bed. "Guests? Why didn't you tell me sooner, Cameron? Who is it? Do I know them? How many are there? I must speak to the cook right away."

Cameron couldn't help laughing. His wife had turned into a blur of activity. "There looked to be about twenty in their party, but only two are nobles. Baron Guy and his sister, Lady Constance. They are probably on their way to Normandy and have stopped for lodging."

"Have I met them?"

"Nay, they were not in London for our wedding. I believe Baron Guy was in Kent at the time."

"Why are you frowning, husband? Do you not like these people?" Kaela asked, a worried frown marring her brow.

Cameron went to her and took her hand in his. "I have no use for Baron Guy. He is at best a devious man, known for his reputation with the ladies. I want you to stay away from him, Kaela. I will not have my wife embarrassing me in front of my men."

Kaela felt as if he had struck her. She stepped away from him and pulled her hand from his tight grasp. "Why would you say such a thing to me, Cameron? I would never behave improperly with another man."

Cameron laughed, a harsh cruel laugh, and Kaela suddenly remembered Andrew's tale about Elizabeth and all the times she had cuckolded her husband. Her eyes burned with unshed tears.

"Women are all the same when an attractive man comes sniffing around. 'Tis for your own good that I warn you. Stay away from him, or you won't be happy with the consequences. Come, we have left them waiting long enough." Roughly, Cameron took her arm in his and led her from the room.

"'Tis wrong of you, husband," Kaela said. "Not all women are the same. I would do naught to shame you."

Cameron felt a twinge of remorse for his words, but shrugged the feeling off.

Kaela shivered with dread at the scene before her. Even though soldiers and servants filled the hall, she saw her guests standing close to the hearth, conversing with Brenna and Andrew. With Cameron still gripping her elbow, Kaela made her way toward them. Even from a distance Kaela could see fire spitting from Brenna's eyes and knew disaster was imminent. She noticed Johnathan and Thorsen leaning against the mantle. Both wore scowls on their faces. Patrick was nowhere to be seen. Kaela took a deep breath, fixed a false smile of welcome on her face, and approached her guests.

Cameron spoke before she had a chance to. She shot Brenna a pleading look, trying to convey her desire that her dear cousin keep her forthcoming outburst to herself.

"Baron Guy, Lady Constance, welcome to Chaldron Castle," Cameron said.

Kaela's eyes widened as she assessed the woman before her. She was really quite beautiful with her pale blonde hair and piercing blue eyes. She did not miss the hot, appraising look Lady Constance gave her husband. The woman acted as if Cameron were the only person in the room.

Cameron was too busy watching the baron to notice Constance. He didn't like the lecherous look in Baron Guy's eyes when the man appraised Kaela. "What brings you to Chaldron?" Cameron's voice sounded harsh to his own ears.

"Thank you for the welcome, Cameron," Guy said, reaching out and clasping Cameron's hand in a sturdy handshake. "Constance and I are on our way back to Normandy. We seek lodging for a night or so. As you know, my holdings in Normandy are quite substantial and I have been away from them too long, I fear. As for Constance, she is desirous to join in the victory celebration William and Matilda are holding at court. 'Tis said the affair is to be quite extravagant."

Shock held Kaela still when the handsome knight took her hand in his. He leaned over and brought her palm to his lips. To her dismay, he turned her hand and placed his kiss on her wrist.

Kaela felt instant revulsion and quickly pulled her hand free, but not before Cameron tightened his hold on her elbow.

"Forgive me, dear Lady, if I have offended you with my talk. I understand you are Saxon." Guy swept her body with his bold gaze.

Kaela felt as if she stood without her clothes. Instinctively, she moved closer to her husband.

"The lady is now a D'Abernon and has given her pledge of fealty to William. Allow me to introduce my wife, Lady Kaela," Cameron growled. He wanted to throttle the randy goat. How dare the bastard look at his wife like that?

"Come, Cameron," Lady Constance said, placing her hand on Cameron's arm, "the chit is still a bloody Saxon and must resent our invasion."

Kaela wanted to slap the stupid woman's hand away. Instead, she put her arm around her husband's waist and stared into the woman's ice-blue eyes.

"Nay, Lady Constance, my father was a great friend to King Edward and King William. He traveled to your country many times and always spoke highly of Normandy. 'Tis a fact he would have much preferred William's rule over Harold's. You and your brother are welcome in our home."

Constance gave her a dazzling smile, but Kaela did not miss the cold dislike in the woman's eyes.

"Kaela, I have ordered rooms prepared for our guests. They must be tired from their journey. 'Tis a fact, poor Lady Constance looks quite bedraggled." Brenna gave her cousin a wicked grin and called out to Maude. "Maude, come and show our guests to their chambers where they can rest and freshen up."

Kaela moved to her cousin's side as their two visitors left the hall. "What have you done, Brenna? You look like the cat who ate the cream," Kaela whispered.

"Why, Kaela dear, I have done nothing that rude

little witch didn't deserve," Brenna whispered back, beaming from ear to ear.

Kaela raised one eyebrow and waited.

Brenna's eyes sparkled with mischief. "I gave them the two chambers closest to the east tower."

Kaela threw back her head and laughed. "Brenna, you know those rooms are closest to the jakes. With the strong winds we are having, they will be quite miserable."

"Aye, that witch deserves to be miserable, as does her lecherous brother. Saint Ambrose's bones, I saw the way he gawked at you. Besides, you should have heard that woman insulting my Saxon heritage before you came down. Worse, she implied Andrew spent too much time with dogs to recognize a true lady's beauty."

"God's teeth," Kaela gasped.

"The old crone won't be here long if I can help it. The jakes were supposed to be limed today, but I have already canceled that order. We shall see how long her delicate lady's nose can stand the smell."

Both women burst out laughing, gaining the attention of Cameron and his vassals.

"I do not see what is so funny, wife."

Kaela moved quickly to Cameron's side as Andrew said, "It seems that Brenna has placed our esteemed guests in the chambers closest to the jakes."

Johnathan and Thorsen roared with laughter, approval shining in their eyes.

His voice cold, Cameron leaned down and whispered to Kaela, "Stay away from him."

Kaela wanted to cry out against the injustice of his words.

❖   ❖   ❖

Later that evening, Kaela sighed, then she motioned for Maude to bring in the fresh honey cakes cook had prepared for dessert. Dinner had been an ordeal. Lady Constance had made several snide remarks, even going so far as to complain about the food. Kaela was fuming. Everyone in England knew no finer fare existed than that served at Chaldron. The woman was a shrew and blatantly flirted with Cameron. Kaela could tell by the intimate looks the bitch gave her husband, she had known him intimately. To make matters worse, she had to slap Baron Guy's hand away twice. Seated to her left, he had the gall to actually place his hand on her thigh. Cameron remained aloof, ignoring Lady Constance's overtures, though he smiled politely at her. Kaela did not know what to do.

She excused herself shortly after the evening meal to put Mattie to bed. She stayed with her niece for quite awhile, letting the child soothe her frayed nerves. Once Mattie had fallen asleep, Kaela stepped out on the parapet for a moment to collect herself before facing her guests again. She heard Lady Constance's voice drifting up to her.

"'Tis truth, Mary, the man still wants me. Why, he can't take his eyes off me."

"Seems to me, mistress, he was much besotted with his new bride," the maid answered.

"Nonsense, the girl is a hag. Why, her hair is a horrible red. I am convinced William ordered Cameron to marry the little slut. I am the one he wanted. With any luck, I will convince him to set her aside. Chaldron Castle deserves a real lady as its mistress, not some little Saxon whore."

Kaela refused to listen to more and quickly stepped back into the room. Shaking with anger, she made her way back to the hall. She intended to find her husband and demand he order these people from her home, but he had disappeared.

"Brenna, have you seen Cameron?"

"Nay, Kaela, he left some time ago with Baron Guy and Johnathan. I have no idea where they went."

As they spoke, Constance reentered the hall and gave Kaela a smug look.

"I have had all I can take of that bitch's company. If you will excuse me, cousin, I am off to the kitchens to compliment cook and see to the preparations for the morrow." Kaela stormed from the hall.

An hour later, Kaela walked to her chamber. A headache pounded at her temples. Praying her offensive guests would depart in the morn, she pushed open her chamber door. There before her she saw her husband with Lady Constance in his arms. The bitch had her body pressed against his and was kissing him. Kaela screamed her outrage and watched Cameron jump away from the woman, his face a storm cloud. But Kaela didn't wait for explanations. She turned and fled the room. She heard Cameron curse loudly and Constance began to laugh. Unable to breathe, Kaela flew down the hall.

She found herself in the north tower, blessedly thankful to find the room unoccupied. Walking quickly to the narrow window, she breathed in great gulps of the night air.

Her hand trembled as she covered her mouth to hold back the sobs that threatened to come forth. Dear God, he had betrayed her. Kaela still could not believe what she had seen. Never had she thought her husband would betray their wedding vows, yet she had seen with her own eyes. He had even taken the bitch to their bed chamber. Kaela felt the slow splintering of her heart and could no longer hold back the sobs. Tears of hurt and frustration spilled down her cheeks. She gasped when two rough hands came down on her shoulders to spin her around.

Cameron loomed over her, his jaw set in fierce determination.

"'Twas not what it seemed, Kaela."

"Oh? Pray tell me then, my lord, what was it? How do you explain being in our chamber with that woman in your arms? You were kissing her!"

"Nay, wife, she was kissing me."

"What difference does that make?" Kaela said, trying with no avail to free herself from his grasp.

"Quite a bit."

"Cameron, you are twice that woman's size. Are you trying to tell me she forced you? By the Virgin's nightrail, you must truly think me a fool."

"Aye, wife, I do." When she would have interrupted, Cameron laid his finger across her lips. "Nay Kaela, close your mouth and listen to me. The woman caught me by surprise. I turned around and there she was. She threw herself into my arms and before I could react, you walked in."

"Ha! I heard her in the courtyard earlier bragging about how much you wanted her. You have slept with her before, haven't you?" Kaela saw the truth in his eyes and she stiffened.

"Aye, I slept with her once. 'Twas long ago back in Normandy and meant nothing. Damn it, I do not have to explain myself to you. I have no interest in her. She is a conniving bitch. Had you stayed a moment longer, you would have heard me tell her so. She and her brother leave at first light."

Kaela felt somewhat appeased at his words, but too stubborn and angry to admit it, she glared at him and said nothing.

"I will not have this foolishness from you, Kaela. Come, 'Tis time for bed," Cameron said, taking her hand and pulling her toward the stairs.

"Nay, Cameron. I am not ready to retire. I would stay here longer."

"I will not discuss this further, wife."

"I have no wish to talk, but hear me well. I want that woman gone from my home by the morn. I promise I will come in soon. Give me these few minutes alone, please."

"I will go and check on Mattie. I expect you in our chamber by the time I get there."

Resenting his demanding attitude, Kaela only nodded. He had no right to give her orders. Still shaking with anger and hurt, she admitted she believed him. Now that he was gone, she allowed herself to feel the immense relief his words had brought.

She walked out onto the wall-walk and let the night breeze dry her tears. Her heart slowed, and she smiled, remembering the look on her husband's face when she had walked in and found him with Lady Constance. What he said was true—he had not betrayed her. Sweet Jesu, she loved him so much. Her love for him grew daily, as the child in her womb did. Their child. The time had come to tell Cameron about the babe. He might not love her, but he cared enough for her to worry about her feelings. He had been frantic to have her believe his innocence. She had seen the anxiety in his eyes. Things had been so good between them lately. Aye, 'twas time to tell him. She prayed, wanting with all her heart for him to be happy about the babe.

"Ah, my little dove, at last I have found you."

Kaela froze at the sound of the voice behind her, then whipped around. Her eyes widened when she found Baron Guy standing very close to her. A sick sense of dread enveloped her when she looked into his eyes.

"You were looking for me?" Kaela winced at the tremor in her voice. She would not show this man her fear.

"I heard what happened earlier. I only wanted to make sure you were all right."

"I am fine," Kaela stated, pleased that her voice was firm once again.

"'Tis a pity, but 'twas to be expected. Cameron and Constance have been lovers for a long time now."

"'Tis a lie."

"Nay, m'lady. 'Tis quite true. 'Twas expected they would marry. My dear sister was most upset upon learning William had forced Cameron to marry you."

"You are a liar." Kaela squared her shoulders and tried to make her way past him, but his arm snaked out and he pulled her against his chest.

"Ah, little dove, you are so soft, just as I knew you would be. Come, let me console you. You will forget your husband in no time." Guy ran his hands down her back and Kaela felt sick with revulsion, she tried desperately to free herself.

"Let me go or I will scream."

Kaela cried out when he grabbed her hair, jerked her head back, then thrust his tongue in her mouth. Although bile rose in her throat, she struggled against him. With all her might, she kicked his shins. At the moment she thought she would suffocate for lack of air, she heard a low growl. Then she was free. She stumbled, losing her balance, and came precariously close to the edge of the walk way before a large hand pulled her back to safety.

Kaela looked up to see her husband's furious face. She had never seen anything more beautiful in her life. Gulping for air, she watched him turn and slam his fist into Baron Guy's face.

"You sorry bastard! How dare you touch my wife?"

Baron Guy steadied himself with one hand against the wall and met Cameron's furious gaze. "Don't fool yourself, D'Abernon. Your wife was consoling herself in my arms."

"'Tis a lie. He attacked me."

"Why are you so surprised, Cameron? Elizabeth loved my touch as much."

Cameron lunged, knocking the man down. Leaping on top of Guy, he slammed his huge fist into the man's face. Kaela screamed, a blood curdling scream that rent the night air and sent soldiers running. Thorsen was the first to reach them and immediately pulled Cameron off Baron Guy. When Cameron lunged for the baron again, Thorsen held his friend back with both arms.

"'Tis enough, Wolf. The bastard is unconscious. Anymore and 'twill kill him."

"'Tis what the whoreson deserves," Cameron muttered, stepping back. "Get him out of my sight, Thorsen. Lock him in the Garrison for the night. I want him and his sister out of here at first light."

"Aye, Cameron, I will take care of him. You had best see to your wife."

Kaela watched in shocked silence as Thorsen threw the man over his shoulder and descended the tower stairs. Her gaze flew to Cameron's face and her body froze at the hatred she saw in his eyes.

"'Twas your wish to punish me for my indiscretion with Constance?" He spoke in a voice so steely soft, she barely heard him, but she did not miss the rage.

"Nay, Cameron. The animal attacked me."

Cameron seethed with rage. He ground his teeth and glared at her. "You lie!"

Kaela sucked in her breath at his words. She felt as if he had struck her. Tears rushed to her eyes. With a shaky hand, she angrily wiped them away. "How dare you call me a liar, you conceited ass. That animal attacked me. Why is it I am expected to believe your innocence when I find you wrapped in that bitch's arms, but you immediately condemn me. God's teeth, Cameron, the man is twice my size. Could you not see I was fighting him? You know how I have struggled with my fear of men, what I have had to overcome since Broderick's attack. How dare you…" Kaela's voice broke and she turned from him only to be scooped up and thrown over his shoulder.

"Put me down, you big oaf," Kaela cried.

"'Tis not the place to have this discussion, Kaela. I am taking you to our chamber," Cameron said, clamping his arm across her bottom.

Kaela kicked and screamed.

"Be still. I just found my wife in another man's arms. I will dare whatever I damn well please. If you persist in screaming, the whole castle will know about this."

Kaela shut her mouth, but only because she desperately needed air in her burning lungs.

Seconds later, Cameron threw open the door to their chamber, strode across the room, and dumped her none to gently on the bed. He crossed the room again and barred the door. Kaela flew to her feet and threw herself at him, pounding her fists against his chest.

"How dare you not believe me, I am your wife!"

"You, my precious wife, are a lying bitch."

Kaela jerked away from him and wiped furiously at her tears. The pain of his words threatened to crush her. She felt a tight band around her chest squeezing the very air from her lungs. She met his gaze defiantly, shocked to see her pain mirrored in his eyes.

"You are wrong, husband. I would never cuckold you. The man attacked me."

Cameron turned from her and walked to the hearth, leaning his arms against the mantle. "It matters naught what you say. All women are alike. But I warn you, Kaela, I will not tolerate infidelity from you."

"You are wrong, Cameron. Your opinion of me matters a great deal. I am your wife, and I deserve your respect. I have done nothing to cause you to distrust me. What you saw was Baron Guy forcing himself on me. I believed you about Constance. Why can't you believe me?"

Kaela's voice was soft and pleading. Against his will, he turned to look at her. Cameron saw the naked pain in her eyes and winced. Strange—Elizabeth had thrown her treachery in his face, doing naught to deny her infidelities. Had he been wrong? Curse the saints, he knew Guy was a lecher. He had no doubt the man would attack Kaela.

"All right, I believe you," Cameron said, his voice clipped and hard. "'Tis late, let us go to bed."

"Nay, husband. I can't live like this anymore. You

will never trust me until you can learn to deal with your past. Talk to me, Cameron. Tell me why you feel such distrust."

Her voice was soft and beseeching, like a caress. She moved closer to him and laid her hand on his arm. He felt like he had been burned and pulled away from her. "I have nothing to say. I do not wish to talk about my past. 'Tis buried and I plan to leave it that way."

"'Tis buried within you Cameron and 'tis eating you alive. Can't you see you will never be free of the pain until you deal with it."

Cameron crossed to the bed and stripped off his tunic. He couldn't look at her. "I know naught of what you speak. 'Tis nonsense. Come to bed."

Kaela took a deep breath. "I know about Elizabeth and Peter."

Cameron whirled to face her. He closed his eyes tightly against the painful memories. "What do you know?" His voice was deadly quiet.

"I know about your disastrous marriage to Elizabeth. I know she was constantly unfaithful to you. I know about Peter, about his death." Kaela's voice broke. She struggled to meet his gaze.

"Who told you?"

Kaela shuddered. "Andrew."

"God's blood, I never thought my own brother would betray me."

Kaela ran to him, clasping his hands in hers. He pulled away from her, and crossed back to the hearth. Throwing himself into a chair, he stared unseeing into the flames. Kaela followed him.

"Andrew did not betray you. Please, you must listen to me, Cameron."

"Nay, I will hear no more of this."

"You have to!" She fell to her knees before him and took his hands in hers. Tears streamed down her face. Taking a deep breath, she said a silent prayer she would be able to reach him. "I am your wife, Cameron. You stood before a priest and took holy vows with me. I have honored those vows, and would do naught to break them. I love you."

"I don't want your love."

"Aye, I am well aware of that. But as your wife I deserve your respect and I deserve to be heard. You are going to listen to what I have to say tonight. Then we will never speak of the past again, if that is your wish." Kaela hesitated, but continued before he could interrupt her. She held tightly to his hand, grateful he did not pull away from her.

"The night I so foolishly told you I loved you, I felt you pull away from me. I was confused with your behavior, but it was not until I overheard your conversation with Thorsen that I began to understand that you did not want my love."

"What conversation?" Cameron looked truly puzzled.

"I was in the North Tower one evening when you and Thorsen stopped below me. You told him that you did not love me or want my love. I understand now that you married me from some misguided sense of duty. Thorsen tried to speak to you about Elizabeth and Peter. 'Tis how I learned of them."

"'Tis why you became so withdrawn?"

"Aye."

"And the reason for your sudden change of heart?"

Kaela did not like the cold control in his voice, but she answered him. "Andrew."

"I see. I do not want your pity, Kaela."

"'Tis glad I am to hear it, my lord, for I would never pity you. Nay, Cameron, let me finish. I was desperate to understand what had happened in your life to make you so cold and uncaring. Without understanding, I could not continue to live with you as your wife. I felt used and betrayed. I approached Thorsen several times, but he would tell me nothing. Finally, in my desperation, I appealed to Andrew. Your brother loves you. He could see how unhappy we were. I told him everything I had overheard and begged him to tell me about your past. He said the same thing Thorsen did."

"Which was?"

"That 'twas your place to tell me."

"He was right."

"Would you have ever told me, Cameron?"

"Nay." His voice was frigid. "I will never forgive Andrew for this."

"You cannot blame your brother. I—I told him something else, which is why he finally consented."

"What could you have possibly told him to cause such a betrayal?"

"'Tis not important now. 'Twas not a betrayal, Cameron. Andrew loves you. Because of his love and concern for us, and his desire to see this marriage work, he told me."

Cameron's face was a stone mask. Kaela pressed on anyway.

"'Tis because of Peter's loss that you refuse to love again?"

"I will not discuss Peter with you. Do not mention his name again."

"Aye, you will. Tonight you will. I will not live like this any longer. You promised never to betray me, and yet you betray me everyday by withholding your love from me."

"I have no love left to give, Kaela."

"'Tis nonsense, Cameron. I can see the love in you. God's truth, look at the way you are with Mattie. You cannot sit here and tell me you do not love the child."

Stony silence.

"You can't hide behind your order and discipline. Open your eyes for, God's sake. You feel guilt over your son's death. Why don't you just admit the truth?"

Cameron lunged from his chair, knocking Kaela backward on the furs that covered the floor. Oblivious to her, he looked lost and far away. "Aye, damn you, I feel guilty. 'Twas my fault."

Kaela rose slowly to her feet. She felt the life within her stir and found courage to continue.

"How can you say his death was your fault?"

"I wasn't there to protect him. I knew what a bitch she was. God's truth, she hated her own child simply because I was his father. I knew, but I left him with her anyway."

"Cameron, you left him with your family. Andrew told me Elizabeth usually had nothing to do with the child. He was in a castle full of adults. Your mother was there, and your brothers. There is no way you could have known what she had planned. No one could know. 'Tis not your fault."

"He was so small and helpless. His face so pale." Cameron raked a shaky hand through his hair. "He called to me over and over in his delirium. I tried to soothe him, but he didn't hear me. When he died, something in me died with him. I have no love left to give, Kaela. Love died with my son." His voice was raw with grief. He raised his eyes to hers and she cringed at the pain she saw there. She went to him and put her arms around his waist, but he pulled away.

"I refuse to believe that," she whispered.

Cameron laughed at her, but it was laughter full of anguish.

"'Tis true, none the less. Nothing you can say will change that."

"Cameron, did you bury your love for your son with him?" Kaela asked softly.

Cameron's head jerked up. For several agonizing seconds, he stared at her. "What say you?"

"Did you stop loving Peter the day you put his body in that grave?"

Cameron gasped, remembering his son's cold lifeless body. "Of course not."

"I see. Do you love him any less now than you did when he was alive?" Her voice soft as a spring breeze, she watched him.

"Nay." Tears ran down his face, but he was unaware of them. "I will always love my son."

"Aye, I am certain that you will. When you truly love someone, husband, it transcends death. True love is eternal. 'Tis forever."

"Beyond death? Forever?"

"Aye. Nothing you could ever do would change your love for Peter. When he was alive, your love for him made his life happy. Andrew told me of the closeness between you. There's naught can ever change that. Peter is not completely lost to you, Cameron. He is in your heart and he always will be. You have precious memories of your son. 'Tis truly my belief you will be with him again someday. His body is gone, but his spirit lives on, just as the love you shared does. In your guilt and anguish over his death, you tried to bury that love, thinking the absence of love would mean the absence of pain. You are mistaken. 'Tis that very love that will heal your pain, husband. You are the bravest warrior I know. You must find the courage within yourself to face your son's ghost. Until you do, you will never be free."

"'Tis nonsense. I will listen to no more." Cameron turned and walked toward the doorway.

Kaela laid her hand on his shoulder, stopping him. "I am right about this. If you will not listen to me, you are going to destroy our every chance for happiness. Look at me, Cameron."

Cameron turned slowly and forced himself to meet her eyes.

"I love you. I cannot help how I feel. No matter what you say, I believe you care for me. I know there is love in you. You have only to free yourself from your anguish. Peter is dead, Cameron, and you are alive. I pray you will not live the rest of your life as a dead man. Peter would not have wanted that. I cannot change what Elizabeth was. I can only tell you I am nothing like her. I will give you my heart, my loyalty, everything that I am, if you will only take the gift. I need your love, husband. So does Mattie. 'Tis the one thing that makes life rich and worth living. Please, Cameron, for the sake of our happiness, won't you stop running away? You are poisoning your very soul by holding so much pain inside."

"You ask more than I can give, Kaela. I told you before that I had no desire for marriage. This is exactly why. You ask too much. I give you my loyalty and my protection. I will never be unfaithful to our vows. There is nothing more I can give you."

"I see. Then I shall do my best to shield my love

from you, Cameron. I will not burden you further."
She walked to the door and lifted the latch.

"Where are you going?"

"I will sleep with Mattie tonight. I cannot bear
another minute in your presence."

"You need not leave. I am going to the garrison. I
want to make sure our guests are gone with the dawn."
He left without another word.

Kaela moved to the bed and lay down, drawing the
furs up over her head. 'Twas a long time before the
tears came, but once they did, they were unending.

Chapter Eighteen

✥ ✥ ✥

The air felt heavy, oppressive. Or perhaps the trouble lay within her heavy heart. Kaela watched the departure of her guests from the wall's walkway. Cameron stood in the outer bailey with Thorsen. He had not returned to their chamber. During the long, lonely night Kaela had not expected him, but she missed him terribly. She watched him now, his legs braced apart, tension in his stance. His face looked as dark as a thunder cloud. To her utter amazement, she saw Lady Constance turn and blow her husband a kiss. Cameron's scowl grew even deeper. He turned and stalked over to the stables. A few minutes later, he came tearing out astride Goliath and galloped across the draw bridge.

Sighing, Kaela entered her chamber to dress for the day. She had no idea what she should do now. Cameron seemed like a stranger to her. She had poured out her heart to him, but her words had fallen on deaf ears.

When she entered the hall she found Brenna waiting for her.

"Well, cousin, 'twould seem our unwanted guests have taken their leave," Brenna said, a smug grin on her face.

"Aye, and good riddance."

"What is wrong? You look like death." Brenna grabbed Kaela by the hand and pulled her over to the trestle table, then pushed her down on a bench.

"Have you eaten anything, Kaela?"

"Nay, I am not hungry."

"You have to eat to keep up your strength. Tell me what bothers you. 'Tis Cameron?"

"Aye, I cannot make him understand, Brenna."

"What do you mean?"

Kaela put her head in her hands. "'Tis a long story, and I am not up to the telling. Suffice it to say, my husband is determined to shut me out of his heart and there is naught I can do about it."

"Nay, surely you are wrong, Kaela. How could the man not love you?"

"Very easily, it seems."

"Nay, I do not believe it, cousin. I see the way he looks at you. Why, when you were so distant from him, he was impossible to be around. I think you are wrong. Surely Cameron loves you. Have you told him about the babe?"

"I planned to tell him last night, but I never—our guest's arrival interfered. Now I am afraid to tell him, and you are wrong. He does not love me. What you see in his eyes is lust, not love. He will lose that look very soon, once he sees me swollen with his child." Kaela's voice caught on a sob and she hastily wiped away her tears, disgusted with herself for her weakness.

"There now, Kaela, don't cry. 'Tis not as bad as that. You are emotional because of the babe. Cameron will want the child. I think you must tell him soon."

"I will tell him nothing. Let him find out for

himself." She stood and tugged at Brenna's hand. "Come, cousin, I will help you with the new tapestries. They are almost finished, are they not?"

Brenna fell into step at her side. "Aye, and they are beautiful. Your husband will be quite pleased."

"Hmph," Kaela snorted. "I do not want to talk about him anymore."

"All right, but I am here if you need to talk to me."

Kaela's eyes filled with tears once more and she hugged her cousin. "I know and I thank you. Now let us get busy."

✣   ✣   ✣

Cameron did not return to the keep until late afternoon. His mood had not improved and his vassals gave him a wide berth.

He was giving Goliath a rub down when Mattie surprised him by running into the stall. She threw her chubby little arms around his leg and squealed. Goliath snorted and started to rear up on his hind legs. Cameron grabbed the stallion by his shiny black mane and soothed him. Then he grabbed Mattie in one arm and strode from the stall.

"Don't ever do anything that stupid again," he shouted, shaking her. "You could have been hurt."

Mattie gazed up at him with wide blue eyes and promptly burst into tears. Cameron hugged her to him for a moment, cursing himself for frightening the child.

"I'm sorry Mattie, but you scared me. Goliath might have injured you." He set her away from him.

"I wanted to play with you, Wolf. I did not see you yesterday."

"I'm busy, sweet pea." God's truth, he did not want to feel these emotions. Kaela was right. He had let himself get close to this child. Their closeness had been a mistake.

"Come on, Wolf, lets play hide and seek in the orchard. I have a new bow and arrow Patrick made for me. Mayhap I can shoot an apple from a tree." Her long black eyelashes spiky from her recent tears, she smiled up at him. Her eyes were so much like Peter's. The realization brought a sudden ache to Cameron's chest.

"Nay, I have no time for you, today. Leave me be, Mattie." His voice sounded cold and cruel, even to his own ears. He watched in dismay as Mattie's lip trembled and fresh tears spilled down her cheeks.

"That will be enough, Cameron."

He turned at the sound of his wife's voice. The look she gave him made him feel cold inside. He watched her scoop Mattie into her arms and carry her away.

He shook his head in disgust, not understanding why he had said the things he had. His emotions had been spinning out of control. He remembered his wife's words the night before. Again, he felt the wrenching pain they had caused.

Cameron cursed and went back to grooming Goliath. He brushed the stallion vigorously, thinking with every stroke about the fiery haired vixen who had upset his life. Fervently, he promised himself he would put the little hellion from his mind, concentrate on his work, regain his discipline. She would learn her place, by God, and she would be happy, damn it. He would see that she outgrew these foolish notions of love.

"I will speak with you now, Cameron."

He winced at the quiet fury in her voice and turned to her. 'Twas no time like the present to start her lessons, but sweet Jesu, she was a vision. Bright spots of color stained her cheeks and her eyes blazed with fire. To his dismay he felt the familiar tightening in his loins. Before he could think better of his action, he reached out and pulled her against him.

Kaela let out an outraged cry and kicked him in the shin. He released her immediately, his loud curse cutting the silence around them. Kaela darted from Goliath's stall, then whirled to face him.

He reached her in three long strides and grabbed for her arm.

Kaela took a step back. "Nay, touch me not, Cameron."

Cameron's mouth flew open in stunned surprise at the venom in her voice. He bit back another curse and glared at her. "That's enough, Kaela," he said, tight-lipped.

"Not nearly enough. How dare you treat Mattie that way." With her fists clenched at her sides, she looked ready to attack.

"I did not mean it the way it sounded. I..."

"Don't lie to me, or to yourself. I don't want to hear your excuses. I know exactly why you treated her so coldly. I won't have it, Cameron. Mattie is an innocent, helpless little girl. You will not punish her because you are angry over Peter's death."

"That had nothing to do with it."

"'Tis exactly why you treated her that way and we both know it. If you feel anger and resentment, take it out on me, but leave Mattie alone. God's teeth, Cameron, that little girl adores you. You have no right to gain her trust, her love, and then turn on her."

Kaela's tears flowed unchecked and she had trouble speaking. Her husband's image blurred before her. She wiped furiously at her tears. "Mattie has lost both of her parents. Brenna and I are all she has now. And y— you h—have let h—her think you c—care about her." Kaela choked out the words. "How could you be so cruel?"

"Kaela, I didn't mean..."

"I won't have it, Cameron. You want a loveless marriage, then fine. You shall have one. You can have all the order and discipline you want, and you needn't worry about problems from me again. I will leave you alone. You shall have exactly the kind of wife you want. I will give my love to the people who want and need it. But you will not hurt Mattie, do you hear me?"

"I imagine everyone in the keep hears you. You are shouting loud enough to knock the walls down, but aye, I hear you. You are right. I am sorry for the way I treated Mattie. 'Twill not happen again. I do truly care about the child. I will make it up to her." Cameron spoke quietly in a very controlled voice, with no hint of emotion on his face. He might have been talking about the weather.

Kaela just stared at him for a moment. She felt very old and very, very tired. Without another word, she turned and left the stable. She didn't glance back as she walked to the keep, but she felt his eyes on her, burning a hole in her back.

Late that afternoon Kaela watched Cameron scoop a laughing Mattie up onto Goliath's back and gallop away with her toward the lake. Kaela felt a moment of deep longing as she watched his broad shoulders disappear from sight. No—she would not long for

something she could not have. She told herself over
and over that she would find a way to live with things
as they were, but she knew in her heart that she would
never be happy.

The evening meal was an ordeal. Everyone sensed
the tension between the Lord and Lady of the keep.
Kaela did not utter three words during the entire
evening. She politely declined Thorsen's offer of a
chess game and retired early. Much later she heard
Cameron come to bed. She lay quietly, feigning sleep.
After several breathless moments, the mattress shifted
and she felt Cameron turn away from her. She didn't
know which was greater, her relief at not having to
face him, or her disappointment. She drifted into an
uneasy sleep, disappointment growing heavier with
every breath she took.

Kaela awoke at dawn to the sound of great commotion coming from the bailey. Johnathan shouted
that riders were coming and she hurried to dress. The
great hall was filled with soldiers when she entered.
She saw Thorsen by the hearth and went to join him.

"What has happened, Thorsen?"

"There has been an attack by Saxon rebels in
Herefordshire," he said.

She could see the anger on his face. "God's blood!
How bad is it?"

"They control one fortress and are laying siege to
its neighbor. I do not yet know the extent of the
damage. Cameron is with the King's emissary now."

Kaela swayed slightly, feeling the color drain from
her face. Thorsen reached out and steadied her.

"Kaela, are you all right?"

The kindness in his voice was her undoing. She was horrified when her eyes filled with tears.

Thorsen wrapped his arms around her and cradled her head against his shoulder. "What is it, Kaela?"

Fighting to control her treacherous emotions, Kaela pulled away from him. She saw so much concern in his pale blue eyes, she tried valiantly to smile, and failed miserably.

"You will be leaving then? To join the fight?"

"Aye, we leave within the hour."

"And Cameron?" Her voice shook despite her efforts to control it.

"He is our leader. He has no choice but to go." His blue gaze bored into her as if he tried to read her thoughts.

Kaela shrugged. "He would go anyway, Thorsen. Have you ever known Cameron to miss a battle?"

"Nay, I have not. 'Tis what we have trained for all our lives, Kaela. Surely you understand. We have a responsibility to our King."

"I understand. 'Tis right that you should go. I only request that you take every precaution for your safety."

Thorsen gave her a reassuring smile. "You can rest assured that I shall, my lady. I shall look after that husband of yours also."

"Thank you." To his utter amazement, Kaela pulled him down and kissed his cheek. He raised his eyes from hers to see Cameron stalking towards them.

"Just what the hell do you think you are doing?" he bellowed.

Kaela stiffened. "I wish you God's speed, my lord," she said, her eyes on Thorsen. Resisting the urge to turn and drink in the sight of her husband, angry or not, she turned without another word and walked quickly from the hall.

"Where do you think you are going?" Cameron ground out the words, and started after her. Kaela had reached the stairs and ran up them at the sound of his voice.

Thorsen grabbed Cameron by the arm. "Leave her alone, Wolf. You have hurt her enough for one day."

Cameron slapped Thorsen's hand away. "What the hell are you talking about?"

Thorsen's face was red with anger. "You tell me. What have you done to her? I see the pain in her eyes. Her eyes used to sparkle, and now she runs as if the very sight of you frightens her."

"'Tis not your concern. You overstep yourself, friend," Cameron said, his voice threatening. "The lady is my wife."

"Aye, she is, but I swear you don't deserve her."

Cameron stared at the empty stairway. "I have to find her, tell her I am leaving," he said, distracted by an overwhelming desire to take her in his arms and comfort her. God, he did not want to be separated from her.

"She knows we are leaving. I told her."

"What did she say?"

"She wished us God's speed."

"Get the men ready and have Andrew report to me within the hour," Cameron ordered, then crossed to the stairs to seek out his wife.

She was nowhere to be found. Furious, Cameron paced back and forth before the hearth in the great hall. She was hiding from him. He couldn't believe it! Why the hell would she hide from him? Didn't she care that he was going off to battle? Didn't she want to talk to him before he left? Wish him well? Ask him to be careful? Suddenly, he felt cold inside. She was giving him just what he had asked for, only this emptiness wasn't what he wanted at all.

"You wanted me, brother?" Andrew came to stand before him.

Turning to Andrew, Cameron gave him a glacial stare.

"Aye, while I am gone you and Jacob have charge of Chaldron. You seem so eager to care for my wife, I leave you to it."

"Fine. I will be happy to care for her. Someone has to, since you obviously are not up to the task," Andrew said tightly.

With tremendous control, Cameron refrained from putting his fist through his brother's face.

"I will ask you once more Andrew, why you told her. What did Kaela tell you that would make you betray me?"

Andrew sighed, a helpless look coming over him. "I told you Cameron, 'Tis Kaela's place to tell you that. I will only say that I stand by my decision. I am sorry you see it as a betrayal. I assure you 'twas never meant as one."

Cameron only shrugged and looked away. "Never mind, what is done is done. I am leaving a third of the men with you. 'Tis possible that there could be attacks here, so stay on your guard. If there is any trouble, send word to me immediately. I will send missives to keep you informed of our progress. I expect this to be a lengthy fight."

"I understand. Do not worry about Chaldron. Jacob and I will see to things."

Cameron wanted to stay angry with his brother, but

he could not leave him in anger, not with the possibility that he would not see him again. He reached out and clasped Andrew's shoulder.

"I know you will, little brother. I will return as soon as possible."

With that Cameron left the hall. He wanted desperately to talk to Kaela, but he could delay no longer. It was imperative that they reach the fighting as soon as possible. He entered the bailey to find his men mounted and waiting for him.

Arik held Goliath's reins as Cameron mounted and gave the signal to depart. He glanced up at his bedchamber window, sucking in his breath when he saw Kaela standing there, watching him. He could see the color of her eyes even from this distance and could tell she had been crying. Looking at her, a terrible sadness overcame him. He could not help thinking about the first time he had ever seen her. She had been in that exact spot, watching his arrival at Chaldron. He remembered well the feelings she stirred in him even then. He longed to dismount and go to her, but he could not. She would probably run from him anyway. He lifted his hand in farewell, comforted when she also raised her hand. Then he turned and rode from the bailey, while he still had the willpower to do so.

At the sun's setting, Cameron and his men made camp. They had kept a fast pace throughout the day and were tired, yet filled with anticipation for what lay ahead.

Cameron had been silent during the long day, his thoughts filled with Kaela. He could not banish her from his mind. He was angry that she had avoided him. He believed had he been able to talk to her before he left, he would not be obsessed with her now. He kept seeing her in Thorsen's arms and the image filled him with rage. He knew in his heart their parting was innocent, but every time he pictured them together, his stomach churned. Cameron clenched his teeth and forced the image from his mind. He would never allow his wife to cause him the pain he had known with Elizabeth.

Patrick brought him from his reverie. "You look deep in thought, my lord. Are you planning our strategy for tomorrow's battle?"

"Tomorrow's battle?" Cameron shook his head. "We will have to wait and see what those Saxon bastards have accomplished before we can plan our counter attack. The missive from William's brother, Odo, said we could expect reinforcements from Barons Frederick and Joseph. Hopefully, they will not be more than two days behind us. We will need the numbers if we want this to end quickly."

Johnathan and Thorsen joined the two men at the campfire.

"I did not see Kaela before we left, Cameron. Was she not feeling well?" Johnathan asked. Everyone had noticed her absence when they left this morning, but Johnathan was the only one to brave the subject. Though Cameron glared at him, Johnathan sat patiently waiting for an answer.

Before he answered, Cameron swung his murderous glare to Thorsen. "I guess you could say she is not feeling quite herself."

"I have noticed an unhappy change in her since Constance and Guy were here. Is everything all right?"

Cameron jumped to his feet, his fists tight at his sides. "My wife is no concern of yours, Patrick. Or any of you, for that matter." Cameron stomped away, then turned. "We leave at first light. See that everything is ready."

He stormed to his tent and quickly stripped out of his hauberk and chausses. Crawling into his bed of furs, he concentrated on shutting Kaela from his thoughts. He willed himself to sleep, but a long time passed before he could. In his semi-drowsy state, he remembered the nights he had spent in this very tent with his wife. Here, she had learned to trust him. Here, he had first kissed her and gloried in her soft, warm embrace. Cameron moaned his frustration, cursing himself for his weakness. Even when he slept, he had no relief. He dreamed of her.

❖   ❖   ❖

Kaela's days fell into a rigid routine. Up at dawn, she did not stop until the sun set, exhaustion the only state in which melancholy could not overwhelm her. With her baby to consider, she refused to let grief over Cameron ruin her health. She forced herself to eat, to smile, to get on with her life.

Running Chaldron kept her quite busy. She ordered all the castle walls scrubbed, and whitewashed before the new tapestries were hung. The rushes were changed and wild flowers filled the rooms. Chaldron had never looked more lovely.

Everyone helped with picking and preserving the precious fruit from the orchards. They would rely on them and the harvested vegetables for the coming year. Kaela and Andrew oversaw the food tithes from the villeins. Her brother-in-law had been upset with her for not telling Cameron about the babe, but he had not been hard on her. Indeed, everyone took, special care to see to Kaela's needs.

More than a month had passed since Cameron's departure, but the pain had not lessened. Even though her days were filled, at night in her bedchamber, Kaela could not keep her feelings at bay. Never more alone, she longed for her husband; for the warmth of his embrace; for the quiet comfort of his presence.

Andrew received two messages from Cameron after his departure. Kaela breathed a relieved sigh to hear he remained unharmed. The battle dragged on and on. She began to wonder if he would return before their child's birth. Growing quite large, she could no longer hide her condition. Other than her immediate family, no one broached the subject with her. Mattie, the most delighted, could not wait for her new baby cousin to arrive.

Kaela silently berated herself for not telling Cameron about the babe before he left. Instead of hiding like a coward, she should have faced him. If anything happened to him, she would never forgive herself for not telling him about his child.

"Please God, let him come home to me. Let him know his child." Kaela prayed with all her heart their child would heal his father's pain.

Herefordshire, two weeks later.

"God's bones, I am tired." Johnathan took a long swallow of ale.

"At least we have made some progress," Patrick said. "Now we control the fortress again, routing the bastards should not take much longer."

Thorsen grunted. "Have you seen Broderick again?"

"Aye, the whoreson stayed behind the lines again today, observing from the ridge. I could not reach him."

"Broderick is a dead man, I promise you. Cameron will kill him before we leave this place. Had not yesterday's sudden storm hidden him, the bastard would never have escaped."

"What is his game, Thorsen? Why doesn't he fight Cameron with honor?" Patrick asked.

"The bastard has no honor," Cameron said, joining the group.

"He plays games with you, Cameron," Johnathan said bluntly.

"Aye, but not for much longer. The battle winds down. We should take no more than a fortnight to regain the last of our lands. Broderick knows this. The cur will run if he can, but he will not escape again. His days of terrorizing my wife are over."

"What do you want us to do?" Thorsen asked.

"Pick three men to scout his whereabouts tomorrow. Johnathan, you direct the battle in my place. Patrick, you and Thorsen ride with me. Once the scouts have located him, we will move in. 'Tis your job to seal off any escape route. Under no circumstances will you challenge him. That pleasure is mine alone."

Cameron turned and strode toward his tent.

"By the saints, I have never seen him like this," Patrick said. "He looks exhausted. I fear he is not up to doing battle with Broderick."

"If he had not slept for months, Cameron could still

take that bastard," Johnathan said in denial.

"What troubles him?" Patrick asked, his voice filled with concern. "He is as grouchy as a bear. The only time he speaks, he criticizes. When he isn't fighting, he stays in his tent. Cameron has always enjoyed a battle. I don't understand him."

"'Tis Kaela," Thorsen said.

"Kaela? Is something wrong with his lady?"

"We all know the problem, Patrick," Johnathan said. "Our Baron needs to come to terms with his feelings for his wife."

"Aye, and unless I miss my guess, that is what he struggles with," Thorsen said.

"How can we help him?"

"We have done all we can. 'Tis up to Cameron now. I believe our Lady Kaela has pushed him to the wall. Cameron must help himself. Let us hope he makes the right decision."

Restless, Cameron paced his tent. Weeks had passed since he had seen his wife. She still haunted him, filled his dreams. To make matters worse, if he didn't dream of her, he had nightmares about Elizabeth's treachery and Peter's death. Over and over, Kaela's words came back to him.

"God's truth, she haunts me, even after all this time," Cameron said, raking his hands through his hair. He looked around the suddenly too-confining tent, threw back the flap, and walked out into the night. He felt restless, and terribly alone. Mounting Goliath, he rode from the camp into the hills. Soon he realized he had unthinkingly ridden toward Chaldron.

Even now he thought of her. He reined in his horse and tethered the animal to a tree. Running water in a stream nearby drew him forward. He watched the full moon riding low on the horizon, then knelt to drink the cold, clear water. Splashing some on his face, he pictured Kaela the way she had been that day on the road to London, sitting by a similar stream, brushing her hair. God, she had been so beautiful. *She is beautiful, beautiful and gentle.* He leaned against a boulder, thinking of her.

"She is loving, loyal, and very stubborn, and I love her," he said softly, surprised by his words. Dear God, he loved her. No longer could he deny the truth. She had been right. He had callously thrown away his last chance at happiness.

Cameron had never missed anyone so much. He couldn't bear to think he might never see her again. Realizing how he had hurt her with his coldness, he cringed. "She is right, Peter," Cameron whispered to the lonely night. "I must face your death. I must face my fear of loving again, for I do love her. God help me, to lose her now would be my death."

Cameron sat quietly, listening to the night, watching the serene moon cross the sky, feeling tears flow unchecked down his face when every memory of Peter rushed into his mind. All the joy, all the sorrow.

"I am sorry I could not save you, Peter, could not give my life for yours. Forgive me, son, for my failure to protect you. I have found someone new to love. I believe you would have loved her, too. And little Mattie, how much alike the two of you are. They need my love now, Peter, even as you once did. Can you understand that, son? Can you forgive me?"

No answer came from the darkness, no words of comfort. Still, Cameron felt comforted. He somehow felt his son was listening. He breathed deeply of the night air. For the first time in more than three long years, something within him began to give, to soften.

He thought of Elizabeth then, of her treachery, and knew he had never truly loved her. Long before her death, she had killed any feeling he had for her.

Kaela. His fiery-haired wife was everything Elizabeth had never been. He could not bear their separation any longer. God grant he had not discovered the truth too late for them to save their marriage.

Tomorrow, he would slay Broderick, rout the other Saxon rebels, and go home to his wife.

Home. Even the word brought a satisfied smile. Home to Kaela and Chaldron.

Cameron returned to camp, feeling better than he had in years, eager for the dawn that would bring him another day closer to home. He slept better than he had in months.

Chapter Nineteen

✤   ✤   ✤

Chaldron Castle, August, 1067

Chaldron's people turned out to welcome their Baron home. The outer bailey, full to overflowing, rang with their greetings and Cameron's men welcoming their comrades home.

Cameron scanned the crowd for his wife. Disappointed, he failed to find her there. He had hoped the time apart would have mellowed her, that she would be anxious to see him. Cameron felt his stomach clench.

"Brother, welcome home!" Striding toward Cameron, Andrew shouted over the noise. "We were not expecting you. Your last missive gave no hint when you might return. Did the battle go well at Herefordshire?"

Cameron dismounted and clasped Andrew's shoulder. "All is well, little brother. The Saxon's have been routed, at least for the time being. We greatly reduced their numbers, but I fear we have not heard the last of them. How are things here?"

"We fare well. Jacob and Kaela have been a great help to me. We had no problems we could not handle."

"Where is my wife? Why is she not here to greet me?"

"Kaela is in the village with Arik and Mattie. She takes her herbs and goes once a month to visit the sick villeins. As I said, we had no idea you would return today." Andrew arched one brow and grinned. "You seem eager to see your lady wife."

"Aye, I am. She should not be in the village unprotected."

"Arik is with her. He would let no harm come to Kaela. Things have been quiet here, Cameron. I send out scouts daily. They find no sign of rebel activity on your lands."

Andrew watched his brother remount Goliath. "Where are you going?"

"To find my wife."

"Wait, Cameron. Kaela will return shortly. You would be unwise to overwhelm your lady wife. Come inside and let us talk first."

Cameron stared at his brother, while prickles of fear raced down his spine. "What is wrong, Andrew?"

"Nothing is wrong, but these last months have not been easy for Kaela. She has a great sadness in her. You did not once send word to her while you were away."

Cameron dismounted and the two men entered the keep.

"I did not know what to say to her, Andrew."

"Do you know now?"

Cameron sighed. This was none of Andrew's business, but he felt too glad to see him to tell him so. "Aye, I think I know what I will say."

"Let me warn you, Cameron, do not do anything that will upset Kaela. She has had enough grief and her condition is delicate."

Alarmed, Cameron asked, "Condition? What condition? Is Kaela ill?"

"Nay, she is not ill, but she should not be upset."

Cameron grew angrier by the minute. "She is my wife, Andrew. I will take care of her. I plan to say nothing that will upset her."

"Does this mean you have had a change of heart, brother?"

"Damn it, Andrew, 'Tis none of your concern. But, aye, I have."

"God's truth, 'Tis about time," Andrew said, chuckling.

"I warn you, Andrew, leave me be."

The men entered the great hall and Cameron stopped short. He turned, gazing around the room, unable to believe the changes. He approached the hearth, amazed at the banner hanging above the massive fireplace. Huge, the brilliant royal blue fabric had been embroidered with a magnificent, snarling wolf in silver and black. Cameron had never seen such intricate stitching.

"'Tis my banner," Cameron said, awed. "Did Kaela do this?"

"Aye, she and Brenna. 'Tis fitting, is it not, for the Black Wolf to have his banner hanging in his keep?"

"'Tis magnificent. I cannot believe she would do this. She was so angry when I left."

"Kaela does not carry a grudge, brother. You are her husband, after all."

"I am." Cameron beamed.

"Actually, Brenna is quite talented with a needle, among other things," Andrew said, grinning broadly. "Look at this tapestry she stitched. Kaela worked out the designs and helped with the stitching, but Brenna has the true talent with the needle."

Cameron turned and carefully studied the tapestry hanging on the far wall. He realized the hall had been completely refurbished. His heart swelled with pride. The walls were clean and freshened with whitewash. The banner, his banner, looked magnificent. Huge tapestries covered both sidewalls. One depicted the battle at Hastings and Cameron could see his likeness and the mark of his shield on the warrior who stood beside William. The other tapestry depicted William's coronation. Again, he saw himself at his King's side. He felt overwhelmed and humbled, by what his wife had done in her effort to make Chaldron his home.

"What do you think?" Andrew asked. "Are they not magnificent?"

"I have never seen anything like them, Andrew. They are wonderful. My wife is wonderful."

"Aye, she is. Did you notice I, too, am in the tapestries?" Andrew laughed. "Brenna would not leave me out."

"Aye, little brother," Cameron laughed. "But I also see Thorsen, Johnathan, and Patrick. Pray tell me, does her heart pine for them also?"

"She had best not."

Cameron again glanced about, more anxious than ever to see his wife. Surely if she had done this for him, he could still hope she would forgive him. Damn it, he wanted to find her, but he was filthy and suddenly aware of how very much he wanted to be pleasing to her.

He ran up the stairs two at a time calling out loudly for hot water for his bath. When he entered their chamber, his gaze went immediately to the new tapestry he found there. Joy filled him when he recognized the scene. 'Twas their wedding. He and Kaela stood facing each other before the Bishop and William. Remembering very vividly the way she had looked coming toward him on Thorsen's arm, he murmured, "My wife, my beautiful wife."

A short time later, clean and wearing his best tunic, Cameron left the keep to go in search of Kaela. When Jacob told him she had returned, he tried the stables, but found only Arik.

"My Lord, welcome home." The blond giant greeted him, throwing his arm around Cameron's shoulder.

"Thank you, Ark. Where is Kaela?"

"She went to her garden. She is probably in the hut where she keeps her herbs. We went to see the sick people today."

"Aye, so Andrew told me. I will see you later, Arik," Cameron called over his shoulder. Making his way toward the hut, his knees turned weak, and he realized how nervous he was.

Quietly, he entered the hut, then sucked in his breath when he saw her. Sunlight streamed through the window, bringing the fiery highlights in her long hair to life. She stood on a stool, her back to him, tying bunches of herbs to an overhead beam. Approaching her, he spoke her name.

Hearing his voice, Kaela whirled and lost her footing.

Cameron caught her and hugged her to him. "Kaela, I have missed you so." He stepped back, still holding her arms, to gaze down at her.

"My God, you—you are with child." In shock, he could say nothing else.

Kaela bit her lip, then her eyes filled with tears.

She tried to pull away from him, but his grip was too strong. "I am sorry, Cameron. I wanted to tell you before you left, but I knew you would be angry. God's truth, I couldn't find the courage."

"No, Kaela, 'Tis I who am sorry," he whispered, drawing her to him.

Overwhelmed, and filled with turmoil, Kaela breathed in his clean masculine scent and felt desire lick through her veins. At the same time, a deep sadness filled her. "I want this babe, Cameron, even if you do not. I will love our child enough for both of us."

He held her tighter, burying his face in her hair. "You do not understand, sweetheart. I am happy about the babe." He looked down at her and kissed away her tears. "Nay, I am overjoyed. I wish you had told me—'twas my thick-headedness that kept you silent. A babe, Kaela, we are going to have a child."

Confused, Kaela saw the pure joy in his eyes. "I don't understand, Cameron," she said in a small forlorn voice.

"I know you don't, sweetheart, but I am very happy about our child, and I am very happy to see you." He laughed and hugged her to him again. "How far along are you? You are very big." Teasing her, he placed his hand on her belly.

"I am huge." Kaela smiled. "Maude says we must have a boy, I am so large. Our babe will be born in late October."

"Holy Saint Ambrose's bones, you must have conceived on our wedding night." Cameron felt dazed.

"'Twould seem so, my lord. Are you truly happy about the babe?"

"Very happy."

She stared at him, unable to comprehend his words.

She must be dreaming. This could not be her husband standing before her.

"I have much to tell you, sweeting, but not here. Let us ride to your lake. 'Tis a beautiful afternoon and we won't be disturbed."

He took her hand in his and led her toward the stables.

"You want to go to the lake?" she asked in confusion. She could not stop staring at him, thinking he might disappear any moment.

"Aye, I want to be alone with my wife." He quickly saddled Goliath and lifted her into the saddle before swinging up behind her. The noise in the outer bailey ceased when Cameron's vassals gawked at their lord and lady. At Cameron's command, Windrey lowered the drawbridge and grinned his toothless grin, giving Kaela a wink. Kaela blushed and buried her face in Cameron's shoulder.

"Cameron, what are you doing? I can ride my own horse."

"Nay, wife, I want you with me," he said, nuzzling her ear. "You should not be riding in your condition."

Cameron stopped Goliath in the shade under the trees and dismounted. Reaching up, he lifted Kaela down before him. With one hand on her swollen belly, he gazed into her eyes, a tender smile on his face. "You are beautiful, wife. I have missed you." Then his mouth descended.

He kissed her, deeply, and Kaela felt her knees weaken with desire.

She laid her head against his shoulder and prayed she did not dream. "What has happened, Cameron?"

He led her to the base of a massive oak and sat down, pulling her into his lap. He held her gaze with his. What Kaela saw there overwhelmed her.

"I have come to realize I love my wife, very much."

Kaela's eyes filled with tears. "You love me?" she asked in wonder. "'Tis not some cruel jest?"

"Oh, sweeting, have I been so cruel you could believe that? Before God, I never meant to be. 'Tis no jest, Kaela. I love you with all my heart. Can you ever forgive me, sweetheart, for the pain I have caused you?" Tenderly, he kissed her and held her to him, reveling in her body's soft warmth. Feeling her tears hot against his shoulder, he stroked her back. "I know this is a tremendous change and 'tis hard for you to believe. I want to explain, Kaela. Will you listen to me?"

Too overwhelmed to speak, Kaela nodded against his shoulder.

Cameron held her for a moment, running his hands gently through her hair, gathering his thoughts. "I have thought of you and little else while I have been away. Your words haunted me, but in my anger I tried to wipe all thought of you and the things you had said from my mind. God's teeth, woman, I have never been more miserable," Cameron said. "Even in the midst of battle, I could not banish my fiery-haired wife from my mind. My men lost all patience with my surly mood." He felt Kaela smile against his neck.

"I realized your words were true. I had been running from Peter's death for too long. 'Twas time I faced his loss. Then I knew, even though I had fought against the feeling from the beginning, I had fallen in love with you. I don't know if you understand this, sweetheart, but admitting I could love frightened the hell out of me. God's truth, I am still afraid."

Kaela looked up at him. When she stroked his cheek, his large hand captured hers and carried it to his lips. "You need not fear husband. For 'tis truth, I will never betray you," she whispered.

"'Tis not your betrayal I fear, wife. My experiences with Elizabeth have nothing to do with us. The infatuation I had for her died long before she did. Her unfaithfulness shamed me, and I admit my bitterness caused me to distrust all women. But I have known for a long time you are nothing like her, or the other women I knew at court. I trust you, Kaela. I could never love a woman I could not trust."

"Then what do you fear?"

Cameron laughed. "I sound ridiculous, do I not? The great Black Wolf afraid. William's fiercest warrior quaking in his boots over a woman."

The tight sarcasm in his words frightened her. She sat up, watching him.

Cameron smiled tugging her back into his embrace. "I am sorry, I do not mean to sound harsh. What I fear, what I have feared for the last three years, is the devastation that comes with the loss of someone you truly love." The words were so soft Kaela had to strain to hear him.

"Oh, Cameron." She wrapped her arms around his neck, pressed her lips to his until he broke the kiss.

"I have run from that pain for a long time, Kaela. You were right when you accused me of feeling guilt over Peter's death. 'Tis mad I know, but I have guilt just the same. Guilt that I am alive and he is not. Guilt that I exposed him to such a vicious woman. Somehow I felt that if I never gave my love again, not only would I be protected, but I would be doing penance for Peter."

Kaela tried to speak, but Cameron stopped her. "Let me say what needs to be said, Kaela. In

Herefordshire, alone, without you, my memories haunted me. Peter, his death, the unhappiness you suffered at my hands... Making peace has not been easy, but my son would not want me to waste my life in bitterness. Peter was a wonderful boy, loving and full of life.

"You would have loved him, sweetheart. He was so like Mattie. You were right, about why I am drawn to her. The realization has been long in coming, but I know Peter would want me to love again, to love you and Mattie.

"God's truth, my love has been yours since the first time we met. Remember? You stormed across the hall, defending your father, attacking the Norman warrior who had come to take your home. By the time we reached London, denying what was between us had me so miserable, I made an ass of myself with William. You should have seen me, objecting to every man the King named as a possible suitor for your hand. 'Twas Thorsen who convinced me I could marry you without loving you. He knew better, knew what I denied. I wanted you so much, to say I married for duty and honor was easy.

"You have my love, Kaela. Though I denied it, you had it when we married, when I turned away from you, when I left for Herefordshire, now, and for always."

Cameron smiled into her eyes and wiped away her tears with his thumb. His lips brushed against hers once, twice, warming her to the very core of her being. She opened her mouth and reveled in the feel of his warm, urgent tongue against hers.

Cameron moaned deep in his throat and pulled back, cradling her head against his shoulder once more.

"'Tis all so new to me, Kaela. I have spent my life training for battle, or fighting at William's side. I know nothing of how to be a proper husband, but I love you and will do my best to make you happy. Can you forgive me for being such a fool? Can you find it in your heart to love me again?"

"Oh, Cameron, I never stopped loving you. You make me happy beyond words. I have been so lonely without you. Not even when my parents died did I know such sadness, feel such emptiness. When you said you would never love me, I feared you would shun our child, never give our babe your love." She burst into tears.

"Hush, sweetheart." Cameron eased her from his lap to the soft green grass. Coming down beside her, he held her in his arms. "Everything is all right now. I will make you happy, Kaela. Please, don't cry."

"'Tis the babe's doing. I never used to cry so much." When she smiled through her tears, Cameron returned her smile.

"God's truth, Kaela, I am the luckiest man alive."

His lips came down and captured hers in the gentlest kiss she had ever known. One strong hand slid down her body to her calf and slipped beneath her gown. He caressed her, his hand warm against her flesh. Slowly, he eased his hand up her thigh. Kaela came alive with desire.

"Cameron, what are you doing?"

"I am loving my wife."

He rose on one elbow and began to untie the laces of her bliaut.

Kaela giggled. "'Tis broad daylight."

"Hmmm… and so warm, is it not?" Cameron murmured.

"Someone might see us."

Cameron laughed. "We are completely alone and you know it. Besides, we are protected by the trees. I have thought of little else but this since I have been away." By this time, he had removed her clothes and was staring boldly at her.

Kaela blushed and tried to cover herself.

Cameron grasped her hands and held them to her sides. "Nay wife, let me look at you. Your body is beautiful."

"How can you say that? I am huge," Kaela said, but the desire in his eyes warmed her.

Cameron leaned down to capture a warm full breast with his mouth and began to suckle. Kaela gasped with delight and pulled him closer. He smiled up at her and ran his hands over her belly. Leaning down, he kissed her round stomach. "Our child, Kaela, only think of it," he said, his tone one of awe. He placed his hand once more on her rounded belly and smiled, a smile filled with love and longing. Kaela's heart overflowed. As if in answer, the babe gave a sharp resounding kick against his father's palm and Cameron's eyes grew wide with wonder. He threw back his head and laughed.

"I think our son is anxious to meet his father."

"And I am anxious to meet him, my love." Cameron sat up and pulled his tunic over his head. Grinning, he tossed it on top of her discarded clothing and began to unlace his chausses. "For now, I have need of my wife."

The desire he read in Kaela's gaze made his heart beat faster. He came to her then, pulled her into his embrace, and kissed her. "I love you, wife."

"I love you, husband," Kaela said, losing herself i

the emotions that flickered in his eyes—the love, the wanting.

"Are you all right? The babe?"

"We are both fine, husband."

"'Tis all right for us to make love? What about the baby?"

"'Tis fine, Cameron. Do not worry. Only in my last month, I am told, will we be unable to love each other."

Cameron groaned, but in an instant he smiled. "Ah, sweet wife, there are many ways we can love each other that will not harm the child."

Kaela answered his smile with her own and reached out, boldly caressing his fully erect manhood. He quivered. His breathing quickened and grew uneven. Passion flared in his eyes, hungry, bright-blue eyes that consumed her. For a moment longer, Kaela allowed herself the luxury of looking at him while she continued to caress him. She drank in the way the sunlight struck blue sparks in the wavy black thickness of his hair, painted golden his handsomely rugged features, and danced over his broad shoulders and wide chest.

Then she released his manhood and pulled him to her. Pressing her swollen breasts fully against his chest, she brought his lips to hers.

"Sweet Jesu, wife," he muttered against her mouth, "I shall never get enough of you." Then his arms came around her, he rolled to his back, and pulled her on top of him.

He kissed her as if he would steal her very soul. His mouth, hot and wet, tasted of mint. His kiss so consumed her, she had no thought save to return his passion.

Kaela thought he kissed her for an eternity. He

sought her breasts with his hand. Heat seared her flesh, making her nipples tighten deliciously. At last he broke the kiss and pulled her legs up to straddle him. Kaela sat up and their gazes locked. He ran his hand one last time over her breast before sliding his long fingers between her thighs.

"I love to touch your skin. Nothing else feels quite as soft," he murmured. His fingers parted and caressed her and Kaela moaned her pleasure, twisting against him until she shook with involuntary tremors. He brought his hands to her waist, lifted and entered her. He began a slow, steady rhythm, gradually building in intensity until they neared ecstasy. Then he thrust for a final time deep inside her and cried out her name.

In the aftermath, they lay entwined, side by side, facing each other. The expression in his eyes left her bereft of words.

Several moments passed before either could speak.

"I never thought our loving could get any better than what we shared before," Cameron said, his voice filled with wonder.

"Neither did I," Kaela replied softly.

"Are you all right? The babe?"

"We are both fine." Kaela smiled.

Cameron rubbed her belly, still awed by the knowledge she carried their child. His eyes were wet when they met hers. "I love you, Kaela."

"And I you, husband," she answered softly.

"Forever?"

"Aye, my knight, forever."

They loved, and whispered, and laughed, and loved some more, and in that afternoon they began to create a paradise that would see them through all the trials and sorrows of life. It was a bonding that was complete.

Hours later, Cameron rose to his feet, swept Kaela in his arms, and carried her down to the lake.

"Cameron, what are you doing?"

"Taking my beautiful wife swimming," he said, striding into the cool, refreshing water. They laughed when he set her on her feet.

"Didn't you tell me you used to swim here with your family when you were a girl?"

"Aye." Kaela splashed him, then dove away from his grasp.

"Now you will swim with your new family." Cameron smiled. "'Tis wonderful, wife. I think we will make this swimming a habit." He lunged after her and she squealed when he caught her in a warm embrace. Their laughter echoed through the stillness of the afternoon.

Late that night, they lay in bed together, exhausted but happy from their lovemaking. Kaela had waited as long as she could, but now she asked him about Broderick. He tensed beside her and she knew the news was not good.

"He was there at Herefordshire," he said, his voice grave.

"Did you fight him?"

"Nay, the coward played a cat and mouse game with me. Then he disappeared a fortnight before the fighting ended."

"Mayhap he fell in battle."

"I had men watching for him, Kaela. I was determined he would die, but he escaped again. Knowing the battle lost, he pulled back to regroup, then deserted his troops. We must be very careful. I fear he is mad enough to try again to take you." Cameron pulled her into his arms and held her close. He felt her tremble and cursed softly.

"No harm will come to you, wife. I promise. I could not survive if I lost you. Don't worry, Kaela, but you must do as I ask and never leave the keep without a guard."

"He will come again, Cameron. His obsession drives him beyond sanity. Broderick will never give up." She shivered and pressed against him, needing his warmth.

"I will slay the bastard first, love. I give you my vow. Already I have men tracking him. When I find his lair, I will draw him out and there will be an end to his perfidy."

"Promise you will be careful. Broderick knows not how to fight with honor."

"Trust me, Kaela. You have faith in me, don't you?"

She smiled into his eyes and pressed her lips to his. "Aye husband, all the faith in the world."

Soon they forgot about their enemy, lost once more in their passion.

August turned to September, bringing a hint of fall to the air. Kaela grew larger and somehow more beautiful with each passing day. She and Cameron were rarely separated. They spent their mornings in their chamber, breaking their fast and making plans for the day. Some days they went hawking. Watching her expertly handle the peregrines, Cameron's admiration grew. He took her with him many afternoons when he rode out to check on the road construction. She and Brenna would often stop their work early and watch Cameron and his men train for battle.

Andrew had finally asked for Brenna's hand. They planned to wed during the feast of winter solstice. Cameron had sent a missive to his family in Normandy, inviting them to share the holiday feast with them. 'Twas a perfect time for Andrew and Brenna to say their vows.

Things had never been happier at Chaldron. Kaela basked in her husband's love and attention. Mercilessly, he teased her as she grew larger and more awkward, but he loved her passionately at night and told her over and over how beautiful she was to him. Kaela felt beautiful and happier than she had ever been. All Chaldron anxiously awaited the birth of their child, the first who would be neither Saxon nor Norman, but a blending of the two. Chaldron acknowledged a new heritage now, one to be proud of.

One evening in mid-September, as they sat down for the evening meal, the horns announced an approaching rider.

Several minutes later, an emissary from London entered the great hall. Cameron excused himself, giving his wife a brief kiss, and closed himself off in the solar with the messenger.

Dread raced up Kaela's spine and she lost her appetite.

"What news do you think he brings?" Brenna asked Andrew, squeezing Kaela's hand.

"The message must be from Odo, William's brother. My guess would be there has been another uprising."

"The Saxon rebels."

"Aye, Kaela, we have expected trouble," Andrew said.

Before anyone else could comment, Cameron entered the hall with the King's messenger in tow.

"Maude," he said, passing her near the hearth, "see that this man receives refreshment."

He strode back to the trestle table and sat down next to his wife. Taking her hand in his, he addressed his men, his voice hard and matter of fact. "The Saxon rebels have started another uprising."

"Where?" Thorsen asked.

"To the northeast, in Kent. They have not yet been successful in taking the castle there. Odo has requested we bring reinforcements without delay. We leave at first light."

Kaela gasped and gripped his hand so hard he thought his fingers might break. He smiled reassuringly. Freeing his hand, he placed his arm around her shoulder and held her to his side.

"Johnathan, you and Thorsen prepare the men. We will take the same numbers as before. Andrew, you and Jacob are once again responsible for Chaldron. With any luck, this skirmish will be far shorter than the one at Herefordshire. Without possession of the Castle, their forces will be easily routed. I do not intend to miss the birth of our child, so you need not worry, Kaela."

Hearing his words, his vassals smiled before they left the hall to make their preparations.

"You have hardly touched your dinner, sweetheart." Cameron still held her against his side.

"I have lost my appetite."

"Come then," Cameron said, and drew her to her feet. "Let us retire. Dawn comes all too soon and I have need of my wife."

To Kaela's surprise, he lifted her and carried her up the stairs. She heard Brenna and Andrew talking quietly, but paid them little mind. She could think only

only about Cameron's impending departure and the possibility he might not return. Cold and shaking, she bit back the pleading words she knew would not keep him with her.

With Kaela still in his arms, he closed their chamber door, and strode to the bed. Laying her down, he stretched beside her. While he discarded her clothing, he rained kisses over her face and neck.

"I will miss you, wife," he murmured between kisses.

Desperate, Kaela clutched at him. "I don't want you to go. I am afraid Cameron." Her voice broke despite her determination to be calm.

"Nonsense, Kaela. 'Tis what warriors do. You have no need to fear. Our troops greatly outnumber the Saxons. Have you lost faith in my ability?"

They were naked now and Cameron cradled her in his arms, her cheek against his shoulder.

"What of Broderick? Will he be there?" Kaela had watched her father go off to battle many times, and Cameron's leaving would be the second time she watched him go, yet she had never felt such sinister foreboding.

"Let us hope so. You know we doubled our scouts and constantly watch the Welsh border, but have seen no sign of him. 'Twill be a good opportunity to rid ourselves of the bastard."

"Promise me you will have Johnathan or Thorsen always at your back," Kaela said, caressing his face.

"You have my promise to be careful. And you must promise me you will take every precaution, Kaela. You must not leave the keep for any reason until I return."

"Not even with a guard?"

"Not for any reason. 'Twill relieve my mind greatly to know you are safe. Do you promise?"

"Aye, husband, I would promise you anything. Besides, I am so large moving about has become awkward. I fear I would break poor Sky's back if I tried to ride her." Kaela laughed, but the sound was hollow and forced.

"Good, I will rest easier knowing you are safe. I won't be gone long, sweetheart. Even if the fighting goes on longer than I expect, I promise you to return in time for the birth of our child."

"I love you, Cameron," Kaela whispered, running her hand over his muscled chest.

"Hmm... show me how much," he whispered, his lips on hers.

A grinding moan came from the depths of Cameron's chest. He touched his tongue to her mouth, first on one side, then the other. He felt primitive in his need for her.

Kaela pulled away from his seeking mouth and tasted her way down his chest, leaving hot wet kisses that fired his blood. She captured his throbbing shaft in her hand and he tensed while she stroked him.

Afraid he would stop her, she raised her head beseechingly. "Let me."

Cameron groaned. Burying his hands in her hair, he gave himself up to her in quiet, magnificent submission. His hands moved frantically in her hair as she pleasured him. Like a man lost in the darkness, he cried out his need for her.

When he could stand the intense pleasure no longer, he pulled her to him and kissed her deeply, turning her onto her back. He came up over her and captured one pink nipple, drew it into the warm wetness of his mouth, and began to suckle. She moaned softly when he caressed her hip and moved his hand to cover her woman's mound.

His fingers parted her and she gasped at the resultant shock of pleasure as he thrust them inside her, all the while suckling at her breast. Wave after wave of pleasure washed over her, slowly building in intensity. When he moved lower, putting her legs over his shoulders, and stroked her with his warm wet tongue, she became completely lost in her desire.

He loved her at a leisurely pace, no matter how she urged and begged. In the moment before she found her release, he turned her to her side, his chest against her back. Lifting her leg on top of his strong thigh, he sheathed himself in one quick thrust. His arms came around her and he found her most sensitive spot, stroking her once more. Her release came, immediate and powerful, so devastatingly sweet, Kaela cried out in wonder.

When Cameron heard her cry, he shuddered, and gave a guttural cry of his own. She felt his warmth spilling inside her and the unbearable beauty made her body climb toward another response, this one unexpected and all the sweeter.

After several minutes Kaela turned in his arms and brought his mouth to her breast once more, teasing him softly with her nipple. He suckled as she stroked her hands through his damp hair.

"I love you so," she whispered.

"I love you, too," he said, continuing to suckle, as if unable to get enough of her.

"Promise me you will be safe."

"I will, sweetheart. I will be home soon." He buried his head between her breasts and she held him tightly to her. Knowing a love so deeply poignant they felt as if their hearts might break, they cuddled close and drifted into sleep.

She awoke early, but dawn had passed. The fire had gone out and, although the room was warm and filled with morning light, Kaela felt cold. Cameron was gone. She was alone.

Chapter Twenty

❖   ❖   ❖

A fortnight had passed since Cameron's departure and Kaela missed him terribly. The days passed slowly and the nights were even worse. Kaela felt consumed with her love for him.

A brisk biting wind ushered in October, hurling the colorful leaves from the trees and promising a harsh winter. The cold snap lasted only a sennight before the weather turned pleasantly cool, bringing days filled with sunshine.

Kaela tried to stay busy, helping to store food for the winter and working in her herb garden. Truly awkward now with the cumbersome weight of the babe, her movements were slower, more deliberate. She had risen early, unable to stand the loneliness in her chamber, and gone down to her garden at first light. She took pleasure in cutting herbs and mixing the curing potions her grandmother had taught her so long ago. Had this been a normal day, she would have called on the villeins with her medicines. Kaela sighed in frustration, knowing she would be unable to go. She had promised Cameron she would not leave Chaldron's walls and she meant to keep her promise.

The terrible foreboding she had felt on the night

before Cameron's departure had not left her. She worried constantly for his safety. They had received his missive the day before. This time he had enclosed a personal message just for her. She smiled remembering his words of love and longing. Her warrior husband's tenderness amazed her. Kaela felt strengthened by his love. He wrote that Broderick had been seen shortly after their arrival, and vowed again to seek vengeance. Relieved her old enemy was far from Chaldron, she still yearned for her husband.

Kaela's thoughts were interrupted by a fierce tug on her gown. She looked down, saw Mattie's black ringlets, and smiled. "Good morn, sweet pea. You're out early."

Mattie tugged impatiently on Kaela's gown. "Can I go with Brenna and Arik to the village, Kaela?"

Kaela frowned. "Don't you want to stay here with me, sweet pea? I thought we would go down to the kitchen and try cook's honey cakes."

"I want to go to the village. Please, Kaela. I want to ride my pony."

"Why don't you let her come, Kaela," Brenna asked as she crossed through the rows of herbs to join them. "She is good with the children, distracting them while I treat their parents. She even helps with the sick children. You know my bedside manner is not as good as yours. I can use her help."

"Please," Mattie begged.

"All right, but promise to stay close to Brenna and Arik," Kaela conceded.

"Hooray!" Mattie jumped up and down in her excitement.

"Be careful, sprite. You're going to smash Kaela's herbs." Brenna laughed.

The three made their way back to the great hall and broke their fast together. A little while later Kaela walked to the gate and watched Arik, Brenna and Mattie leave. Mattie waved until they were out of sight. Again, Kaela felt a shiver of dread. All the way back to the keep, she reprimanded herself for being silly. When she entered the great hall, she found Jacob there and crossed to his side. Mayhap his cheerful smile would banish her fears.

Several hours later Kaela heard screams in the outer bailey. She dropped the urn she was polishing and ran through the hall, knowing in her heart something dreadful had happened.

The scene in the courtyard made her blood run cold. Hearing Maude's keening wail, Kaela tore her way through the huddled warriors. When she reached the center, she found her old nurse on her knees in the dirt. Jacob bent over her, apparently trying to calm the woman. Kaela's gaze flew to Brenna's bruised cheek and bleeding lip. Even with Andrew's arms around her, Brenna tried to reach out to Maude.

Kaela felt her world spinning out of control at the despair and utter horror she saw in Brenna's tortured gaze. She clenched her fist, her nails digging into the palms of her hands. "Tell me, Brenna."

Brenna gazed down at Maude for a moment, then raised her eyes to Kaela's. Though, she tried to speak, for a moment nothing came out, but Kaela knew.

"Broderick?" Kaela spoke the name in a voice so soft she could barely be heard over Maude's hysterics.

Brenna nodded as fresh tears streamed down her cheeks. "H-he h-has M-Mattie," she stammered, and buried her head in Andrew's shoulder.

Kaela grabbed her, whirled her around, and gripped

Brenna's shoulders so hard she knew she caused her pain, but could not stop herself. "Tell me!"

"We had just left Phoebe's hut. I had given her the tea like you told me to. We were riding home and suddenly, out of nowhere, they c-came at us."

"How many?" Andrew had turned pale.

"At least a dozen, I think. I don't know for sure. One minute we were laughing and singing a song, and the n-next they were on us. I saw Broderick right away, Kaela. He attacked Arik and knocked him from his horse. Arik staggered to his feet to fight, but he didn't last long. Broderick struck him several times with his sword. God's teeth, there was so much blood… he is terribly hurt, probably dead." Brenna swayed on her feet and Andrew reached for her again to steady her.

Maude cried out again, screaming over and over, "My baby, my baby."

"Get her inside, Jacob," Kaela ordered, and watched numbly while he carried the old woman away.

Taking Maude toward the keep, Jacob spoke to Andrew. "Have some of the men ride out for Arik."

"What about Mattie?" Kaela asked.

"H-he has her. Oh, God, Kaela, he holds her in ransom for you," Brenna cried. "He knocked me from my horse and grabbed Mattie. When I begged him not to harm her, one of his men struck me. Broderick ordered me to say you have one hour to meet him on the east ridge. If y-you don't come by then, he will kill her." Trembling, with great sobs racking her body, Brenna collapsed in Andrew's arms.

"May God damn that whoreson to hell." Making his way back to Kaela's side, Jacob bellowed. The soldiers in the bailey, a grim lot, cursed loudly.

Kaela turned on her heel and stormed back toward the keep.

"Where are you going?" Jacob bellowed.

Kaela never looked around or slowed her step.

"To get ready."

Jacob, Andrew, and Brenna followed on her heels.

"You can't mean to go, Kaela. You know what that bastard will do to you," Andrew said.

Brenna gasped. "But what about, Mattie?"

Grave, Andrew met Brenna's gaze. "She can do nothing to save the child anyway, Brenna."

"Don't say that!" Kaela trembled from head to toe. Holy Mother of God, Broderick had her baby. Little Mattie, so innocent and trusting, in that devil's hands. She fought to keep from collapsing on the spot. Taking several deep breaths, she steeled herself for what she had to do.

"I will go after the bastard," Andrew said, his voice cold. He looked to Jacob. "We can take a dozen men, circle around the lake, then come up behind them. With any luck, we will have the element of surprise on our side."

"Nay," Kaela said. "He would kill her for sure then. Broderick knows the land too well. He grew up here, Andrew. He expects you to give chase. He will have men watching. I know my cousin, believe me. The only way we can assure Mattie's safety is for me to go to him."

"Kaela, you can't. Cameron would never allow you to leave the keep under these circumstances," Andrew argued. "You carry his child. God's truth, he loves you. He would never survive if anything happened to you or his babe."

"And if I stay here and an innocent child is murdered?

What then, Andrew? How will he live with that? How will any of us live with that? Mattie is like my own. She's Brenna's sister. God's truth, even Cameron has grown to love her as if she were his. After what happened to Peter, do you really think Cameron could live with Mattie's death?"

Andrew stared at her for a moment. Anguish filled his voice when he answered. "What are the chances of saving her, Kaela? Be reasonable. We would only lose you, too. Don't you see?"

"Nay, I do not see! 'Tis truth, Andrew, I know Broderick better than anyone. Believe me, he will not harm Mattie as long as he thinks he can use her to get to me. He wants me very badly and has waited a long time for this. His vengeance will not be swift, but slow and painful. We will have enough time to get word to Cameron, and he will come for me." Kaela's voice no longer quivered. She was deadly calm.

"Broderick has no idea I am with child. I am too far along for him to harm my child without also risking my life. He will never kill me before he has his satisfaction."

"Oh, God," Brenna cried.

Kaela stared them down. "I am going. We waste precious time with foolish arguments. Brenna, go get my cloak. Pack a change of clothes for me, and send a servant to the stables to saddle my horse." Kaela walked to the trestle table and sat down, Jacob and Andrew right behind her.

"This is what we will do," she said, calmly. "I will ride out to meet him. With luck, I will be able to talk him into leaving Mattie behind. He has no reason to harm her, not once he has me."

"Since when has that whoreson ever needed a

reason?" Jacob asked, tight lipped.

Kaela met his gaze, then looked away. "We must hope for the best. Andrew, I need the best tracker you have."

"'Twould be me, Kaela. No one is better, except for Thorsen."

"'Tis settled then." Impulsively, she reached out to take his warm hand in her cold one. "'Twill be a comfort knowing you follow me. You must ride alone, I think, leaving after I do. Ride north towards Kent. Broderick will assume you've sent a messenger for Cameron. Circle the lake and head for the Welsh border. Our best guess says Broderick's hideout lies somewhere near there. Will you be able to find our trail?"

"'Tis a promise," he said, squeezing her hand.

"Good, I am counting on you. Due to my condition, Broderick will not be able to travel as quickly as he would like. Hopefully, 'twill slow us down enough for Cameron to catch up. We must send a message to him immediately."

"I have already sent the missive, Kaela," Jacob said. "'Tis a hard two days ride to Kent."

"We will have time, Jacob. My babe will guarantee that." Kaela spoke with more conviction than she truly felt. "Andrew, once you are sure about our general direction, you must ride back to Chaldron and meet your brother. Cameron will know what to do then. Now, time is quickly running out. Jacob, will you get me a quill and parchment? I want to leave a message for my husband."

Once Jacob left, Andrew took his new sister into his arms and held her. "God's truth, Kaela, this is going to destroy Cameron."

"I know, Andrew, but we have no choice. 'Tis what

Cameron would do. I have every faith my husband will rescue me. I have out-smarted Broderick before, you know." She tried to smile, but failed miserably.

Jacob returned with the parchment, and they left her alone for a moment. Kaela prayed her plan would work. Terrified for Mattie, and filled with sorrow for Cameron, she knew he would be devastated. "Please God, let him reach me in time. Don't separate us now. 'Twould be more than either of us could bear."

Kaela met Jacob, Andrew, and Brenna in the court-yard. She gave them each a brief hug before letting Jacob help her mount, then gave the parchment to Brenna. "See that my husband gets this immediately upon his arrival. Do not worry, cousin, I will bring Mattie home."

"I know you will, Kaela. God's speed!"

Kaela rode out swiftly. She did not look back. To do so might have weakened her resolve.

Riding to meet her enemy, she tried not to think about what lay ahead for her. She thought of Arik instead, praying that by some miracle he might live. The soldiers had not returned with his body before she left. She had no way to know his fate.

Twenty minutes later when Kaela reached the ridge, Broderick waited for her. She breathed a relieved sigh at the sight of Mattie. Thank God the child still lived.

Broderick's cold pale eyes bored into hers. Immediately, his men surrounded her. He held Mattie to his breast. Her eyes were red and swollen from crying. Dismounting, he shoved the child into another soldier's arms, and approached Kaela.

"Get down."

Kaela dismounted, clutching her cloak around her.

When Mattie began to cry for her, Kaela stepped forward to reach for the child. Broderick clutched her arm, his strong fingers digging into her flesh.

"I have waited a long time for this moment, Kaela. You are finally mine."

"I will never be yours, Broderick." She stood ramrod straight, meeting his stare with cold defiance.

"We will see how you feel after tonight, cousin. You will pay dearly for your escape from Ralston. Aye, you thought you were clever, running from me while I fought that whoreson you married. For that you will pay the greatest price, Kaela. You gave yourself in marriage to that bastard." Raging, he reached for her so suddenly Kaela had no time to evade him.

Grabbing her hair, he pulled her to him, clamping his other hand painfully around her jaw and forcing her lips to his. His hot tongue invaded her mouth and bile rose in her throat. With all her strength, she pushed against him and bit down on his tongue. Broderick yelped and pulled back. In the same instant, he back-handed her across the face. When she tumbled to the ground, her cloak fell away from her shoulders. He stared down at her, his shocked gaze on her extended belly.

"God damn you to hell, you bitch! You carry that bastard's whelp!" Advancing on her, he screamed the words.

Kaela scrambled to her feet. "Aye, Broderick, I am with child and there is nothing you can do about it."

"You think not? I can beat the hell out of you, you bitch. 'Twill be a pleasure to watch you lose D'Abernon's child." His eyes were wild with fury.

"You can beat me if you wish, Broderick, but if

you cause me to lose this child now, you will kill me at the same time," she said to him, her voice icy calm. She could tell by the confusion in his eyes that he struggled with her words.

"What say you?"

"I am too far along in my confinement to abort this child easily. You can see the babe is due to be delivered very shortly. If you force me to lose it, more than likely I will die with my child."

"You would like that, wouldn't you Kaela? To escape me so easily? Well, it won't happen. You will deliver that bastard's child, and I will have the pleasure of watching your face while I kill it. Then, my dear, I will use you until I tire of you. Your death will be painful and slow when the time comes, Kaela, and I will enjoy every minute of it."

His laughter held an eerie sound. Kaela shivered. She had bought the time she needed. Now she must try to save Mattie.

"Prepare to ride," Broderick ordered his men.

The soldier who held Mattie approached with the crying child. "What do you want to do with this one?"

"Kill her."

"Nay, Broderick, you cannot," Kaela screamed, lunging for the child. Mattie struggled in the soldier's arms, crying for Kaela. Kaela reached for her and, with a nod from Broderick, the soldier released her. Mattie buried her head in Kaela's neck, clinging for dear life. Kaela held her tightly and turned back to her cousin.

"She is only a child, Broderick. She can do you no harm. Release her, I pray thee. Someone from Chaldron will come for her after we leave."

"You plead with me for her life, Kaela?" Broderick's

strange laughter rang out again.

"Aye, I do. Please, Broderick, she is an innocent child."

"Hmm… one you care for greatly, I see. 'Twill give me pleasure to hurt someone you love. Aye, and better control of you. The brat goes with us. Do exactly as I say, and I will spare her. If not, she dies."

"Broderick, please…"

"'Tis decided. Stop whining, bitch, and mount your horse. The child rides with you, if you can stop her wailing. If not, I may kill her if only to shut her up." Taking a rope from his saddle pack, Broderick tied it around Kaela's neck.

"What are you doing?" she asked, her eyes wide with surprise.

"Securing my prisoner. You will not escape me again." When he tugged, she stumbled forward.

Broderick laughed. "Aye, this will do nicely." He mounted his horse and looped the rope over the saddle horn.

Kaela mounted clumsily and the soldier passed Mattie up to her. She held the child in her arms, whispering soothing words. "Hush, sweet pea. I have you now, but you must be quiet, Mattie. 'Tis the only way I can keep you safe."

"I'm scared, Kaela. The devil hurt Arik bad and hit Brenna, too. I want to go home."

Kaela felt her little body trembling. "I know, sweet pea, but we can't go home yet," Kaela crooned, rubbing the child's arms.

Moving now, they rode single file, Kaela and Mattie behind Broderick. She had to be careful to keep up with him or the rope would jerk painfully on her neck.

"I want Wolf, Kaela," Mattie whispered. "He will make the devil man leave us alone."

Kaela smiled at that. "Aye, he will, Mattie, and Cameron will come for us, sweet pea. But you have to be patient. 'Tis going to take a while for him to find us. Until then we must be very quiet and do what these men tell us. Do you understand, Mattie?"

Nodding the child leaned into Kaela. She had stopped crying for the moment. Kaela said a quick prayer of thanks. A few moments later, she heard Mattie's even breathing and knew she had fallen asleep.

The babe sat heavily in Kaela's belly and riding was difficult. Mattie's added weight pressed into her. The rope, heavy and uncomfortable, weighed on her flesh and on her spirit.

"Come soon, my love," Kaela prayed. "And please give me the strength, Lord, to keep Mattie and my babe safe until Cameron finds us."

Sick with worry, Cameron slowed Goliath and galloped across the draw bridge into the outer bailey. The messenger had reached him late the night before last and he, Thorsen, and Johnathan had left immediately for home. They had ridden hard, stopping only to rest the horses. The message had been short and cryptic, stating only that he return to Chaldron immediately. Terrible things had gone through his mind. Had something happened to Kaela? Had she gone into labor? 'Twas too soon for the babe to be born. He would know soon enough.

Dread settled around his heart when he saw Brenna

running toward him, with Jacob at her heels. Neither Kaela nor Andrew followed them. Something was very wrong.

Brenna hesitated for a moment, looking every-where but at Cameron. He noticed her bruised face and dismounted, stepping forward to close the distance between them. He took her face gently in his hands, forcing her brown gaze to meet his.

"What has happened?" Cameron fought to control his panic, but his voice shook.

Brenna sobbed and collapsed against him. Jacob came forward and quickly gave an accounting of Broderick's treachery. Cameron, filled with shock and rage, could barely think.

Thorsen and Johnathan stepped to his side. "Let us go inside, Wolf. We have plans to make," Thorsen said, putting a hand on Cameron's shoulder.

At Cameron's nod, they all moved at once to enter the keep.

Jacob continued, telling Cameron he expected Andrew back at any time. Cameron felt calmer, knowing Andrew had tracked her. His brother would not let him down.

When Brenna pressed something in his hand, he looked down at the parchment for a moment before he raised his gaze to hers.

"Kaela left a letter for you."

Cameron heard his heart-beat roar in his ears. He looked down at her missive, now crumpled in his hand. He rose slowly and walked across the hall to the solar, closing the door behind him. Slowly, he broke the seal and opened the parchment. Reading her precious words, he could almost hear her soft, sweet voice.

My Dear Husband,

As you know by now, I have gone with Broderick. 'Tis sorry I am that I broke my promise, but I could not leave Mattie to suffer at his hands. I know in my heart I have done what you would have me do.

I have every confidence you will come for me, my love. I vow I will stay alive until you find me. I know this in my heart, husband. This knowledge gives me the courage to endure any trial.

Hurry, my love, and Cameron, take care! Broderick has no honor—you must remember that.

I love you, husband, and will think of you and pray for your safety every minute.

Your loving wife,

Forever,

Kaela

Cameron dropped into a chair before his shaky knees gave way. He read her letter again, the writing blurred by the mistiness in his eyes. "Forever, Kaela," he whispered softly.

Her words gave him comfort. She was too stubborn to die and he was too stubborn to let her. "Dear God, I cannot lose her now." He stood, his resolve renewed and firm, and joined his friends. He carefully folded the letter before he tucked it in his belt.

They had decided to leave on the morrow, when Andrew burst into the hall and made his way to his brother.

"Broderick has taken her over the border into Wales, even as we thought he would," Andrew said, then opened his arms to Brenna. He held her to him, but his gaze never left Cameron's. "The bastard has a rope tethered to her neck, but she seems unharmed, as far as I could tell from so great a distance. Mattie is with her."

Cameron's face turned to stone, but his hands clenched in his lap.

"Their camp?"

"'Tis high in the Black Mountains. From what I could tell, they hide in a large cave. Facing east, the opening looks down on a large valley. They are no more than a half-day's ride beyond the border, Cameron."

"How many men?" Thorsen asked.

"No more than fifty, and they are battle weary."

"Aye," Johnathan said, "we saw the bastard no more than a sennight ago in Kent. Once he saw we were engaged in battle, he must have come directly to Chaldron.

"'Tis to our advantage his men are worn, but that whoreson will be expecting us. He knows I won't give up Kaela this easily," Cameron said.

"What is your plan?" Jacob asked.

Cameron felt a steely calm come over him. "Johnathan, prepare the men. We take five score with us, enough to keep Broderick and his men busy."

"They will see our approach several miles out, Cameron. He could take Kaela and flee once he realizes you know his location. Worse, he could kill her."

"Nay, Kaela was right about that. He will not kill her before he has the chance to sorely abuse her," Jacob said.

"I want him to see our men approach. This is the plan. Thorsen and I will go ahead of you and reach the camp area undetected."

"If anyone can do that, brother, 'twould be you and this Viking." Andrew clapped both men on the back.

Cameron smiled grimly and directed his words to

Johnathan. "You, my friend, are to wear my armor and shield. I want you to ride Goliath."

Johnathan smiled broadly. "Ah, I begin to understand."

"You will take the men and camp in the valley below the cave, sending out search parties every few hours. We want the bastard to know we are looking for him, but he must think we do not know his exact location."

"He will think Johnathan is you?" Brenna asked.

"Aye, that way he will not be so guarded. He will think he has Cameron right where he wants him." Andrew grinned.

"They will be outnumbered, but will think they have the advantage of surprise when they attack," Thorsen said.

"Once Broderick's men have moved into position in the valley, Thorsen and I will rescue Kaela and Mattie."

"Much could go wrong."

"Nothing will go wrong. I will not allow it," Cameron said.

"Kaela told me the same thing. Her faith in you knows no bounds, Baron. I believe she was right. You will bring her home to us." Jacob rubbed his hand across her eyes.

"How is Arik?" Andrew asked.

"He is alive, but I do not know for how long. Maude tends his wounds. He lost much blood and there is infection."

Cameron felt his gut tense at Jacob's words. "He will be avenged. I will look in on him before we leave, which will be within the hour. You have your orders."

"What about me, brother?"

"You ride with Johnathan once we reach the border, but first you help Thorsen and me to pick up their trail."

"Brenna, I will need provisions for Thorsen and myself. Jacob, you see to the soldiers' supplies," Cameron ordered. He took Brenna aside and told her to pack dried venison strips, small bags of meal, and skins of water.

He left the hall and made his way to the chamber he shared with Kaela. His eyes went to the empty bed when he entered. He remembered the passion they had shared on their last night together. Turning, he gazed at her likeness in the tapestry on the wall, then placed his fingers on the finely woven threads. "Soon, my love, I will bring you home," he whispered, then stripped out of his mail.

He dressed quickly in the Viking tradition that was best for the work he had ahead of him. He pulled a tunic of soft doeskin over his head and added a rough jerkin of wolf fur that would keep him warm in the cold mountain heights. On his feet he wore doeskin boots that would make no noise as he tracked his prey. He pulled on warm fur leggings and bound them tightly to his muscular legs with soft leather laces. He added a leather belt in which he hung his broadsword and well honed dagger. Then he crossed the room and took the fierce looking Viking battle ax from its hook on the wall and secured it to his side.

Cameron found Thorsen in the stable, tying sacks of grain behind his saddle for the horses. His friend, also dressed in the Viking manner, nodded.

"We will bring her back safely, my friend, and the little one, too."

Cameron didn't trust his voice not to break so he

said nothing as he mounted his horse. The chestnut stallion, not trained as well as Goliath, would have to suffice.

They rode into the outer bailey where Johnathan, Andrew, and the chosen soldiers waited for them. Cameron had ordered Jacob and a spare crew to stay behind to man Chaldron's defenses. A messenger had already been sent to Kent with instructions for half of Cameron's men fighting there to return to Chaldron.

Cameron spoke quietly with Brenna for a moment before giving the signal to depart. He was the first to ride out across the drawbridge.

Chapter Twenty One

❖   ❖   ❖

The men rode hard, not making camp until late that night.

Cameron, close to exhaustion, found sleep impossible. He was a man tormented. Every time he closed his eyes he pictured Kaela with Broderick. Only by sheer willpower did he maintain the iron-clad control he needed.

They rode out again at dawn. With the setting of the sun, they reached the border and made camp. Johnathan and Andrew joined Cameron and Thorsen at the fire. Andrew had already shown Cameron where Broderick had crossed, his trail still visible. Cameron and Thorsen would leave at first light. The four men ate their meager meal in relative silence and sat for a while reviewing their plans. After a time Andrew and Johnathan retired, leaving Thorsen and Cameron alone.

"She has been with him for well over a sennight," Cameron said, His voice was filled with anguish. "God alone knows what he has done to her and little Mattie. God's teeth, Thorsen, Mattie is only five summers, not much older than Peter when he died. She is like him in so many ways, innocent and trusting, full of life and laughter." His voice broke. "If he has hurt them in any way, I swear I'll—"

Thorsen cut him off. "Kaela's reasoning was logical, Cameron. Broderick has waited long to have her. He won't risk losing her so soon. He will be forced to wait until she delivers the babe. As for Mattie, we know Kaela will find a way to protect her."

"I pray you are right, Thorsen. I can't lose them now. If anything happens to them…"

"I know, friend, I know. We will bring them home safely. Kaela will give you a fine son. I have already ordered a broadsword made for the lad."

Cameron smiled at that, a weak smile, but a smile just the same. His thoughts turned back to Kaela and what she must be going through. His innocent wife was back in the devil's hands. The thought chilled his soul.

"The moon is full," Thorsen stated.

"Aye, let us take advantage of its light." Cameron rose to his feet.

Without another word, they saddled their horses and slipped across the border.

Wales

Kaela rolled over in her sleep. The sharp pain in her head woke her. Tentatively, she raised one hand to touch the swelling around her right eye. The bump was still there, but not quite as bad as it had been earlier. She shivered with cold and held Mattie tighter, pulling the fur securely around them. The precious child still slept, snuggled into her side.

Nearly a fortnight had passed since Broderick had taken them. Kaela's fear grew stronger every day. Broderick was losing his patience. He taunted her constantly and flew into a blind rage over the smallest thing. She needed all her concentration to keep him calm and away from Mattie. Thus far she had been successful, but she sensed her time was running out.

Aching all over, she greatly feared she would give birth to her babe before Cameron reached her. Broderick would kill her child. She and Mattie had to escape before that happened. "God, Cameron, where are you?" she whispered softly. Mattie brushed her hand against Kaela's neck and she winced against the pain.

Broderick had kept the rope around her neck until the day before yesterday. Her wrists and ankles had been tied since they reached the cave. For some reason, he had untied her yesterday. She supposed he grew more confident as each day passed. Where could she go? They were high in the mountains and her time was very near. At least she had managed to steal a dagger from one of the soldiers. She had hidden the blade in her boot.

The men had been excited about something during the day. Most had ridden out of camp. Even Broderick had been gone for most of the day, but had returned before nightfall. He seemed almost gleeful, though he said nothing to her. She noticed he had only one guard posted at the cave entrance this eve, instead of the usual two.

She could not wait any longer. Broderick was too restless. He would hurt Mattie soon. She could sense his need to inflict pain. Straining to hear the lightest sound, no longer willing to cower in the darkness, she shook Mattie awake.

"'Tis time to leave, little one," she whispered in the child's ear. "You must be very quiet, Mattie. Do you understand?"

Mattie nodded her head and took Kaela's hand. "Good, sweet pea, you have been so brave," Kaela whispered to her as she gathered up the fur they had been using to take it with them.

Slipping the dagger into her right hand and, placing the fur under her left arm, she took Mattie's hand. Very slowly they made their way toward the entrance. Only a handful of Broderick's men remained, snoring loudly where they lay huddled in their furs. She wondered again where the others had gone. Broderick slept in his usual place, directly across from her. She could hear his heavy breathing.

Kaela approached the opening, every nerve stretched to the limit. She stopped and listened for several minutes. Hearing nothing but the snores around her, she gritted her teeth and crept forward. Amazed and relieved, she found the guard asleep. She and Mattie scuttled past him and out into the cold, dark night.

No sign of life, human or animal, met her. Engulfed with mind-numbing desolation, she pulled Mattie along behind her while she made her way farther up the mountain. She didn't relish the climb, but if she descended, she would be more apt to run into Broderick's men. Nay, the safest route was to climb, then circle around to the other side before she descended. With any luck they might find a cottage or other shelter once they reached the valley. Mayhap she could find help, or if not, steal a horse.

Cold and pungent, the air smelled of damp moss

'Twas a living smell, with the slightest hint of salt from the sea. They moved along as quietly as possible until they reached the foot of a ridge. The terrain grew rougher, the wind more biting. Kaela stopped and took the shivering child into her arms, wrapping the fur around her and tying it with her own belt.

"You did so well, Mattie. 'Tis proud I am of you."

"I thought we were going to wait for Wolf to come."

"I was afraid to wait any longer, sweet pea. I thought we could meet him half way." Mattie smiled at that idea, and Kaela felt relieved. The child's resilience amazed her.

They started slowly up the steep incline, Kaela pushing Mattie up in front of her. Her long skirts and the babe slowed her progress, and Kaela cursed fluently under her breath. The two scrambled over boulders, dislodging small rocks as they climbed. The sun had begun to rise when they topped the ridge. Kaela had not realized dawn was so near. She had hoped to be much farther from the camp by daylight. Broderick always awoke with first light. An able tracker, her cousin would soon be after them.

As if her thoughts conjured him, she heard a noise. Looking back the way they had come, she saw him advancing toward her. Oh, God, no! Still a distance away, he had seen them and moved far more quickly than they. "Please, God," she prayed, "don't let him catch us."

Along the ridge top, tall firs forested a gently sloping incline. Kaela fled into the dense foliage. She soon stumbled onto a natural fissure carved into the rocky mountainside. The opening just big enough for Mattie to hide in. Shrubs covered the face of the low-hanging crevice.

Kaela dropped to her knees and drew Mattie into her arms. "I want you to hide in here for me, sweet pea."

"Alone?" Mattie's blue eyes grew huge with fear.

"Aye, but not for long. I will come back for you, I promise. I have to make sure we were not followed," Kaela said, lying, for she didn't want to frighten her any further. "Do not come out Mattie, no matter what you hear. You must promise me, you will not come out until I come for you."

"All right, Kaela, but hurry." Her mouth quivering, Mattie crawled into the narrow space.

Kaela heard Broderick crashing up the ridge. She snatched her dagger from her boot and ran back to intercept him.

❖   ❖   ❖

Cameron and Thorsen had ridden through the cold night and located Broderick's hideout before dawn. They surveyed the area with a critical eye. The Black Mountains were unforgiving with hostile peaks and naked ridges, but the cave Broderick had chosen for his lair, though not as high as it could have been, offered no way to approach from the front without being seen. They walked soundlessly amongst the towering oaks that seemed to close in on them. Their soft doeskin boots made not a whisper against the damp heather and bracken.

They decided to circumvent the ridge, climb the mountain's steep face, and approach from behind the cave entrance. The climb would take precious time, but they saw no other way to reach Kaela without being detected. They found a heavily wooded area near the Usk river and tethered their horses there, ate a quick meal, and started to climb. They forged their way upward the remainder of the day and into the night, stopping only once for a short while to rest.

"Johnathan and Andrew should have reached the valley by now," Cameron said. The men had hardly spoken throughout the long day, both lost in thoughts of what was to come. They didn't need words to communicate. They had been together so long, 'twas easy to read each other's mind.

"Aye, they should have reached the valley by midday. By now Broderick has sent his men down the mountain to lie in ambush."

They continued to climb, reaching the top around midnight, when they began their descent. Close to dawn, they had the cave in view. Cameron scanned the nearby slopes for signs of movement. Satisfied there was no guard posted, he turned to Thorsen.

"If we make our way to the ridge below, we should be able to see the cave entrance. Once we are certain the Saxons have gone down to meet Johnathan, we can be about rescuing my wife." Cameron glanced down to the ridge in question. His heart stood still. He couldn't breathe, but stood there gaping while his wife pushed a fur bundle up over the ledge and scrambled up behind it. In disbelief, he watched her disappear behind the cover of the trees.

"Holy Mother of God," he whispered. Then, as one, he and Thorsen started to make their way toward her.

Kaela reached the ledge, her dagger in hand, her heart pounding so loudly she knew Broderick could

372   LEE ANN DANSBY

hear the sound. Stopping a few feet from the edge, she
tried to decide how best to meet him.

She heard not a sound and was quite shocked when
she felt a strong arm steal around her and clamp down
over her mouth. She almost passed out from fear when
the huge brute who held her whirled her to face him.
She stared into the most beautiful blue eyes she had
ever seen.

She tried to speak, but Cameron shook his head
and lifted her in his arms, running for the cover of the
trees. Kaela saw Thorsen then, and her heart sang with
pure joy.

They heard Broderick scrambling up the mountain,
screaming orders to a soldier who clambered up the
ridge behind him.

Cameron shoved Kaela behind a huge fir tree and
kissed her. Although she clung to him, he pulled her
arms from his neck, "Don't move one inch from this
spot until I come for you. Where is Mattie?"

"I hid her in a crevice."

"Good girl, now stay put." Cameron kissed her
again, then started toward the ridge with Thorsen.

"Be careful," she whispered to his retreating back.
Watching them move back to the ridge, she couldn't
believe they had found her.

Cameron and Thorsen ducked behind two large
boulders as Broderick crested the ridge line.

"Kaela, you bitch, come out! There is no way you
can hide from me." Screaming the words, he stormed
forward. "You will pay for this! The child is dead, do
you hear—you have signed her death warrant."

Cameron stepped from his hiding place and smiled
at the pure shock he saw on Broderick's face.

"I think not, Broderick. I believe 'tis your death

we will see this day." Cold-eyed, his mouth set in a grim line, he drew his sword and advanced on the Saxon.

Recovering quickly, Broderick drew his sword from its sheath. "I will see you in hell, D'Abernon. You will never touch the slut again. She is mine!"

The two men charged, their broadswords crashing blade against blade, the sound of metal against metal singing down the mountain. From the distance, Cameron could hear other sounds of battle, and knew Johnathan had engaged Broderick's men. Thorsen had followed Cameron into the open and stood, silent, to watch Broderick meet his death.

The two men matched each other blow for blow, but Broderick tired quickly. They circled each other, wielding their swords with deadly accuracy. Cameron slowly forced Broderick backward, closer to the edge of the ridge.

Broderick's man came hurling over the ridge, a battle cry on his lips, his sword drawn. He lunged toward Cameron.

Thorsen grabbed his battle ax in both hands and, raising it over his head, he let the weapon fly. The honed edge buried itself in the Saxon's skull dropping him instantly.

Cameron met Broderick's sword once again and muttered between gritted teeth, "You will burn in the fires of hell for all eternity for what you have done to my wife."

His eyes wild, Broderick laughed and met Cameron's next blow. With the blood lust racing strong in his veins, he attacked with greater fervor.

Cameron moved quickly to the right, missing a blow to his arm. He spun, thrusting his sword forward at the same moment Broderick stumbled on the loose gravel. Cameron's sword rammed into Broderick's chest, piercing his heart. Surprise and dismay chased across Broderick's face as Cameron withdrew his sword.

"Burn in hell, you whoreson," Cameron said in an icy, hate filled voice, then lifted one booted foot and kicked the dying man over the ledge.

"'Tis done," Cameron said, satisfied.

"Aye, my friend, 'tis done."

Cameron turned at the sound of Kaela's cry. Smiling broadly, he watched his very pregnant wife make her way toward him. He reached her in three long strides, hugged her to him, and buried his face in her hair.

"'Tis over, sweetheart." He placed wild kisses all over her beautiful, dirty, bruised face. He blanched at the ugly bruise around her eye and swiftly ran his hands over her body. "Are you hurt, sweetheart?"

"Nay, only a little," she said, tilting her face up to look at him.

He gasped when he saw the raw welts around her neck. "God's teeth, I wish that bastard would get up so I could kill him again."

"Hush, Cameron, 'tis over. Thank God, 'tis over," Kaela whispered, kissing him with desperate urgency.

She pulled away from Cameron, then ran to Thorsen. Standing on tiptoe, her arms around his neck, she kissed him. The Viking blushed to the roots of his hair and Cameron and Kaela both laughed.

"Thank you for keeping him safe for me."

"Ha! I was taking care of him" Cameron replied.

"I see. Pray tell me, husband, whose battle ax is that?" Kaela asked, pointing to the dead Saxon.

Cameron only shrugged.

Thorsen laughed as he pulled away from Kaela's embrace.

"What were you planning to do with that dagger, wife?"

"Why, kill Broderick, of course."

Cameron and Thorsen scowled at her. Cameron realized his knees were shaking. He caught Kaela in his arms once more, and tried not to think how close he had come to losing her.

"Where is Mattie?" Cameron asked.

"Mattie! God's truth, she must be so frightened." Kaela turned and started back up the slope.

Cameron swept her off her feet and into his arms. "Show us where she is. You have to rest, Kaela, or have you forgotten about our babe?"

Kaela smiled and laid her head against his shoulder. She pointed the way, but Cameron carried her until they reached Mattie's hiding place. They stopped in front of the crevice and Kaela called softly to the little girl.

"Mattie, 'tis safe now, sweet pea. Your Wolf has come for us. Thorsen is here, too. He's going to reach in now and pull you out."

Thorsen pushed the brush aside, reached in, and brought Mattie out, then held her in his arms. She beamed up at him, tears streaming down her dirty little face, and placed a sweet, wet kiss on his mouth. Thorsen gave her a huge smile.

Cameron took Mattie from Thorsen.

"I knew you would come, Wolf," she whispered. He hugged her, placing soft kisses against her hair.

"Of course I came, sweet pea. I could not let my two best girls get away from me." His voice cracked with emotion. He didn't even notice the tears that dampened his face.

"Can we go home now?" Mattie asked, grinning from ear to ear.

"Aye, right now." Cameron handed Mattie back to Thorsen. With great care, the men helped Kaela descend to the cave. Mattie rode on Thorsen's back, giving him orders all the way.

"Where were you going with her?" Cameron finally thought to ask Kaela.

"To find you," Kaela said, smiling. Then she sobered and buried her face in his neck. "I was so afraid, Cameron. Broderick became more violent with each passing day. He would have hurt Mattie. I could not wait any longer. I feared I would run into his men if I went down the mountain, so I went up instead. Are you angry with me?"

"Angry? Never. You made my task a lot easier by coming to me."

"I love you so much, Cameron. Promise me we will never be parted again."

"I will never again let you out of my sight, wife. You are my life. When I thought I might have lost you, I nearly went insane. I love you, sweetheart, more than my life."

He kissed her then, long and hard, and when he lifted his lips from hers, their soldiers applauded with a rousing cheer. Kaela blushed a bright red when she found herself surrounded by Cameron's men. Smiling broadly, Andrew held out his arms, and Cameron passed her to him. Her brother-in-law kissed her and handed her to Johnathan, who did the same. When he started to give her to Thorsen, Cameron interceded.

"'Tis enough. She already kissed him on the ridge,"

he said, grumbling when the men laughed.

Andrew took Mattie up on his shoulders and the company made its way down the mountain.

Cameron took Kaela up in front of him on Goliath. He wanted her in his arms. He worried, knowing she was far too pregnant and too exhausted to be riding.

When they made camp, Kaela stayed awake only long enough to eat. She curled into Cameron's side and slept restlessly through the night. By dawn, they were on the road again. Cameron was relieved to see the torch lights on Chaldron's walls when night approached. Kaela, awake most of the day, had been very quiet. She'd spoken only when he asked her a question. She sighed when he told her they were home.

"'Tis glad I am, husband. I was beginning to think our babe would be born on this horse."

"God's teeth, Kaela, why didn't you tell me?"

"Because I was busy trying to calm myself. I did not need to have to calm you, too. That's why." She squeezed his hand tightly as she felt another contraction.

"How long have you known?" He couldn't hide the concern in his voice.

"Since this morn."

"Curse the saints, woman, you will yet be the death of me." He kissed the top of her head. "Hold on, sweetheart, we are almost there.

Chapter Twenty Two

✣ ✣ ✣

They entered the bailey to be greeted by thunderous cheers. Brenna, Maude, and Jacob stood in the forefront, then ran towards them. Cameron dismounted with Kaela in his arms.

"Thank God you are safe," Jacob said when he reached them.

"Kaela's time is here. We need to hurry," Cameron told Maude, striding toward the keep.

"What did he say?" Brenna asked. Reaching for Mattie, she hugged her sister.

"I believe he said that Kaela is having her babe." Leaning over, Andrew kissed her lips.

"Oh my God!" Brenna thrust Mattie into Andrew's arms and ran after Maude, who followed on Cameron's heels.

Cameron took the stairs two at a time. In their chamber, he gently settled Kaela on their bed.

"I'll take over here, Baron. Ye can wait down stairs," Maude said briskly, and pushed him aside.

"Nay." Kaela reached for her husband.

"Don't worry, sweetheart. I'm not going anywhere." Cameron sat beside her on the bed and took her hand in his. "'Tis my babe, too. I will see him born." He smoothed her hair from her brow, kissed her forehead.

"I am afraid," Kaela whispered.

Maude frowned.

"So am I, a little, but I am excited, too. Think, sweetheart, our first child is about to be born."

"I would rather you do it, Cameron."

He laughed. "I would if I could, sweeting, but I think you will be better at this than I."

Kaela smiled until another contraction hit her, and she moaned.

Blanching, Cameron took her hand in his shaky one. Looking at Maude, he said, "Tell me what I can do."

The old woman scowled at him. "Not much, except stay out of my way. Never in my life have I heard of a man staying for a birthing."

"I'm not leaving," Cameron said sternly.

"All right then, stay by her and hold her hand." Grumbling, Maude turned to Brenna with her orders. "Get some hot water up here, girl, and extra bedding."

Brenna ran from the room to do her bidding.

"Maude, how is Arik?" Kaela asked, her green eyes wide with worry.

"He's alive, mistress. I didn't think he could live when I first saw him. There was so much blood. Both sides were pierced, but the thrusts missed anything vital. He still has a bit of the fever, but he'll pull through." Two giant tears slid down her wrinkled face.

Kaela beamed. "Oh Maude, I am so relieved."

"I know ye are, milady. Don't worry your head none about my Arik. Let's get this babe born."

They spent the next hour on preparations. Maude stripped the bed and put on several layers of fresh bedding, while Cameron, with Brenna's help, stripped

Kaela, bathed her and put her in a fresh nightrail. Every time she had a contraction, they stopped what they were doing. She would cling to Cameron for dear life while he whispered soothing words in her ear.

When they were done, Cameron helped her to the bed, but she didn't stay there long. Nervous and in pain, she walked instead, back and forth across the room. Cameron took every step she took, while Maude grumbled and Brenna smiled.

Near midnight the contractions were strong and close together. Kaela finally consented to lie down. Relieved, a worn-out Cameron sat by her side and leaned against the head rest. Kaela leaned against him, and gripped his hands tightly.

Another contraction took her and she cried out with the pain. Cameron felt all color drain from his face. Sweet Jesu, the babe was killing her. Please, God, he prayed, don't take her from me.

He opened his eyes to see Maude's frowning face.

"Don't ye go weak on me now, Baron. Kaela is just fine. 'Tis natural to scream when ye are birthing a babe."

Cameron gave her a doubtful glance, but he felt relieved just the same.

Difficult and unending, the last hour of labor dragged by. Kaela screamed in agony. Sick with fear, Cameron swore he would never again get her with child. Kaela bore down with all her might during each long, excruciating contraction. Maude placed Cameron's hand on Kaela's stomach and had him push down with each contraction, but the babe didn't cooperate and the pain grew worse.

They repeated the process with the next contraction. Tiring quickly, Kaela trembled with exhaustion.

Tenderly, Cameron wiped her face with a damp cloth. Maude knelt to check her progress.

"Praise God," Maude said. "I can see the babe's head."

Kaela smiled weakly and clutched Cameron's hand when another contraction gripped her.

"Push, sweetheart, push," Cameron urged.

Amazed, he saw a tiny head appear. Maude clasped it with both hands, pulling gently while Kaela pushed one last time. Maude grasped the babe and placed him across Kaela's stomach.

"Ye have a fine son."

Kaela cuddled their babe. "Isn't he beautiful?"

Cameron stared, open-mouthed, at the tiny, squalling babe. Heavy, black hair covered his small head.

"He has a roar as loud as his father's," Brenna said.

"He's perfect. A son, Kaela, a son," Cameron whispered, his eyes filled with tears.

When Brenna began to clean the babe, Kaela gasped, unexpectedly in the throes of another contraction. Brenna jumped back in alarm and Cameron grabbed Kaela's hand.

"What's wrong?"

"Nothing," Maude muttered, catching the beautiful baby girl. "'Twould seem ye also have a daughter."

Feeling very weak, Cameron collapsed on the bed. "Two babies?"

Smiling at her husband Kaela took her daughter in her arms. The baby had as much black hair as her brother.

Brenna handed Cameron his son. She cleaned the little girl and returned her to Kaela while Maude finished with the birthing, cleaned Kaela and made her comfortable. Then she followed Maude downstairs to tell the news.

Cameron and Kaela heard the cheers from below. Exchanging tender smiles, they placed the babies side by side between them.

"Twins. I can't believe it," Cameron said, kissing his wife.

"Oh, Cameron, are they not the most beautiful babies?" Kaela said, laughing.

"Aye, wife, as beautiful as their mother. Let me see my daughter."

Kaela lifted the blanket away from her little girl's face. Cameron leaned down to place a gentle kiss on his daughter's brow. When her tiny hand reached out and grasped his finger, he stared in wonder.

"What shall we name them?" Cameron asked.

"We should name our son after his father, I think. He will inherit your lands, why not your name?"

Cameron grinned. "Aye, I will be proud for him to have my name, but I think he should have one of his own, also."

"How about Charles?" Kaela suggested. "After my father."

"Charles Cameron D'Abernon. I like that. What about our beautiful daughter? Should we name her after her mother?"

"Why don't we name her after our mothers, instead?"

"Marisa Kathlin."

"I like that," Kaela said, her eyes misting.

Cameron took his sleeping son in his arms and carried both babies to the cradle that Andrew had built for Chaldron's heir. Then he went back to the bed and lay down beside his wife, taking her in his arms.

"You have made me the happiest of men, wife."

He kissed her so tenderly Kaela felt her heart would break with joy.

"I love you so much, Cameron," she said, cradling his head against her breasts.

"And I love you, sweetheart."

"Will you love me forever, my knight?"

"Forever, my love. Forever."

THE END

Author's Note

Dear Reader,

I hope you enjoyed reading Cameron and Kaela's story as much as I enjoyed writing it. I have always been fascinated with the medieval time period and I learned a great deal while doing research for this book.

Chaldron Castle is fictional and I took historical liberties with its architectural structure. It is conceivable to me that a forward thinking and well traveled man such as Kaela's father would have been influenced by the Norman castles of his time, and by his friendship with King Edward the Confessor, who appeared to love almost all things Norman.

In truth however, it was during William o Normandy's reign that the first stone castles were buil in England. Prior to William, England did have ston forts, churches, and roads, some dating from Roma times.

The Norman influence redefined the Saxon concep of a military fort and lead to the construction of castle as large all encompassing residential fortresses Castles became a very important part of feudalisi which was also introduced by the Normans. Mo castles in England were held by the Norman knigh who were favored by King Edward the Confesso

They were made barons and allowed to keep their holdings after the conquest, as they did not bear arms against William at Hastings.

On a lighter note, I took liberties with the addition of ladies undergarments which were not worn until the fourteenth century. Knights however, did wear a garment under their armor to protect from chafing.

If you enjoyed *Forever, My Knight,* please write and let me know.

Lee Ann Dansby
P.O. Box 1912
Alvin, TX 77512

Lee Ann Dansby
c/o LionHearted Publishing, Inc.
P.O. Box 618
Zephyr Cove, NV 89448

Dear Reader,

We hope you enjoyed this LionHearted novel. You may have already noticed some differences between our books and many others, beginning with our covers. I was always embarrassed to read books with 'bodice-ripping' covers in public, so I had our team of artists create covers I wouldn't even hesitate to recommend to my male friends.

You may also notice that necessary violent scenes in our novels have been toned down or take place out of view of the reader. I personally enjoy empowered heroines and heroes who show that honesty, integrity, high values, persistence and love will ultimately triumph over adversity.

We have a different vision of what constitutes excellence in romance fiction, and hope you agree. It takes authors with talent, skill, and imagination plus a diligent and caring editorial staff to produce entertaining and memorable stories. And it also takes *you!* Please write and let me know what you like so that we can keep providing quality and entertaining stories. And, don't forget to tell a friend about our books.

Mary Ann Heathman
President & CEO
LionHearted Publishing, Inc.

The LionHearted Story

♥　♥　♥

When forming LionHearted, we discovered that approximately 50% of all paperback books go unsold and are destroyed, often being dumped into our oceans as wastepaper. Yet more book titles are being released each month than there is space for on book store shelves. As the number of books increases, their shelf life decreases, severely limiting their exposure time to customers, and limited exposure means limited sales and lower author royalties. Also, many books being released now are actually re-issues of earlier titles that consumers have already read.

It appeared to us that there was a need for an alternative approach to the marketing and distribution of paperbacks, and in the methods of author compensation in the publishing industry. So we chose to create an environment where authors can earn better than average royalties and receive them sooner, and readers can turn their romance reading into an income producing activity by simply telling their friends about LionHearted books!

How often have you recommended a great movie, an excellent restaurant, a good book, or even a brand name you liked? All the time! But has any restaurant, movie theater or author ever reimbursed you for the highly effective "advertising" you did on their behalf? LionHearted does!

We will publish six new romance titles each month, and readers can purchase the books at discounted prices saving $1.00 or more per book over what they would expect to pay in stores.

Customers purchase their monthly six-pack from the LionHearted Romance Network (LRN), LionHearted's marketing division. Each six-pack will contain an entertaining and memorable variety of romance sub-genres such as contemporary, historical, Regency, time-travel, suspense, intrigue, and more.

By selling and shipping the books directly to our customers, the money that would otherwise be paid to large book distributors, wholesalers and stores can now be paid to you. Independent LRN Representatives can turn a favorite leisure activity from an expense into a profit making business, and write off any business related expenses.

As a LRN Representative, each month you purchase a six-pack from LRN, you qualify to earn a referral fee on the purchases made by all of the customers you personally refer, and on all of the customers those customers refer, etc. extending to five levels of customers.

LRN Representatives are not required to maintain

an inventory, and there are no required meetings or trainings to attend. LionHearted wants you to spend quality time with your family and do what you love most. We hope that includes reading and telling your friends about LionHearted so they can get their own books—and we will pay you to do it!

This marketing approach presents an interesting opportunity to anyone who builds a network of readers. Authors, for example, can now earn beyond their own royalties, earning referral fees on the sales of all LionHearted's books. And, the referral fees will not run out as royalties eventually do, income will continue year after year with the release of each new monthly six-pack.

Since LionHearted does not withhold royalties in reserve against returns, we can also pay authors their royalties monthly right along with the referral fees paid to our Representatives.

Our humanitarian project is a literacy video that can teach people how to read in the privacy of their home. One out of five adults in this country can't read, and illiteracy has been found to be the biggest link to the rise in crime. Unfortunately, many adults won't attend public reading programs because they don't want others to know they can't read. Let us know if you are interested in this project, or know others who would be.

Whether you are an author, an avid romance reader, or know someone who is, we would like to hear from you.

To receive more information on LionHearted Publishing, The LionHearted Romance Network, becoming a LRN Representative, or to request our author guidelines, contact us at:

LionHearted Publishing, Inc.
P.O. Box 618
Zephyr Cove, NV 89448-0618

888-LION-HRT (546-6478)
702-588-1388
702-588-1386 fax

admin@LionHearted.com
LionHrtInc@aol.com
75644.32@Compuserve.com

Visit our Web site on the Internet at
http://www.LionHearted.com

Or fill out one of the information request pages that follow and mail or fax to the above address.

Note

If you don't subscribe to *Affaire de Coeur,* a popular romance industry trade magazine that reviews novels from publishers of romance, you have likely missed their reviews of our books. They have given LionHearted the highest rating awarded any romance publisher.

Affaire de Coeur
3976 Oak Hill Rd.
Oakland, CA 94605-4931
510-569-5675, 510-632-8868 fax
SSeven@msn.com

LionHearted Romance Network

____ Please send me your six-pack of romance novels for $29.95 + $3.55 s/h. I am enclosing a check, cashiers check or money order for $33.50, + 6.5% ($1.95) sales tax if purchased in Nevada.

____ Please send me the following number of copies of book #1____, #2____, #3____, #4____, #5____, #6____, + 6.5% Sales Tax in Nevada + $2.00 s/h for one copy and $1.00 s/h for each additional copy.

PLEASE PRINT CLEARLY

Name _____

Addrs _____

City _____

St/Zip _____

Phone1 _____

Phone2 _____

eMail _____

I was referred by:

Name _____

LRN PIN _____
Personal Identification Number is the last 7 digits of SS#, or Employers Identification Number (EIN) if a business.

Mail to:　　LionHearted Romance Network
　　　　　　PO Box 618
　　　　　　Zephyr Cove, NV 89448-0618

Or call:　　888-LION-HRT (546-6478)

LionHearted's First Six Books

1) UNDERCOVER LOVE Lucy Grijalva   ISBN 1-57343-002-1 **$5.99**
   The last thing undercover cop Rick Peralta needed was a tempting but off-limits school teacher poking around in his business. The biker low-life was everything Julia Newman disliked in a man. He was dangerous but irresistible. Soon she found herself in deeper trouble than she—or he—could handle. *"Way to go Lucy! You have a winner." Affaire de Coeur*

2) DESTINY'S DISGUISE Candice Kohl   ISBN 1-57343-006-4 **$6.99**
   Lord John, the earl of Farleigh, never expected to inherit title or lands. He arranges to marry the youngest daughter of a neighboring lord. Lady Gweneth is the eldest daughter, a widow bitter toward men. She saves her younger sister from the warrior's hands by impersonating her sister and marrying him herself. John doesn't discover her lie until after the wedding.
   "A deliciously convoluted romance. Believable characters and true to period situations." — Affaire de Coeur

3) FOREVER, MY KNIGHT Lee Ann Dansby ISBN 1-57343-007-2 **$6.99**
   It is 1067 and Cameron D'Aberon, a Norman knight, is in service to William. He does not need or want another wife, his first having betrayed him and caused the death of his son. Kaela of Chaldron distrusts the Norman knight almost as much as she hates and fears her evil and lustful Saxon cousin, Broderick. Now she is the King's ward and it is Cameron's duty to escort her to court where the king will choose a husband for the spirited young heiress.
   "Tension filled... pulls the reader forward to the end." — Affaire de Coeur

4) IF WINTER COMES Millie Baker Ragosta ISBN 1-57343-003-X **$6.49**
   Her husband's deathbed confession shatters Laura Fortunato's world and begins a journey of self discovery, forgiveness and the power of healing love. Ian McMurtry pursues the reluctant Laura as she battles the lingering ghost who must make things right before he can go on to The Light.
   "Truly remarkable. Charming. A keeper." — Affaire de Coeur

5) THE MARPLOT MARRIAGE Beth Andrews   ISBN 1-57343-004-8 **$5.99**
   Widow Lady Phoebe Bridgerton wakes up in bed next to her cousin by marriage, the last man she'd ever want to marry. Charles Hargood believes her late husband fortunate to be dead rather than alive and married to her. Caught, then jilted by his current fiancée he now has a new fiancée: Phoebe.
   "Pure enchantment from cover to cover." — Affaire de Coeur

6) THE SIPÁN JAGUAR Joan Smith   ISBN 1-57343-005-6 **$5.99**
   A week before the wedding Cassie Newton is unexpectedly invited by her fiancé to join him in Canada. John Weiss, an insurance investigator, has traced a stolen art object and is in deadly pursuit of the thief. But something has gone wrong with the case, and he fears he might not survive.
   "Inventive. Delightful. Bright, witty and loving." — Affaire de Coeur

LionHearted Romance Network

____ Please send me your six-pack of romance novels for $29.95 + $3.55 s/h. I am enclosing a check, cashiers check or money order for $33.50, + 6.5% ($1.95) sales tax if purchased in Nevada.

____ Please send me the following number of copies of book #1___, #2___, #3___, #4___, #5___, #6___, + 6.5% Sales Tax in Nevada + $2.00 s/h for one copy and $1.00 s/h for each additional copy.

PLEASE PRINT CLEARLY

Name _____

Addrs _____

City _____

St/Zip _____

Phone1 _____

Phone2 _____

eMail _____

I was referred by:

Name _____

LRN PIN _____

Personal Identification Number is the last 7 digits of SS#, or Employers Identification Number (EIN) if a business.

Mail to: LionHearted Romance Network
           PO Box 618
           Zephyr Cove, NV 89448-0618

Or call: 888-LION-HRT (546-6478)

LionHearted's First Six Books

1) UNDERCOVER LOVE Lucy Grijalva   ISBN 1-57343-002-1   **$5.99**
The last thing undercover cop Rick Peralta needed was a tempting but off-limits school teacher poking around in his business. The biker low-life was everything Julia Newman disliked in a man. He was dangerous but irresistible. Soon she found herself in deeper trouble than she—or he—could handle. *"Way to go Lucy! You have a winner." Affaire de Coeur*

2) DESTINY'S DISGUISE Candice Kohl   ISBN 1-57343-006-4   **$6.99**
Lord John, the earl of Farleigh, never expected to inherit title or lands. He arranges to marry the youngest daughter of a neighboring lord. Lady Gweneth is the eldest daughter, a widow bitter toward men. She saves her younger sister from the warrior's hands by impersonating her sister and marrying him herself. John doesn't discover her lie until after the wedding.
"A deliciously convoluted romance. Believable characters and true to period situations." — Affaire de Coeur

3) FOREVER, MY KNIGHT Lee Ann Dansby   ISBN 1-57343-007-2   **$6.99**
It is 1067 and Cameron D'Aberon, a Norman knight, is in service to William. He does not need or want another wife, his first having betrayed him and caused the death of his son. Kaela of Chaldron distrusts the Norman knight almost as much as she hates and fears her evil and lustful Saxon cousin, Broderick. Now she is the King's ward and it is Cameron's duty to escort her to court where the king will choose a husband for the spirited young heiress.
"Tension filled... pulls the reader forward to the end." — Affaire de Coeur

4) IF WINTER COMES Millie Baker Ragosta   ISBN 1-57343-003-X   **$6.49**
Her husband's deathbed confession shatters Laura Fortunato's world and begins a journey of self discovery, forgiveness and the power of healing love. Ian McMurtry pursues the reluctant Laura as she battles the lingering ghost who must make things right before he can go on to The Light.
"Truly remarkable. Charming. A keeper. " — Affaire de Coeur

5) THE MARPLOT MARRIAGE Beth Andrews   ISBN 1-57343-004-8   **$5.99**
Widow Lady Phoebe Bridgerton wakes up in bed next to her cousin by marriage, the last man she'd ever want to marry. Charles Hargood believes her late husband fortunate to be dead rather than alive and married to her. Caught, then jilted by his current fiancée he now has a new fiancée: Phoebe.
"Pure enchantment from cover to cover." — Affaire de Coeur

6) THE SIPÁN JAGUAR Joan Smith   ISBN 1-57343-005-6   **$5.99**
A week before the wedding Cassie Newton is unexpectedly invited by her fiancé to join him in Canada. John Weiss, an insurance investigator, has traced a stolen art object and is in deadly pursuit of the thief. But something has gone wrong with the case, and he fears he might not survive.
"Inventive. Delightful. Bright, witty and loving." — Affaire de Coeur

LionHearted Romance Network
Representative

Name _____

LRN PIN _____

Write: LionHearted Romance Network
           PO Box 618
           Zephyr Cove, NV 89448-0618

Call: 888-LION-HRT (546-6478) or
           702-588-1388

Fax: 702-588-1386

eMail: admin@LionHearted.com

Web site: http://www.LionHearted.com

Lee Ann Dansby

The middle of five children, Lee Ann grew up in Alvin, Texas, where she discovered her love for reading at an early age. Combining her love of writing and her fascination with knights and maidens, she began writing her first historical novel, *Forever, My Knight* in 1991 and has recently completed her second novel, *Forever, My Love*, for LionHearted Publishing.

Lee Ann started her own catering business out of her home in 1984. With a lot of hard work, creativity, and an eye for detail, she has watched it grow into a successful business with a reputation for excellence.

No matter how hectic her schedule, Lee Ann finds time to write every day. "I have always wanted to punch a button and go back in time for a day. Writing romance novels is my way of living in another time. In my books, I am able to experience life and romance in a way that is no longer possible in the modern world."

Lee Ann brings her belief that one should pursue excellence in all areas of life to her catering and writing careers. She is a member of Romance Writers of America and the Houston Bay Area Romance Writers for which she serves as chapter President. She also actively supports her community's literacy program.

Lee Ann's other passion is traveling. When she is able to get away from her hectic businesss she spends her time in Europe where the land's rich history inspires her to create stories and characters that bring the middle ages alive for herself and her readers.